Redemption's Grace

THE REDEMPTION SAGA
BOOK FIVE

Redemption's

Grace

E. L. CROSS

Redemption's Grace
Book Five in The Redemption Saga

Copyright © 2022 Erin L. Cross

Scripture both paraphrased and directly quoted from the New
King James Version®. Copyright © 1982 by Thomas Nelson.
Used by permission. All rights reserved.
Scripture quotations marked (NIV) are taken from the Holy
Bible, New International Version®, NIV®. Copyright © 1973,
1978, 1984, 2011 by Biblica, Inc.™ Used by permission of
Zondervan. All rights reserved worldwide. www.zondervan.com
The "NIV" and "New International Version" are trademarks
registered in the United States Patent and Trademark Office by
Biblica, Inc.™

Cover Design by

Ebook ISBN: 978-1-7363603-8-5
Paperback ISBN: 978-1-7363603-9-2

Other Books by E. L. Cross

※　※　※

The Redemption Saga

To learn about new releases and read exclusive content,
connect with E. L. Cross at www.elcrossbooks.com

Epigraph

"Here is a trustworthy saying that
deserves full acceptance:
Christ Jesus came into the world to save sinners—
of whom I am the worst."

1 Timothy 1:15 NIV

※　※　※

Contents

PROLOGUE

TIRZAH

December 16th

I came to court to find a husband, not find a traitor. Yet as I press my ear to Lady Silla's closed door, I fear there can be no other explanation for what I overhear.

"Do you want the kingdom to burn?" Lady Silla exclaims.

"What I do is for the greater good!" The unfamiliar man bellows. "It is abhorrent that the backside of a peasant should fill one throne while another is sullied by a Limban queen. That should have been *your throne!* You allowed two princes to slip through your fingers. Had you married either prince, you would have secured our family's power for generations."

"I tried. You know I did," Silla argues.

"And failed! But now, when presented with an opportunity to redeem your worthless name, you balk."

I lean into the door trying to catch his fading words.

"Honor your blood!" He barks, causing me to startle back, which is just as well since I hear his booted feet stomp toward the door.

I scuttle into my adjacent room nearly missing Silla's rejoinder. Thankfully, he opens her door allowing her plaintive words to carry. "I have cast suspicions elsewhere, you cannot ask more than that."

The man steps into the corridor. "Nay, I do not ask. I demand it." He bangs her door shut, causing me to jump again. The older man pauses outside my door, permitting me a perusal of his face from the crack between the hinges. There is naught remarkable about him—lean build, average height, greying brown hair—excepting his frown that promises death to whomever crosses him. His head rotates slowly, glancing both ways down the corridor. Does he sense I watch him?

His eyes meet mine. Pressing a hand to my mouth, I shrink back against the wall, praying the darkness covers me. My heart tries to escape through my throat when he sticks his head into the threshold of my room, peering into its black corners.

No one. There is no one here, I silently plead. *Be gone.*

Air whooshes against my face as he shuts the door, leaving me alone in the night shrouded room.

CHAPTER ONE

TIRZAH

Winter Solstice Celebration, December 21st

The Queen of Malesiir is mad. There is no alternative explanation. For what other reason could she possibly think her hastily concocted scheme is workable?

Mad. Utterly Mad.

But as long as she holds up her end of the bargain and I am not affected by her lunacy, then I shall go along with it.

And she scares you, I reluctantly admit to myself. There is something about her, a sharpness, a lethal edge to her personality that is frightening. Her lover has it too, but his is easier to explain—a short temper coupled with his imposing size. He is a man not to be crossed. But the queen is neither short tempered nor imposing in stature. There is something about her, however, that is different. If the noblewomen's gossip is to be trusted, the queen has killed without remorse more than once.

I glance back at the door to her office that has remained closed since I stepped out several minutes ago.

She was detached, cold even, while she explained how it would be done. Not even her lover's outrage roused her from that place. Only when I dared to question her mental acuity did she come snarling to life.

Well done, Tirzah. Well done, indeed. This is the woman you spent the better part of a month heckling. In her own castle!

But it was simply too much. In a blinding bit of unforeseen possibility, I was offered the chance at a future as the wife of the king's Hand. But that vanished the moment the widowed queen arrived and

4

stole his affections. I was angry at first, but I was not attached to him, and he vowed to make amends to me by bringing me to court where I could choose a husband from hundreds of candidates.

That was more than possibility. That was probability.

But the queen ruined it again.

A week before I arrived, she came out of mourning. All that I have heard from the moment I arrived at court was that the noblemen were vying for her hand in marriage.

Again, she is the prize. I am merely the beautiful object to dance with, to flirt with, even trifle with, but she is the one all the noblemen want.

That is not fair.

The door creaks open bringing me around in time to see Queen Erianna and Commander Ironforge striding from the office as though they are strangers.

I fall into step with the queen, aiming for the great hall.

How could she have gone from kissing him wantonly before the entire castle to questioning his fidelity within the span of a day?

Mad. There simply is no other explanation.

I cast a sideways glance at her. Torchlight warms her cold features that are presently flushed and her lips that are not usually so full or red. So the queen and commander are back to kissing.

Unbelievable. Is there nothing he will not forgive her for?

Not because I care about her, but because my reputation is balanced upon her addlepated plan succeeding, I say, "Press your lips together. They are too red."

The queen does so without comment.

I feel all the eyes in the room settle on us the moment we enter the great hall. Though the winter solstice celebration is at its peak, a hush settles over the place.

This is not the sort of attention I wanted when I imagined arriving at court. Being acquainted with the queen, a guest of the queen's Hand, a friend to the prince's wife and a bevy of the highest ranking military officers, I thought for certain I would be welcomed at court and have at least a decent chance of meeting one or a dozen eligible men.

That did not happen. Now with this apparent scandal of which I am at the center, *Thank you kindly, Your Majesty*, I doubt I will leave with the hopeful acquaintance of *any* eligible men

I should have stayed at home. Valor's offer was too good to be true. I should not have accepted him, but I have become increasingly determined to marry. It is the only path I can see around my difficulties.

I remain with the queen as she whispers something to Prince Lorennt and his wife, Lady Nev. Moments later, Commander Ironforge appears with Captain Anders at his side. The pair of men clear a path toward the vestibule by their imposing size alone. At the door, Valor turns back revealing a bleeding split lip and a contrite expression directed at the queen he loves. Her scornful glare given in answer drives him into the freezing night. If I did not know they had been kissing seconds before she split his lip, I would believe what they are purporting. Except for quivering when the door bangs closed, the queen's act is flawless.

Then the real cause of this scandal approaches the queen—Lady Silla.

How the queen manages to speak evenly to Lady Silla, I have no idea. I am afraid I will give away the plot unconsciously by my expression alone. Never mind, *speaking* to her which I will be forced to do sooner or later. Cuyler Trent, Lady Silla's deceived suitor, looks between me and the queen, trying to unravel the mystery. I avert my gaze from his inquisitive eyes and miss trouble pushing her way into our group in the form of our friend, Leelah Tareth.

"Where is Valor going?" Leelah questions, grabbing for the queen's hand. One glance at her swollen red knuckles has Leelah shouting, "Did you do that to him?"

"I do not want to talk about it," the queen murmurs coldly.

But Leelah cares too much about all of us to let it go. "Erianna..."

"Yes, I did that to him. I told him to leave the castle," the queen snaps.

"Tirzah?" Leelah turns to me for answers.

I nearly reply with the queen's flat tone, but recall I am supposed to be playing the victim. Fortunately, or rather *unfortunately*, I have a bit of practice in this role. I drop my eyes and hush my voice. "Can we talk about this later?"

Leelah recognizes my tone and demands, "No, I think we need to discuss this now."

I look at the queen to see if now is an appropriate time to bring Leelah into our conspiracy. She nods her consent. Just as well. I would rather escape further scrutiny on this wretched evening that I expected to be one of the best of my life.

Leave it to Queen Erianna to ruin this for me too.

"Start at the beginning," Leelah instructs seating me upon the couch in her sitting room. Unlike me, Leelah is a favorite of the queen and was given a spacious room for her large family in the royal wing of the castle. Not that I am jealous of that. The room I was given adjacent to Lady Silla's is larger than my entire cottage.

"The beginning," I repeat, wondering how far back I ought to go.

How about to when you made eyes at the commander to irritate the queen? My conscience unhelpfully suggests.

She deserved to be irritated, I argue with myself. *After all, I apologized and told her I had no designs on Valor. Still she was rude to me and watched me like I might try to steal him away.*

"Well?" Leelah says impatiently.

Best skip that part, I decide. "I overheard Lady Silla speaking with her father several nights past. It sounded as if they wished harm to Erianna and Nev. They also spoke of the kingdom burning. When I tried to tell Erianna, she would not listen."

"What do you mean she would not listen?"

"I mean she threw me out of her office."

An exaggeration, my conscience nags.

"Well, she asked me to leave," I amend, "because she said that she trusted Silla implicitly. I told her it was a mistake and tried to wash my hands of it, but I could not. I was afraid for their lives. Thus, despite being warned away by the noblewomen, I told the whole of it to Valor this evening. He, at least, had the decency to listen. But then Erianna made a spectacle of us by acting as though Valor and I had dallied in the shadows! Can you believe that?"

Leelah huffs. "Poor thing. She must learn to let go of the past."

For a moment, I think she is sympathizing with me, but she is not. She is sympathizing with her "best friend." Never mind that Leelah and I are the dearest of friends or that we have known each other for years. Oh, no. As soon as Erianna arrived on her doorstep, *she* was Leelah's "best friend."

"Well, I think she behaved abominably. It was wrong of her to mistrust Valor—not that he rebuked her as he should have. They decided that Silla and her father, Lord Hugler, are likely colluding with the Ruphiri to destabilize the kingdom. They think the Huglers had a hand in the attack on the west side of Malsihra a few months past and might even be hiding the Ruphiri on the Hugler estate."

"Almighty," Leelah gasps in horror. "But Silla is Erianna's spymaster. If she has betrayed Erianna to the Ruphiri then heaven knows what else she has lied about."

"That was their concern."

"Then Valor's dramatic exit?" Leelah asks.

I shake my head. "It was all for show. They do not want Silla or Lord Hugler to know what they suspect."

"So everyone will think Valor left because he and Erianna had a fight."

"A fight about me," I grouse. "They want the court to think Valor tried to kiss me, that I rebuffed him, and Erianna threw him out of the castle for it."

"That is ridiculous!" Leelah exclaims. "Anyone who knows Valor will know that is not true. What makes them think this will work?"

My conscience prods me again. I try to ignore it. "Well... Apparently, there has been some gossip about Valor and I. The nobility think that because Valor brought me to court and bought me a dress, it means he has designs on me. Some women were also saying it is Erianna's fault because she is a cold lover. That is why the king took a mistress while they were married."

"What rot! Those despicable noblewomen will say anything out of jealousy."

"It is not a leaping assumption," I point out. "Erianna *is* cold and haughty. Why else would the king have taken another mistress?"

Leelah's amber eyes flash. "She is no more cold than I am. Nor is she haughty. And you should know better than to listen to gossip. The king keeping a mistress had nothing to do with how warm Erianna was."

I shake my head. Of course Leelah would side with her.

"If she would let you know her, it would be obvious to you that what you describe as 'cold and haughty' is only a mask to keep people from knowing how sensitive she is. But she is afraid of you, so you have not seen that side of her."

My guilty conscience must show on my face because Leelah fixes me with the look that causes her children to confess their misdeeds.

"Tirzah. Does Erianna have any reason to fear you? I thought you did not have any particular affection for Valor."

"I do not."

Leelah pins me to my chair with her prying gaze. "But..."

I cross my arms. "I might have been a bit coy with him a few times."

"Intentionally so?"

I shrug.

"Tirzah, how could you!" Leelah scolds. "Valor and I have been chastising her daily for not befriending you! Why did you taunt her?"

"She has been nothing but critical of me since the moment we met! And for what? She has everything a person could possibly want and still she watches me like I would have the indecency to try to take Valor from her!"

"This is absurd!" Leelah jumps to her feet, throwing out her hands. "You are both jealous of each other without a bit of reason for it!"

"Without reason? She will never know what it is like to live from hand to mouth and work hard every day of her life. She was born into a life of privilege."

"And she hates the shackles that came with that birth!"

"She has the love of Valor and the attention of every nobleman in the kingdom! Not to mention that she is reasonably proportioned." I gesture to my indecently curvaceous figure.

"And she is jealous of you because she thinks you are more desirable than she is and because you can give a husband what she cannot!"

"Oh? What is that?" I smirk and pat my bosom. "A nice pillow for his head?"

Leelah glares at me. "I have had my fill of the both of you. You are both ungrateful for what you have and wanting what the other disparages. I will not be in the middle of it anymore."

We glower at each other for long moments until I relent. There is no point trying to change Leelah's mind about Erianna. Like everyone else, she is unduly smitten with the queen. "Fine. But we all must pretend that Valor and Erianna have fought. She says that we must not correct any assumptions that the nobility make and Trent cannot be told the truth. Only you and Kragorn, Nev and King Lorennt are to know what truly happened."

"What of Trent? He is courting Silla. If she has betrayed us, he must be told."

I sigh. "They said it is too great a risk for him to know. They want to keep it all a secret until they know for certain what part Silla played in this."

Leelah's brows shoot up in dismay. "But that could take weeks for them to discover all the answers."

"It could."

"That is unacceptable. Trent's heart is set on Silla. I have never seen him court someone like he has her."

"Maybe you can talk Erianna around on it then," I suggest.

"Do not think I won't." Leelah sets her mind to it. "But what is to be done about you and Erianna? What is everyone supposed to think where you are concerned?"

"Apparently," I drawl, "Her Majesty thinks she can protect my reputation by making nice to me in front of the court and pass me off as a victim of Valor's 'unwelcome advances.' We are going to be taking meals together and spending time together."

Leelah gloats, "Well, it serves you both right. Had you been nicer to each other you could have avoided most of this unpleasant business."

CHAPTER TWO

TRENT

December 22nd

After breakfast I extricate Erianna from the group of nobility who have cornered her. The court rats try to hold on to her so they may continue harassing her for answers about exactly what happened between her and Valor last night at the solstice celebration. With a bow, a regretful smile, and a reminder about a nonexistent meeting, I offer Erianna my arm and set a course for the stables followed by her guards. The noble class will not venture into the frigid winter unless forced. Excepting Queen Erianna. But she is a wholly different class of noblewoman. She is as hardened as the ice glittering from the eaves of the castle and would never let a measly thing like chill wind keep her from what she wants. Which leaves me puzzled as to why she has let a misunderstanding separate her from the man she has pined after for years. There must be more to it.

"Where has Valor gone?" I ask conversationally.

"Elsewhere." Her tone forbids further questions on the subject.

"When will he return?"

She pulls her heavy fur lined cloak tighter. "Eventually."

"That makes sense. You finally agree to let him court you for all of what? A week? And at the first misunderstanding you toss him out of the castle."

"Trent…"

I do not let her beleaguered tone stop my conjecture. "There must be more to it. How did you convince him to go? It would take a sword to remove him from your side."

"Trent…"

"Whatever happened between him and Tirzah last night was not what the court thinks. He would never seek her favors."

"Trent!" Erianna jerks her hand from my arm and shoves me with it. "I do not want to discuss this! Not with the court and not with you! Just leave it be!"

I hold my hands up, feigning surrender. Erianna proceeds toward the stables.

"I am surprised you called a truce with Tirzah. Especially considering how she played coy to Valor."

Erianna draws breath to flay me. Then my words settle, striking a chord.

She tries not to be drawn in, but cannot help herself. Tentatively she asks, "You think she has been coy, too?"

"Too? Did Valor not perceive it?" I happen to know he did not. Silla has kept me apprised of all the developments where these three are concerned. But this is the only thread with slack to draw Erianna in.

"No. Neither did Leelah."

I shrug. "That makes sense. Tirzah has no real interest in him. She simply wanted to heckle you."

"But why? I have been nothing but—"

"Patronizing?" I supply.

She glares. "Welcoming."

"Horse apples."

She snorts.

"Which makes me wonder," I lead her back around to my first question. "Why? What is this all about?"

Erianna holds close her words. The warmth of hay scented air wraps around us as we stroll down aisles lined with the best horseflesh in Malesiir. I lift the iron latch and open the stall door to a hardy chestnut mare. Erianna passes me her cloak over the stall door after pulling it closed. Her guards take up opposite positions down the aisle where they may watch the doors.

Her slender fingers grip the top of the door as she quietly admits, "Valor and I fought. Though there is more to it, I have not come to an understanding of my own feelings yet. Please do not press me, Trent. When the time is right, I will explain it to you, but it may be a few weeks until Valor returns."

Her weary expression is the glimpse of honesty I was searching for. Peeling back Erianna's layers takes time. She does not show her true self to most people. That she allows me to know her and call her friend is not something I take lightly. Valor also entrusted me with his woman's care while he is away. That makes me dually responsible for Erianna.

"Alright. I won't ask again. I am here for you, though, if you need to talk." I glance about her mare's stall where she will probably want to hide for a while. With snow still piled high in the city from the vicious storm two days past, there is little for Erianna to do besides wait for the streets to clear and daily life to resume. I whistle to a stable boy wheeling a barrow full of hay. He hustles forward. I pitch a pile of hay into the corner of the stall then spread Erianna's cloak atop it. My peculiar queen drops onto her makeshift bed and pulls her knees up beneath her skirts.

"I think I will *loudly* tell Silla that the queen is taking air on the ramparts where anyone may ambush her."

"Thank you, Trent. You are a good friend."

"Enjoy your solitude, Majie." I reach over the stall door to squeeze her shoulder and add in a whisper, "Valor did not see Tirzah's smiles because his eyes are always on you."

Her chin trembles, but she nods.

Valor had better have a benighted good reason for leaving Erianna in a flurry of gossip like he did. If not, I will do my level best to beat the life out of him.

CHAPTER THREE

TIRZAH

December 24th

The evening's diversions extend later than usual with Prince Lorennt overseeing the evening. He seems to be enjoying his conversations with the other men congregated around the fire.

I have long since bored of the card games the noblewomen play. They are far less intent upon the games than the gossip to be had. I expected them to tire of the same topics which they repeat night after night, but they do not.

"Ladies, I fear that I am not equal to the length of this evening. I wish you all a good night."

The expected forced pleasantries follow my exit, but not a single word is genuine.

Longings for my tidy cottage and the sincere friends I made in Parse Kítaran twist my heart. The glitter of court is not as bright as when I first arrived. I simply want to go home. I miss the niche I carved for myself in the valley. Though a tad lonely at times, the excitement of aiding the midwife and fulfillment of caring for the ailing members of our community gave me a purpose. I anticipate becoming a healer in full.

That desire cannot become something tangible until I am rid of my brother's guardianship. Until then, I am limited in the things I may learn and do. I honestly believed catching a husband at court would solve that and more of my problems.

What a pointless venture I have indulged in.

I set my hands to the productive activity of sewing before going to bed. This day ought to count for some measurable success, even if it is only a hem mended.

In the corridor outside my room, Silla's laugh tinkles. It always carries a note of falsity to my ears. The one thing I have not become accustomed to since being redeemed by the Almighty is the ability to hear lies. This discernment grows deeper with each passing year. For some, the gifting is deeper than others, but all possess it. The elders say it is no different than the gifts of peace and joy that also come from the Spirit of Truth indwelling our hearts. I like those gifts and many others. I like the discernment, too, but with it comes an awareness of lies.

Lies unsettle something deep within me. Sometimes they feel like sadness. I feel it when I hear a lie. When I choose to tell a lie, it is even worse.

Cuyler Trent's genuine laugh blends with Silla's tainted one. How could she have duped Valor and the queen for so long? Surely they can hear what I do. Salome's admonishment comes to mind. *Sometimes we ignore Truth's whisper because we do not like what He has to say.*

It is always a foolish thing to ignore Truth. In the case of Silla, it is proving downright dangerous.

Usually Cuyler bids Silla goodnight without delay. Tonight, he lingers.

I feel a deep prompting in the core of my being. *Cuyler needs to leave.*

I return to my sewing, whistling a tune to myself. It is none of my concern what goes between Silla and Cuyler.

The unsettled feeling grows.

No, I sternly tell myself. *I will not interfere. See where it got me last time?*

I push the needle through the fabric and straight into my finger. "Woe's sakes!" I mutter, sucking the pad of my finger while hearing Silla's door open.

Urgency adds to the prompting.

"Oh, confound it!"

I leap from my chair, dashing toward my door without any clue what I ought to say. I do not have time to consider it before my door is open and I am walking into the hall.

Cuyler takes a startled step back from the threshold of Silla's room. It looks like he meant to follow her inside.

"Tirzah. Good eve." His expression reads like a man caught doing something he shouldn't.

Silla is annoyed. "Tirzah. Did you need something?"

I say the first thing that comes to mind. "Would you help me with my hair in the morn? I wanted to try something different."

She glares at me. "I am no lady's maid. How dare you presume—"

"Silla," Cuyler chides with a note of astonishment.

She masks her irritation in an instant and offers, "Perhaps I can send my maid over when she has finished with me?"

"Thank you. I would appreciate it," I reply. "I will say goodnight then." I smile at Silla then look at Cuyler longer, letting him know that I know what he was about.

His guilty countenance intensifies. "As will I. Good eve, ladies." His boots echo smartly in the hall as he strides away.

Silla fixes me with her sour dislike. There is nothing false in that.

TRENT

I owe Tirzah a debt of gratitude. Her well-timed appearance saved me from doing something I would have regretted. Though the lady was willing.

I roll the ruby studded ring between my fingers then return it to my pocket. Tonight would have been a mistake. When I first love Silla, it will be on the night of our wedding. Not before.

I am done making mistakes with women.

CHAPTER FOUR

TIRZAH

December 25th

"You need to tell him." I enter the queen's office and declare with out preamble.

"We have already discussed this. You know it is not possible. It would undermine all that we have set in motion," she calmly replies.

"It is not right. How would you feel in his place?"

The queen's flawless control slips. She flinches.

After a measured pause, she looks at me with eyes far older than her twenty years. "I would feel betrayed. Heartbroken. Sick with myself for not seeing through the lies of the one I loved. Trent will feel all that whether I tell him now or in a few weeks. My hope is that Valor will find some evidence implicating only Lord Hugler and not Silla."

"You truly think she is not involved?" I know what I heard. She is involved.

"No. But to what extent and to what end?"

Queen Erianna's loyalty to one who is clearly not loyal to her baffles me, but I hold my counsel.

"How have you fared?" She asks.

"Well, considering. The attention seems to be on you and Valor."

"As hoped." Erianna seems determined to not allow her prior distrust to infect her opinion of me. Still, it surprises when she asks, "Have any of the noblemen caught your eye?"

I prop my hand on my hip. "Would you understand if I say that I am disenchanted with court?"

"Perfectly." The queen pulls her plaited hair over her shoulder, undoes the crossings and nimbly reworks them. "What of the castle guards?"

"Being the wife of a soldier does not appeal to me. They are nomadic and notoriously unfaithful." I made an exception when I considered a future with Valor because of who he is and his position, but I do not wish to marry a soldier.

The queen raises a scarred brow but does not comment.

The silence between us stretches uncomfortably. She returns her attention to the papers before her. "You are welcome to stay, but I must attend to this."

"Then I will not disturb you." I incline my head to her, feeling dismissed.

"If it would not be an imposition," she rushes to say as I reach the door, "I could use help."

"*My* help?" I must have misheard.

She pushes the papers toward me. "I am memorizing the words to the coronation ceremony. Would you listen while I recite? I must say them perfectly." The humility in her request is directly opposed to the aloofness I have come to expect. Maybe she truly does want to call a truce on our private battlefield.

"Certainly. I have the time."

TRENT

Erianna and Tirzah engage in what seems earnest conversation with each other throughout dinner. I am seated too far away to overhear their conversation, but it piques my interest. I know the court's suppositions on recent developments are false, but I cannot sort out the truth of the situation no matter how many plausible explanations I concoct. That alone irritates me. What does that say of me as a spymaster?

"What do you make of that?" I ask Silla.

Silla discreetly glances at the high table. "Oh, do not think it is so complex. Erianna is compensating for her guilt. She accused Valor of infidelity, and he left because of it. She probably hopes he will forgive her if she makes nice to Tirzah."

It is the most plausible explanation, but it only takes into account Erianna's actions. I know how completely Valor loves Erianna. *Only* if she forced him to leave would he go. Even then, I cannot believe there is anything that would take him far from her side, yet I learned he has left the city. "I am not so sure. And what of Tirzah? I did not think she liked Erianna anymore than Erianna liked her."

Silla titters. "Oh, Cuyler. You are naive."

I rest my arm across the back of her chair giving her my full attention. "How so?"

She leans against my arm. "You fail to account for a woman's calculation. Tirzah and Erianna do not care for each other in the least. They are simply using each other. Erianna wants to make amends with Valor. Tirzah wants an advantageous marriage. Ingratiating herself to the queen makes for a short step to the choicest noblemen."

"Is that why you called a truce with Erianna? You needed to make an advantageous match?"

She daintily shrugs one shoulder. "Would that be so wrong?"

Her light eyes tell that she does not mean a word of what she says. My lady likes to play games. "I suppose that depends on your definition of 'advantageous.'"

"That is an ambiguous statement? Very well, I shall define it." She taps her lips thoughtfully. "He should be well-off, possessing vast holdings. He absolutely must cut a fine figure." Her finger moves from tapping her lips to draw a line across my arm. "I could not abide a man I did not like to look at. Besides that, he must be somewhat intelligent and able to carry a conversation. Not that I expect him to be as keen as me."

I smirk. "No one is."

"Exactly. He must be capable of making me swoon from his kisses."

My fingertips stroke her shoulder. "That is a lengthy list."

"Fortunately for me, I have found such a man." She sighs dramatically. "If only Lord Ormount would look my way... I am afraid that I will have to ambush him in his bed if he is going to take my interest seriously."

I laugh loudly. Lord Ormount is a dullard, a glutton and on the edge of poverty from his overindulgence. Silla would not look his way in a thousand years. "Your standards are high indeed, my Lady."

"Rightly so," she sniffs. "I am quite desirable."

I pluck at the brocade sleeve of her gown, rubbing it between my fingers. "Excessively desirable."

She smiles flirtatiously.

"But I wonder. Are you negotiable on any of your criteria?" Namely the bit about being well-off with vast holdings. I am well paid, but not by noble standards. I am also landless.

"Well..." Silla sighs. "I suppose I could set aside my hope for swoon worthy kisses."

"I think you can leave that on your list."

Her brows pinch slightly. "I will not sacrifice his appearance. He must be handsome."

She is not lack-witted. She is teasing me. But since she has told me before that she finds me attractive I am not worried about that either. "That is understandable. I also hope for a beautiful wife."

Just saying the word "wife" to Silla makes me nervous. She does not alleviate my anxious thoughts when she says, "What else would you have me remove from my definition?"

I look hard into her eyes trying to judge if she is tormenting me or being serious. I truly have no idea. My quick tongue fails me, and I back away from the topic. The ruby ring feels like a lead ingot in my pocket. "You will have to decide that for yourself. I only hope you won't be too harsh with Lord Ormount if he does not meet all of your high standards."

She turns away, lifting her goblet of mulled wine to her lips. "Perhaps he will find a way to give me what I want."

I pick up my own goblet, wondering if there are any modest estates for sale that I could purchase. Likely not within my means. Not with half of my earnings going to my support my widowed mother and siblings. Maybe it is time to ask my older brother to take on the responsibility of them. As the eldest they *are* his responsibility, especially since he is to inherit the small family farm.

Unless he were to turn the land over to me... That would save me the purchase of property.

I try to picture the immaculate lady seated at my side feeding my mother's flock of chickens from the backdoor of our dilapidated farmhouse. I cringe.

Perhaps I could knock the old house down and build a new one. Having been involved with the reconstruction of the west side of this city, I know what such an endeavor would cost. I could reasonably undertake it, but the home I could build would not be grand by anyone's standards. Certainly not worthy of the title of "estate."

My original plan was to purchase a furnished home here in Malsihra. Silla would be able to attend court as much as she likes without living on the generosity of the royal family, which is fine for now, but not something I could ever stomach for my wife. I will provide for her on my own merit, not from the coffers of another, no matter how good of friends I am with Erianna and the rest of the Rodiharians.

I toss aside the idea of purchasing an estate. My original plan still seems the most sound.

I only hope Silla agrees.

CHAPTER FIVE

TIRZAH

December 27th

I read the directions the queen gave me at breakfast. Despite living in the castle for the last month, I have explored a mere fraction of the vast premises.

Turn right off the stairs of the fourth floor. Continue on this corridor until you see the picture of the royal family with sour expressions wearing scarlet clothing. Turn left at the next corridor. When you see the statue of Lorennt's ancestor who thought much of himself, turn left again. The library is the third door on the right.

I snicker at the bronze statue of a king in full armor who did indeed think much of himself judging by his idealized features and disproportionate attributes.

Had she not told me which door was the library, I would have known it by the royal guards stationed outside. They merely nod at my warm greeting, but I am not offended. Her guards are a stoic lot.

After answering the queen's polite inquiries about my interests, she became eager to show me the collection of medical books in the castle's library. A plethora are related to botany while another section is dedicated to the healing arts. Not possessing expendable income, my own shelf of medical texts consists of only four tattered books. As I step into the library illuminated by tall paned windows, I squelch jealous grumblings in my heart.

The wealth of the royal family is summarily displayed in the extravagance of their personal library. Ceiling high shelves of books wrap the interior walls while cozy seating areas are tucked between the windows on the exterior wall. As if they had filled up the laddered shelves generations ago, two rows of chest high shelves were built in rows across the middle of the room. I could lose myself in here for weeks reading for pleasure and filling in the gaps in my education. What a privilege to live with access to all of this!

When my shock wears off, I scan the room for the queen. It is the murmur of a man's voice that leads me in her direction. I tiptoe along the shelves wondering what man would be allowed an audience with the queen without her guard present.

I discover them sequestered in an alcove in the midst of an intimate exchange. She is tucked into a chair with the handsome Lord Sigure leaning over her, his face inches from hers, hands braced on the arms of her chair.

I cannot see her expression, but I know why Lord Sigure was permitted entrance without escort. Besides being a relation of her deceased royal husband, he is the other man who was given permission to court the queen. Though she has steadfastly rebuffed his suit, with Valor away, has she secretly welcomed his advances? It appears so.

How despicable!

Just when I began to think she might not be altogether entitled and haughty, she compromises herself with Lord Sigure. Wait till Leelah hears this! She will be furious over the affront to Valor. And then she will stop acting as if any of this is my fault.

I creep backward, leaving the queen to her dalliance and feeling nicely vindicated. All the ridicule she has received seems—

"You deserve this."

My head snaps up at the malicious words spoken not by me, but rather issuing from Lord Sigure.

"Is that why he left you? Because you are barren?"

Barren?

"You do not know of what you speak," Erianna replies in a detached tone.

"Don't I? It makes perfect sense now. Why Leer kept a mistress... Why Ironforge brought his own woman to court... You cannot give them what they want."

"You are wrong," Erianna's voice is quieter.

"Acting as though you are above my touch all the while knowing you are not woman enough for me. Deceitful, barren tramp! You deserve the humiliation of Ironforge's scorn! You have wasted my time, and I am glad to see you suffer for it."

My own complaints against the queen shrivel at what I hear come from Lord Sigure's mouth with such animosity.

I wait for the queen to defend herself and put the brute in his place with one of her scathing retorts.

She says nothing.

"Was it truly Jaleh's fault that you miscarried Leer's child or did you blame it on her to hide you own failing?"

Cold washes over me at the appalling accusation. Valor warned me that I did not possess the full story and should not be passing judgments on Erianna. I should have heeded him. Of all people, I ought to know better.

And so should Sigure. Yet here he stands attacking his cousin's widow for rejecting his suit. Hot anger propels me forward. "How dare you speak to the queen like that!"

They startle at my sudden interjection and Sigure steps back from Erianna. Her face is stricken and pale. It makes my anger burn hotter.

"Apologize and leave immediately!" I demand.

Indignation darkens his countenance. "You have no right to make demands of me."

"Leave or I will fetch the queen's guard!"

Which turns out to be a needless threat because at my raised voice the door to the library opens admitting that man. "Do you have need of me, Your Majesty?"

"Lord Sigure is leaving," the queen says evenly.

How she maintains her composure under this duress I cannot imagine. Yet she waits impassively for Sigure to leave which he does without a backward glance.

To her guard she says, "Sigure may not speak to me privately again."

He bows his way from the room.

My thoughts reel at the implications of what Sigure said.

"I selected a few books that I thought might interest you," Erianna intones.

"What?"

She lays a hand atop a short stack. "You are welcome to search for yourself. I can show you where the medical texts are located if that is your main interest."

The queen makes no move to rise. She stares vacantly.

I kneel in front of her and take her cold hands in mine. "Erianna. Are you alright?"

"I just need a moment."

"You miscarried a babe?" I ask, suddenly wanting to understand.

She focusses on me. "The gossips do not like that part of the story. It is sad and makes me less of a monster." She sighs deeply and takes her hands from mine, wrapping her arms around her waist. "No. I did not miscarry her. Half-way through the pregnancy, I was poisoned with opium and pennyroyal."

"Almighty," I gasp. "That could have killed you!"

"It very nearly did," she says. "For a long time, I wished it had."

I feel the worst sort of wretch for the hateful thoughts I fostered toward Erianna. "The pennyroyal…"

She nods. "My physician believes I was rendered…" She retreats from the word Sigure spat. "I am damaged. Quite a problem for a queen who is supposed to produce heirs. Thus, we never disclosed my condition to the court."

I remember Leelah saying that Erianna was jealous of me for what she could never have. This was it. "But Valor…"

"He knows. He wants me anyway." She shrugs her brows as if she thinks he is foolish for it.

"He loves you."

"He loves me," she repeats to herself, touching a blue sash tied at her waist. "He did not leave me. This is real." Her left hand makes a fist then she rises. "I am sorry for being maudlin. May I show you around the library?"

Maudlin? That is how she describes what she feels discussing the murder of her unborn babe and ruining of her body for more children? No, I cannot believe she feels something as benign as self-pity. The ashen color of her cheeks and dull of her eyes that are usually sharp describe her emotions with better words. Words like *devastated* and *heartsick*.

The Spirit of Truth takes this opportune softening of my heart to point out my culpability in the attack Erianna endured from Sigure. I only meant to nettle her for finding what I have not yet secured with one who might have been mine.

Might have been mine only if this woman's first husband had not been murdered after their babe, the sensible side of me further chastises. *Isn't the consolation of the return of her first love the least of what she is due?*

Aye. Never again will I begrudge her this present happiness that others persistently try to taint.

"I am sorry, Erianna, for the part I played in our…" I struggle to find a word.

"Our private war?" Erianna's mouth smirks but her eyes are still sad.

"Aye. Our private war. I am surrendering."

"It is called a truce when both sides accept their part in the fighting and lay down their weapons."

I smile and teasingly ask, "Ought we draw up a contract of some sort? Like a peace accords."

She returns my smile and extends her arm. "Actually, I rather hate paperwork. Shall we make it official like the men do?"

I clasp her forearm and she mine. "There. It is official."

"Now then. If we are truly to come to terms, I can think of no better way to do it than to become acquainted over books. They make for good common ground."

If I am not careful, I could actually grow to be more than peaceable with the queen. I might even like her. "I quite agree."

Erianna tours me around the library and invites me to make use of it as often as I like, though she cautions me not to come alone as it is quite out of the way and someone of an ill bent could seize such an opportunity. I nearly contest that someone in her castle would not dare do such a thing, but her own cousin just railed at her because of his own stupidity.

We wind up sitting on the floor like children with a pile of books between us. Erianna's humor is restored over an outdated medical text that details a range of cures for illnesses. Some of the recipes are more ridiculous than others.

"Here, look at this!" Erianna points to a portion of text with crudely drawn diagrams. "'If the child's cough persists, pass the infant over and under a braying donkey as often as needed to steal the cough from his chest.'"

I laugh and turn the page. "Oh! This is gruesome! 'If the patient is light of head and suffering an imbalance, place leaches upon his temples to draw blood upward and restore balance.' Can you imagine all those slimy things on your face?" I shudder.

"You have never been leached?"

"Have you?"

She nods. "They are still used in Limba. It is not bad as long as you do not look at them."

I gape. With perfect factuality she explains, "Limba is decades behind the rest of the Continent. There has been no social progress within King Arcto's reign."

King Arcto? Is not the Limban king her father? How strange she does not name him as such.

In due course, we come to a segment on treating broken bones. Erianna studies the page intently. "This is how bones are treated in Limba. Would you do it differently?"

The illustrations depict properly aligning the bones, applying plaster, and reducing mobility for breaks that have not penetrated the skin. Detailed instructions follow the depictions.

"Aye. That is still how it is done. Not much changed there."

I move to turn the page, but an inward nudge stops me. "Have you much experience with broken bones, Your Majesty?" Her privileged royal life could hardly have put her in the way of such dangerous situations to grant her that knowledge.

She turns the page. "King Arcto holds no paternal affection for me nor I for him."

Her father… *beat her?* A princess?

"How many of your bones did he break?"

She shrugs noncommittally. "They were fractures mostly, not complete breaks."

I begin to construct a picture of Erianna's life that holds more darkness than mine. In fact, hers seems to be a bleak study of darkness excepting a few brightly painted figures.

One of them being Valor.

Valor in whom I feigned an interest to make her jealous because I am jealous of the fictitious life I imagined her to have.

All our friends warned me that I was judging Erianna wrongly. Even though she aided in my misperception, who can blame her for looking sideways at everyone with snakes like Lord Sigure hiding in the grass?

CHAPTER SIX

TRENT

January 5th

My inquiries about homes for sale within the capital yielded fruit. I rode out to tour a few yesterday while the ladies were occupied with their afternoon sewing in Queen Celiea's solar. One in particular met all my requirements. Situated in an elite area of the city, the home was smaller than the rest, but not reproachably so. It was elegant, furnished, and boasted a lovely rooftop view of the city. Neighbored by a wealthy tradesman and a noble family, I felt confident that I could picture Silla contentedly making her home there. Thus, I placed a deposit on the home straightaway. If all goes accordingly, I will take her into the city today and ask for her hand from the rooftop of our new home.

"What has set you in such a mood?" Silla glances at me over her paltry breakfast. Her keen eyes miss nothing though they conceal much.

There is always something new to learn about her. A look or flash of intelligence hinting at more but never revealing all at once. I love that about her. The mystery. The intrigue. I look forward to the years to come when I can unravel her mysteries and leisurely learn what makes this woman different from all the rest.

The press of her lips against the rim of her goblet leaves a pink stain.

"You are lovely without the artifice, Milady."

She smiles to herself. "I am glad you know it."

Last eve, I kissed all the stain from her mouth leaving it the prettiest shade of blush. High on the taste of her and the excitement of purchasing our home, I nearly asked her to honor me with her hand in marriage on the spot. However, I was held back by a feeling that I can only describe as hesitancy. The closer my fingers came to my pocket with the ruby ring, the more uneasy I became. After bidding her goodnight, I decided that I hesitated because she may have mistaken why I asked. I want Silla to know I love her, not only for the physical intimacy she can give me.

I turn at the tromp of an approaching guard. He presents me with a note from Anders. I scan the few lines quickly. He requests me to meet him outside the jail. He and Valor have returned at last and with a Ruphiri prize no less.

"What is it?" Silla wonders as I rise.

"We'll know soon enough." I softly touch her cheek. "I will find you before noon."

"Until then," she replies with a coy smile.

Aye. This day, I will ask her.

TIRZAH

Queen Erianna startles back from her plate. "How can you not like riding? Do horses make you nervous like Leelah?"

"No, it is not that at all." I wave away her astonishment, then note, "But isn't it funny that Leelah will stare down a fully grown cow without flinching, yet horses make her nervous?"

Erianna grins. "She says she prefers her animals to be on the dumb side of intelligent. An animal that could be plotting her demise unsettles her."

We share a laugh.

"If that is not it, then why do you so dislike riding?"

I lean toward her and lower my voice. "Does all that bouncing atop a horse not cause you discomfort?"

"What do you mean?"

I quirk a brow meaningfully. "Your breasts do not ache after you ride?"

Seated on the queen's other side, King Lorennt chokes on his watered wine.

Erianna looks round at him with a scornful glare. "Serves you right. Keep your ears on your own conversation."

Being next to her humor rather than opposite it is so much more entertaining. "Or perhaps the king finds his wine not watered sufficiently for the noon meal?"

The handsome king turns annoyed eyes on both of us. "Lovely, Erianna. You recruited another member to your sardonic army."

"Every army needs a healer, Majesty," I smile sweetly.

He turns back to his own conversation, muttering about expanding the ranks of *his* army.

Erianna dismisses the king with a toss of her thick braid. "Do not mind him. Having a newborn interrupting his sleep has made him grumpy. You were saying that riding causes you discomfort? I had no idea."

"Running does the same. All that bouncing," I explain then look past her to see the tips of the king's ears turning red. "I assumed most women felt the same way. That is why I suggested a little pony cart for your mare."

Erianna laughs. "I thought you were attempting to insult my mare. She is far too fine an animal for a pony cart."

I chuckle. "Well, I did not mean it as an insult the first time, but I saw it bothered you, thus, I kept saying it. Truly though, I do think she would look so pretty with a fancy little cart."

The animated woman sighs dramatically. "*Ah,* I like riding far too much to even consider it. I do wonder if you, too, would like riding on the right horse. Granite, Valor's stallion, has a gait so smooth it puts me to sleep. Perhaps a specially gaited horse would suit you. If I can find such a horse, would you try it?"

"Perhaps." Though I doubt such a thing would make a difference, I have a hard time saying no to Erianna's enthusiasm.

"We could walk through the stables later to—" With a sharp inhale, Erianna abruptly turns away from me to stare across the great hall.

I follow her gaze to find Valor stalking across the distance between them. His stern expression forebodes that what he discovered will not be of a pleasant nature. With his hand fisted over his heart, he bows to the king and queen.

"He looks whole, does he not?" Erianna murmurs.

"He does," I assure her.

Nevertheless, she tucks her trembling hands beneath the table and shores up her expression.

"Commander Ironforge," King Lorennt formally welcomes Valor, the joviality of moments earlier erased from his person. I begin to grasp the workings of these Rodiharians. They are genuinely likable people, but their sovereign duty to Malesiir comes before that. "You have returned from your assignment. Come forward."

My gaze darts down the table to the one unlikable Rodiharian who is glaring at Valor. I lean close to ask Erianna, "Will you tell Valor what Sigure said?"

She shakes her head. "No. His words do not matter. Best to leave that alone."

I disagree wholeheartedly. Valor would want to know what has happened these past weeks, and I want to see that temper of his unleashed on the ones who have made Erianna's life miserable.

I catch his eyes as he draws near the dais trying desperately to make him understand, but, apparently, only the one he calls beloved can he converse with absent words. He attends while I think of a way to explain. He is a smart man. Maybe this will not be so difficult. I look pointedly down the table at Sigure who seems hopeful for another spectacle that makes the queen appear scorned. I take my fork and smash the tines into a roasted potato, glaring at Sigure. Valor nods his head in understanding, but I want him to *truly* understand. I move my gaze slowly around the room at large to encompass the lot of nasty gossips. Then I cut the food on my plate into tiny pieces just like they cut Erianna with their hurtful words.

Erianna's hand appears atop mine, ending my silent conversation with Valor, but not soon enough to conceal what she wished. Valor's thunderous eyes the color of steel meet mine. Message relayed, I sit back in my chair and primly fold my hands in my lap.

"Your Majesties," Valor bows again. "I hope you will forgive my absence from the coronation and for leaving the solstice in such a manner. It was a regrettable necessity to rout the traitor from your court."

I hide a satisfied smirk that I had a hand in setting Valor's path to face the gossip head on instead of giving it some credence as Erianna planned.

Dear, sweet Nev also adds her own commentary to Valor's absence and how the royal family felt about it. "You were missed, Commander."

Valor takes the opportunity to further display his intentions toward Erianna. "Thank you, Milady. I hope I am permitted the time to be where my heart always is from now on."

Though given the perfect opportunity to reciprocate, Erianna seems to want to hold to her own plans for the gossip and does not reveal her heart. Instead, she asks after the success of his mission. "You found what we suspected?"

"I did, my Queen," he replies.

"Then let us proceed." She rises from her seat, shifting fully into the Queen of Malesiir. "Lord Hugler, Lady Silla. Come forward."

Cuyler is no longer seated by Silla who pales at the impending exposure of her conspiracy. In fact, I cannot spot him anywhere in the great hall.

"What is the meaning of this, Your Majesty?" The ignoble Lord Hugler demands of the king.

The sovereigns ignore him. Erianna asks, "Commander Ironforge, please present the evidence you have uncovered."

Valor's voice is loud and implacable. "On October the Eleventh, Malsihra was breached and attacked by the Ruphiri. We have long suspected that they were aided from within the city, though we could not find proof. Our investigations into the matter were assisted by Lady Silla who has served as an informant to you. A few weeks past, a witness overheard an incriminating conversation between Lady Silla and Lord Hugler then brought it to my attention."

I glare at Silla to ensure she knows precisely who bore witness to her treason. She winces and withdraws her gaze from mine, no longer the haughty lady.

Valor continues, "Not wishing to insult a respected member of the nobility, on my Queen's orders, Captain Anders and I left to investigate the allegation that pointed to collusion between Lord Hugler, Lady Silla, and the Ruphiri."

Lord Hugler raves, "This defamation of my character will end immediately! I will not allow such—"

"Be silent!" King Lorennt snaps. "We will hear all the evidence before coming to a decision."

At his nod, Valor proceeds. "We discovered a tunnel leading from the inside of one of Lord Hugler's derelict properties on the west side beneath the curtain wall with clear signs of the tunnel being used by wolves." The nobility are shocked and frightened by the discovery of this weakness in their home which forces Valor to speak over them. "Not feeling this to be sufficient proof, I set out for the Hugler's family estate near Port Veritae."

This declaration visibly frightens Silla. But why? What did she hide there that would prove more her downfall?

"We apprehended eleven Ruphiri men at the Hugler estate, ten mercenaries, and five members of the household who resisted our search of the property. They are being held in the castle's jail. In addition, we found Lady Hugler at the estate. She claims to have been kept against her will—"

"There!" Lord Hugler points at Valor. "My wife was a hostage so it is impossible—"

"After being sent there on Lord Hugler's order," Valor inserts the words like a knife. "The rest of the evidence I uncovered is more conclusive. Here are letters found at the estate from Lord Hugler to Reuel Zavaan. Zavaan's corresponding replies were found this morning at Lord Hugler's residence in the city. They detail what Lord Hugler receives in exchange for his collusion with the Ruphiri." Valor presents those letters to the queen who takes them in shaking hands. If she can read the words on the paper I would be surprised. I want to reassure her, but it would make her appear weak.

The king takes the letters from Erianna and becomes visibly angry.

"Your Majesty," Silla humbly interjects, "if I may—"

"You may not," the queen declares, sharply eyeing the woman she trusted. "I find this information most disturbing and sufficient to have you both incarcerated until a trial can be held. Do you agree, Your Majesty?"

King Lorennt is so irate that I lean deeper into my chair in an attempt to escape the waves of fury rolling off him. With a restrained nod, he gives his consent.

Erianna motions the guards forward. "I shall attend to this task personally," she assures the king. Without hesitation, Valor steps forward to take her on his arm. Sigure looks none too pleased over it.

"Do remember," the king growls, "we do not afford noble lawbreakers privileged treatment. Treason is treason."

Silla could be hanged.

Until this moment, I did not realize how directly my information changed the course of history. I did not want anyone to be killed, namely Erianna and Nev, but in exchange for their safety, Silla is going to die.

And she knows it.

The controlled woman nearly faints where she stands while her father yells at her. "Cease your dramatics ere you make fools of us!"

A guard takes charge of Silla, clasping her arm to keep her upright and marching her from the freedom of her previous life toward the jail meant for traitors.

TRENT

Anders awaits me outside the jail with a grim look about him. "Where have you and Valor been? I saved up a few choice words for our commander." Poor Erianna has dealt with the worst rumors these past weeks. The gossip has been unmanageable even for Silla and I, though we tried to temper it with plausible excuses that cast everyone in the best light.

"Afore you get to that, let me show you what we caught." Anders leads me into the dark gloom of the jail toward a cell full of Ruphiri.

"Nicely done," I commend him. "This brings their numbers down significantly. How did you snare these wolves?"

"First question that needs answering is *where* we caught them," Anders says.

"Alright. Where?"

He takes a weighty breath. "At Lord Hugler's estate."

"They attacked his estate? Why?"

"No," Anders corrects my assumption. "They took shelter there."

I am dumfounded. "Hugler was aiding the Ruphiri?" Silla has told me enough of her father to know that the old cur is a hateful man, but for him to have plotted treason... "How will I explain this to Silla?"

Anders grimaces. "Lad."

"How did you learn of Lord Hugler's involvement with them?"

"Tirzah warned Valor at the solstice," Anders slowly replies.

"Well, that explains a few things. I knew Valor wouldn't run out on Erianna, no matter how bad a fight they had. How did Tirzah learn of it?"

"*Ah*, Lad," he groans. "She heard Silla and the old man plotting outside her door."

"Impossible. Tirzah must have misheard. Silla would never aid her father, let alone the Ruphiri. She has been helping us rout them." The denial makes more sense to me than the pitying look of my friend.

"Maybe. That's why Majie sent us to investigate. We found a tunnel in an abandoned house on the west side that Hugler owns. That's how they got into the city." He tips his head toward the cell.

Before I can explain it away, I recall Silla asking me not to go that night. She was fearful for me. Because she cares for me.

Or because she knew what awaited us? She kissed me when I returned the next day. It was that moment when I became certain the flirtation between us meant more to her, as it had come to mean more to me.

"There's something you missed. Some simple explanation," I argue. "She did not betray us."

"Majie thought the same. But we found letters between Zavaan and Hugler—"

"Anders, if you say one more word against my lady…"

One of the Ruphiri chuckles to himself. The man sits apart from the rest, reclining in a corner, changing the bandage around the recently severed stump of his finger. "Your Malesiirian women are a treacherous lot."

Rarely must I fight to control rage. It is not part of me like it is Valor. Now I wonder if it is because I have never been wounded so deeply. In this moment, rage builds as too many oddities I dismissed, too many trails that suddenly disappeared, too many subtle manipulations I fell prey to spring to my mind. Denial at this point is useless.

Silla played me.

Enraged, I rattle the iron bars of the cell while reaching for weapons to gut the miserable carps who poisoned our kingdom. Their toxic presence ruined our lives. I know they are responsible. Them and Silla's wretch of a father. Anders hauls me away from the cell as I fit a narrow blade into the lock that separates me from the enemy who ruined my future.

In the stark daylight, Anders relates what was found on the documents. Plans. Schemes. Strategies that would see Queen Erianna stolen as war booty, Lady Nev killed along with her babe, and Silla wed to King Lorennt. She meant to purchase herself a crown through bloodshed.

My heart is mute with pain. My sense of reason, however, is not impaired. Silla's role in all this is only too clear. She was to throw us off the trail, keep us running in circles.

When I returned from the attack on the west side, was her kiss a means of concealing tracks I would have otherwise seen? What else did I miss?

After all these months the hart I thought I chased turns out to be a clever fox who led me far afield.

Time cruelly mocks me, not granting me the benefit of another moment before the castle guards approach dragging Lord Hugler and his daughter. Lord Hugler is spitting curses. His daughter walks sedately behind them until she sees me.

"Cuyler! Cuyler, listen to me, I can explain. Let me explain!" The outburst is so unlike her that I scowl. She is pulled into the jail, still pleading with feigned emotion.

How many times does she expect me to be duped?

CHAPTER SEVEN

TIRZAH

January 6th

Valor's dramatic entrance and the Huglers' more dramatic incarcerations throw the great hall into an uproar that King Lorennt quickly silences. He declares a public trial will be held within a few days time with swift punishment should those once-trusted members of his court be proved treasonous. Then he dismisses the court. The nobility scurry from the great hall, relocating to secluded corners of the castle to discuss what transpired. If King Lorennt meant to keep them from gossiping, he failed miserably. Likely, he only meant to get them out from underfoot as he summons a core group of generals and advisors to the war room, including Kragorn.

I replace him at Leelah's side, herding the children back up the stairs while they air their grievances at the injustice of being confined to a room larger than my house when they could have had the run of the great hall.

Leelah calmly reasons with her unreasonable brood. "King Lorennt has ordered everyone from the hall and that includes us. We obey our king."

"But I am hungry!" Micah complains.

Leelah huffs. "We just ate, Micah."

"Not enough! I want an apple!"

"Me too!" The girls chime. "And cookies!"

I squeeze Leelah's arm. "I will run down to the kitchen and gather a basket, the sooner to see them settled."

Fialla begins to whimper and squirm in her mother's arms. "Aye. Do that. I shall get this one to sleep then we will have a nice long sit down."

I return with what is hopefully a day's worth of snacks for the children and help Karris settle them in the parlor with food and entertainment, but it becomes necessary to separate Micah from the girls when he takes his fun by putting their dolls to the sword while shouting, "Traitors!" The wails of the girls set Fialla to crying again in the next room which makes me seriously reconsider my desire to have a large family. I confine Micah to the unbelievably large space that was once the queen's dressing room, then help Ivy and Lois reorder their dolls till they are playing quietly.

Leelah slips out of the bedroom to meet Karris and I in the foyer. We turn about, searching for a quiet corner for our own use, but all the rooms are occupied by her children.

With a roll of her eyes, Leelah pushes open the bathing room door and ushers us inside. "Now, then! Find a seat, Ladies."

Karris drops a towel on the cold floor and plops down, leaving me to perch on the edge of the tub and Leelah to claim the little bench next to it.

"I never liked Silla," Karris does not hesitate to assert. "It makes perfect sense that she was treacherous."

"That is ungracious," Leelah chides. "Though I hold no fondness for her either, we will not rejoice in another's downfall. We will pray she has a change of heart and time to repent ere…"

Leelah's voice trails off, with the weighty knowledge that "ere she dies" may not be very long at all. I shudder.

"Poor Trent," Leelah sighs. "He must be heartbroken."

"I hope he does not come to hate us for keeping this from him these past weeks," I worry.

"Was it you that heard the plot? The witness Uncle mentioned?" Karris asks.

I nod.

"Well, that explains much. Like why you and Erianna are suddenly friends."

Leelah is smug on this point. "Aye. That and—"

Before she can warm to her topic, a knock interrupts us. We step into the foyer while Leelah opens the door to find one of the queen's guards.

"The queen wishes to see Healer Tirzah immediately," he announces.

"Of course," I follow him into the hall.

With the door shut, he says quietly, "The queen bids you fetch your healer's things then I am to escort you to her."

"Is she well?" I ask, quickening my steps to deliver me faster to Erianna.

"I cannot say."

The basket containing all my medicinals is in my room, always ready to grab at a moment's notice. Thus, it is not long till I am knocking on the newly designed bathing room, anxiously awaiting assurances of Erianna's health.

After a prolonged minute, I knock again. "Erianna?"

Erianna cracks the door, looking more shaken than I have ever seen her. When she simply stares at me, I prompt, "You asked for my help. Are you well? Your guard found me with Leelah and will not say what is wrong."

She nods mutely and widens the door allowing me to enter. I make it only two steps inside the antechamber before drawing up at the sight of Valor hunched on a stool in the middle of the room and bared to the waist. Cords of muscle form his arms and grooves define the muscles beneath the flat planes of chest and stomach. It is not that I have never seen a bared man before, but they are usually farmers. Men strong through the arms and shoulders, but often rounded through the middle. Nothing like the warrior before me.

At whom I am gaping.

My mouth works to say something instead of hanging open catching flies. Something sardonic ought to be safe. "Well! You certainly don't have a paunch."

Valor barks a laugh, harkening back to when I offered that same teasing compliment the day we spoke of courtship. Now, I halfway wish I had fought Erianna for his affections.

Oh, rot! I guiltily shift my gaze to that woman, hoping she is not offended by my admiration of the man she is courting. If she heard my words, she gives no acknowledgement. She only calls my attention to why she brought me here.

"The wound on his shoulder is the worst. I cleansed it but perhaps not well enough? It is beginning to fester. Please..." Her voice quavers. "Can you help?"

Her forlorn expression now makes sense, though I presume she is over reacting. I offer her my reassurances and cross the room. "I am certain you did the job perfectly. I will check to see what else needs to be done."

Valor huffs at my indulgent tone. "I know what needs done. I simply did not have the supplies to do so. It needs to be packed and —"

"Valor!" I exclaim, staring at the severe laceration on his shoulder that has begun to fester. It truly is a testament to his impressive form that this injury did not immediately come to my notice. I know he has a solid foundation of medical knowledge, and it makes me all the angrier that he disregarded treatment for himself that he would have insisted upon for another. "No! You know better than to have let it get so bad. At this point you do not get to tell me what needs doing. You know the risks from not treating a muscle wound properly. It can cause permanent damage to the arm. It can poison your blood. Or you could lose your arm if the tissue blackens and dies. How could you have ignored such a thing? It is absolutely un—"

"Tirzah!" Valor barks, interrupting my tirade. "None of that is going to happen, is it? This is nowhere near so serious. You are being unnecessarily dramatic to prove your point." With a glare that promises he will shut my mouth for me if I do not close it, he nods toward Erianna.

The touted Warrior Queen appears no more than a terrified young woman. In truth, I am afraid any more words from me will take the spine out of her then I will have two patients to attend.

I smile apologetically at Erianna, postponing my lecture till Valor is the only one who can hear it. "Yes, I was only being dramatic." The half-truth comes out of my mouth without much effort. "Forgive me. A few days and this bit of infection will be resolved. A few more and it will only be a little scar. It is certainly not the worst place to be injured. These sort of injuries heal quickly because of the strength of the muscle." All true, even if the few days prediction was an optimistic exaggeration.

"You see, there is nothing to worry about." Valor draws Erianna to his uninjured side. Sending a complacent grin my way, he says, "As my beloved has so often noted, I do maintain an impressive build. I have that to my advantage."

"To be sure," I agree, holding his gaze with a bit of effort.

But Erianna mutters, "Conceited," at Valor's boast.

This time my spoken admiration earns me a critically arched brow from her.

I blush and temper my words about his build. "Medically speaking, of course."

She sighs the sigh of the long-suffering. "Do not encourage him. His confidence does not need bolstering."

Though her words match her typical humor, they are forced and breathy. It causes Valor to pull her closer. His fingers stroke her face. The tenderness of the massive warrior surprises me. To further distract her from her fear for him, Valor goads, "Are you saying that I have never left you speechless?"

Erianna retorts, "I have never been speechless. I simply choose not to express my thoughts."

Unfortunately they seem to have forgotten that I am bearing witness to their exchange.

Valor's voice deepends to a rumble. "I dare you to voice them next time."

Oh, heavens! Erianna truly did not stand a chance of resisting Valor's pursuit of her indefinitely. I begin whistling to drown out their flirtatious interlude while inspecting Valor's shoulder and taking supplies from my basket.

"Can I help?" Erianna volunteers.

Smiling, I note that Valor returned all of the color to her cheeks and then some. "Certainly. The rest of his cuts need to be cleansed and treated with a salve. Will you do that while I pack this nonsense and make a poultice to draw out the infection?" I give her a jar of salve infused with calendula, rosemary, chamomile and honey to reduce the healing time and guard against infection. "But first, more water."

I draw a fresh pitcher of warm water and in it dissolve a sachet of salt to cleanse the wound. Never have I taken any pleasure in the pain of others. But seeing how much anguish Valor has caused Erianna by neglecting to care for himself, I feel a sort of satisfaction at the task before me.

Valor groans when I brandish the saltwater over his shoulder. "Hush!" I scold. "You knew this was coming. It is your own fault."

He gives me a narrow eyed look. I smile pleasantly and tip the pitcher slowly to flush the wound. For a moment, I am afraid Valor will not remain upright.

I pour a bit faster as he sways on the stool, grumbling, "Unsympathetic sadistic woman."

Erianna and I quickly set aside our pitcher and basin to prevent Valor from sliding to the floor. Suddenly, I am not so appreciative of his bulk.

When he has mastery of himself, I smile widely at the sulking man.

"There. The hard part is over."

While I pack the wound and Erianna cleanses his lesser ones, they discuss the warlord who dealt Valor these injuries. It makes me exceedingly curious about this enemy whom Erianna does not believe is fully an enemy. Above all, I find one thing exceedingly strange.

After dressing Valor's wounds and answering Erianna's candid questions about the severity of them, we step into the corridor to allow Valor to bathe while I prepare his poultice and she fetches him fresh clothing though he jested that he would not mind crossing the castle in naught but a towel.

Before she hurries away, I ask, "Majesty, there is something I wondered while listening to you talk about the Ruphiri warlord."

"What is that?"

I phrase my question carefully to prevent shocking any who might overhear. "Why did the Ruphiri warlord tell you Valor was injured?"

Even Erianna's guards who follow the queen day and night believe she and Valor are intimate. Somehow from their brief interaction, the warlord intuited what others have not. If Erianna were to learn of the wound on Valor's should, she must be told. She would not discover it by undressing him. Thus, he informed her of the injury he dealt Valor.

Comprehending the weight behind my question, her brows wing upward. "That is an excellent question."

Still pondering the answer, I go to the kitchen to make Valor's poultice. I grind dried calendula, chamomile, and oregano into a fine powder with mortar and pestle. From a sealed jar, I add a hefty pinch of charcoal to draw out the infection. To this, I add enough boiling water to form a paste. Then I bundle the paste in a clean strip of linen and return to the bathing room. Thankfully, because the bathing room is adjacent, the poultice will not lose its heat before I can pack it into Valor's wound.

As I approach the bathing room door, I do not have time to dither about knocking or waiting for Erianna. She appears trotting down the corridor, skirts swishing about her legs. It seems the queen ran across the castle to have returned with Valor's clothing so quickly.

I did not give any credence to Valor's jest about crossing the castle in naught but a towel, but perhaps she did. I decide not to ask.

Erianna sets the bundle of clothing in her guard's hands and orders him to deliver it. Quickly masked surprise passes over his face before accepting his queen's order, further proving he believes there would be nothing untoward that has not already transpired were she the one to deliver Valor's clothes.

Who is this warlord? What makes him different from all others, even an anomaly among his own people? I wish that I could meet him, to judge for myself. Not that I believe my observational powers are superior to the queen's—certainly they are not—but still, I am curious.

The guard steps out, and after another minute, Valor opens the door for Erianna and I.

"What is in that?" He eyes the poultice in my hand.

"Healing herbs that I hope feel like a coal against your flesh as punishment for your stupidity."

"Pain is the best teacher," Erianna agrees.

Valor makes a face and mimics her words like a child. *"Pain is the best teacher... Do not quote Kragorn to me."* He drops onto the stool. Its protest he blames on shoddy craftsmanship.

"Then you build me one, if you have so much spare time laying about," Erianna snaps.

Despite what I said, I genuinely doubt this poultice will pain more than it soothes. With a gentle touch, I form the sachet to fit into his wound, ensuring good contact with the sides and bed to draw out the infection. As I always do, I entrust my healing work not to the skill of my own hands, but to those of the Great Physician, whispering a prayer as I wrap a bandage overtop the poultice and under Valor's arm to hold it all in place.

With a shuddering breath, Erianna echoes my quiet "Amen" as does Valor.

"We shall reapply this at least four times a day to more quickly see you healed. Valor, if you can meet me in the great hall at those times, I feel it would be best." When he agrees, I lay down one more absolute. "Do I need to tell you to keep your arm immobilized as much as possible or can you tell that to yourself?" I ask with a hearty dose of reproach.

He sighs, some of the wind taken out of his prideful bluster. "I can tell myself. Thank you, Tirzah, for your excellent ministrations."

"Aye, thank you," Erianna seconds.

I gather my basket and walk toward the door. In the most loving tone, Valor asks Erianna, "Do you feel better now? Good. There is something you promised once my injuries were tended..."

I peek over my shoulder as I slip out of the room to see Valor gather Erianna close and touch her face, bringing her closer still.

Closing the door as quietly as possibly, I sigh. My heart is happy for them and relieved to see Erianna cared for, but I also ache at being reminded just how far I am from finding for myself the one who will love me like that.

CHAPTER EIGHT

TRENT

January 6th

I delay for eighteen hours. Obsessively I examine the evidence condemning Lord Hugler and Lady Silla. There is no question that he aided Zavaan. However, Silla's direct involvement *is* questionable. With evidence firmly in mind, I rattle the bars of Silla's cage. She starts awake from the hay pallet on which she huddles with her mother. In her entire life she has never slept on anything so humble.

"Cuyler?" She rises, careful not to disturb her mother. The rat nosing at her slippered foot is not so considerate. She leaps back with a hand clapped to her mouth. Stripped of her lavish existence, she is unremarkable. Simply another noblewoman who never learned how to exist outside the privileges afforded by her class.

Why did I ever think she was brave?

"Cuyler." She repeats my name sounding relieved. She knew I would come eventually. It makes the pitiable tone of her voice a farce. "You are here."

"You wanted a chance to explain. Go ahead." Terse words given all that is between us and the leaden weight of the ring in my pocket.

"What have you heard?" She asks fearfully. But I, too, know the game.

"No, Silla. I'll not let you craft a shinier version of the truth. Tell me what happened."

She blinks twice. The affected part of her fearful demeanor falls away. What remains is raw and real. Genuine regret hangs about her, but she is no longer fishing for sympathy. She is controlled. "I did not want it to be like this, but my choices were taken from me. The night of

45

Lorennt's wedding, my father told me that he purchased the throne for our family since I failed to do my part to secure it. He warned me against going into the city that night. He said all would be managed and that I was to wait for the opportunity to present itself, then seize it. He would not tell me what he had done. When I heard from you what happened in the city, it was too late."

"But not too late to reveal the traitor in our midst," I point out.

"I told you I was without choice. I could not."

"I would have protected you from him."

"You could not have protected her," Silla murmurs, glancing back at her sleeping mother. "Days before Lorennt's wedding, he sent her to our estate. *He sent her to Zavaan.* He knew I would need impetus to do what he required."

The bitter voice of Lord Hugler sounds out of the darkness. "Why shouldn't I? The worthless woman only gave me you for an heir. If being your incentive is all she could do for our family, then it is the least she should do. Not that she went willingly."

I know that to be false. Lady Hugler birthed three other babes after Silla, all sons, all died in their first year of life.

"Your grasping at power knows no bounds!" Silla hisses. "Mother loved you in spite of you though the kindest thing you ever gave her was your absence."

"You worthless females ruined our family's chances. You could have done your duty long ago to further our family name, but you were weak!" Lord Hugler's hands ball into fists that are too far away to strike the tender flesh of his daughter.

Silla's venom reaches farther. "Because I refused to climb into the bed of a man with years enough to be *your father*? He was repulsive! Unfit to sleep in the piggery!"

"You have no spine! You would have outlived him and been the keeper of all his holdings!"

"After you murdered his grandson!" Silla mocks. "What an excellent plan that was! Then there was—"

"Quiet!" I snap. "We are discussing why you were party to treason."

Silla recoils. "He had my mother! I had no choice!"

"You could have told me," I reiterate. "I would have found a way to free her before Zavaan hurt her."

"No, you could not. You do not have that kind of power, not even the ability to lead a contingent without the commander's permission."

Her belittlement of me more than stings, but I set it aside. Now is the time for answers. "You keep company with the Queen of Malesiir. She would have acted on your behalf."

"I could not take the chance," Silla argues. "What is the safety of one woman compared to the capture of the Ruphiri? The queen would have had no choice but to act. Even if she did not wish to, her generals would have forced her."

"Therefore you did your father's bidding and aided Zavaan?"

"I had no direct contact with Zavaan or any of the Ruphiri. My task was to direct your attention away from my father. Make certain you did not see what he did."

The jagged question fights its way free before I can stop it. "Was inviting me to your bed part of it?"

Pain marks her face. I do not trust it. "No, Cuyler. I care for you. That was not part of my deception."

"Is there anything else you wanted to tell me?"

She searches my eyes in the scant light. "I wanted you to know why. That is all."

"Now I know." My feet carry me away from the sounds of Lord Hugler's insults at his daughter, and the soft sounds of her crying. I hate that I cannot even trust her tears.

TIRZAH

I wait in the corridor within the jail, pondering my own stupidity and believing again that Queen Erianna is mad. For certain, there is no other explanation for what she has asked of me.

Apparently, my tending of Valor has placed me as the primary healer of whom she thinks when needing to treat battle injured warriors. Ironically, if all goes as planned, I will be treating the wounds Valor inflicted on the man who inflicted Valor's wounds. How delightful it would have been had I been there when they stood opposite each other. I could have asked them to save me and themselves a good bit of grief by tucking those honed blades back into their scabbards and using words like learned men.

I huff a breath up my face. Yet another reason I have no interest in binding my life to a soldier.

The door swings inward, my cue that the warlord whom I foster a great deal of curiosity about has proven himself worthy of receiving medical treatment. The first thing that startles me upon my entrance is the Limban tongue in the Queen of Malesiir's mouth. In this context, she seems as foreign to me as when I first met her. I wonder if her various personas make Valor dizzy with the effort to know her.

The second thing of note is the Limban warlord himself. He is lanky, in need of several solid meals to fill out his frame that when stretched to its full height might be as towering as Valor's.

Erianna abruptly switches to the common tongue. "I trust you like women sufficiently that you will not harm this one who has consented to tend your injuries?"

The warlord queries in the common tongue of which he has such mastery that no accent is detectable, "You would not poison me, would you, *Královna*?"

The queen grins with a ferocity that reminds me she has earned her place among the warriors of my acquaintance, even though she often dons the soft clothes of a wealthy noblewoman. "That is not my style, Warlord. If I decide to kill you, I will do you the honor of informing you death is coming."

I shiver at the veracity in the playfully spoken, cold words.

The warlord eyes the queen then shifts his gaze to me. He is a striking man. Narrow of face and form, but with balance in features that make him attractive in a peculiar way. Hazel eyes sit above high cheekbones and level brows. The nose is long and narrow save for the telltale bumps at the bridge where it has been broken. Or perhaps what arrests in his features is the intelligence shining from his eyes.

We stare at each other for a long moment, me clutching the pitcher of warm saltwater and basin covered with a cloth, him peering at me with preternatural stillness. Softly, he says, "I will not harm her."

The warlord crosses his arms so that his empty hands rest palms up on his opposite knees. I look to Erianna whose brow is drawn in consideration, but she nods me forward. The tension goes out of the warlord which sets me at ease though I should not be.

I place the basin at his feet and wet a cloth. "I will treat your finger last. Please direct me to your other injuries."

"On my right arm is the deepest of many minor cuts."

Noting the bloodied sleeve, I reach in my basket for scissors. "I must cut open your sleeve to reach it."

"You may," he replies, as calm a man as I have ever seen.

I snip my scissors across the grimy fabric to reveal wounds that are angry and red. With the wetted cloth, I reach for his arm. He does not flinch away though I know it is painful to remove so much dried blood and dirt.

I become absorbed in my task, a thing easily done with the relaxed demeanor of my patient. I cleanse, apply salve, and move about him to see the thing done right, no matter how small the laceration.

"Finally, your finger." I bend to take his left hand in mine, unwinding the cloth from his middle finger. It sticks to the stump Valor left him. I frown.

"Healer?" He questions, the breath of his words fanning the small hairs hanging about my face.

I sigh. "You and the Commander. Much damage you did to each other. I wonder what the point of it was?"

The smile in his voice holds fast though I wet the old bandage on his finger and loosen it till it lifts free, definitely causing him pain. "The most obvious point is that I am incarcerated while the commander's head is still atop his shoulders."

Why does he not sound regretful of such?

I murmur regret over the ruined state of his finger that was cleanly severed and cauterized. Though cauterizing was not necessary if a tight wrap could have been applied to stem the blood flow, what is done is done. I pour water over the finger and lightly abrade the wound to loosen whatever dead tissue is clinging to the blackened surface. Only when I begin to abrade the wound do I notice a shift in the warlord. He holds his breath while I tend his finger, likely from pain. Another pour of the water, then I cleanse his whole hand in an effort to protect the finger from contamination. More salve, more bandages, these dusted with charcoal for drawing infection, then I rise.

No word of thanks passes his lips, but I feel it hanging about him as if he makes an effort to hold it back.

Thus begins my daily care of the Ruphiri Warlord.

TRENT

Erianna finds me perched on the fence of the training yard, watching the soldiers practice at swords late in the day. The ring of steel echoes off stone buildings and walls, preventing her softly spoken words from traveling farther than the two of us.

"Lorennt has agreed to a private audience with Silla. Would you like to be there?"

"To what end?" Bitterness edges my question.

She taps her boots against the lowest rail of the fence to dislodge the snow crusting the leather. "My heart says Silla would not have done what she did unless her position was untenable."

"The evidence stacked against her says otherwise."

"What evidence? The letters drafted by a murderer or the letters of an abuser of women? Both of whom are voracious for power. No, Trent. I want her story."

Likely Erianna already knows I spoke with Silla in the dark hours of this morning, yet she does not ask if I learned anything. Thus, I volunteer it. "She claims she did it to protect her mother, not that it will make a difference in the end. She has still committed treason." I saw the documents. I saw that Nev and Laszlo, the king's infant son, were meant to die, clearing Silla's path to the throne. "Lorennt will not forgive her after what they planned."

Erianna rests her head on her hands, gripping the top fence rail. It is answer enough.

Silla will hang next to her father. The knowledge is a fist in my gut. I may never be able to look past her betrayal, but that does not mean I want her dead. "She should have trusted us to help her."

"It no small thing for a person to bestow their trust when they have seen the worst in mankind."

My silent dissent is a shout in my mind. *But Silla knew me! She should have known I would not betray her trust.*

"I am sorry you are hurting, Trent. And I am sorry for not finding a way to tell you what we suspected."

I watch a young soldier batter himself against someone of superior skill. Again and again his sword is knocked from his hands. The futility of his efforts will not make him a better swordsman, no matter his wish to change the outcome. The weapons master observes the pair, then rearranges the soldiers with different partners, more evenly matching them with an opponent who complements yet challenges each of them. Thereafter, the young soldier's stance and technique rapidly improve. Simply knowing that he has a chance at victory makes him strive for it.

From the corner of my eye, Erianna stretches her hand toward my arm. The deepening of my scowl causes her to abandon her attempt at consolation and reconciliation.

"Let me know if you wish to attend Silla's hearing."

The queen leaves me to my solitude, accepting the distance I maintain between us as her due.

CHAPTER NINE

TRENT

January 7th

It is not until Lorennt is striding across the great hall with his guard in tow that I make my decision. Rising from the alcove in which I have been stewing, I intercept the king.

"Your Majesty. May I accompany you to the hearing?"

Lorennt appraises me. "Will you interfere or can you remain impassive?"

"I will remain silent," I assure him.

"Then come."

I fall in with him. Erianna and Valor stand outside the jail, the former exuding anxious tension.

The king takes one look at her and grumbles, "I do not know why I have agreed to an audience with this traitor. She cannot sway me from my belief in her duplicity."

Valor gauges my reaction to the king's declaration, which is a total lack of surprise, then says on Erianna's behalf, "Silla's duplicity is unquestionable, but she may possess additional information we need. And I, for one, hope she can explain her actions in such a way that will lessen the severity of her sentencing tomorrow."

Lorennt is incensed. "Do not hope for that."

Then Silla's fate is predetermined, no matter what comes to light as a result of this hearing. The accursed ruby ring hangs heavy in my pocket. My hand slips inside my pocket that my fingertips might touch my sundered future again.

In taut silence, the four of us wait in the jail. I stand in as Lorennt's guard while Valor keeps watch over Erianna which feels thrice foolish when my Lady Silla is led into the room begrimed and shackled. She is no threat to any of us. The only strength she has ever possessed is her keen mind and network of informants.

Lorennt and Erianna direct the interview, Lorennt with an extreme prejudice that causes Erianna to ignore him and Silla to speak directly to her queen.

The story is the same as the one she told me yesterday. Her father's lust for power became so great that he sought to gain a throne through her marriage to one of the princes of Malesiir. I know that Lorennt used a lengthy flirtation with Silla as a means of staying aware of the court's gossip, but she told me it never meant anything more to either of them. Once King Grandileer was murdered, Lord Hugler pushed Silla harder to secure Lorennt's affections. She refused. He became desperate and somehow connected to Reuel Zavaan, the leader of the Ruphiri. Through that connection, he began plotting to kill Lady Nev and the infant Prince Laszlo while trading Queen Erianna to Zavaan. Silla's task in this was to lead astray our investigation of the Ruphiri attack and make it impossible for us to discover her father was the traitor.

Silla shudders through the accounting of how her mother was beaten by Zavaan in recompense for Silla having foiled her father's plots to poison Lady Nev. How Silla also smuggled servants out of the castle and rescued their loved ones from her father's home in the city, I have no idea. But she would not lie about this, not when I could so easily verify her story. Which I shall do.

However, her recounting of disrupting her father's plans to capture Erianna needs no verification. Multiple times Silla told me that Erianna had grown restless and was planning to sneak into the city. I, in turn, made that an impossibility by ensuring Erianna had a surfeit of guards to protect her from her impulsivity.

But Silla should have confided in us! Confided in me. No matter what, I would have done anything for her.

When Lorennt presses the issue of her subterfuge, Silla relents. "I have given that matter considerable thought and realize I should have confided in Queen Erianna, but at the time, I was too afraid for my mother's life."

Again, confided in Erianna.

Not in me.

I draw my hand from my pocket, attempting to forsake my attachment to the future I thought was mine for the claiming with a fictitious woman. How can I possibly pick apart Silla's tale to discern when she was leading me away from uncovering her father as the traitor and when she was being genuine in encouraging my pursuit of her?

It serves me better to view all of what transpired between she and I in the same light—Silla was a desperate misguided woman doing whatever she must to protect her mother, Erianna, and Nev. In that light, I think I can make my peace with being a tool used by her. But the way her eyes dart to mine, seeking some sign of sympathy, some sign of concern, I have a hard time believing that is all I mean to her. Nor will the hollow ache in the middle of my chest allow me to ignore what she means to me.

Erianna is deeply moved by Silla's tale. I know that given the chance, she would show compassion to Silla.

However, for King Lorennt, it all comes down to one point. "You chose the life of one over the hundreds that have died at Zavaan's hands since then. You chose wrong."

Anger boils in me at Lorennt's hypocrisy. He is not sentencing Silla because of the hundreds of commoners that have died. He is damning Silla because it was his wife and child that were singled out by Lord Hugler for death.

It is painful to watch Silla realize she is without recourse. The clever fox is cornered. There will be no escape for her. For an interminable moment, desperation fills her eyes. Then she exhales it, accepting her fate with quiet dignity.

I nearly break.

Why did she not tell me what was happening to her! How her father was extorting her and using Zavaan's abuse of her mother to force her to betray her conscience.

Coldly, Lorennt inquires, "Do you have anything else to tell, Lady Silla?"

"Your Majesty," Silla addresses Erianna, "I do not deny frustrating your investigation or hiding my father's involvement. However, I also endeavored to protect you and Lady Nev at great cost. I ask that you recall our arrangement, all of the favors I have accumulated by aiding you which stretched beyond this business into dealing with the court and other matters. In spite of my complicit deeds, you are indebted to me, Your Majesty."

Erianna hushes Lorennt's argument to the contrary then encourages Silla, "Go on."

"As such," Silla calmly continues, "I wish to claim all favors owed to me in exchange for my mother's freedom and provisions for her after my father's death. You cannot object to her release as she played no part in my father's plots. She is innocent but by the unhappy association of being married to a villainous cur."

Erianna does not take long to consider Silla's bargain. "Granted."

Silla exhales, settling back in her chair.

"Do not look so relieved, Lady Silla," Lorennt ominously cautions. "You have not been granted clemency."

Silla smiles tightly. "This I know."

The pain in my chest is unbearable.

I am going to watch the woman I love hang for treason.

The castle slumbers when I move on silent feet, becoming another shadow in the bailey. Rats pay me no mind within the torchlit confines of the jail, continuing their nocturnal hunt for sustenance.

Silla sits awake, her head leaning back against the wall, staring vacantly. From the depths of shadow, I gaze upon her. Her mother's arms are wrapped around her, dozing almost peacefully. Knowing Silla, she probably gave false reassurances to her mother that clemency would be granted them at tomorrow's trial. For that reason, I am here.

Stepping from the shadows, I come to Silla's notice. "Cuyler."

She carefully extracts herself from her mother's arms and stands before me. "I am glad you have come."

I reach between the bars and touch my fingertips to her cheek.

She shudders, her eyes dropping closed. "You believe me. You understand."

Not wanting anymore half-truths between us, I say, "I believe you. I do not understand why you could not trust me, but I believe you."

Conflict plays across her face that seems more open than ever before. Finally, she says, "It hardly matters now. This cannot be undone."

Though my plans are barely formed, I offer her what I have. "It cannot be undone. However, it must *not* be done. I will take you from here after the trial. That way, your mother's freedom will be publicly secured. You will not need to worry for her."

Silla shakes her head. "No. Cuyler, if you are caught—"

"I will not be."

She reaches her hands toward me, then closes them, pulling back at the sight of her own filth. I capture her hands and set them upon my face.

"Cuyler. You cannot do this. I am snared in a web of my own making. I accept that. It means my mother will be safe. I cannot risk Lorennt changing his mind about her verdict."

"Then I will take both of you. We will go to the Commonwealth. The Sutherlands. Somewhere far away."

She shakes her head. "You have your own mother and sisters to look after. You cannot also bear the burden of me and my mother."

"I can," I insist. "I will see you and your mother settled, then I will return for my family or provide for them at a distance." Something I do not wish to do, but I will.

Doubt fills Silla's eyes. "You are not thinking clearly. You are not being reasonable."

"What is unreasonable is this," I grip the bars of her cell. "Silla," my voice cracks. "I cannot watch you hang. I cannot."

Tears spill from her eyes, glistening in the dark. "Promise me something."

I withhold my agreement until I hear her request.

"Promise me you will not be at the trial tomorrow."

"No."

"Cuyler, please. I will not be able to bear your grief, not when I must first contend with my mother's." She looks backward at the sleeping woman. "I told her we were both going to be granted clemency. She does not know—"

I nod my understanding.

"Please. Promise me you will be far away tomorrow."

"Alright, Silla. I promise." The lie rolls easily off my tongue. I hold her eyes when I say it, giving no indication that I am not being truthful.

And she believes me. "Thank you. Now go. Before you are discovered."

I kiss her hands and slip back into the shadows, knowing that if I do not go, she will be the one to pull away from me.

Convincing Silla to follow me on the course I have plotted will not be easy, but there is no alternative. She is out of options. Which is why her whispered words haunt my steps leading away from her cell.

"Farewell, Cuyler."

CHAPTER TEN

TIRZAH

January 8th

The excitement in the air disgusts me. That anyone in this room is anxious to see one their own convicted of treason is unthinkable. Yet here they all are, watching the drama unfold with the same excitement that vibrated the air during the tourney matches.

"Lord Galderon Hugler," King Lorennt raises his voice to proclaim the verdict at the end of the trial, "I find you guilty of all charges. You are sentenced to hang at dawn on the morrow. All your property and possessions are hereby confiscated by the crown excepting a stipend for your widow."

Murmurs of approval run through the crowd.

"Knew he was guilty," the noblewoman sitting adjacent says to her companion.

"Of course, he is guilty. We all know the sort of beast he has been to Lady Felice these past years," her companion replies. "But then again —"

"*Shhh!*" The first woman silences her companion when the king calls Silla's mother to approach the dais.

A guard takes Lady Felice by the arm and helps her walk toward the king. "I find you innocent of any involvement in these dealings with the Ruphiri and clear your name of all charges brought against you. You are free to go." The clank of manacles springing open and Lady Hugler's thanks echo loud in the great hall.

The second noblewoman sighs, though it is far from genuine. "Oh, good. Felice is such a dear. It would have been ghastly to see her hang."

"Oh, aye. Ghastly. But that Silla…"

"She is a nasty thing, isn't she? Spying on us and reporting to Erianna."

"Serves her right if she swings."

"Be quiet!" I hiss.

They glare at me like an insect. "Who are you?"

They know who I am. Every noblewoman has marked my face for having the audacity to befriend the aloof Queen Erianna. I speak though their hateful glares attempt to cow me. "Have you no compassion for what is happening? These people are going to *die*."

Their derision fouls the air. "Aye. They deserve it."

I shake my head in disgust.

"Lady Silla Hugler. Come forward."

My heart pounds as Silla approaches the dais then bows to the king. "Your Majesty. I thank you. I accept your judgment of me as just."

"You have not yet heard my sentence." The king's cool tone says plainly what it will be.

"I do not need to," Silla replies. "Thank you for allowing me to call your court home these past years. It was a kindness I shall never be able to repay." Silla bows again then walks toward her father, knowing the death sentence also awaits her. A cry of dismay cuts through the crowd's satisfied murmur. Weeping, Lady Hugler struggles futilely against the guard restraining her then collapses in his arms, reaching for her child.

The mother's anguish tears at my heart. I clench my hand over my chest, aching because I am directly responsible for what is happening. Though I had to reveal Silla as a traitor, I did not think how my actions would carry forward to this moment.

To Silla's death.

Searching the faces of the crowd still does not reveal the man whose heart must also be breaking. But I cannot believe Cuyler is absent. Slower, I look to the edges of the rooms, the places away from people like the ones next to me. I turn all the way around on my bench and spot a narrow stair clinging to the edge of the great hall leading upward to the musician's gallery. There, far above the hateful voices, is Cuyler.

"Lady Silla," King Lorennt calls out, pulling my attention forward again. "I did not grant you your leave. Return to the dais." After another long minute of expectant silence, Lorennt rises to his feet and descends to face Silla. "Lady Silla, I find you guilty on the counts of lying to the queen, abetting a criminal and interfering with our investigations. However, I do not find you guilty of treason. Furthermore, on the other counts, I believe that you were extorted into committing them upon the verified mortal peril of your mother. It is my judgement that as such you will receive a lesser sentence. Effective immediately, I strip you of your title and all the privileges thereof. You shall be reduced to a penniless commoner and sentenced to work in the castle until such a time as we are satisfied with the recompense for your crimes."

My gasp of disbelief is drowned by the raucous shock in the great hall. People leap to their feet, some cheering as King Lorennt personally unlocks the manacles on Silla's wrists, some raising an outcry that she will not be hanged for treason. How did this come about? Leelah told me that it had been decided there was no hope for Silla. Lorennt would not be moved to show mercy.

Yet he did.

The tightness in my chest eases, freeing my breath that was stuck. No matter what changed, I am glad for it. I hold no affection for Silla, but hearing the evidence presented, I can readily believe she acted to protect her mother and never truly wanted Nev or Erianna to be harmed.

I look upward to Cuyler. He is folded over, head resting on the banister in relief. The sight makes my eyes burn. Aye, many people would have been hurt if Silla had been sentenced to death.

TRENT

January 9th

"It would seem I am in need of a new wardrobe."

Silla's droll tone scrapes my raw nerves. She nearly died, was nearly hanged as a traitor alongside her father this morning, yet she greets me with insouciance.

A full day after the trial, the clamor in my mind has not calmed, only magnified. My thoughts kept me awake through the night, tracing the paths of my choices and her choices. What did happen. What could have happened.

And there is this anger.

I do not know what to do with it.

Thus, I ignore it. "You should encourage your mother to leave court for a time. This place will not be good for her."

Silla comes close to where I stand staring into the undulating flames. This parlor has been our quiet meeting place to confer over the goings on within Malsihra. We chose this particular parlor because, unlike most, it has a fireplace rather than a brazier, and the atmosphere is better for it. Using it today seems like a travesty since I have no way of knowing if anything she said to me within these walls was genuine or if it was all part of her schemes.

"Erianna has permitted me a few days with Mother before I begin working as a lowly chamber maid. Afterward, Mother will travel to Port Veritae with her friends. My Aunt will look after her, this time, in truth."

"Good."

"I confess, Cuyler, I expected a warmer greeting from you, considering what you offered the last time we spoke."

"Then you mistook what I said. My not wanting to see you die does not mean I have reconciled what you did." If the undeclared courtship between us was real, she would have trusted me to help her. But Silla relied only on herself.

"I see." She laces her hands before her, projecting a relaxed demeanor while maintaining her perfect posture. Is she relaxed or does she want me to think she is? I thought I could tell the difference with her. Clearly, I do not know her at all.

Her voice is steady, but her breaths are shallow. Nervous, perhaps? "When you have reconciled it, do you think you will lower yourself to be seen with a chamber maid?"

I scowl at her, lacking my usual temperance of word and expression. "You think it is your station that upsets me?"

Regret softens her eyes. Or is it only that I wish to see regret? "No. I know you are too honorable to concern yourself with such things." Her face becomes carefully blank. "Will you be able to reconcile what I had to do?"

"*Had to*, Silla? You *had to* lie to—" I snap my mouth closed, turning back to the fire.

"To you?" She finishes my question and answers it. "Indeed, I did."

My eyes follow the lines of the wood grain in the mantle. Straight, then bending back on itself. Here and there a knot. The way forward for us seems like that. An abrupt stop and switchback. It will take redefining what is between us. Even if we do, will Lorennt allow Silla to improve her circumstances by marrying? Does it even matter? Can I reconcile what she did?

"I cannot speak to the future. I need time." Time away from her. Time away from this castle and my friends who let me be deceived. Time to think.

Making an impulsive decision, I voice it before I can reconsider. "I am going to see my family. It has been too long since I visited my mother and sisters. Working for Valor has kept me occupied of late."

"I know," she murmurs. "It would be good for you to see them. To take the time you need." Her hand settles on my arm. "I will be here when you return."

CHAPTER ELEVEN

TRENT

January 11th

My restless gaze searches the woods for any threats to our party. Though Valor dealt the Ruphiri a heavy blow, it would be foolish to believe they will be long in retaliating. For that reason, Kragorn pushes his family to ride farther each day. At this pace, we will reach the Valley day after next. Hours in the saddle usually provide more time for reflection than they presently do owing to Kragorn's children and the women's chatter. Soon, however, I will have the road to myself and time aplenty to know my mind.

After the noon meal, Tirzah falls into pace alongside me. "It was good of you to escort us. I know you could make better time without us slowing you."

"I am happy to be of service to my friends," I respond amicably. "Besides, it is hardly an inconvenience since I pass by Parse on my way to my own family's home."

Tirzah's eyes remain on the road before her, not rushing her reply. "That is convenient. However, were I you, I think I would be put out with the lot of us and more than a bit angered over what we suspected but did not tell you."

I glance at her profile to find it hidden by the sweep of her brown hair falling in a plait over her shoulder. "Are *you* angered over the part they asked you to play?"

She shrugs her shoulder making the plait spill behind her back affording me a partial view of her expression. "I accepted responsibility for the path I set my feet upon. Had I chosen to be circumspect, there would have been much less cause for the court to make the assumptions that they did."

Knowing how she taunted Erianna, I cannot argue with her assessment. Still, I find her decision to own her mistakes refreshing.

"But you, Cuyler? I think you were dealt the most wrong with the least cause. I am sorry that a way was not made to tell you."

Bitterness sours me though I struggle to be reasonable. "I know how the games are played. I would have made the same decision that Valor and Erianna made." Though that is what I tell myself, I do not truly think I would have. I cannot imagine allowing my friends to experience what I have. To think how close I came to asking Silla to marry me! Would she have accepted despite all her lies?

It does not matter. Even if she had, we would have still come to the same place. Thankfully, I do not have more to regret in having gone to her bed though she invited me. Happy chance prevented me when Tirzah stepped into the corridor...

My eyes shoot toward the woman at my side. "It was not a coincidence that you stepped into the corridor when you did, was it?"

She ducks her head, not needing to ask for more specifics to know the moment I reference. "It seemed wrong to let you do something you might deeply regret once you knew her duplicity. Besides, the Spirit of Truth would not leave me be till I blundered into the middle of your affairs."

Of my closest friends, it was this woman with whom I am barely acquainted that took pity on my ignorant state and saved me from a great error. "Thank you, Tirzah. Truly. Thank you."

She looks at me from the corner of her eye. "Like I said. It did not seem fair to you. I hate when life is unfair."

I find myself smiling at her sense of fair play that is in direct opposition to the way of the world.

We lapse into silence and eventually Tirzah is called upon to help with the children.

I consider what she said, that the Spirit of Truth urged her to intervene to keep me from going to Silla's bed. If that is true—and I know that she believes it is—I wonder why He would trouble Himself to keep me from making that mistake? I am not entirely sure I believe there is a Creator that speaks directly to people or has a relationship with them. An aloof deity that set the world in motion then left us to our own devices seems more likely. In this circumstance, I doubt Tirzah's intervention can be attributed to anything more than her own conscience. Either way, I feel like she has removed one of the sticks from the load bowing my shoulders simply by proving that there are people in the world who care for the burdens of others.

TIRZAH

January 13th

The valley unfolds in one snowy hill after another. I am beyond anxious to see this journey to its end. My little cottage beckons. First, I will lay a merry fire in the hearth then set water to boil for my tea. The absolute mundane of airing out my cottage and washing my laundry after unpacking my belongings sounds like the choicest of pleasures. Then tomorrow, I plan to be up to my elbows in the herbs that will have finished drying in my rafters this past month.

My patience frays as the children become whinier the closer they come to their home. Nevertheless, I aid Leelah as best I can by settling them. Finally, *finally*, the high wall comes into view. We wait outside with the few soldiers trusted to enter the valley while Kragorn and Cuyler draw swords and inspect every nook and cranny within the Tareth home for intruders. It seems a small eternity until the men emerge and declare the place safe. The children nearly trample them in their haste to gain their freedom within the walls of their own home.

"You mark my words," Leelah says, "though all we have heard for days is how they cannot wait to have all their toys and be allowed to romp around, I will be sorting out fights before dinner time and hearing how they wish they were back at the castle."

I stifle a groan as Cuyler catches the bridle of my mare and reaches to help me dismount. He must see my weary expression for he winks then asks Leelah, "What can we do to help you get settled so that Tirzah may also go home to her rest?"

Leelah drops into her husband's arms. "Actually, there is little to be done today that we cannot do for ourselves. The livestock are all with neighbors. We only have the children to care for."

The soldiers begin unpacking the horses and toting the Tareth's belongings inside. I left the castle with far more belongings than I went with, yet still, there are only a few additional bags tied to my mare.

Cuyler's hands drop from offering assistance, leaving me in the saddle. "Should I take Tirzah home?"

Kragorn's words put a smile on my face. "Aye. And after you all take your meal," he nods to include the other soldiers, "it would be good if you could head to Chishelm and allow us time to settle in."

Cuyler passes the mare's reins back to me and turns her in a circle while heading for his destrier. "Kragorn, your hospitality is appreciated, but I can speak for all of us when I say we will eat on the way to Chishelm."

The men clasp arms. "Safe travels, then. And thank you."

I wave to Leelah where she follows her children into their home then kick my mare into a trot, heading back down the tree lined path.

"I thought you hated riding at anything above a walk?" Cuyler laughs, drawing even with me.

"I do." Not that I will explain the why of it to him. "But I will do absolutely anything to sooner get home."

"Lead on then," he waves me ahead.

My cottage sits across the river on the opposite side of the valley from Leelah's home. My brother Mather rents it from a farmer named Brick for a fee made reasonable by my maintaining the place and Mather making any necessary repairs.

"Normally, I cross here." I point to the stone fishing weir that serves as a bridge across the river, "but with the horses, we probably ought to go round to the bridge near the chapel. The water is hip deep in the middle."

We take the long way, riding farther into the valley to double back once we cross the stone bridge. The path from there is well marked beneath the thick layer of snow leading alongside a dense copse of trees and up a hill. My cottage sits back from the rise of the hill providing a lovely aspect of the valley spreading down toward the river. Behind it, rolling pastureland covered in snow appears like tufts of pristine wool.

I catch sight of my snug cottage framed by deep snow drifts. How the snow has piled up without me to manage it after each storm! Brick said that he would tend the cottage in my absence, but it seems he has neglected it. Perhaps it is not so much work as it looks from here. A few days of shoveling ought to be sufficient to set it aright.

Unfortunately, it is much worse than it appears at a distance.

"No!" I gasp, seeing the snow piled high upon the roof excepting one corner where the roof collapsed beneath its weight. Without awaiting Cuyler's help, I drop to the ground sinking up to my knees in snow. Working my legs free, I locate the crust of frozen snow under the fresh powder to hasten my way forward.

At the door that has been knocked from its hinges, Cuyler catches hold of my arm. "Wait!" He points to the tracks in the snow. The boots of a man crossed the threshold going inside then back out along with the massive paw prints of a bear.

"Oh, Sow!" I exclaim. "This is what comes of being neighbors with a bear."

Cuyler's alarm is marked. He urges me behind a snowdrift to wait while he draws his sword and enters my cottage. After only a moment, he calls for me to follow.

The last of my happy dreams evaporate as I take in the state of the single room. It is in such shambles I do not know where to begin. The roof collapsed in the front corner leaving my bed buried beneath a mountain of snow. The strain of that must have tweaked the wall and upset the door frame allowing Sow, the mother bear, to push open the door despite the lock. She overturned the table and benches near the fire and raided the cupboard that serves as my larder. I emptied it before leaving the month past excepting some jars of preserved food which she smashed. The top shelf of the cupboard that usually boasts neat rows of herbs in jars has been wiped clean. The clay jars are scattered about, most broken, leaving me without a way of earning money by selling them. The bunches of herbs I hung in the rafters to dry are desiccated from exposure to the weather.

I turn slowly, trying to decide what to do first. Angry tears leak from my eyes. I howl against the wretched feeling of helplessness. Set back two years from the progress I made toward independence all for a season's indulgence at the castle in a fruitless search for a husband. What a waste!

"Cursed Sow! Lazy Brick! And foolish me! Foolish!" I scream my frustration, forgetting I have an audience until Cuyler sets his hand on my arm, startling me.

"This can be solved," he assures me. "Who must be told to begin the repairs?"

I can barely think past the destruction. "Brick, I suppose. He owns this cottage. My brother Mather rents it from him. Brick said he would look after it while I was away, but clearly that did not happen."

"Alright. Let's begin there." He tugs me toward the door and sees me mounted before going for his destrier.

It does not occur to me until we are led by one of Brick's children into his barn that this does not concern Cuyler whatsoever. Now is not the time to point that out, however, so I default to gratitude at his assistance in setting the repairs in motion.

"Tirzah," Brick rises from the shavehorse he straddles, setting his carving tools on the seat. "I take it you have come from the cottage."

"I have," I say as the men exchange greetings and Cuyler introduces himself.

"Shame about the roof. Snow has been heavy this year. Have you contacted Mather yet?"

"Actually, I came to see you first. I thought you might help with repairs until he can arrive." Whenever that may be.

Brick's expression is sympathetic yet stern. "You know that is not the arrangement I struck with him."

"Aye, but you did say you would tend the cottage while I was away."

He does not accept the serving of blame I push his way. "Not that it was my responsibility, but I did go over there to knock the snow off the roof. After that, the snows came too quickly to be helped with my own house and barns to tend. Had you been here it would not have happened."

"But you knew I was not here and agreed to—"

Brick's chin juts out. "I am sorry, Tirzah. But our arrangement was that Mather would make any repairs to the cottage and you would maintain it. The responsibility of it is yours alone. And since it had a roof when you let it, I insist you repair it to at least the condition it was in when I entrusted it to you."

My face falls. I knew there was little chance he would aid me. But better asking Brick than the alternative. "I understand."

Once we are outside, Cuyler asks, "Where is your brother stationed?"

"He was at Old Fort. I think he mentioned being posted somewhere else. I shall have to locate his letter for the direction." Not quite the truth, but close.

"You do not keep in regular contact with him?"

I quirk a brow. "Do you keep regular correspondence with your siblings?"

"Not directly, but through my mother, aye. But had my sisters only me to look after them, you can be assured I would not neglect my responsibility."

"Mather does not neglect me," I retort.

"I misspoke—"

"You did." I take the reins he hands me and set off to forestall anymore questions on the subject.

Perhaps I was overreacting to the damage. This time I am prepared for what I will find. I can be objective and formulate a plan that does not involve Mather. Likely I can set aright the majority of what is wrong. After that, I might find one of the families willing to trade my labor for lending me one of their sons to repair my roof. It is the usual way we trade in Parse Kítaran. Labor for labor.

Do not overreact, I admonish myself as we approach my cottage.

I wait for Cuyler's assistance, presenting him with a collected smile and gratitude for his help. This is not his problem, after all. It is mine.

Do not overreact, I repeat to myself while stepping through the door. I set my hands on my hips, facing the destruction. It is every bit as bad this time as the first time I saw it, even without the shock.

"Where do you plan on staying until Mather arrives?"

Cuyler's question catches me off my guard causing me to answer honestly. "Stay? Here, of course."

"You cannot be serious. Tirzah, this place is not inhabitable."

I dismiss him with a wave of my hand and begin searching the wreckage for any of my belongings that survived.

"A bear wandered in! You are not safe here."

I hold up a jar of Valerian that is intact. "Sow never bothers me. Besides, I will bar the door." I look about for a place to deposit my rescued items. I drag the upset table back into place.

Cuyler assists me, still fussing about the state of my life as if I cannot clearly see my predicament. "What if more of the roof caves in while you are sleeping? You will be crushed."

He presents a valid point. I ought to clear the rest of the snow from the roof before I set about the interior. I drop the Valerian onto the surface and head toward the lean-to on the back of the cottage.

"What are you about?" He asks as I wade through the drift blocking the lean-to.

"Taking your suggestion. I mean to clear the roof."

The ladder is right where I left it as are my garden rakes. Since Cuyler is still standing about, I hand him the rakes and haul the ladder out. He objects immediately and takes the ladder from me.

His indignation amuses me. "Why, thank you, Spymaster Trent."

He glowers. "That is supposed to be a secret."

I smile. "These walls are excellent at keeping secrets. They have never betrayed mine."

He leads the way around the cottage then firms the ladder against the edge of the roof that is undamaged. I push past him, placing my feet on the rungs and taking a rake from him at the same moment.

"Tirzah!" He shouts, bracing the ladder as I climb steadily upward.

"Calm yourself. I am not some wilting court flower. I know myself and my limits." The rake sinks into the sheet of snow. One hand on the roof for balance, I use the other to wiggle the rake side to side, back and forth, until the snow slides off the roof in huge sheet. Adjusting my position, I attack the next mound of snow near the peak. It too slides free. Unfortunately, it knocks loose a sheet that falls into the gaping corner of my roof. Timbers crack and groan beneath the weight, widening the hole.

"No!" I throw my hand toward it as if by my will alone I can halt time.

"Hold to the ladder!" Cuyler shouts.

My hand returns to the topmost rung. Frustrated, I toss my rake into the fresh drift of snow. It sinks deep, leaving a rake shaped hole. Skirt clenched in my fist, I descend the ladder. As soon as I alight, I grasp the ladder to move it around to the other side of the cottage to clear the remaining snow, but Cuyler will not relinquish it.

"No, Tirzah. I admire your grit but not so much that I will watch you risk yourself for no reason. You will go inside and draft your letter to your brother then I shall deliver you to Salome's house. I am sure she will welcome you until your brother arrives."

"I have decided not to send for Mather. I will see to this myself and barter with my neighbors to repair the roof."

"Why?"

"Because it is what I wish to do."

TRENT

When did all the women in Malesiir become detrimentally independent? What could possibly make them want to prevent the men in their lives from helping them?

"This is too much for you to manage alone. I am certain your brother would want to be made aware of what has happened so that he can help you."

Tirzah huffs. "I have already acknowledged it is too much for me to manage. That is why I will seek help from my neighbors."

"Aren't they all occupied with their own farms and families like Brick? How long until someone will be able to help you?"

She casts her eyes to the ground. I expect another evasion or an outright lie, but she is candid. "It could be some time. If no other snowstorms appear, perhaps less."

"Are you willing to wait that long to avoid involving your brother?"

She bobs her head.

It does not sit well with me that she will not let her brother help. I doubt it is a matter of pride since she so readily asked Brick to mend the roof and will accept help from her neighbors. Is she afraid of him? Working as a spymaster has taught me how to convince people to confide in me. I do not use such tactics against my friends, but if Tirzah is in some danger from her brother, then I will not suffer remorse for using whatever means are at my disposal to uncover it. I gentle my tone, speaking slowly. "Tirzah. Is there something you want to tell me?"

Her brow rumples. I wait. She shifts away from me, trying to keep her secrets. I am all the more determined to see them exposed.

"You have done nothing wrong. What happened to the roof was an accident, one you tried to prevent."

"Mather will not see it that way," she says to herself.

On a suspicion, I ask, "Did Mather approve of you going to court?"

She crosses her arms defensively. "No. Or, he would not have had I bothered to tell him."

"He did not know you went to court? But you left here two months ago. Has he not been in contact with you in all that time?"

Her eyes snap up to mine. She goes on the offensive. "Have you sent letters to your family in the last two months?"

I nod. "My mother and I exchange letters regularly."

"Oh." Her argument topples.

I return to my original suspicion of some neglect on his part. "Would he come if you write to him?"

"Probably. Eventually." She straightens, firmly closing the discussion. "It hardly matters. This is a mess of my own making. I will sort it out."

Far from allowing the door of this conversation to be permanently shut, I stick my toe in the threshold. "I am sure you will. Mather will be pleased with your resourcefulness when he sees the new roof when next he visits."

She snorts. "I doubt that." Then in a muttering voice that I do not entirely catch says "…wonder how I managed…"

My lips twitch toward a smile. That is the second obvious time she has spoken to herself. Does she do that often?

She stares into the ruined shell of her home and pats the doorframe. "Do not worry. I will straighten you out."

I smile in earnest. "Is there anything you need from here?"

"I do not suppose so. I have gone two months without it. What is one more day, *hmm*?"

The thought of her crawling through the wreckage tomorrow concerns me. I consider the cottage. Could I make it safer for her between now and then? The only way to know is to climb on the roof. Once she is settled with Salome, I will come back to see what can be done.

The ride across the valley to the widow's house is quiet. More of my attention shifts to considering Tirzah amid the silence. When I help her dismount, I notice how nicely my hands fit in the valley of her narrow waist between the generous hills of bosom and hips. She is the sort of woman that would fit well in a man's arms. She looks made to be held. All the soft of her paired with a pretty face and wide violet eyes is quite tempting. It is a wonder that she has not resolved herself of her difficulties with her brother by marrying. Though, that was her intention in going to court. "Was your search for companionship at court successful?"

Her brows shoot up. "Companionship?"

"That was your intention… To find a husband?"

"Oh!" She laughs. "A husband, aye. Not *companionship*."

"You thought I meant—"

"Well, considering the many offers I received to be a *companion*, I thought perhaps you misunderstood my intentions as well."

I frown while unbuckling her bags strapped to the mare. "Not for a moment did I think that of you."

"That is reassuring. And, no. My search was not successful. Apparently, noblemen prefer to marry within their societal circle."

"You were looking only for a nobleman? What is wrong with—"

"Is that my favorite healer come to call?" Salome Brighton asks from the raised porch across the front of her house.

"It is," Tirzah answers with a grin. "But you best wait for me inside. It is too cold out here."

Salome dismisses Tirzah's concerns while tightening the shawl draping her shoulders. "Nonsense. These old bones have lasted me this long. Who is that you have with you?"

Hefting Tirzah's belongings, I stride toward the house and announce myself. "Sergeant Cuyler Trent." Though I am well acquainted with Salome, her eyesight is failing her. "How fare you, Widow Brighton?"

Her kind face creases with deep age lines when she smiles. "Well enough to take you to task for greeting me so formally." After weeks of sleeping in Salome's great room to guard Nev this past August prior to Nev's return to the castle, Salome and I are beyond being formal acquaintances.

Her eyes focus on the bags slung over my shoulder. "Am I to have guests?"

Tirzah hugs Salome and kisses her cheek. "They are mine. The cottage roof collapsed while I was away. May I take advantage of your hospitality until it can be repaired?"

"Oh, that is a shame!" Salome squeezes Tirzah's shoulder. "You know you are always welcome here. What of your medicinals? Did they survive?"

"They might have if Sow had not taken liberties with my larder."

Salome's face reflects her sympathy. "You worked so hard for those. Do you have enough monies saved to repair the roof and feed yourself until you can begin harvesting this summer?"

I cut Tirzah a stern look causing her shoulders to jump to the level of her ears like a child caught in a fib.

"Probably not," she mutters.

"You relied on those herbs for your income?"

"Everyone works, Cuyler."

I pin her with the question she has danced around answering. "Does Mather not provide for you?"

Salome returns inside her house saying, "I shall go put the tea on."

Tirzah draws herself up and faces me boldly. "Mather pays Brick directly to let the cottage. I earn the rest of what I need through assisting the midwife and selling my medicinals. Occasionally, I work with the women to bring in their harvests and put up their produce as well as other things here and there."

"How are you going to feed yourself if the repairs require all of your money?"

She shrugs. "I will make do. Might be a bit thinner come summer," she says wryly, "but I certainly will not starve."

My eyes skim her beautiful figure, imagining it thin from hard work and rationing her meals. It would be like ruining a painting by cutting the finished canvas too small for the frame that it was created for. I cannot abide the thought. "Get inside. It is cold."

CHAPTER TWELVE

TIRZAH

January 14th

I thought I would never escape Cuyler's questions about Mather, but after he learned that I am self sufficient save for the cost of letting the cottage, he relented. Those closest to me, like Salome and Leelah, know of my complicated relationship with my brother and what happened to make it thus. Cuyler will not be in my life long enough to need such explanations, though I appreciated his willingness to assist me as much as was reasonable. Salome pressed him to accept a light meal, then he was on his way.

I return to my cottage this morning with renewed optimism. My skin protests the rough texture of the thick woven wool of my winter dress, but I am grateful for the warmth it provides. Returning to Parse Kítaran also means a return to homespun fabrics and long days filled with work. Without a doubt I will complain of my lot eventually, but at present, I am grateful for the sense of purpose that comes with it.

Had my cottage been in the condition I expected to find it, today would have been spent processing my dried herbs, and I would have notified Mamey, the midwife and resident healer, that I have returned and am ready to resume my work as her assistant. However, that happy normalcy is not what is in store for me this day. This day, I will fill the baskets on my arm with my salvageable possessions from the cottage then set about clearing snow from the roof and searching for someone willing to help me repair the damage.

When I crest the rise that brings my cottage into view, I learn that my day will be far different than I anticipated. Standing on the cottage roof that has been cleared of snow is Cuyler Trent.

"Oh, dear," I say, stumbling to a halt.

Cuyler pries the broken wooden shingles away from gaping hole in the roof, tossing them into a pile on the ground. With a deep breath to calm the rhythm of my heart, I approach the cottage. "Had I known spymasters were proficient in carpentry I might have offered you the position."

He looks up with a smile. "This spymaster was reared on a farm."

"Then that makes you highly overqualified to be atop my roof and far too costly for me to employ."

"Aye, I suppose you don't have need of most of my skills. Fortunately for you, the cost of my labor is only a decent meal each day. Do you think you can manage that?"

"Cuyler," I drawl, "I cannot accept your charity."

"Then do not think of it as charity," he argues with a charming smile that probably convinces most people to agree with him.

I cross my arms, shaking my head. "I am grateful, truly, but I cannot take you from your family."

With a resigned look, he slides toward the ladder braced against the eaves. I prepare myself to be stern in the face of his kindness. There is simply no way he can convince me that he is not putting himself out by helping me.

Yet standing before me with an easy confidence that a woman could learn to depend upon, Cuyler sets about persuading me. "You have your reasons for not contacting Mather, reasons you do not want to share with me, correct?"

I nod the affirmative.

"Then you will understand if I say that I have my own reasons for not wanting to visit my family. I, too, have a brother that I would prefer to avoid, though contending with him seemed the lesser evil when weighed against staying in the capital." *With Silla*, he does not say, but it is the obvious completion of his sentence. "You will be doing me a service by giving me a temporary purpose. You can see that, can't you?"

I feel myself nodding along, unable to argue with something he claims to want to do for reasons that extend beyond a charitable inclination.

"Alright, Cuyler," I hear myself say, though the cautionary voice in my head calls me a fool.

"I knew you were a reasonable woman." He gives me another of those charming smiles that could get me into trouble.

TRENT

January 16th

Tirzah takes hold of the end of the split log I point out. "Are you certain Valor will not mind my raiding his lumber? I still do not feel right about it."

After two full days of removing damaged timbers from the cottage roof, I have discovered why Tirzah was so certain she could manage on her own. She has worked just as hard as I have at any task that needs doing, be it shoveling snow or hauling wood. I tried to keep her from the most strenuous tasks, but she only laughed at me and kept working.

"I am certain he would want you to use it. Besides, did Erianna compensate you for healing Valor and the Ruphiri?"

"No. I did not allow her to. It was the least I could do to make amends."

We carry the log to the sled, stacking it with the others I have already selected. "Well, Valor would have insisted upon it. Think of this as your compensation."

She considers it, then teases, "I suppose. And I can always blame you for the pilfering if he is angered."

"You go right ahead." Because the more days that pass, the more I want to trade blows with Valor. If he had not been so single minded about finding Erianna's enemy, he would have considered the others being exploited by the Ruphiri. Maybe he would not have let his friends become casualties of his war.

"How many of these do we need?" Tirzah waves to the logs.

"Those four are the purlins, these seven are the rafters, and then you will need another dozen or so to split into battens for the shingles."

She blinks wide violet eyes at me, then the corners of her mouth hitch in a slow smile. "Perhaps I could not have managed this alone."

I chuckle. "You know, I have come to think the opposite. You have grit."

"That does not mean I know what a *purling* is."

"A *purlin*." I correct. "Come here."

She rounds the sled, tracking my finger to where I point in the roof of the shed above us. "Do you see that horizontal board there? That is a purlin. It provides structural support for the rafters. There was only a single purlin on each side of your roof. I am going to put an additional one on each side."

"Was that why the roof collapsed?"

"As best I can tell, the only reason your roof has not collapsed prior was your dedication to knocking off the snow between storms. The purlins and several rafters were cracked, a few were even rotted. They needed to be repaired. I am glad you were not sleeping in your bed during that snowstorm. It would have crushed you."

"Then you do not think it was my fault?" Tirzah looks at me over her shoulder, seeking absolution.

"No, I do not."

She sighs, her hand pressed against her chest. "What a relief. Thank you, Cuyler."

My eyes follow her hand's unconscious movement, but I flick them back to the roof where they cannot gawp at her. "Those vertical poles are the rafters, though your roof uses split beams instead of rounded poles."

"Is that good?"

"Aye. It provides a flat surface for the battens, which are those narrow horizontal boards."

"And the shingles are nailed to the battens?"

"Exactly. You see, I knew you would have managed without me."

Tirzah sobers. "Not everyone can manage on their own. Nor should we."

I pretend not to know what she means and try to divert her attention with a smirk. "Right you are. Thus, if you will help me with —"

"Cuyler."

I meet those violet eyes that miss nothing.

"She should have confided in you."

Maybe it is because we are utterly alone or because she is sympathetic or simply because I need someone to see this thing that is gnawing at my insides, I feel my hand reach into my pocket and draw out the ruby ring. "I wish she had told me. My life would be very different if she had."

Tirzah lifts the ring from my palm, watching the light dance on the facets of the gem. "You were going to offer for her hand in marriage."

"I was." Though Tirzah could do more harm than good, I chance letting this healer see a bit more of my pain. "It is foolish, but what is still bothering me is wondering if Silla would have accepted. I honestly have no idea if she has a genuine care for me or not."

Tirzah does not mock me for toting the ring about in my pocket. Nor does she belittle the feelings I have for Silla by offering the conciliatory platitudes I half expect. "She made a terrible mistake. Sometimes, it feels like there are nothing but bad choices left to us, yet I am sure she regrets the one she chose."

I swallow, trying to ease the tightness in my throat. "Again, my life would be very different if she did."

Tirzah's surprise is marked. "She does not regret lying to you?"

It takes me a long moment to be able to answer, still, my voice quivers with bitterness. "She hopes that I will come to accept what she did. To see that she did 'what she had to do.'"

The skepticism in Tirzah's eyes has me tucking the ring back in my pocket. Before I can end the discussion, she says, "It is alright if you cannot do that. You do not have to agree with what she did."

"Don't I? If I want a future with her, I have to make my peace with what she did." Which plays a large part in my absence from Malsihra.

Tirzah considers that. "If you join your lives, I suppose you will. But you can have peace by forgiving her, even if you do not come to a place of agreeing with her."

"She has not asked for my forgiveness," I contend. "She does not deserve my forgiveness if she won't ask for it."

Tirzah's gentle answer slips beneath my anger, getting to the ache in me. "None of us deserves forgiveness, Cuyler. That is what grace is for. It is not earned. It is a gift that speaks of the heart of the giver not the receiver. That same grace spared Silla from a traitor's death and gifted her a second chance."

Though I already feel she has given me much to chew on, Tirzah offers me one more thing.

"You can choose to forgive Silla even if she does not ask for it. Forgiveness grants the wronged person a measure of peace in spite of the circumstances. It will save you from the bitterness consuming you."

CHAPTER THIRTEEN

TIRZAH

January 18th

After a day spent sawing, planing, and setting a few of the rafters, I appropriated goods from Salome's larder to prepare Cuyler what he declared to be a meal fit for the queen's table. I bid him goodnight thinking on what I could cook next for him. Since Salome only keeps an amount of food suitable for an elderly woman, I leave her house with my coin purse tucked in my basket to purchase some staple items while I am about my errands today.

Cuyler is already at work when I arrive, splitting the halved logs into square boards. With a large mallet and iron wedges, he sights the grain of the wood then hammers each wedge into the log, spacing them down its entire length in a straight line. After all the wedges are set, he alternately pounds each deeper into the log until it cracks. I have come to appreciate the fibrous tearing sound of the wood splitting nearly as much as I take pride in the papery crunch of a perfectly dried herb. Cuyler flips the log and begins again, splitting away the curved edges. Those are set aside for firewood.

"Purlins?" I guess. That was the next task after setting the remaining rafters.

He looks up at me with a smile that makes my stomach somersault. "Aye. Breakfast?" He nods at the basket slung across my arm.

"Aye. You aren't hungry, are you?"

"Did you make it?"

"I might have," I drawl.

He sets aside his tools. "Then I am starved."

I try not to be overly pleased that Cuyler enjoys my cooking. Mather rarely compliments it, and the only other people that I typically prepare meals for are the sick or elderly. Those meals must be made bland for their weak stomachs which does not allow me to take advantage of my extensive knowledge of herbs to flavor a dish.

I spread the simple fare on my little all-use table that Cuyler helped me bring outside while the house is in a state of chaos. Once the rafters and purlins are in place, he will allow me to go inside to begin cleaning the cottage while he cuts the batten boards for the shingles. He does not want to chance another collapse of the roof with me inside.

I wipe my hands clean on my apron. "I will get the bucket and—"

"No need. I already drew water. Do you still mean to let the midwife know you are returned today?" Cuyler asks, rising to retrieve the bucket after motioning me to sit.

I set slices of salt cured pork on top of a thick slice of bread slathered with jam. "Aye, after I have helped you seat the remaining rafters."

Cuyler lifts the dipper from the bucket and drinks deeply before refilling it and passing it to me. I look at the place on the dipper where his lips touched. If I turn it to drink from the opposite side, would he attribute it to the peculiarity of healers? Setting my lips where his were seems an intimate thing...

Stop being foolish! I scold myself and put the dipper to my lips.

My stomach ignores my scold and flips once more.

If Cuyler notes my little hesitation, he does not comment. "That would be helpful. It goes much better with you to steady the beams while I place them."

Which is what we spend the rest of the morning doing. When we break to eat the noon meal, I proudly admire the work we have accomplished. "If we continue at this rate, the roof will be repaired in a matter of days."

"I like your optimism, even if it is rooted in inexperience," Cuyler teases, dropping onto a bench.

I prop a hand on my hip, waiting for him to elucidate.

"The rafters are the big pieces. With them in place, the tedious work begins. Splitting out the batten boards and shingles could take the better part of two weeks. The door also must be repaired and hung correctly."

My face falls. "But that is so much of your time."

"Do not look so glum," he cajoles. "Keep feeding me meals like these, and I promise to be good company for you while I mend the roof."

Which is something I am deeply concerned about. Cuyler is too amiable. And I am too easily snared.

So get on with your errands and leave the man be! The sensible side of me insists.

I heed that voice, efficiently unwrapping our meal from waxed cloths. "If at any time you must leave, I will understand. Please do not put yourself out on my account. I *can* find someone else to help."

"But not Mather?" He inquires with that charming smile.

"Maybe," I drawl, pausing over the food I lay out.

His smile holds, but a layer of eager interest shows beneath.

I shoot him a knowing glance.

He sits back with a chuckle.

"Leave it be, Cuyler. I do not want to discuss this. Please do not try to trick me into answering."

He sobers. "I apologize."

I cant my head. "Why are you determined to know?"

"Honestly?" He gives me the chance to withdraw my question.

"Honestly."

All his charm falls to the wayside revealing the disillusioned man who has traded in secrets and lived in a world of shadows for too many years. "Because I have seen how powerless women are to protect themselves from dishonorable men. I have seen girls sold into slavery. I have seen sisters and daughters neglected by the ones who ought to care for them. Tirzah, if you are one of them, I swear I shall do something about it."

I swallow the lump in my throat, lowering to the bench opposite him. A memory falls free of my tangled thoughts. "You and Valor found Ivy. You rescued her, didn't you?"

Cuyler's usually warm eyes darken to coals. "The way we found Ivy still haunts me."

Leelah's sweet adopted daughter was being prostituted by her uncles at the tender age of seven. It was the unmistakable guidance of the Creator that led Valor and Cuyler to that dilapidated tavern where they discovered Ivy, carried out justice against the wicked men, then delivered her to Leelah.

Maybe Cuyler would understand after all. Maybe he would not look at me differently if he knew. A tremble rolls through me. This secret was the one thing Mather forbade me from telling. He did it to protect me more than himself. Still, I want to give Cuyler something, some assurance that I am not in any sort of danger.

"Mather and I have a complicated relationship. Some of that is my fault, some of it is not. He and I had a… a falling out several years past that well and truly ruined any familial affection on his part. After, we decided to spend as little time together as possible. He provides for me out of duty. If the cost of my living here were to be any higher, he would simply move me to keep house for him to spare the expense. I do not want that. I like my life here, being an assistant healer. It is something Mather allows me to do, though he disapproves. He has a strong sense of propriety where I am concerned. And…" I sigh, deciding that I may as well admit to my subterfuge. "Mather would not like that I went to court. Had I asked, he would have said no. Thus, I did not ask. If I asked him to repair the damage to the cottage that occurred because I was somewhere of which he disapproved, he would settle with Brick and move me to live with him."

"Which is why you were adamant that he not be involved," Cuyler summarizes.

"Aye."

"But he will learn you went to court eventually. What then? What will he do to you?"

Do to me. I have not sufficiently eased his mind. "Mather has never raised a hand to me nor would he." If he did not do it three years ago, he certainly won't do it because of this. "Deep down, I know that he loves me."

"But he might relocate you?"

"He might. But I knew I would never have the chance to go to court again. I decided it was worth it." I smirk. "I regret that choice now, of course, as I am sure you also wish I had not gone to court."

Cuyler takes my hands in his atop the table, pulling my gaze along with them. "Silla's choices were her own. You did right by bringing it to Valor. I do not regret that she was found out. I only regret the trouble it brought on you. Alright?"

"Alright."

He releases my hands but continues gazing steadily at me. "As far as Mather and the cottage roof are concerned, I will finish helping you repair it. Hopefully, he will have no cause to remove you from Parse Kítaran. But if you do run into trouble with him, I will do whatever I can to help you sort it out, if you ask me."

"Thank you, Cuyler. That is far too kind an offer." Especially since he has not met Mather.

I take my leave shortly after the noon meal, first to find Mamey, second to procure the best foods my limited resources can afford. If food is the only repayment Cuyler will allow me to give, then I shall make certain it is the best food I can possibly prepare.

"Where have you been?" The deep wrinkles of Elder Eloham's face pull into a frown. "I kept asking after my daughter, but no one could tell me where you had gone."

If I thought the guilt brought on by my vain pursuits these past two months would be alleviated by the fulfilling work of healing, I was deluding myself.

I straighten Eloham's tunic that tries to slide off his frail shoulder. He has lost noticeable weight since I left. Not surprising if he was distraught over my absence. More than the other elders to whom I give care, Eloham has taken to me. "Are you cold?"

"Of course, I am cold. That boy is always stingy with firewood. Don't know why. We live in a forest."

Calling his attention to the fire that is burning oppressively hot would not sway him from his belief that "that boy"—his neighbor's twenty year old son—has been stingy with firewood. Instead of arguing, I tuck a quilt around his legs. "Why don't you warm under this while I check the fire and start some tea."

"I don't want any tea. I want to know where you have been. A father ought to know where his daughter has been."

I wince. Changing the subject often works when he is being obstinate, which is most of the time. "I am sorry I was away, but I am returned now and have no plans to travel again."

Eloham huffs. "Good. No one else can do anything right."

"Are you hungry?" I put a nourishing soup in a pot over the fire then check on the overall state of the house while it heats, straightening and cleaning as I go.

"No! You come here and tell me where you have been, Mirande."

It was a short time after I began helping Mamey care for the growing number of elderly that Eloham decided he liked me. As the aging mind sometimes does, he assigned me the role of his daughter. Sadly, his real daughter Mirande passed away in childbirth decades ago. Since it brings him a measure of peace to think of me as his daughter, I allow it and have learned to answer to her name. "Alright. I will tell you, but it would make me so happy if you would drink some broth while I do." I use my sweetest tone to convince him. "It was someplace special."

He grunts. "Suppose that would be alright."

"I was at a castle."

"A castle?" He looks across the room at me. "There is not a castle here."

"It was several days journey to get there. That was why I was gone for a while. It was so beautiful, set low on a mountainside behind a large city with paved roads."

"Truly?"

I smile. "Truly."

Eloham eats the soup one spoonful at a time while I tell him about the castle and the tournaments, our Warrior Queen and High King Lorennt. His eyes droop as soon as his body's need for nourishmennt is met. I help him with his personal needs and tuck him into bed before the sun has set.

"You are not going anywhere are you, Mirande?" Eloham's worried tone breaks my heart.

"I am going home to sleep for the night. You only have one bed here, remember?"

The expression of childish surprise on his aged face is comical. "Oh. I forgot."

I kiss his forehead. "I will return tomorrow. Sleep well."

"Goodnight, Mirande."

The whole way home I fight the guilt of abandoning my charges for the sake of a hopeless cause. A few tears escape when I think of how upset Eloham has been without me.

I hang my cloak on the hook inside Salome's house and set my basket on the table before going to her.

"Tirzah, what is wrong, my sweet girl?" She greets me with a hug that looses a few more tears.

She is sturdier than Eloham, but not so very much. "Promise me you won't get old."

Salome laughs brightly. "You seem not to have noticed, but I am already old."

"Well, you are not allowed to get any older. I forbid it."

She guides me across the great room to her favorite chair by the fire. "Tell me of your day."

I settle on the floor at her feet and lay my head in her lap. She strokes my hair like my mother used to when I was worried. "Eloham is not faring as well as when I left. He is so thin. And he is very upset with me for leaving."

Salome listens patiently before offering consolation. "You must recall that he accuses you of leaving him or being gone even when you are there day to day."

"I know, but this time I *was* gone. Even if he does not know the difference, I do."

"If you had returned and he had not been worse, would you be well with having left?"

The question makes me look at my guilt a different way. "Probably. Maybe not. I do not know."

"I think it was your reason for going to the castle that has your conscience nipping at you."

For as long as I have lived in Malsihra, I have turned to Salome for counsel. I have shared my heart with her, and she has unfailingly gifted me with her wisdom. Not that I availed myself of it this time. I went to Malsihra for misguided reasons. "I was selfish."

"Did you feel that way before Eloham?"

"Aye, but seeing him made it worse."

Salome continues gently stroking my head. "Would you like to know my thoughts?"

I nod, closing my eyes to listen to what I did not want to hear before.

"Your heart has the capacity for so much love. You find a great deal of joy in pouring out your love onto the sick and physically ailing, but they are not capable of returning that love in the full measure you give it. Thus, you have undertaken to find that love by searching for a husband."

"There is nothing wrong with that." I am quick to defend myself instead of listening as I said I would.

Salome soothes me, unswerved by my interjection. "No, there is not. However, I am afraid that you are placing more significance on the love of a husband than on the love you have already been given."

Have I?

I could never forget the love that wrapped around me the day I was redeemed. In one breathtaking moment, I went from feeling alone and unworthy of love to knowing that I was unspeakably precious. I fell into the arms of a Love so perfect that there was nothing He would not do to be with me. The Saving Son fought for me and died for me so that nothing would separate us. Not heaven or earth or the grave or even my sin can stand between He and I. Through the Holy Texts, He told me of His love and grace that were waiting if only I would let Him in. So I did. I could not do anything else. I needed His love more than my next breath.

I weigh my recent actions against those memories. There is nothing wrong with wanting to marry. The Creator Himself declared that it is not good for man to be alone. Is there truly something wrong with my pursuit of the tangible love of a husband?

TRENT

I anticipate the warm greeting I will receive when I enter Salome's home. It reminds me of my mother's house with her and my sisters fairly celebrating each time I walk through the door. Perhaps it was Salome's insistence that I stop knocking before entering or the way Tirzah smiles and orders me to sit at the table the moment I remove my cloak, something my mother and sisters also do. Whatever it is, I am glad for the decided change from the forced politeness of the Malesiirian court.

The house is quiet when I step through the door. Are the women out? They are always chatting or making some domestic noise. A glance across the great room answers the question of their whereabouts in a way that concerns me. Tirzah is seated on the floor like a child, dozing with her head in Salome's lap.

"Welcome, Cuyler." Salome's normal quiet timbre is not enough to wake Tirzah.

I crouch before them, searching Tirzah's face for an explanation. Her brow is pinched as if, even in sleep, she is deep in thought. I realize that she is several years older than I previously estimated. I placed her at the same age as Erianna and Silla. Without the look of perpetual amusement livening her features, I can see that she is probably five years past that, placing her at the same age as me. That reanimates the question of why she is not married, but I can wonder at that later.

"Is she unwell?"

Salome strokes her hair affectionately. "She is a good healer, but it costs her at times."

What happened today that left her drained? "Why don't I carry her to bed—"

"No!" Salome's hand splays protectively on Tirzah's head. "No, it is best for her to wake and finish out the day."

Before I can protest, Salome gently rouses her.

Tirzah's wide eyes strain against the light, then focus on me with confusion.

"You fell asleep while we were talking," Salome informs her.

Tirzah is distressed. "But I have not prepared dinner!" She pushes to her feet then gasps.

I catch her beneath her elbows before she can stumble. Her feet undoubtedly fell asleep from being folded beneath her. "Hang dinner. You should rest."

"But..." She sets her hands on my arms, letting me steady her.

"You can impress me with your skills in the kitchen tomorrow. I will make something for all of us tonight."

When she still looks uncertain, I tease, "I *am* an overqualified farmer, remember?"

She grins and looks ready to accept, but Salome sighs. "Make a decision, Tirzah."

"Oh!" She steps away from me, sparing a guilty glance at Salome. "Thank you, but I had best see to it."

For the first time in the course of our acquaintance, I am irritated with Salome. I have never seen her come anywhere close to scolding anyone, and it was hardly Tirzah's due for being tired. "I will be sure to leave straight after dinner so she can go to bed." Though additional waking hours spent sitting on Valor's porch before retiring to the loft of his barn hold less appeal than the women's company.

"Very considerate," Salome acknowledges. "How go the repairs?"

CHAPTER FOURTEEN

TRENT

January 19th

A light snow fell during the night dusting the world in clean white powder. Tirzah takes one look at the accumulation of snow inside her home then glares skyward through the hole in her roof.

"I thought we discussed this and I persuaded You to hold back the clouds for a while longer." She heaves a sigh. "But I suppose You know better than I about the necessity of snow. Though perhaps You would consider covering my house with Your hand that I might have less work when it comes time to clean it?"

"Tirzah," I call her attention back to earth. "With whom are you speaking?"

Her frustrated expression turns my way. "The Almighty. I prayed He would hold back the snowfall, but it seems He saw necessity in loosing the clouds."

"Or perhaps He does not trouble Himself with such requests." I did not mean to let the cynical words escape. Thankfully, Tirzah is not offended in the least.

"Oh, but He has done so for me before! Just this summer I was harvesting my herbs when a big storm gathered over the mountains. I watched it build, oh, it was black with thunderheads and moving fast. It was the sort of storm that ruins crops. I could feel the rain on my face when I began to pray that the Almighty would hold back the storm. I desperately needed that harvest. Suddenly, a strong wind blew out of the west and halted the storm. I could see the rain falling in sheets right there in that field," she points across the distance, "but it did not come any closer. The west wind blew steadily until every last bundle of my herbs was brought inside. Then it stopped. The storm was upon my house moments later—hail followed by a driving rain." She stalls, caught up in the wonder of her own story. Her wide, earnest eyes fix on mine. "Don't you see, Cuyler? It was not a silly thing to think He might hold back the snow. He has held back the storm for me before."

I want to tell her it was a coincidence, that it is impossible her prayers swayed an aloof Creator.

I cannot.

"It is not silly, though I do wonder why He did not do it again?"

She smiles. "That is easy to answer. He sees something that I do not. The snow needed to fall more than I wanted to not clean up the ensuing mess. Maybe even in my life he used the snowfall in a way I cannot see. He has a reason."

Tirzah's simple faith is so genuine, providing her with such reassurance in her daily life that for a moment, I want to grab hold of it, to capture it for myself. How much peace would I have if I could see the world the way she does?

But the dangers of this world are bigger than thunderstorms. She cannot explain them away as being necessary. If that aloof Creator was present, the world would be different.

"What are you thinking, Cuyler?"

I don the winsome smile I have perfected to turn conversations the way I want them to go. "That I like your story, and I hope you will soon know the reasons for the snowfall."

She crosses her arms, a stubborn pout on her lips. "That is not what you are thinking."

I feign a laugh to make her feel unsure of herself, though it is my heart that beats faster at the thought that she might see through me.

She frowns at me. "I asked you not to manipulate me like that."

I nearly swallow my tongue. Twice she has unerringly pierced my perfected disguise. "I do not—"

She huffs. "Let me be clear. Since you insist on shamming me, I am going to walk into that cottage and spend my time in a more productive manner. If you would like to be honest, you know where to find me. In the future, if I make you uncomfortable and you do not want to discuss something, simply say so. I won't pry."

Tirzah does exactly what she says. She turns on her heel and marches across the snow dusted ground.

TRENT

Confound these Judges and their uncanny ability to sense a lie! It is an unfair advantage over the rest of us.

I leave Tirzah to her snit and set to work on the battens. My attack on the logs with the maul is more enthusiastic than yesterday. If Tirzah wishes to make a man miserable, she is clearly capable of doing it with a few choice words. Undoubtedly, our next meal will be an unpleasant affair.

Gah! Women.

This particular one appears in her doorway with a trunk she places outside. Again and again she pops out the door to deposit handfuls of belongings into the trunk. I ignore her. I certainly don't notice her smile growing brighter with each rescued belonging. Or the agreeable sway of her hips as she returns inside her cottage. Or the way she whistles cheerfully to herself as she works.

I straighten, bracing myself on the long handle of the maul as she steps outdoors again. How upset can she be if she is whistling?

I prod my courage to life and walk to the cottage. While Valor likes courting trouble, I have always thought Kragorn takes the more intelligent route of handling women. Growing up with two sisters firmly taught me that it is best not to cross a woman in a temper. I stand in the crooked doorframe using the subterfuge of inspecting it to watch Tirzah work for a moment, though the frame does need to be repaired before the shingles go up or I risk creating a leak in the new roof.

Tirzah seems decidedly pleasant.

It makes me decidedly cross with myself.

I don't like to think that I intentionally manipulate people, friends especially, but perhaps I do. Maybe I never step fully out of the spymaster's cloak.

Tirzah catches sight of me before I decide what to say to her. "Oh, good! I was about to come find you. Do you think I ought to remove the furniture before shoveling the snow or just get to it?"

"Are you asking for my opinion?" I am truly confused. I thought she was angry with me. Women never want a man's opinion when they are angry.

Her mouth hitches up in an amused smile. "I asked for your opinion."

I glance out the door to the place she delivered my reproof then back at her, wondering if I imagined it. "Why?"

"Because I do not want to waste my time and thought you might have a suggestion. Which I begin to doubt the longer you stand there gaping like a trout."

"But you are cross with me."

Tirzah props a hand on her hip. "Why, Cuyler! Are you nervous?"

"I try not to land on the bad side of women." Yet this one has me off kilter.

She quirks a brow. "Is that why you speak what you think people want to hear?"

She has taken my measure rather quickly.

"I can see that I am right, thus, now that I understand you, let me help you understand me. I tend to be overly candid. You will never have to wonder what I am thinking. I assure you. You will know."

My smile answers her declaration. "Then I ought to play fair and not 'sham' you again?"

"If you can help it." Her expression says she doesn't think I can.

I duck my head, feeling chagrinned. "You are probably right, but I give you leave to call me out for any future shamming."

She collects another armload of belongings. As she brushes past me, she gives me a saucy grin. "Don't worry. I will."

CHAPTER FIFTEEN

TIRZAH

January 21st

Salome has long since gone to bed while Cuyler and I sit up late into the night talking at the table. My tongue is loosened by the lateness of the hour. I find myself answering questions I would not otherwise.

"How many years older than you is Mather?" He wonders.

"He is seven years older than my twenty five which, I suppose, is part of why you asked."

He throws me that charming smile. "Guilty. I will be more direct with this next question."

The more often I call out his conversational maneuvering, the quicker he is to acknowledge his mistake. "Go on."

"Mather sounds like a surname. For whom was he named?"

This line of questioning is dangerous. I cannot let him delve it too deeply. "Mather *is* his surname. John Mather."

"You call your brother by his surname?" Probably especially strange to him since I call every other soldier by their given name. It is an obstinance on my part.

"He prefers it, to be known by the name of his father rather than the name his mother gave him."

"Yet you do not use your surname. I have never heard you called Tirzah Mather."

"We have different fathers. I have no surname to be known by."

Cuyler's expression relays his surprise. He is too clever by half to not realize the circumstances of my birth were less than ideal, but not even he could guess at what they actually were.

"Your turn," I declare. "How many siblings do you have?"

Cuyler folds his hands over the table. "An older brother, two younger sisters, and a younger brother."

"A large family. Do you hope to have as many children of your own?"

He frowns, studying the table. "I suppose it depends upon the woman."

Poor Cuyler. He may have only considered the topic of children in the context of a marriage to Silla. "Your brother. You said that you had difficulties with him. Of what origins?"

He shakes off my previous question. "My older brother, Hale, will inherit the farm. I was obliged to make my own way. He married the tavern keeper's daughter shortly after I joined the army and took over the tavern from his father-in-law. I had become committed to a soldier's life by the time our father died a year into my service. When that happened, Hale wanted me to return home to steward the farm, but I refused."

"Why did he want to relinquish his inheritance?"

"He didn't. He doesn't. He wanted me to be its caretaker and look after my mother and siblings while he reaped the benefits of the lucrative tavern."

"But that is not fair!"

Cuyler smiles indulgently. "Since I refused to return, I consented to help him financially support my mother and siblings. That money goes directly to my mother. I do not have to worry that she will use it unwisely."

"Why did Hale not offer you the farm if he also owns the tavern?" It does not make sense that he would ill use Cuyler or be so greedy.

He turns mischievous. "Hale is still piqued that his wife asked me to marry her before I entered the army."

My interest flares. "Well, that sounds like quite a story!"

He shrugs. "Only when I say it like that. As a boy, I was a flirt—"

"Unthinkable!"

He chuckles, an unsettled edge to the sound. "Right. You have seen through me."

I lean closer, giving him my attention without censure.

"Millie was one of the girls I was most often talking sweet to. When word got around that I was leaving, she asked me to stay and take her to wife instead. But I was young and did not have a care for her, though it shames me to admit I made her think I did. The next letter I received from my mother told that Hale had wed Millie."

The poor girl. How easy it would be to fall for the charming Cuyler Trent. "Why did she settle for him?"

"No, no. It was nothing like that." He banishes my concern. "It is a love match and a good marriage by all accounts."

"Then why the hostility?"

Cuyler stares at me a long moment before admitting, "Because my brother cannot abide the thought that I kissed his wife before he did."

"Oh," I drawl the single sound. This is the possessive side of love. It must sit especially badly with Hale that it was his younger brother who kissed his wife, even though Millie was not his at the time. Considering how quickly they wed, perhaps Hale had esteemed Millie while Cuyler was toying with her.

The older and wiser Cuyler tips his cup to view the dregs swirling in the bottom. "Sakes, Tirzah. What did you put in this tea? It has me talking looser then three pints of ale."

My heart sighs. *He confided in me.*

The sensible side of me harrumphs.

I rise to retrieve the tea kettle. "It is a healer's secret blend."

He watches me refill his cup. "I think it has more to do with the healer."

I dare a glance at his smile. One single glance. My swooning heart cannot remain upright if I dwell on it.

"What of yourself? You cannot convince me you have not laid claim to a few hearts."

My hand trembles as I refill my cup. "No. I have not."

"Be fair," Cuyler wheedles. "After all I have confessed, you must give me something."

"I am being truthful." The one time a man professed to love me he proved false. But since Cuyler has been honest with me, it would be unfair not to do the same. "However, I have received several offers of marriage."

He perks up. "*Ah*! How many is several?"

I settle back in my chair, pushing the tea kettle to the center of the table between Cuyler and I. "When I worked as a laundress in Chishelm and before that in Juniper, probably a dozen. I am not sure precisely. I stopped counting. Since the offers were bookended with an invitation to spend the night in the traveler's bed till we could marry the following morning, I found those offers insincere."

Cold silence fills the space between us. Eventually, Cuyler's tight reply claims it. "Attention from lechers is not what I was asking after."

"Is it not? It happens with regularity. Even at court."

Cuyler pushes the kettle aside, leaning towards me. "Not all men are dishonorable. Was there no suitor in your youth?"

I shake my head.

"No soldier that could not leave Chishelm because he was smitten with you?"

"No soldiers," I adamantly state.

He raises a brow. "You said you have lived here over two years. Has no one here payed court to you?"

I smirk, trying to convince him leave off this conversation by employing the irreverent expression I have seen Erianna use. "Valor nearly did. Does that count?"

"No. It does not."

Apparently, I need to practice the expression.

I shrug. "I have had a few offers I considered. Twice since moving here, widowers have asked for my hand. Each had a passel of children and made it clear that I would need to give up healing to become mother and wife."

"You are not opposed to the idea of a marriage of convenience," he states, having likely deduced it from my receptiveness to Valor. "Thus, I assume it was the part about giving up healing?"

"It was," I admit, finally able to look him in the eye again. "In healing, I have found my calling. I cannot give it up. Not entirely. It seems wrong to abandon it for a marriage of convenience."

"I can understand that," he sympathizes.

"Mather does not," I say quietly. "He lets me do it, but he does not approve. I think it is difficult for the men here, too. Of course, they are happy to accept my help if they are injured, but I think they also view it as indecent. For me to be a wife, my husband would have to be well with my healing hands touching his neighbors."

Cuyler ponders that, then admits, "As a man, I am forced to agree with your assessment. It would be hard for me to accept my wife touching my friends. Could you limit your healing to women and children only?"

I frown. "I could say aye, but if a man was injured and needed my help, then I could not refuse him."

"That would be a dilemma," he acknowledges. I am grateful he can see it from my perspective.

Wanting to turn the mood, I offer a lighter anecdote. "What I need is a permissive husband. I thought I had found one last year. He was a respectable man with a smallholding. He even agreed to allow me to continue healing since his children were long grown."

"How 'long grown'?" Cuyler catches on quickly.

I grin. "Long enough that he said he was fairly certain he could give me children of my own, but he could not make any promises."

Cuyler laughs with me. "Oh, that will not do. At least he warned you."

"People will tell a healer absolutely anything." I cast my eyes heavenward. "If I am to marry, I think the Creator must intervene. My efforts have yielded as much reward as fishing in a field."

"It will happen, Tirzah," he assures me. "Someone is going to lay claim to you and count himself the most fortunate of men that all the rest were too foolish to make you their own."

The more days I spend in his company, the more a part of me wishes he could be that man, even though he is a soldier. "Thank you."

We lapse into silence once more. He pats the table and rises. "It is late. I will say goodnight."

As I lay in bed, my attention is pulled away from my prayers. I spend my time repeating our conversation and wondering if Cuyler could eventually make his peace with me being a healer.

CHAPTER SIXTEEN

TRENT

January 23rd

The doorframe was not as difficult to repair as I anticipated. Less than a day was spent correcting the lintels and rehanging the door. The bear did more damage to it than the collapsing roof.

So much do I dislike the thought of this gregarious bear neighboring Tirzah, whose sole defense is a locked door, that dawn greets me high in a tree with my bow clasped between my hands.

The forest awakens first with birdsong. From their perches, they sing in the new day, flitting from branch to branch, picking at depressions in the bark to extract insects. A trio of grouse burst from their shelter beneath a blanket of snow to gorge on the buds of a cedar. Chipmunks dart across branches while chattering to one another and feasting on autumn's bounty that they stashed away. A hare reveals its den, ambling slowly from beneath a bush. Another returns to its home under a downed tree. The wild things are not bothered by my still, silent presence as long as I do not interfere. It is the peaceful part of hunting, becoming an observer of nature.

However, that is not the reason I am here.

The fresh signs point to the sow bear having passed by recently. That she has forgone her winter sleep to continue feeding is not good. She must have learned to pilfer from the surrounding farms and possibly their livestock. I am hopeful that she will return to eat the mast from the acorn and walnut trees hidden in the leaf litter under the snow.

Like the soft whisper of a woman, an animal moves through the evergreens. Though it is too delicate a noise to be the bear, I nock an arrow. The anticipation of this moment never wanes. Blood pounds in my ears. Sweaty palms clench the bow. Dry tongue sticks to the roof of my mouth.

I hold my breath as its each step brings it closer to my view. A flicker of mottled grey that could be excused as tree bark except for its progressive forward motion. The animal stalls, flicking the white tail characteristic of its kind. I do not dare to twitch.

It picks up its feet, placing them daintily on the snow. The rustle it makes brushing on pine needles masks the stretching sound of my bow string as I draw it taut, anchoring it to my jaw. I focus on the break in the trees where it will appear, steadying my breathing and forcing my muscles to hold the weight of my drawn bow without quivering.

Another stride brings the magnificent hart fully into view. Even without his antlers, recently shed judging by the depressions in his pedicle, there is no mistaking this buck for a doe. Thick through the body, deep in the belly, round in the rump, he is a beautiful mature male, the sort that has fought and won many battles, sired many young, and evaded many hunters. He browses the buds of a dogwood tree, taking his sustenance however he can during the lean months.

I am momentarily awestruck, my first inclination to slowly ease the tension from my bow.

But I must not let him go. His life will sustain Tirzah for months.

Trusting my accuracy to the consistent placement of my fingers on my jaw and the touch of the bowstring on my lips and nose, I aim slightly behind and below his shoulder where a single arrow through his lungs and heart will fell him. I inhale and hold my breath in preparation for the shot. Then he looks up.

Keen, glassy eyes the color of earth meet mine. He stares unflinchingly at me.

His life for Tirzah's.

I loose the arrow.

Scarlet soaks snow.

I bear the weight of the kill on my shoulders as I climb the road to Tirzah's cottage, feeling grateful for the animal's sacrifice. The sun is getting on well in its morning ascent when I hear a now familiar whistling headed toward me. Rounding the copse of trees reveals that the whistling matches the tempo of a swishing skirt and empty bucket swinging from Tirzah's hand. It is a cheerful image.

Tirzah calls a greeting followed by a wide smile when she notices what I carry, though she does not alter her leisurely pace. Again I doubt that she told me the full truth the other night. It is unbelievable that someone has not tried to court this beautiful, pleasant woman and keep her for far longer than a night. She simply did not want to reveal it to me. Nor does she have to. She owes me nothing.

"The overqualified spymaster is also an accomplished hunter," she drawls with that teasing look when she comes even with me. "I begin to wonder if there is anything you cannot do."

What magic does this woman possess that makes even the burden of the deer seem lighter with just a few words? I flash her a conspiratorial smile. "Can you keep a secret?"

She returns my playful smile, but it looks better on her. "Maybe. Tell me and I will let you know if I can keep it or not."

I laugh. "Suppose I will have to take my chances. This is not something I ought to confess to a healer, but there is one skill I lack. I have earned a reputation for being terrible at suturing. Even Anders prefers to stitch himself than trust me with the job."

Tirzah is aghast. "Imagine if we were in a dire situation and I unwittingly called on your clumsy hands to assist me! That is absolutely something a healer ought to know." Her eyes twinkle. "Along with everyone else."

"Unfeeling woman!" I bemoan. "It is not as bad as that. I am not clumsy."

She raises her chin to a stubborn angle. "I will not hear it, Cuyler. There is nothing you can do to change my mind."

I have a sudden urge to change her mind by setting my fingers on her skin and proving my hands can be exceedingly skilled given the right circumstances.

I give my head a hard shake to dislodge the thought. No. I will not allow myself to think there. Though my eyes urge me to notice that Tirzah can make even homespun fabrics look appealing, she is a distraction from contending with the wake of Silla's choices. Once my good deed is done and I do not have to worry over Tirzah being left to fend for herself, I will face what Silla did.

"Did you fell this magnificent beast here or farther off?" Tirzah asks, sinking her fingers into the thick winter coat of the deer.

"Nearby. I intended to fell the bear that thinks raiding your larder is permissible."

Her hand flies to her throat in distress. "Oh, you did not hurt Sow, did you?"

"I would have, but I did not find her."

"Please leave her be," Tirzah begs. "She does not do any harm. I enjoy watching her raise her cubs in the summer."

"Yet another reason to do away with the bear. A sow with cubs is the most dangerous. What if—"

"Please, Cuyler." Her wide violet eyes blink up at me without artifice or manipulation, merely an earnest request.

"Alright." I hear myself reluctantly agree. Sakes, she is going to run roughshod over whatever poor sop marries her. I feel bad for the man.

With a smile, she squeezes my arm. "Let me collect the water then I shall return to help you dress it. We best take a quarter to Brick since it came from his land, but the rest we can smoke and parcel for you to take with you."

I am glad she reminded me of taking payment to her landlord, but she is mistaken about the reason for my hunting. "Tirzah, the venison is for you."

"For me?"

How have I taken her by surprise? "Your larder was empty. I could not leave you without food."

Her eyes shine brightly. "Thank you, Cuyler. Truly. You have gone to such trouble for me. I appreciate all that you have done."

Her gratitude pleases me, more so because she did not take for granted that the venison was for her. "You are welcome."

She touches my arm again as she steps past on her way to the river. "I must take extra care with dinner tonight. Such a fine animal ought to be thoughtfully prepared."

I turn to watch her proceed and catch the smile she throws me over her shoulder.

Maybe I do not feel badly for the poor sop she will marry after all. A man could do far worse.

CHAPTER SEVENTEEN

TRENT

January 24th

The pleasant odors of the smokehouse curing the joints of salted venison float in a warm haze on the frigid air. Another few days of the smoke imbuing the meat will complete the curing process enabling it to be stored for continuous use. Tirzah has amused me with her hen-like tending of the little smokehouse beneath the lean-to. At any moment, she is likely to jump to her feet to ensure the fire is properly fed, even though it could not be otherwise since she fed it an hour past.

Early this morning, she carried a crock of rich stock made from the bones of the hart to the tanner to trade him for processing the animal's luxuriant winter cape. She was nearly giddy at the prospect of having such a thick hide to make into a lined cloak for herself. Happy as I was to have a hand in her simple joy, I realized that the gift would have been lost on Silla had I done the same for her. Silla would never look at a deer hide and call it grand. She would not even deign to wear such a common animal as the lining in her shoes. At least, not prior to her downfall.

I place the next half log on the chopping block to split into shingles. With the froe and mallet, I mark lines across the end of the log, dividing it into sections. Alternately tapping the blunt edges of the froe, I slowly drive it through the wood until the shingle splits away from the log. I toss it into the pile of unfinished shingles alongside Tirzah. Seated on the shavehorse that I brought from Valor's barn, Tirzah pulls a drawknife across both faces of the rough shingle, shaping them into the smooth, slightly angled finished product. She has proved herself a quick study in the skill and saved me considerable time.

Once we have amassed a respectable stack of shingles, I set aside the mallet and froe in exchange for hammer and nails.

"Is that enough then?" Tirzah asks hopefully.

"Probably not. But it is enough to make a good start." I hang two buckets filled with shingles on the ladder. "You may work inside if you like. I know you are anxious to see your cottage righted."

Tirzah grins. "Call for me if you need me."

I agree, though I know I won't call her away from feathering her nest without dire need.

She has no sooner disappeared inside then she gasps and reappears hustling toward the smokehouse. I chuckle. If she cares for her patients with half the attentive diligence of that little smokehouse, it is no wonder she makes a good healer.

I clamp several nails between my teeth and lay the first shingle against the batten, losing myself in the mindless repetitiveness of the task. Row after row of shingles I nail in place. My pride is bolstered by the fruitfulness of work that yields immediate results. I may not have lived the life of a farmer for a several years, but my hands have not forgotten the honest work.

The telltale whistling of Tirzah's good humor fills the gaps between the tapping of the hammer. I climb onto the edge of the roof to lay the next row of shingles. Beneath me, Tirzah glides around the single room of the cottage cleaning every nook of the abode. She stops whistling to mutter something to the table then begins pulling the benches away from its sides. More than once I have overheard her talking to herself when she thought I was not listening, a habit I suspect developed from living alone. She seems to dislike total silence. If she is not whistling, she is talking to herself or making noise with some domestic implement. Even her skirt provides a relief from silence, swishing along the floorboards when she walks. At first, I suspected the swing in her gait was meant to draw attention, a small flirtatious sort of behavior. The ladies at court have a litany of such idiosyncrasies. But I have come to realize that Tirzah's steps only swing when she is happy and primarily when she is alone. The sound of her skirt swishing over the floorboards of Salome's kitchen has drawn me to seek her out more than once to watch her cook. She exudes such contentment with her simple work.

From my current vantage, I observe something I missed before. Tirzah weaves between the table and benches, swinging her skirt from one side to the other in tempo with her renewed whistling. She swipes the cloth across the table's surface, takes a step back, then turns in circle. A grin splits my face. She is dancing.

I begin to tap the hammer in subtle rhythm to her steps. She curtsies to the table, her stationary partner, then steps around it in the pattern of a common dance. I lean my elbows against the battens, yielding to the fun of watching her.

Tirzah dances the table clean then turns to the benches.

"Do all your partners have wooden legs?" I call out.

Her hands startle to her chest. "Cuyler! I forgot you could see me."

"You forgot I could see you?" I laugh. "You are a funny one."

"Did you need something?" She asks, marshaling her dignity.

"I was only going to suggest that the broom looks a bit more spry. Maybe try dancing with him next."

Her scolding expression dissolves into laughter.

I pick up the tune she was whistling and resume laying shingles. Tirzah continues cleaning in a more traditional way, though her skirt still sways with her unique dance-walking.

Late in the day, a youth hastens across the hilltop toward the cottage.

"You have a visitor," I relay down to Tirzah.

She steps outside to greet the lad. "Hello, Liam. Does Mamey have need of me?"

"Aye. Mistress Gildner says she's having the baby," the lad answers. "Mamey wants you to see if it's so."

"Tell her I am on my way!" Tirzah calls back excitedly.

The lad is off in a tangle of limbs he has not yet grown into.

"Shall I saddle the horse?" I ask, descending the ladder.

"No. Rochlin lives nearby. This is her first babe. She is quite nervous. I promised I would stay with her through the whole birth." Tirzah pushes back her sleeves, scrubbing up to her forearms in the wash basin. "Am I covered in wood shavings?"

Evidence of her shingle planing clings to most of her dress. "Aye."

She huffs and digs out a fresh dress from her trunk. I pull the door closed then wait outside lest she forget I am present again.

Moments later she appears with her healer's basket on her arm and tugs a cloak around her shoulders. "I could be a while. Will you tell Salome where I am? I left a stew at her house so you two won't be hungry."

"Don't worry about that now. I will tell her where you have gone."

How can she think about such a trivial thing as a meal with the urgency of bringing a babe into the world before her? Her compulsion to care for people must feel consuming at times.

"Thank you!" She catches up a handful of skirt and breaks into a jog, becoming only a smudge against the white landscape.

I refill the buckets with shingles then kneel on the edge of the roof. I calculate the number of rows left to lay against how long it has taken to accomplish these. My days in this agreeable pursuit are nearly at an end.

❖ ❖ ❖

TIRZAH

I barely knock on the door when it is flung open. A harried young husband drags me inside. "Tirzah. Thank the Almighty! She's been having pains for the last few hours. I was afraid the babe would come afore you got here."

"Breathe, Zimeon." I loosen the man's grip on my hand. "All will be well. Women have been having babes since the beginning of time." Salome's great nephew is not appeased. I give him a task to make him feel useful. From my basket I withdraw a sachet of tea and written instructions for its preparation, a little trick I learned from Mamey. "I need you to prepare this tea and follow my instructions exactly. Can you do that for your wife?"

"Aye, I will have this done straightaway!"

Unlikely since I built time-eating extra steps into the instructions such as *Hold the water at a boil for seven minutes* and *Steep tea in water for five minutes*. The truly ridiculous instruction is *After steeping, remove sachet and stir slowly twenty times to thoroughly mix tea*. But no one has caught on yet, so I keep providing anxious husbands with the busywork.

I find the young woman in her bedroom resting against the headboard of her bed. "Hello, Rochlin. How are you feeling?"

The anxiety on her face is considerably less than that of her husband, but what remains mostly abates at seeing me. "Oh, Tirzah! Thank you for coming so quickly. The pains have been coming and going for the better part of the day, but they have gotten worse the past hour. I think it is time."

I do not, but I ask her to lay back on the bed nonetheless. After examining her, I am nearly certain the babe will not be making an appearance this day. "Tell me, what have you been doing?"

"Well…" She looks a bit sheepish. "I was scrubbing the kitchen floor. Zimeon said it was plenty clean, but it had to be done before the babe comes. Then I started having pains, and I could not remember if I had washed our second set of bed linens. But the pains became so bad while I was washing them that Zimeon made me lie down and sent for you."

"Rochlin, I have never seen a home as clean as yours. Truly, you have nothing to worry about. Zimeon was right to put you to bed."

"Then the babe isn't coming today?" She asks with equal parts relief and disappointment.

"Probably not," I smile. "Let's see if we can get these pains to go away so you can rest."

I stumble across Salome's threshold not bothering to cover my open mouthed yawn. My cloak finds its home on the peg and my basket on the shelf by the door. Footsteps approach from the kitchen. "Salome, your great great niece or nephew did not make their appearance this day."

Salome chuckles. "Poor Zimeon. His mother said his nerves have been taut as a bowstring over the birth. How fares Rochlin?"

"Cleaning everything in sight and exhausting herself. Her labor pains finally went away after I made her lie down and drink copious amounts of water. I told Zimeon to keep her abed tomorrow and left her with red raspberry leaf tea. Hopefully the next time her pains come, they will be strong enough to bring forth the babe." I try to kick off my boots without bending over, but my feet cannot pull free. "Cooperate, will you?" I grumble at the leather stiff with cold. I unlace them with equally stiff, cold fingers. "Did Cuyler enjoy the stew?"

A masculine voice answers my query causing my fingers to fumble on the laces. "Cuyler did enjoy the stew and wants to know why you crossed the valley alone at night."

I look to Salome for reinforcements, but she is no help. "No, Darling. You know I do not condone you traveling after dark either." She kisses my cheek and trundles off to bed.

The ache spanning my shoulders is too intense to bother with good posture at this late hour. I slouch my way into the kitchen and drop onto a bench at the table. Cuyler stands over the sink full of clean dishes with his sleeves rolled up to his elbows, drying them with a rough towel. I prop my head in my hand taking the opportunity to gawk while he stacks the dried dishes neatly in the cupboard. He is quite nice to look at, especially doing something as kind as washing an old widow's dishes.

He tosses the towel aside and fixes his reproachful gaze on me.

I suppose his question was not rhetorical. "Well, I keep telling these babes to arrive at reasonable hours, but they will not heed."

He is less than amused. "You should not take your safety so lightly, Tirzah."

"We are in Parse Kítaran. What could happen?"

"Beyond the obvious danger of bears, boars, wolves, and mountain lions? A man could easily overpower you." The shadows in his eyes make me shiver. He is not speaking of possibilities. He is speaking of things he has seen.

I reassure myself as I always do when fear makes prey of me. "I live here partly to avoid such danger. Most of the Continent does not know this place exists, and none of my neighbors would harm me."

Cuyler sighs, crossing his arms. "I do not want to shatter your naivety, but men, even the ones here, could do you unspeakable harm."

"I am not naive, Cuyler."

"Foolhardy, then?"

I glare at him. "If you are opposed to my walking home, what do you suggest? That I spend the night in the homes of these would-be evil doers? Or perhaps I could simply sprout wings and soar over all the dangers?"

"Can someone not escort you home? Or at the least let you borrow a horse to speed your way?"

"At times someone does walk me home, but I could not ask Zimeon to leave his wife in a delicate way when I am relatively safe."

Cuyler is not satisfied. Why does it matter to him what I do? It should not, yet he is plainly worried, far more than anyone one else except perhaps Salome. The simple fact that he is here, making my welfare his concern when he could be anywhere else in the kingdom still confounds me. He does not have to be here. Why has he gone to all of this trouble for me?

My heart wants to believe it knows his well enough to answer those questions, but I have been wrong before. I do not want to make such a dreadful mistake again. I summon my courage to ask him. I will make him plainly state why he cares what becomes of me. "Is there any stew left?"

Coward, my inner critic accuses. *Wasting a perfectly good opportunity to disillusion yourself.*

Cuyler deposits a brimming bowl before me. "Why don't you sleep late in the morning. You look exhausted." He is gone before I can protest.

I drop my forehead to the table with a groan. "I am beginning to think I should have sent for Mather."

CHAPTER EIGHTEEN

TIRZAH

January 25th

"I have something to show you," Cuyler announces when I appear at sunup. "Wait here."

He takes the two baskets from my arms and carries them inside. His hand settles on my back bringing an immediate smile to my lips as he guides me toward the ladder. "I will go first then I want you to follow me."

Cuyler climbs onto the roof, steadying the ladder from the top for my ascent, then takes hold of my hands, hauling me onto the sloping surface. I roll to my backside, scooting farther from the edge.

From this vantage, I can see the glittering river trimmed in ice winding through the valley like a line of crystals set in the snowy white folds of a gown. "How beautiful! You know, I never can grow bored of the views in this valley."

His gaze waits mine when I glance higher up the roof to his perch. He studies my face then looks past me to the valley dressed in winter finery. "I agree."

Doubtful that he brought me up here to admire the scenic qualities of my home, I shift my attention to the roof. The progress he has made is impressive. Nearly half of the gaping hole is covered by new shingles blending into the jagged teeth of the existing rows. "I am impressed, Cuyler!" I touch the old shingles then the new. "See how well they are joined!"

"Thank you," he says, holding his head a bit higher. "But what I wanted to show you was this." He clambers to the peak of the roof, takes hold of a thick canvas tacked there and unfurls it, covering the unfinished portion of the roof. "I discovered this canvas among the detritus in Valor's barn last night."

"Is that a sail from a ship?" I have not seen such a large, thick swath of fabric before.

"I think it is, though I have no idea why he has it."

"Why did you bring it here?"

"You have not guessed?"

I shake my head.

He grins, savoring what he is about to tell. "It means you can move back into your cottage today."

"I can move back..." My mouth works silently, repeating the statement he made.

"Today," he concludes. "Between the canvas and the additional rows of shingles I will lay today, there will be sufficient cover to keep out the snow and trap the heat in your cottage. You can come home."

I squeal my glee and fling myself across the distance into his arms. At least, that is what I meant to do. Instead, I slip sideways on the frost slicked roof, falling onto my belly with arms splayed wide.

"Whoa!" Cuyler shouts, moving toward me. "Stay put!"

He keeps a hand on my back, then my leg as he passes me, stepping onto the ladder. "Push back toward me. Slowly."

I feel my skirt ride up to my knees exposing my stocking clad legs. Still, Cuyler's hands stay on my legs sending warm tingles racing along my limbs, though I doubt he intends for more than securing my safety. He helps my feet find the top rung of the ladder, descending ahead of me. His hands grip my ankles, placing my feet on each rung. I would tell him he is being overly cautious if I could get my wildly beating heart to release its grip on my tongue. There is little chance of that happening as I take the last three steps into the shelter of Cuyler's arms braced on the sides of the ladder.

"Are you alright?" He spins me around, running hands down my arms, turning my palms upright searching for scrapes. Every touch sends pleasant prickles into my skin.

No. No, I am far from alright.

He tips my chin up, reading my expression. "I have frightened you. I am sorry."

You have. I am terrified. Because how can I feel this for you when I have no notion how you feel about me?

"I only meant to surprise you with the canvas. That was not well done of me. I did not consider how difficult it would be for you in a dress."

I nod mutely.

"Come. I will start a fire. You are shaking terribly." Cuyler's arm wraps around my shoulders leading me inside my cottage.

I shouldn't do it. I know better. Even so, I cannot stop myself from leaning into his touch, imagining for a moment that his solicitous behavior means something more. Which is absolute foolishness.

I get hold of myself while he lays a fire in the cold hearth. "Thank you. I am quite alright." In the sense that I am not harmed. "I am not usually so clumsy."

"It was the frost," he agrees. "Shall I get you a blanket?"

"No, that is not necessary." I open the basket containing our food. Cuyler watches me with a frown from the place at the table that I have begun to think of as his.

I am in such trouble. My heart has cast him in a role he has never claimed to want. Thankfully, I recognize that. I can avoid further entanglements if I am stern with myself. *He is not encouraging your affectionate thoughts, leastwise, not intentionally. Stop pretending otherwise.*

"Thank you, Cuyler. I am grateful you found the canvas and for all the work you have done. How long do you think it will be until the last of the shingles are laid?"

His lingering concern hides behind his lighthearted teasing. "Two, maybe three days. Can you tolerate me for that long if I promise not to put you on anymore slippery roofs?"

"Certainly."

His charming smile makes me doubt the veracity of my claim.

CHAPTER NINETEEN

TIRZAH

January 28th

The *tap, tap, tap* of a hammer wakes me. I roll from beneath my covers smiling. Cuyler is nothing if he is not diligent. Only a sliver of sky can be seen at the very peak of the roof and that is quickly disappearing with each shingle he affixes.

The best way I know to say thank you is by starting breakfast before I go down to the river. I then take my time with my ablutions, scenting the water with sweet woodruff before washing and braiding my hair more intricately than usual. I squelch the feelings of regret as I slip into my simple homespun dress, reminding myself to be grateful for serviceable garments. Though would it have truly been such a blow to my pride to accept the gowns Erianna offered to gift me?

"Stop this nonsense!" I rebuke myself. "You are supposed to be suppressing this misplaced attachment, not encouraging it. Do not forget."

With renewed resolve, I step into the crisp new day, bright blue and sparkling with a fresh layer of powdery snow on the ground. The castle was lovely swathed in winter white, but I do not think there is a more beautiful place in all of Malesiir than this valley.

"Good morn!" Cuyler calls out from atop the roof, dispersing my resolve like chaff on the wind.

I turn to him with a smile. "Good morn!"

He waves his hammer before taking a nail from his mouth and returning to his good deed. I meander down the path to the river, whistling merrily. The talkative river does not focus my mind as it usually does. Though I try to rein my thoughts to attend to my prayers, I am woefully unsuccessful in light of the distant tapping I can hear echoing down the hillside. There is simply no putting that man from my mind.

I dip my bucket into the water, feeling the drag of the current as it fills. Holding fast to the rope handle, I resist the pull of the water. Droplets sharp with chill splash my hand encouraging me not to linger. The cheer of my cottage beckons.

Though precious few hours remain to be spent in Cuyler's company, there is nothing different this day than any of the past two weeks. We work, we talk, we sit across the table from each other, until the only thing that remains is returning the tools to Valor's barn.

The destrier is hitched to the sled and the tools loaded when my plans are dashed on the rocks of circumstance.

"Tirzah! Tirzah!" Liam races over the ridges of the hills.

"Not now," I mutter and wave to the lad.

"It is Mistress Gildner! She says it's time!"

"I am on my way!" I call back.

"Do you think it is true labor?" Cuyler asks, following me into the cottage.

"Most likely." I slip my basket into the crook of my arm then bank the fire.

Cuyler holds my cloak open for me. "I will be on my way to Chishelm after I return Valor's tools and sled."

My heart pinches in my chest. "I cannot thank you enough for all that you have done for me, Cuyler. If you had not made my problems yours, I truly do not know what I would have done."

He smiles. "Which is why I intervened."

I stand quite close to him in the threshold, giving him a chance to make more of our parting.

He pats my shoulder. "Farewell, Tirzah."

My hopes crash into my stomach. I watch him walk away. "Well, that was anticlimactic."

"You must keep going, Rochlin. I know you are exhausted, but you cannot give up."

The young woman cries through the next round of pain, not trying to bring forth the babe.

"I can't!" She wails. After hours of this, I do not blame her at all for feeling defeated, but if she quits, it means the lives of both her and the babe.

"You can. You must."

This is not the most difficult birth I have attended, but the longer it continues, the higher the risk becomes. It frightens me, though I would never let Rochlin see my worry. Mamey was called away from the birth to tend to a broken leg leaving me to deliver this babe into the world on my own. For the first time.

Rochlin's mother in law, Eva, dabs a cool cloth across her brow. "It will be over soon. Then you will hold your sweet child in your arms, and you will forget all about this pain."

The wave of pain passes leaving Rochlin whimpering.

"Deep breaths now. When the next pain comes, I want you to give it your all."

"I can't," she wails. "I have nothing left."

"Then it is good that you do not have only your own strength to draw from." I take her hand in mine. "Almighty Creator, please flood Rochlin with Your strength. Give her back her breath. Refresh her with Your Spirit." I pull her hand down to touch the crown of her babe's fuzzy head poised to enter the world if only she will not give up.

Her belly tightens with the next wave. "Now, Rochlin! Everything you have!"

She grips the arms of the birthing chair, holding her breath and bearing down through the length of the labor pain. I guide the babe out, cradling its head, adjusting its shoulders, and catching its fragile body as it slips free in a final rush.

"You have a son, Rochlin!"

The new mother sags in the chair, gasping for breath. Quickly, I inspect the babe for anything of concern while I wipe his nose and mouth clean. He blinks hazy blue eyes up at me, but does not immediately take a breath. I blow on his little face, startling him into his indignant first breath followed by a hearty wail.

I laugh at his expression and lay him against Rochlin's breast. "Oh, Sweet One, here is your mother."

Rochlin is instantly smitten with her boy, holding him like the most precious gift she has ever received.

I go through the motions of tending mother and child then see them abed. Mamey returns while Eva and I are cleaning. After speaking with Rochlin and admiring her son, Mamey comes to me. "How do you feel the delivery went?"

"It went smoothly. Rochlin did so well, and her son is perfect."

Mamey smiles kindly. "Indeed. Well done, Tirzah. You are growing into an excellent healer."

My eyes fill with mist. "Thank you."

Zimeon's delight in his wife and firstborn was the crescendo of the evening. Eva stays the night to watch over the little family, granting Mamey and I the reprieve of a night's sleep before returning on the morrow to check on them. The older healer wastes no time in climbing into her pony cart and heading for home, but I need a moment.

I exhale the breath I have been holding, letting all my feelings wash over me. The trepidation. The uncertainty. Then the confidence that I was meant to be with Rochlin in that moment. The exhilaration. The sense of purpose. And through it all, the overarching wonder of bringing new life into the world. "Thank You, Father. Thank You for being present. Thank You for this beautiful calling on my life, this gift that I never grow tired of unwrapping."

Joy burbles up in me followed by a fit of giggles. I skip down the steps of the porch, sinking up to my ankles in snow that mires my steps.

"Well, if my feet cannot dance..."

I catch the ribbon at the end of my braid and pull it away, dragging my fingers through my hair, setting it free to fly in the night breeze. I throw my head back, marveling at the glittering vastness of the heavens. My breath forms a veil before my face, softening the silhouettes of the night when my eyes return to earth.

Through the veil, a figure peels away from the night. I shake my head, trying to clear the effects of exhaustion and my wild imagination, but the form solidifies rather than dissolving.

My heart is thrown into a chaos the likes of which I have never known. Cuyler Trent stands in my path.

"I take it the birth went well?"

I nod. "Rochlin has a beautiful boy."

"Good." Cuyler takes charge of my basket then extends his arm to me.

I hold onto him with both hands. "What are you doing here? I thought you meant to leave for Chishelm."

Cuyler shrugs, my hands moving with the gesture. "I could not let you walk home alone."

My smile is surely too wide to fully conceal what this means to me. "You are rather overqualified to be a simple escort, Cuyler Trent, but I am glad you are here."

This night could not be any more perfect.

TRENT

I could not do it.

I made my way as far east as the mouth of the valley before I turned back. Knowing that Tirzah would be walking through the dangers of the night alone gnawed at me. It could have been weeks until I knew for certain she was safe. So I turned back. Salome directed me to the Gildner's smallholding where I waited beneath an oak for her to appear.

I am glad that I did.

If only to have witnessed the radiant joy shining from Tirzah, my time was well spent.

I understand, now, why she perseveres through the draining aspects of healing. It is for these moments filled with immeasurable satisfaction.

With rapt attention, I listen to her recount the birth. If I could find half as much pride in my own work as spymaster, I imagine my view of the world would be very different. Tirzah's exuberance makes me want to take hold of something in my own life that brings me such fulfillment.

But what?

"Have I bored you?" Tirzah asks. "I suddenly realized how dull this must sound to you."

"Hardly," I assure her. "I envy your enthusiasm for your work."

"Do you not feel the same about being a spymaster?"

"I thought I did. It used to be exhilarating to discover secrets no one else could find, by fair means or foul."

"But no longer?"

"I feel more mired than passionate."

She angles her head to fully capture my expression. "Mired? That is a telling choice of word."

I offer her my unfiltered thoughts, letting her help me examine them. "I have been slogging through the tasks associated with my work. There is no enjoyment in it."

"Why not?"

"The fruitlessness of these past months may be at play. It is hard to feel any sense of accomplishment when all my efforts were undermined."

"Then it is only since you have been working to unmask the traitor that you have felt thus?"

Is that true? Has chasing my tail in the castle left me dissatisfied? The affirmation I want to give sticks in my throat. I answer in the negative, following the mental paths Tirzah chooses. "No. My dissatisfaction has been present longer." I try to work backward to locate the beginning of this feeling.

Tirzah takes me there faster. "When was the last time you were proud of something you accomplished?"

My smile is too smug. "I am quite proud of the roof on your cottage."

She strokes my complacency. "As well you should be. If you decide to pursue a different career as an overqualified man-of-all-trades, I will highly recommend you. Although," she tightens her hand on my arm, "I might decide to keep you all to myself."

I chuckle at her jest and build upon it. "I might let you. I'd be a fool to willingly give up my place at your table."

"Then don't be a fool," she says quietly before jumping back to our place in the conversation. "When did you last feel pride as spymaster?"

"Recently. Frequently, even. There is always some tidbit of information that I have uncovered to give me a rush of pride." Saying that aloud causes me to rethink my stance. "Perhaps it is only this last assignment. I certainly do not go through my day hating every portion of it."

"Cuyler, don't dismiss this. It is important." She tugs me to a stop to face her, unconcerned by the chill wind blowing on her red tipped nose. "You said you feel 'mired.' That you have been 'slogging.' To me, that sounds as if you have found yourself knee deep in a bog. When did you leave the road? When was the last time you had a sense of pride-of-place? That you were exactly where you were supposed to be, doing something worthwhile. That you in particular brought skills to the work that no one else could."

Here. With her. Tirzah needed me to help her set her home to rights. I stayed and helped.

Why can I not shift my mind from these few weeks? Has this truly been such a singular experience?

No. It has not. Many times I have aided my friends with similar tasks. Why does this one stand apart from the rest?

Tirzah shivers in the night air while awaiting my answer. I tug her closer to me, making my back a windbreak for her.

In the midst of my present time in Parse Kítaran, I doubt I will know what makes it unique. Given some time, however, I am certain I will know. Setting aside this fortnight, I think further back. When did I feel as if I was exactly where I was needed, bringing skills no one else could?

The answer comes as a surprise. It was not working as Valor's spymaster. It was working as *him*. "Last winter, Valor was—" I cut myself off to guard his honor. She does not need to know that he was drinking himself into incoherency after Erianna wed Grandileer. He could not fulfill his duties as the Hand of the Prince, and he no longer cared to try. When Kragorn called him to account, they agreed he needed help while he sorted himself out. "Valor assigned me a heavy portion of his work as Hand. Rather than spying upon our people, I was seated across from them, negotiating and bargaining for peace. It was my responsibility to discover why the cities were attempting to secede from Malesiir and encourage them to see reason."

"Were you successful?"

"In truth, no, not most of the time. There were a few towns that wanted restoration as a result of change. I helped them articulate what those changes were. It proved significant eventually, but even in the thick of things, I knew there was no one else Valor could have entrusted with his responsibilities that would have had the necessary skills. My position as the interim Hand of the Prince was vital. *I* was vital."

Tirzah smiles. "Again you prove how overqualified you are."

Her praise makes me stand taller. Despite being able to claim no rank higher than that of Sergeant, Valor entrusted me with his responsibilities.

"I think," Tirzah continues, "that you have come to a place where the things that give you greatest pleasure are affirmative actions. You take pride in improving the state of those around you. You enjoy serving others in a lasting way. I do not question that your current work is meaningful, however, I think it has left you disillusioned with humanity as a whole. Your eyes tell the toll it has taken on you. Perhaps, weighed against the darkness you must encounter, the thrill of being a spymaster has worn off."

I stare at her. Not a single person has questioned if there are burdens that come with my position. Yet Tirzah has stated it as fact. "You might be right. But what should I do knowing that?"

Her expression sobers, reminding me again that she is not as youthful as she appears. "Perhaps you ought to consider a change in occupation."

Which is a frightening thought. In one sense, I am not encumbered by much, though I did pay a goodly sum toward the house I have agreed to purchase. But assuming that was not an issue, I could transition into another position within the military. I could apply for the position of master of trade within a city, perhaps in Gistin, with my family. That idea I quickly discard. My elder brother would make my life a misery if I did so.

I return Tirzah's hand to my arm, leading her toward the cottage. She remains companionably quiet while I turn over the idea she has instigated. It has merit. The question is, what occupation would provide me with, what did she call it? *Affirmative actions.* I doubt pursuing the rank of captain would be the significant change I am considering. Being a weapons master might suit if I had the qualifications for such a position, but my faculty and passion for the subject is simply not there.

I plant my feet firmly on the icy stoop of the cottage should Tirzah's slip. Though the fire is banked, the relief in being sheltered from the wind is marked. She hangs her cloak while I lay a log in the hearth and coax the fire to life beneath it. She pours water into the kettle then pushes it into the flames to heat.

"My toes are numb," Tirzah explains when she drags a chair to the hearth and removes her boots, setting her stockinged feet on the warm stones.

I stretch my hands toward the blaze. Looking at her nearly bare feet from the corner of my eye, I feel safe in asking, "Would it be presumptuous of me to ask to pass the night in the lean-to with my horse? I would rather not make up a stall at Valor's for the one night." Or tack my horse and trek across the cold valley to do so.

She is quiet for a long moment.

"If you are worried what your neighbors will think—"

"No, I am well with it. You may even sleep in here, by the fire, if you would like. The lean-to is not nearly so warm as a barn."

It is a request I would not have made, but if she is offering, I will not refuse. "Thank you."

We thaw by the fire until steam rises from the kettle hanging over the flames. Tirzah lifts the kettle from the hook. "You will be leaving in the morning?"

Her question is an opportunity to make better on that lousy farewell I gave her. It was another reason I turned back. After her kindness to me, I could not leave letting her think I was ungrateful. "Aye. It is time for me to visit my family before I am needed back in Malsihra." I trade my seat next to the fire for one at her table. "I cannot express how grateful I am that you allowed me to help you these past two weeks."

She casts a skeptical look my way paired with her amused smile but says nothing.

"Truly. Your world has been a respite from mine."

A trivet lands on the table followed by the kettle. "Certainly. All overqualified spymasters long to fill their days of rest with strenuous labor."

"Honest work," I insist. "A day's labor in exchange for food."

"That you also helped provide." She chuckles. "You are a good man, Cuyler, and I am glad that you take pride in the work you have done here, but I know that mine was the better end of our deal."

I watch her glide about the simple room, taking mugs from the cupboard for the tea. Of a sudden, the reason why I have found such pleasure in these past weeks comes to me.

It is her.

Simply watching her go about her day, a woman confident in her routine, graceful in her movements, earnest in her speech, has eased a great deal of the anger I felt. I never anticipated the boon her companionship would be. Greatly have I enjoyed fitting myself into her world. *That* is what I should have told her earlier.

"If you cannot accept that, will you accept this?" I push out of the chair and circle the table, stilling her busy hands with mine. "*You* have been a respite for me."

Her smile slides away, replaced by uncertainty.

"Your company and candid way have refreshed a body weary of half-truths and deceit. I am grateful to you, Tirzah. You have blessed me." I press a kiss to her hands that well know hard work but equally as often bestow her healing touch on needy souls.

Tirzah's eyes follow the path of my lips down to her hands. The gesture is one of such common currency to convey favor and gratitude among the noble class that I do not question what it will mean to her until it is done. For a moment, she is startled. I begin to formulate an apology, but then a hesitant smile moves her features.

"Your presence has been a blessing to me, too. You are always welcome in my home, Cuyler. I hope I will see you again?"

The tentative question from one so confident compels me to offer exaggerated assurance. "Undoubtedly." I squeeze her hands. "Likely so often you will ask me to leave."

Her fullest smile—pleased and bright—makes an appearance. It satisfies me to know that my being here has caused it, that I was able to stay and make her world better rather than leaving her to solve her problems alone.

Then it is my turn to be startled. She returns the kiss I gave her, rising on her toes to press it back to my lips, her own still curved in a smile. It is lighter and sweeter than any kiss I have ever received and entirely unexpected.

The press of her lips to mine is brief, but she does not immediately retreat from me. I must be wearing an expression of such dumbstruck surprise that Tirzah's full smile vanishes, quickly replaced with contrition. "I should not have. Please, let's forget I did that."

She pulls away, turning to face the cupboard, reaching for a jar on the upper shelf. "Chamomile tea will be nice. Don't you think? It is what I prefer when I return late in the night. It helps me sleep. Truly, I could use some help with that tonight. Perhaps I ought to add some sage and lemon balm. My mind is obviously slipping."

The feel of Tirzah's lips lingers, sinking deeper, making me aware of heat where I thought to find mere warmth from my physical attraction to her. I fight the question that begs for an answer.

How much heat is there?

I have to know.

Tirzah returns to the table to prepare our tea, continuing to babble with her back to me, only a step away in this small room. My hand brushes aside the cascade of her hair that the wind had its way with on our walk home. She goes still, clasping the jar of tea as the chestnut locks glide through my fingers. I softly kiss her flushed cheek, attuned to her reaction. A sigh parts her lips, encouraging another kiss. This one I move to her neck, just below her ear. She shivers when I nuzzle her neck, coaxing her toward revealing the answer. *How much heat is there, Tirzah?*

Her head falls back against my shoulder, and she turns her face to meet mine. The jar clinks as it tips from her hand, spilling chamomile across the table's surface. Its delicate fragrance teases my senses before they are overwhelmed when I claim her offered kiss.

Her soft lips yield to the pressure of mine, moving with me, answering my question with emphatic clarity.

Heat. And much of it.

My arm circles Tirzah's waist, pulling her back to my chest. My body concurs with what my eyes long ago determined—Tirzah was made to be held. She fits perfectly to me. One of my hands settles in the curve of her waist while the other cradles her face, holding her close while the heat of our kiss builds. There is no pretension about her. She kisses as earnestly as she speaks.

My eyes open on her thick lashes that flutter against cheeks lightly dusted with the sun's gift of freckles. My fingers caress that soft skin as my eyes follow it down the column of her throat to skim the modest neckline of her dress that reveals little, not that it needs to. There is nothing modest about Tirzah's proportions. She is all sensuous woman. Oh, so tempting…

That thought shakes another free. *This must stop.*

I break our kiss and force myself to let her go. She is no trollop to lust after. She deserves better from me.

"Cuyler," Tirzah murmurs, turning to wrap her arms around my neck. She rises to her toes, trusting my hands to steady her while she bestows a kiss I think I am prepared to meet with reserve.

But I am not prepared.

Nothing could prepare me for the way her kiss sears through my limited self control. The taste of her intoxicates me. The genuineness of her soft sighs drown me.

I make more of it than I should, leading us farther than we ought to go. Desire chokes the life out of my honor. My conscience rails till, finally, I take heed.

"Tirzah," I set her back, "We should not go any farther."

"I do not care," she argues, closing the distance I placed between us, laying her hands on my chest. "I burn, Cuyler."

Aye, heat. Too much heat. Stoking it has birthed flames.

"As do I. Which is why we must stop before we have something to regret." Rather, *more* to regret, I realize as my eyes stray downward to the splayed lacings of her dress.

She lays her head on my chest, both of us struggling to regain our breath. I stroke her head, smoothing the fall of her hair as she trembles in my arms. I feel shaken to my core as I breathe her in. I want her in a way that I have never wanted another. That should make me more cautious, cause me to think on why that is. But the flames beckon me closer. The taste of her is on my tongue. The softness of her fills my arms.

Into the quiet I should leave undisturbed, I ask a question that will come to plague us both. "What do you want from me?"

Tirzah meets my gaze with a sincerity that matches the candor of her words. "I want you to love me."

I use her words to put a muzzle on my conscience. How wrong can this be if it is what we both want? The way Tirzah kisses does not lead me to believe I will be the first to lay with her. Perhaps that is the real reason she has not married. Thus, there is no cause to feel guilt. She desires me as I desire her. It is that simple.

I frame her beautiful face with my hands. "Then I will."

CHAPTER TWENTY

TIRZAH

January 29th

Was it a dream? I recall in exquisite detail the feel of Cuyler's hands on me. The way he kissed me. The ardent sound of my name on his lips. The wondrous things he made me feel. I have had pleasant dreams before, but nothing that imaginative. I peak one eye open in the early morning light. Cuyler's arm is draped over my bare waist beneath the covers. His other is a pillow beneath my head.

I relish the feel of being held so close. His chest rises and falls at my back, strong and even. I would be content to stay wrapped in his love like this all day.

My happy sigh at that thought is quiet, but he notices.

Cuyler's fingers come up to brush my hair back from my face. "Are you awake?"

The gentle touch makes me smile. "Maybe."

He sighs, but it is not a happy sound. "I'm sorry."

Sorry? "You did not wake me."

"Not that. For the other."

I think back to last night, moving through the memories a little faster this time. I recall a fleeting pain—sharp but quickly over—then only pleasure. That must be what he means. "I am fine."

He carefully slides his arm from beneath me. "If only that was true."

I roll onto my back, expecting him to kiss me again. That is what lovers do, after all. But Cuyler will not meet my eyes. Disturbing me as little as possible, he rises from the bed and searches for his clothes.

Wondering if he is correct, I stretch beneath the covers. What aches I have are minor. Certainly nothing that would prevent me from

123

welcoming his touch. I smile as I set my feet on the floor and go to him, eager to draw him back into my arms. He buttons his pants while facing away from me. I set my hand on his back, admiring the way his muscles move beneath his skin. My hand remembers the feel of him, too, at once strong and gentle.

Cuyler bows his head, speaking to the floor. "I am so sorry."

"For what?" I ask, stepping around to face him.

His eyes move over me, then he grimaces, averting his gaze. Why is he acting strangely?

"I think your dress is by the trunk."

My modesty is what concerns him? It strikes me as adorably funny. "You wish me to be modest now? After you have seen and touched all of me? I am not bothered by my nakedness."

"How can you not be?" He tries to hold my gaze, but fails and turns abruptly to the bed. He snatches up the thick coverlet then stops, staring at the sheet beneath stained with my blood. Horror mars his face.

"It is not much at all, Cuyler. Truly, I am fine."

"No, you are not. I ruined you." He wraps the coverlet around my bare shoulders. "I am so very sorry, Tirzah."

I do not know what to say. All I can do is stare at his contrite face that I covered in kisses.

"Why did you let me do that to you?" Desperation fills his voice. "Why?"

Understanding begins to creep in, and I do not like it at all. "You regret last night."

"Of course, I do!" He throws his hands wide, stomps across the little room. "I stole your virtue! What sort of man does that?"

I clutch the coverlet tighter around me, trying to hide from my own guilt that was waiting for the opportune moment to spring upon me, forcing me to acknowledge it. Last night was not my wedding night, though I behaved with wanton abandon as if it was.

What have I done?

Part explanation, part defense of what happened between us, I speak the only thing I can think to say. "I kissed you first."

He turns his pleading expression on me again. "But you would never have taken it any farther had I not seduced you. It was a mistake. I am so sorry, Tirzah."

I feel worse each time he apologizes. Another realization pounces on me that makes me understand why my heart hurts—Cuyler does not feel for me what I feel for him.

But he changed his mind about leaving! He stayed to walk me home last night. He said he would return to court me, that he would see me again soon. He even said he cared for me. Didn't he?

I recollect his exact words, examining them without my own desires biasing my interpretation. He thanked me. He said he was grateful for my company and the time he spent here. He said he would return frequently to see me. Yet now I doubt he spoke truth. His words had the dull sound of falsity to them. I wanted him to be earnest so badly that I let him sham me.

But he asked what I wanted from him. He made love to me. Why do that if he knew he could not give me what I wanted? My words tremble with fear of the answer. "Why did you do it?"

"I don't know."

Desperation raises the pitch of my voice. "Don't you? You would have gone to Silla's bed that one night." I watch as his guilt piles higher. I feel ill. "But that is not why you came to my bed, is it?" *Tell me I am wrong, Cuyler. Please tell me you feel* something *for me.*

He hangs his head. "No. It is not."

My last petal of hope is crushed.

He will not become my husband.

He is not even my lover.

He is merely another man who wanted my body.

I am suddenly aware of how very little covers me. Like Eve in the garden, I am naked. And I am ashamed.

"You lusted for me."

"No, it was not lust," the denial is hardly off his lips before he contradicts himself. "Well, not *only* lust."

Aye, it was. I feel despicable for it. Mather was right. I am destined to be lusted after, never to have my love returned. That ugly truth makes me miserable.

I want Cuyler to be miserable too. I sharpen the most hurtful weapon I have and hurl it at him. "Then it was also a transaction."

Confusion furrows his brow. "A transaction?"

I force myself to locate my dress and shake it out. "Certainly. You repaired my roof, and I gave you my body. Are you satisfied with the one night or do you require another? Of course, I also gave you my virtue. I suppose that ought to count for something."

"Do not say that!" Cuyler shouts. "It was nothing like that!"

I drop the coverlet so he does not know how deeply ashamed I am then pull my chemise over my head, smooth it down my hips. "My mother was a harlot. I know the way of things."

He is stunned into silence.

I push my arms into my dress and draw the lacings tight across my breasts, concealing what I so waywardly bared. The hem of my dress skims the floor, but it does not restore my feeling of modesty. I drive the last of my verbal knives into Cuyler as deeply as I can. "Tell me," I turn to him and set my hands on my hips. "Did I satisfy you? I must know if I can ply my mother's trade."

Cuyler sickens. He picks up his shirt and steps into the snowy morning without pulling on his boots. I hear him retch forcefully then the sounds of water splashing in the horse trough.

I toss the coverlet onto the bed that was not disheveled with love but something much baser. With jerking movements, I straighten the pillows and the sheets. I will need to melt snow to wash them later, but at this moment I cannot stand to see the evidence of my sin. My stomach threatens to betray me too. I will not allow it. I will not relinquish the shredded remains of my dignity.

The kettle sits on the table filled with cool water from my interrupted tea making last night. Dead chamomile flowers are spilled across the table. I poke the fire awake and set a log in the embers. After placing the kettle over the fire to warm the water for my ablutions, I bar the door. It would be mortifying if Cuyler returns while I am bathing.

His boots sitting neatly next to mine inside the door draw my eye. I pick them up and set them outside on the narrow stoop before barring the door once again. Not that I want to show him consideration of any kind, but I cannot help thinking how cold his feet must be.

Once bathed, I stare into my cup of tea. The aromatic peppermint cannot fill the hollowness inside me. I am carved out. Empty.

Salome cautioned me that I had become destructively desperate in my pursuit of love. Could there exist greater proof than this? Even knowing Cuyler habitually tells people exactly what they want to hear, I trusted him. There must be something wrong with me. With him too. I warned him not to sham me. Why didn't he listen?

He has not come back yet. That is just as well. I have no desire to see him. Pushing away from the table I pair that lie with actions, gathering his belongings and packing them into his saddlebag along with a day's meals. He can purchase the rest of his food in Chishelm. When I open the door, his boots are gone replaced with the jingle of a bit and squeak of leather from the lean-to.

He means to leave me.

Though I had already decided as much on his behalf, it hurts like a blow to my belly that he has chosen to walk away from me.

Why shouldn't he? My inner critic attacks. *He does not feel anything for you. His lust is slaked. He has no need of you any longer.*

I drop his belongings outside the door and again bar it.

Tears sting my eyes. Was it only lust? The memories from last night that were so sweet bring pain. It felt like more. Not that I have anything to compare his touch and whispered words to, but I thought...

Fool! I wanted it to be more so I made more of it. It was nothing to him.

I hear Cuyler's footfalls on the stoop. He pauses there. My foolish woman's heart raises its bruised face, desperately hoping he will knock on the door. Call to me. *Something.*

I pad toward the door. My hand hovers over the bar, ready to raise it if he asks...

Cuyler collects his belongings and walks away, soundly rejecting me.

My heart shrivels. I bite down on a sob.

Be strong! Do not succumb!

Against my commands, the tears come streaking down my cheeks. I press my hand to my mouth, sliding silently to the floor.

TRENT

Tirzah has every right to throw me out. I used her so badly. After her kindness and the favor of her company when I needed a friend, I stole something irreplaceably precious from her. Once more, I let my body make decisions for my head, but this is the worst decision I have ever made.

I fit the leather straps into the buckles on the back of my saddle, pulling the bedroll tight. Never will I forget how she looked standing in her little cottage, hair still mussed from my hands, asking if I was satisfied with our transaction.

Transaction.

The word makes my gorge rise. I know what that is like. The sweet, trusting way Tirzah gave herself to me was nothing like trading coin for the favors of a harlot.

My mother was a harlot. I know the way of things.

She skirted around that detail in our many, lengthy conversations, but it fits solidly into her narrative.

Her mother's trade.

After what I took from her, what worthy man will overlook her loss of innocence? Surely no one in Parse Kítaran. Nor any of the noblemen she danced with at court. Maybe a soldier. Maybe a tradesman in a village. She is not without options.

The reassurances I feed myself are empty. I try a different one.

Tirzah kissed me first. She might not have taken it farther, but she should not have done that. She invited trouble on herself. This is not solely my fault. I tried to do the honorable thing. She asked me to love her. Had she told me to stop at any point, I would have. It is not as if I forced myself on her. She enjoyed last night too. She was downright brazen with me this morning. At least, until I covered her and told her it was a mistake.

Wait.

Why did she ask if I regretted what happened? Doesn't she? Actually, she never said she regretted it. She asked if I regretted it. She asked why I laid with her and compared it to when I nearly laid with Silla.

Oh, no.

No, no, no.

I am a bigger scoundrel than I knew myself to be when I woke and found her in my arms. Tirzah kissed me because she has feelings for me. She lay with me because she thought I shared them. She smiled at me this morning until I explicitly told her that I do not love her like I do Silla, that I only lusted after her.

When I asked what she wanted from me, she said she wanted me to love her, not *make love* to her. With a woman as candid as Tirzah, that distinction is everything.

Smite me! The self loathing I feel after trading with prostitutes is nothing compared to the loathing I feel for ruining Tirzah and trampling her heart. I push the heels of my hands into my temples. *What am I going to do?*

I ought to go apologize to her again. Maybe I can ease some of her hurt. By saying what, though? I have already told her I do not love her. That is not something I can undo. Did I try to claim otherwise, she would hear the lie. I cannot blunder in there without something acceptable to say. How do I begin to apologize for this? The things that come to mind are trite.

Maybe I should go. That seems to be what she wants. She did toss out my belongings. That is a definitive statement.

I fit my foot to the stirrup, swinging up to the saddle. Though the road calls to me, offering reprieve as it ever has, I draw up outside the front window of the cottage. If I could catch her eye, ask her permission to return inside and discuss this...

The curtains are shut, withholding even a glimpse of the beauty within.

If she does not want to see me, I will not force my presence on her. I have done enough.

I cluck to my destrier, moving him into a trot. The thing to do is put this behind us.

Pounding hooves draw my eyes farther out. Cresting the hilltop is a girl galloping bareback. She flies over the field of snow heading this way. I pull back on the reins, waiting.

It is Karris. A little closer and I discern her screaming for Tirzah. I ride to intercept her. Leelah's pony is blowing hard. Karris must have run her the whole way.

"Trent! They took Mother! I couldn't stop them! She made me shut the gate! They tried to get in, but Tamraz... Then they killed him too!"

There is no sense to what she is saying. "Slow down, Karris. Start over. Slowly. What happened?"

"Mother went out to bring the goats inside last night because Tamraz had herded them near the wall. He was barking and growling. Mother thought it must be wolves. And it was. But there were men there too. They ran at mother, but Tamraz attacked them. She tried to make it to the door, but they were too fast. A man attacked her and she fought him and screamed at me to close the door." Karris bursts into tears. "I didn't want to! They hit her and took her staff."

"Did they get inside the wall?" I ask, thinking of all the little ones.

"No, they beat on the door, but I locked it before they could come in. I could not understand what they were saying, but they tied mother to a horse and took her away."

Leelah... The babe...

"Where are the children now?"

"At home. I made the girls lock me out when I left to get help."

I wheel my horse around, charging across the short distance.

"Tirzah!" Snow sprays in a wave as I slide to a stop. "Tirzah!"

She flings open the door, wiping red rimmed eyes. "What's wrong?"

I jump from the saddle, brushing past her as I run into the cottage. "Leelah was taken by the Ruphiri. I need you to stay with the children so I can go after her." I use the poker to put out the fire in the hearth. "You have one minute to gather whatever you need."

Tirzah springs into action, grabbing a bag and hastily filling it. I toss her cloak, stockings and boots on the table. She drops into a chair after passing me the bag. I run out the door tying it to my saddle.

I guide my horse to the stoop as Tirzah exits, locking the door behind her. She falters for only a moment when I reach for her to lift her to my saddle, then I follow her up, pulling her tight against me. "Hold on." She obeys gripping the pommel.

CHAPTER TWENTY-ONE

TRENT

Karris is already galloping across the hilltop when I ask for every drop of speed my destrier possesses. We overtake her tired pony, pressing on to sooner reach the children. Karris did right by coming for help, but the youngest child is but a year old, far too young to be left for long.

My mount's hooves break through the crust on thick snow, sinking up to his knees. I feel Tirzah tense in my arm with the jarring movements. Her knuckles are white from her grip on the pommel.

When we jump a small creek she gasps. I check our pace, loosening my hold on her. "Turn toward me."

I do not have to tell her twice. She pivots to face me, wrapping her arms around my waist.

"Better?" I ask in her ear as I let out the reins, increasing our speed.

I feel her nod. "Thank you."

Gratitude is the last thing she owes me.

The path up to the Tareth house is churned by more than just Karris's pony. That is promising. Plain tracks will make this all the easier.

Tirzah jumps to the ground as soon as I stop. "Lois! Ivy!" She calls to the children. "It is Tirzah. Let me in, Darlings."

"Is Karris there?" Lois asks. Though she is younger than Ivy, she often speaks for the both of them.

"Aye, Dear. Trent is also."

The heavy bolt groans in the lock as the children fight to move it. The snow here is stained red. I follow the signs of the struggle where Leelah's smaller boots spread in a fighting stance guarding the door to her home until she was knocked unconscious. I touch the depression in the snow where she slumped to the ground. Near the forest, I discover the mighty Tamraz fallen, defending his family. I pat the loyal dog's head. He was not slain easily. Goats bleat mournfully in the forest. Several of their flock mates were also killed. The gluttonous hunger of the wolves is revealed in the ripped out bellies and strewn innards. Only the soft organs were eaten before they moved to another kill. Leelah's prized, matron dairy goat scampers toward me, the little bell on her collar tinkling. I catch her by the collar, beckoning the others out of hiding. A few obey. It is better than nothing.

Karris lopes over the clear cut lawn as the sally port swings outward. The children huddle around Tirzah's skirts, crying and helpless. She hurries them back inside while asking where Fialla is.

I lead the goats toward the door. They sprint for safety. Several more tiptoe from the woods then break for the open door as I usher Karris and my horse to the safety behind the wall. I slam the door and lock the bolt.

"Tirzah! Gather the children in the great room," I instruct, drawing my sword. It sings gleefully as it rises from the scabbard for the first time in weeks. "Go, help her," I urge Karris. I will not leave them until I am certain the home is secure.

Though I am thorough in my search, I am expedient. Every moment Leelah is captive is a moment too long. I only pray—

Pray? I ask of myself. *Aye, pray.*

Almighty, if You are listening, if You are there, do not abandon Leelah to the Ruphiri. Let that sharp tongue of hers hold them at bay until help arrives. Please, protect her.

Tirzah holds all of the children on the couch near the fireplace. Even Karris is snuggled into her side, crying. Micah spots me and buries his face in Tirzah's skirt, clutching his wooden practice sword.

Tirzah nods meaningfully at the lad. I crouch at her knee, setting my hand on his back. "Micah, I shall bring your mother back."

"It's my fault! I couldn't get my sword fast 'nuff to help Mother! I'm not a warrior like Father!" Man sized tears drip from the boy's chin.

I bring him in close, speaking soberly to him. "You did what your mother wanted you to do. You were here to protect your sisters. Your father will be awfully proud of you for that."

"You're sure?" He drags the back of his hand under his snotty nose.

"Without question," I promise. "Warriors know what battles to fight. You did as you should."

"Can I come with you to get Mother? I've got my sword now."

Micah very well may be the bravest warrior Malesiir has ever seen. I hope I am alive to see the man he becomes in another few decades. "That is a generous offer, but if I take you with me, who will be here to protect the girls? Isn't that the charge your father has given you? To protect your sisters?"

He looks at them, considering. I look, too, and find Tirzah watching me with a tender expression. For a brief, unguarded moment, her heart shines from her violet eyes. I am jolted to see it. Abruptly, she looks away, unwilling to give me any more pieces of herself. I do not begrudge her for it. I have stolen much.

Micah turns back to me. "I should stay here, shouldn't I?"

I nod solemnly. "It is the right thing to do, even if it is hard."

"That's what Mother says. The right thing is usually the hard thing." He puts his sword into his belt. "I'll protect my sisters. You find Mother."

"Good man," I clap him on the shoulder. "Tirzah will be staying here. I need you to promise you will also protect her." I catch her gaze and hold it earnestly. "She is special to me."

Tears glisten on her lower lashes. She bows her head to hide them, placing a kiss on Fialla's wispy crown. The babe pats Tirzah's cheeks with pudgy hands.

Micah grips his leather wrapped sword hilt, mimicking exactly the habit of men who live by the sword. "I promise."

"Karris, take Fialla. I must speak with Tirzah before I go."

Tirzah accompanies me to the sally port while I state the rules. "Do not leave this home. Do not open the door for anyone or for any reason —not even if the goats are standing right outside. It is not worth the risk. You may only open the door for me, Kragorn, Valor, or Anders. Do you understand?"

"I do. Can you find her?"

"The trail is fresh. I should be able, but they are good at hiding their tracks. I will go straight to Chishelm and send word to Kragorn and Valor. Time is on our side. Hopefully, we can undercut whatever scheme they are planning."

"Why take Leelah of all people?"

I sigh, hating that likely answer. "To draw out Erianna. Zavaan wants her, but Valor has kept her safe in Malsihra since she left Parse. Leelah and the children's visit to the castle enabled Lord Hugler to inform Zavaan whom Erianna cares about."

"Erianna will leave Malsihra for Leelah. She will trade herself for Leelah, if it comes to it." Tirzah pales hearing her own words.

"We will not let it come to that," I declare, though I have no idea if it is true. "I shall take a contingent from Chishelm and rescue Leelah before then."

"Will they hurt her? Will they…"

"Pray," I cup Tirzah's chin, undone by her forlorn expression. "You pray like Leelah is always saying to do. We *will* get her back." I am gripped with the overwhelming desire to hold her, but I do not think she would welcome it. "Bolt the door behind me."

I lead my destrier outside the wall and swing into the saddle.

"Cuyler," Tirzah calls, peeking around the door. "Be safe."

I nod then fix my eyes on the trail when I hear the bolt fall into place.

The Ruphiri do not attempt to conceal their tracks nor hide their intent. They galloped in a pack out of the high valley, never slowing their pace. The tracks funnel into a single column through the narrow ravine. They sweep outward from there, moving two and three abreast following the descent of the ice trimmed river. I drop to the ground when the road comes into view. The tracks scatter in multiple directions on the road, confusing the trail. My horse takes water while I analyze.

Some of the tracks lead into the woods. A trio point toward Malsihra. More follow the road to Chishelm. I consider those as they seem most likely to me. If the Ruphiri mean to trade Leelah for Erianna, they will want to be as close to the Ascent as possible when they make the trade to minimize the chances of us taking her back.

One set of horse tracks skitters more than the rest. The horse prances sideways following a pace off another horse. The distance between the two does not vary, likely because it is being led. The skittish horse must be Leelah's. If she is being difficult, then the horse would naturally prance in response.

I mount, beating the path toward Chishelm and our new fort.

"What do you mean '*no?*'"

"The full connotation of the word, Sergeant Trent."

I grit my teeth at the insignificant title. My pride is not the greatest of things at stake in this moment, but *his* sore pride is the source of the denial. My lesser rank is, however, a barricade to securing what I requested of General Kannik. Were I possessed of the legitimate title of spymaster within the royal army, my request would be an order that could not be denied.

"General Kannik, it is of utmost importance that I set out immediately with a company to wrest Leelah Tareth from the Wolves. She is with child and has already suffered a night in their clutches. We cannot abandon—"

"Why should she be of more concern to us than any other Malesiirian who has been killed by the Wolves?" He shuffles the papers on his desk, not giving me the outward respect of his full attention, though I know I have it. He is relishing this opportunity to strike Valor through me after Valor figuratively parted Kannik from his manhood and literally had him thrown from the castle. The stab at Kragorn by refusing his wife assistance is an added benefit. Many times Kragorn has been chosen over him for promotions and given the choice of assignments.

"*Anyone* taken captive by the Wolves is of utmost concern to us! It is our honor bound duty to protect and defend Malesiir from its enemies!"

Kannik spares me an irritated glance for bringing honor into the discussion. "You have no evidence that she was taken by the Wolves."

"Her children described the men, and I saw the place of her attack. I then tracked them to the forests outside Chishelm. If we do not make haste, the tracks will be lost to the next snowfall!"

He returns to his papers, dragging a finger down the duty roster. He taps the list. "As I have been tasked with hunting Wolves in this part of Malesiir, I will lead a contingent to investigate your claims."

My ire comes to a boil. "A contingent! It will take a full company, possibly two to ensure Leelah's rescue."

"A company! Not for any woman, not even the esteemed Mistress Tareth, will I leave this fort vulnerable to attack. That might be the Ruphiri's plan. Did you consider that, Trent? The likelihood that they are using her as bait to draw us away from Chishelm so they may pillage the city?"

"Zavaan does not care a horse's hind about this city or any other! He

135

wants our queen. That is why he has taken her friend. By the fiery depths, General! You must see reason!"

He leaps to his feet. "Be gone from my fort! If I hear of you attempting to commandeer any of my soldiers I will have you jailed!"

A deep breath produces the restraint to evenly state, "I act on behalf of Commander Ironforge. I have full authority to—"

"You have no authority! Produce a writ from the commander, and I shall grant your request."

I cannot. He knows I cannot. There has been no time.

"Leave, Sergeant." His order smacks my face with flecks of spittle.

My salute is begrudging. I give it only to deny him the least excuse of jailing me for insubordination.

Furry whips through my chest on hot winds. General Kannik's quarrel with Valor will cost Leelah her life if I do not intervene. Silla's disparagement haunts me. *You do not have that kind of power, not even the ability to lead a contingent without the commander's permission.* Still, I must do something. I will not abandon Leelah.

Back at the stables, I dig my hand into my saddle bag, stringing a plan together. A lumpy bundle blocks my search for pen and paper. I withdraw it then untie the knotted corners of the unfamiliar fabric. Inside are strips of smoked venison and a thick slice of coarse bread. Tirzah must have placed it in my saddle bag. But when? My stomach rumbles at the hearty scents. I tuck the bundle under my arm while I locate the paper and pen.

I lay the paper against my destrier's saddle while I draft the letter.

January 29th

Leelah was taken captive by the Ruphiri at dusk yesterday. I was in Parse when she was taken and have followed their tracks past Chishelm toward the Ascent. General Kannik has denied my request for a company to pursue them. He plans to lead a contingent in pursuit later today, but it is a token gesture. He claims that the Ruphiri are using the capture of one woman to leave Chishelm and the new fort vulnerable to attack. He does not care that it is Leelah who was taken. In fact, I think he is glad of it.

I will track the Ruphiri and not rest until I have Leelah in my sights. If I can rescue her, I will. At the least, I will prevent them from harming her.

All the children are safe. Tirzah is watching over them.

My pen stops moving. I know when Tirzah placed the meal in my bag. She could not prevent herself from caring, no matter that I had grievously wronged her. Taking care of others is too much a part of her nature.

Look for the trail I will mark for you.
  Come quickly.

I sign the letter. Fold it. Dash Valor's name on the paper. Seal it in the messenger's shop. The coins I plunk on the counter will pay for the most expedient delivery possible. So expedient that the owner of the shop is calling for his lightest messenger and swiftest horse as I push out the door into the grim day.

My teeth sink into the venison first, grinding the dried meat. The smoky flavors that burst across my tongue are a reminder that my duty to Tirzah is not finished. Not until I make amends with her. Somehow.

TIRZAH

I cannot sleep. They cannot sleep.

Most of the day was spent in fits of tears. Karris tried to be strong, to hide her tears from the rest. I told them it was alright to cry. I cried, too, for a time. Then the necessities of living rushed in to claim the day. Feeding this hearty brood is no small task.

Unanswerable questions swirl through my mind in the dark. Is Leelah hurt? What of her babe? Leelah is strong, but the babe places her in a delicate state. Has Zavaan inflicted the same misery on her that he did to Erianna? Father, forbid it! Has Trent found her? Please let it be so.

My bruised heart aches when I think of him.

She is special to me.

I want to believe him. That makes it impossible to do. My feelings blind me. Instead of trusting the undertone of truth in his words, I apply to reason to decipher why he made a point to tell me that. I do not have to think on it long. It is sadly obvious. Cuyler is not a fool. He knows I hold him in my affection. Again, he told me what I wanted to hear. This time, not to lure me to bed, but to assuage the guilt he feels for having done so. He would have said anything to erase what he did.

Why must men be like this? Where are the men of honor who

respect women and would never take advantage of our tender hearts?

The only ones I encounter these days have already wed virtuous women, of which I am no longer. The hollow place in me swallows more of my hope. I try to imagine meeting such a man, being courted by him, then confessing that not only was my mother a harlot, but I have no proof that I am not one also. He would walk away from me. Last night, I squandered whatever vague chances I had at marrying for love.

Ivy whimpers at the foot of the bed. Her cries slice through my self pity, piling it up in heaps like a scythe through grass.

I sit, pulling her into my lap. Her tears wet the bodice of my gown.

"Will they hurt, Mother? Like they hurt me?"

Raw anguish stifles my reply. This young girl should not know of what she speaks.

"Mother is bigger and stronger than me. They can't do that to her, can they?"

Leelah is indomitable in her children's eyes. I do not want to lie to them, but more, I do not want to burden them with this. "Your mother is strong. She will be alright. Trent shall find her, and bring her home. I have no doubt that your father is also on his way. Try not to worry."

Wracking sobs shatter our pretense of sleep.

"Tamraz is dead! They killed him, and we'll never see him again!" Micah's wails send the girls into another round of tears. So fretful have they been for their mother and from the traumatic events that their well of grief for their faithful dog was as yet unopened. Now realized, all the children cry for Tamraz. Even Karris's stoicism cannot hold.

I rise from the bed to light a candle and collect Fialla. It was foolish of me to think sleep would find us this night. Instead, I lean against the headboard with the children piled around me, holding each other and letting the grief flow unchecked.

CHAPTER TWENTY-TWO

TRENT

January 30th

Midday arrives with the best gift I could have hoped for—warm horse manure.

The steaming piles left by the Ruphiri mounts precede the noises of their party by an hour. I trail them at a cautious distance. When they make camp for the night, I circle wide and tie my destrier parallel to their camp. He should be well outside the range of their night patrols. Once I learn the exact radius of their patrols, I can reel my distance in closer. While waiting for the fall of darkness, I inspect my weapons, tightening loose buckles on armor, running a hunk of beeswax down my bowstring. In Chishelm, I augmented my quiver of arrows with a sheaf now tied to my saddle.

The hush of night settles on the forest, bringing a fresh blanket of chill air. I bend to the earth, digging through the snow to the mud beneath. I smear a fistful on my face concealing my skin that does not match the surrounding night. Hiding my face beneath my hood would be equally effective, but it would hinder my sense of hearing. I must not impair a single one of my senses.

Far from the road, the Ruphiri fires blaze in the night, glinting red on the frozen ground. My path is deliberately jagged. Slow. The outliers of the group appear first. They are likely the men of lower rank who serve as sentinels and living barriers to protect the life of their overlord. I tally the enemy soldiers to just north of a hundred. Thankfully, Valor ordered the destruction of the tamed wolves at the Hugler estate, otherwise, skulking through the camp would be impossible. Among the harsh Limban tongue, I tune my ears to pick out the softer cadence of Leelah's voice. For a woman that is rarely silent, it is disconcerting that I do not hear her.

The deep shadows beneath the boughs of a cedar allow me to draw close to the central fire. Seated near the heat of the flames is the only figure I recognize. Her wrists are bound, yet she holds her head at a defiant angle, promising a fight to anyone fool enough to get too close. Her mouth is gagged.

I grin. That makes more sense.

Leelah glares across the fire at a man who pointedly ignores her. Even if I did not have a description to match him to, I would know that he is Reuel Zavaan by the deference shown him by the others, his location at the center of the camp, and the aura of power surrounding him. There is also something vile in his eyes. He scans the camp as if looking for something to devour. Erianna refers to him as "the murderer." It suits better than his given name.

Leelah scoops snow in her bound hands and flings it at him. In the space of a breath, I pull my bow from my shoulder, grasp an arrow, then nock it. Leelah is going to get herself killed before I can rescue her.

Reuel Zavaan turns her direction. "Does our guest require another lesson in respect?"

Her attempts to speak around the gag bring an amused smile to his face. She kicks snow at him.

Zavaan springs across the fire, lifting Leelah by the throat before she can flinch. I feel my arms strain against the weight of the drawn bowstring. It was instinct to ready an arrow for the predator, but killing him now will not ensure Leelah's escape. I fear her violent death at the hands of all these men, especially, yet excepting, Zavaan. He has a use for Leelah. He will not hastily kill her. By the defiance in her eyes, she knows that he is bluffing.

But that does not preclude her from all harm, as Zavaan reminds her. "Be careful how much of your fire shows. You offer something we have not had in weeks—an object to pour out our lust upon. You tempt men already in a way of being sorely tempted." Clutching her by the throat, he pulls her fully against his body. Resentment flares in her eyes. He draws upon it.

"Who else would like to sample her? Orjek?"

A Ruphiri unfolds from the opposite side of the fire, his attention rapt on Leelah. His head is shorn of hair excepting the crown that falls down his back in a skinny plait. It is the detail I fixate upon as he presses against Leelah's back, pinning her between himself and

Zavaan. Within Leelah's gently rounded belly is her innocent babe, caught in the midst of this depravity. Poison burns in my gut to bear witness to this.

I *won't* be a witness to this! The sheaf of arrows I carry within my quiver will fell two dozen men without a wayward shot. My sword could defend Leelah's life while she flees from harm's way, but she would be on her own thereafter. It is the best I can offer her. A chance to die fighting.

At a nod from Zavaan, Orjek pulls the gag from Leelah's mouth. Zavaan's hand slackens on her throat. "Take a breath, Leelah. I want to hear you scream."

Pressed between the vile Ruphiri, Leelah fills her lungs then expels her costly breath not on a scream, but a vow. "I will forget this as one forgets an ant bite the following day."

The men share a flummoxed expression. Zavaan attempts to reclaim the power over her that fear gave him. "There will be nothing to forget if you are dead."

Her voice rasps from her abused throat, losing none of its potency. "I have already passed from death to life. What the Almighty has resurrected, wicked men cannot kill. You, however," she derides, "are an object of wrath destined for destruction in the fiery abyss."

Leelah's words possess a power greater than Zavaan's. His grip on her throat fails him. He steps back. Leelah tries to advance, but Orjek restrains her. Realizing he retreated from a captive woman, the back of Zavaan's hand flies through the air, knocking Leelah across the cheek so fiercely that Orjek must hold her upright.

Zavaan strides through the camp, calling over his shoulder, "Food and water for the prisoner. Our bait must not die on the hook before the fish arrives."

If there was any doubt why Zavaan captured Leelah, there is no longer. The blood charging through my veins makes my soul feel loosely tethered to my body. The repulsive things done to Leelah infuriate me. I am further infuriated that I cannot immediately free her. Were it a matter of trading my life for hers in a guaranteed escape, I would not hesitate. But it is more complicated. Too many enemies stand between her and freedom.

I watch as Leelah is unbound and provided sustenance. The Ruphiri sit apart from her, eyeing her as though they have made the mistake of capturing a mountain lion and must now keep it alive. Somehow, they miss the obvious trembling of her hands as she drinks from the water skin. When she lays down to sleep, I settle against the tree, keeping my eyes fixed on the jackals surrounding her throughout the night while plotting her rescue.

❖ ❖ ❖

January 31st

By morning, my eyelids scratch with every blink as if sand has formed a film over the glossy surface of my eyes. It is an unfortunate thing that exhaustion has claimed me so thoroughly, because my rapt attention is more necessary now than it was through the third and fourth watches of the night. With the coming dawn, my hiding place that was chosen amid darkness becomes precarious. One boon is that the Ruphiri's own footprints conceal the ones I made stealing into their midst.

They rouse from sleep, moving into the edges of the woods to relieve themselves, causing me relief that I did not choose a hiding place on the fringes of their camp. A man tramps past my hiding place, brushing against the lower limbs of the tree and knocking loose some of the snow. I fear that I am dead. If any of them were to gaze directly my way, they would surely see me sitting at the base of the tree. I remain stock still, breathing shallowly, doing nothing to draw attention to myself. Again, I am thankful that my hiding spot is not on the edge of their camp for it is there they train their watchful gazes, never suspecting that someone made it to the dead center of their camp under cover of night.

The harsh cadence of their speech and difference in garb leaves no doubt that these men are foreigners in our land. But for all the differences, the routine of the Ruphiri is the same as any company of Malesiirian soldiers. Some of the men wake with energy. Some wake groggy, snapping at their companions. Breakfast is made. Horses are tended and readied. Fires are smothered. The higher ranking men dole out orders. It is all uncannily familiar excepting one glaring difference. Malesiirian soldiers would never dare to raise a hand against a female captive in sight of a ranking officer.

Leelah is woken with a kick to her back. She comes upright immediately, leaping to her feet despite her bound hands. They jeer at her response. She composes herself, rolling her shoulders and stretching her arms as much as the binding around her wrists allow. She does not complain, but I am certain she must be miserable. I recall the care with which Kragorn made her pallet each night on the road from Malsihra to Parse Kítaran. Her condition with child makes her more sensitive to the discomfort of the hard ground. Not that the Ruphiri have a care for their captive. They take enjoyment from causing her pain.

I must free her.

Carefully, I mark each man, noting their apparent hierarchy and responsibilities. Though it is unlikely, I hope to find someone sympathetic to Leelah's plight. Quickly I realize there are two categories the men fall into regarding Leelah. They look at her with either indifference or predatory intent. In the latter category is the man holding her leash. Zavaan watches every breath she takes until he falls into conversation with the lanky Ruphiri with the half shaven head, Orjek. That man also eyes Leelah, but his intent seems different than Zavaan's. Zavaan's dead eyes view Leelah as one would view a commodity. He claimed her as a point of utility to gain what he truly wants. Orjek looks at her like she is a fatted calf prior to a feast. And he is slavering.

For her part, Leelah is dignified and controlled. She ignores the Ruphiri as much as possible, eating the food dropped at her feet, calmly bowing her head in prayer when she is finished. It is not until Orjek is entrenched in ordering the breaking of the camp that she approaches Zavaan.

"I must see to my needs."

I laud her wisdom in discerning that Zavaan is of less immediate threat to her person than Orjek. She has always been sharp.

Leelah is of the same height as Zavaan which denies him the ability to intimidate her with superior height. Instead, he taunts her with an indolent smile. "Say, 'Please, Master.'"

Leelah ruins his intended humiliation by quirking an eyebrow and drawling in a placatory tone, "Please, Master," as if she has made a great concession on his behalf.

Zavaan's eyes pinch at her mockery, calculating the best retribution.

Leelah yawns. Loudly.

He smacks her across the face.

She winces as little as possible from the blow, then snorts. "How original."

"Some things do not need to be original to be effective. As a mother, you surely know the power of pain to correct a disobedient child."

Before she can rally a rejoinder, he grips her upper arm and propells her to the edge of the camp, affording her no privacy. Leelah shrugs as if it is of no consequence, but I know the shame she conceals. For all her brassy temperament, Leelah is a modest woman. This costs her.

I *must* free her from these wretched Ruphiri.

But the problem of the moment is this: How will I keep pace with them without being discovered while I wait for the opportunity to rescue Leelah?

By far the riskiest thing I can do is to repeat what I did last night by stealing into the camp. Luck was with me this time, but I risk discovery if I do it again. Moreover, I do not see how I can free Leelah if I, too, am in the thick of things. Unless, I could go unnoticed indefinitely…

In the course of my assignments I have posed as all manner of men —tradesman, wayfarer, nobleman—to ferret out information. Nearly two years ago, I was in the midst of the most elaborate disguise I had ever undertaken. Valor had placed me in Port Veritae to infiltrate what he suspected was a smuggling operation. Before I could complete the assignment, Valor withdrew me to accompany him across the Continent to retrieve Prince Grandileer's bride from the Kingdom of Limba. Though I never completed the mission, I had successfully insinuated myself into a group of roughnecks connected to the smuggling. That experience causes me to consider the viability of disguising myself as one of the Ruphiri.

They might not realize their numbers have increased by one. However, though they might not notice an additional man, they would undoubtedly notice a Malesiirian man. So different do they dress and gird themselves that the only possibility of infiltration would be by way of replacement. Even their compact, fleet-footed horses are blatantly different from my bulky destrier.

I scan the men, searching for one of comparable build and coloring to myself. Preferably one of insignificant rank. The difference of language is an insurmountable hurdle if the man I replace is expected to dole out orders. I need someone whose mannerism I can mimik, whose clothes I can don, whose horse I can ride, all without arousing suspicion. If I were a man of exceptional height or distinguishing features, the task would be impossible. But I am unexceptionally ordinary, forgettable even, if I maintain a neutral expression.

I select a target. He is of nearly identical stature and only a bit narrower through his shoulders. An additional boon is the length of black cloth wrapped around the lower half of his face to protect it from cold.

He will suit. Under the cloak of night I will trade places with that Ruphiri.

TIRZAH

I dive into the mess of a kitchen after sending the children outdoors and laying Fialla down for her nap. The task is not so engrossing that I can force my mind to attend solely to it.

For three days, I have been with the children. The more days that pass, the slimmer my hope that Cuyler—

"Trent," I correct myself aloud. He is *Trent* to me. *He* is not *Cuyler*, should never have been *Cuyler*.

In between all my worries for Leelah, I have had to take a stern voice with myself about my thoughts toward that man. I can hardly fit more concerns into my head than those of the Tareth family. Those that concern myself and what passed between Cuyler and I—

"For shame, Tirzah!" I scold myself, plunging the dish rag into the sink.

Trent will rescue Leelah from the clutches of the Ruphiri and bring her home, though later rather than sooner. My optimistic belief that he would track the Ruphiri, steal her away in the middle of the night, then return with her after a day has expired. I attempt to resuscitate it by amending the time frame I allowed for him to execute my plan from afar.

One day to gain on the Ruphiri.

Two days to shadow them and rescue Leelah.

One day to evade them.

One day to secure an escort in Chishelm.

One day to journey home.

That makes six days. I wipe my brow on the shoulder of my dress. Three more days. It would be reasonable to expect Leelah's safe return in as few as three days.

"Hasten the day," I plead with the Almighty.

A commotion in the garden pulls my attention toward my charges. They have not been themselves since their mother was taken. It has been everything in me to manage their daily care and constant spats.

"Tirzah! Tirzah!" Ivy hurtles through the garden door. "Mistress

Lourna is coming up the walk!"

Going to the courtyard, I hold my breath until I also see Mistress Lourna approaching the wrought bars of the lowered gate. This pillar of our community is a welcome sight after days of worry. Her husband, Thad, is an elder of great standing and happens to be Valor's neighbor. If ever a woman could be trusted within these walls, it is Lourna. But I heed Cuyler's order to not open the gate for anyone.

"Tirzah?" She greets me with a question in her voice. "I feared that someone had taken ill since I did not see Leelah at Gathering. If you are here—"

I shake my head, cutting off her conjecture. "The truth of the matter is not so simple." In the sparest details, I explain what happened to Leelah.

Lourna is aghast. "But that means..." Her suppositions trail off before getting their footing when she looks at the children clustered around my skirt.

"Aye. It could mean that, but I pray not. Sergeant Trent is a capable man. I do not doubt the Almighty will use him to guard Leelah from harm." Even as I espouse the belief, I recall Erianna's stricken face when she spoke of the wickedness of Reuel Zavaan. A man that could brew such turmoil in our Warrior Queen is not a man that I want to exist in the world, let alone be the captor of my dear friend.

Lourna takes my hands between the bars of the gate. "I shall add my prayers to yours. May I share this information with the rest of the community?"

I shake my head. "No. Not at present. I do not know enough to make a qualified judgment. Share it with Thad only."

"Leelah's other friends may also call on her," she cautions. "What will you tell them?"

"The truth, I suppose, at least part of it." Nothing else will do. They will hear a lie. "Leelah is not at home. I do not know when to expect her back."

Lourna nods her agreement. "I will do what I can to divert her friends. How can I help you in the meantime?"

I stare at the faces of the Tareth children. My deepest wish is that I could remove the distress marring their countenances. But I cannot.

Sensing my floundering, Lourna asks, "Do you have plenty of food? Supplies? Clothes for yourself?"

My mind, ever capable in crisis, seizes upon the practical. "The larder is well stocked, but I could use more clothes. They are in the trunk in my cottage. If you will wait, I shall fetch the key."

While inside, I decide there is one more task Lourna can do for me. I drop to Leelah's desk and begin writing.

CHAPTER TWENTY-THREE

TRENT

February 1st

The opportunity I awaited tarried. But no more.

My target patrols the forest, alert to the sounds of enemy soldiers who would attack his people. He does not suspect that he himself is prey. I bend my bow, anchoring the string to my face. Perhaps I should feel the same aversion to taking his life that I felt when I slew the deer for Tirzah. But I don't. At another time, if I saw him with his family, with his friends, perhaps even a wife, I might sympathize. But not now. Not knowing that he aided in the capture of my friend and the murder of Malesiirians who had no part in this war over thrones.

He is guilty.

My arrow pierces his eye, burying itself into his brain.

The enemy soldier slumps into a heap in the snow.

I lower my bow, listening for sounds of alarm from his fellows. Beyond the sound of my blood rushing in my ears, the silence of the night is unbroken.

I sling my bow over my shoulder and descend the tree. Rapidly, I exchange my clothes and weapons for the Ruphiri's. His naked body I push into a snowbank. I have a moment's regret discarding my armor and weapons beneath a bush. Wrapped well in my cloak, hopefully they will survive the elements. I fix their hiding spot in my mind so that I may return for them after rescuing Leelah. Turning loose my nameless horse is more difficult still.

A memory pricks my mind of Tirzah scolding me for his nameless state. Though not a great lover of horses, she is a compassionate woman and thought it was unkind that such a faithful animal did not bear a name. I suggested she name him. After conversing with my horse and whispering in his ear, she said that she had, but refused to tell me what it was. In retrospect, I recognize her smile that was normally teasing had turned flirtatious. I should have taken notice then. Selfishly, I let her beauty and pleasant company distract me from my troubles without a thought toward how I might affect her.

I pat my destrier's neck, urging him away from the Ruphiri camp. With luck, he will make his way to Chishelm where the brand on his flank will identify him as a Malesirian soldier's mount. Or some fortunate yeoman will claim him and cut the brand from his hide. He disappears in a westerly direction. I send my thoughts of Tirzah with him.

I can only help one ill-used woman at a time. At present, that woman is Leelah.

❖ ❖ ❖

February 2nd

My name is Brynjar. I learned that much before killing the Ruphiri that bore the name. I fit myself into his place, taking his patrols, rations, weapons, and horse.

For two things I am grateful. The first is that he owned a fine bow and a quiver filled with arrows, some stolen from Malesiir or perhaps provided by Lord Hugler to fell our own people—a dark thought, that. It is the work of a moment to blend Ruphiri arrows with the nondescript sheaf of arrows I obtained in Chishelm. Mixed among Brynjar's bedroll and pack, I take the calculated risk that the addition will go unnoticed. The second thing for which I am grateful is that of the hundred-odd Ruphiri, only Brynjar's horse takes note that a Malesiirian has assumed the cloak of his master.

The compact dun gelding whuffs at my hands and stolen clothes, puzzled as to why I smell familiar yet not. He decides that it is not too great a problem and carries me without complaint through the first day.

From the moment my arrow pierced Brynjar, my ruse began to decay. I have mere days before the Ruphiri scent the stench of deception. Of all the Ruphiri, it is Zavaan's attention I fear. His keen eyes are like the wolves for whom the Ruphiri are named. He is as willing to feast on carrion as he is willing to tear out throats.

I plan for the event of my discovery setting awry Leelah's rescue.

There is not much to the plan—a pair of arrows for Zavaan, another pair for Orjek, Brynjar's sword and forty-four arrows to provide cover for Leelah to flee. Leelah must lift a dagger from the fallen Zavaan to cut through the bindings on her feet, or she will be subdued before she can leave the camp. It is a contingency plan that will end with my death and little chance at escape for Leelah, but it is better than no chance at all.

My worry for Leelah increases when she continues to provoke Zavaan. "Trading me for the queen is a fool's plan. It reeks of desperation and weakness."

A few heads turn toward her, scowling. I wager those are the few who comprehend the common tongue. I do not know if Brynjar was among them, thus, I remain impassive.

Zavaan's smile is venomous. "That you try to convince me it is so serves only to convince me I am right." His hands flex on the reins. "Soon, I shall have my wife."

Leelah chuckles. "So you say."

Zavaan eyes Leelah with dark malice. At his unwavering gaze, Leelah shifts in the saddle and hunches her shoulders. The ravenous wolf surfaces behind Zavaan's veil of humanity.

Keep silent, Leelah. Remain stalwart, I urge.

Had I whispered the words into her ear, she could not have obeyed better. She fills her lungs with winter air and straightens her spine. I watch for the opportunity to convey my plans to her in person.

The miles separating us and the Ascent melt faster than ice on a hearth. Erianna attributed their speed to the compact, hardy horses that can ascend the Spire Mountains with the sure footedness of mountain goats. I have also observed the Ruphiri have one peculiarity of routine compared to Malesiir's soldiers that explains their speed of travel—they are not dictated by the sun. As if born of the darkness that clothes them, they rise ere dawn to eat and ride, they break to eat again long past noon, and the day is fully gone when they hobble their mounts for rest. They ride an additional five hours each day without suffering ill effects. Their horses are likewise conditioned to the pace. It is good that I traded my destrier of unknown name for this hardy mountain horse of equally unknown name. My destrier could not have maintained this ferocious pace.

Though I told Valor I would lay a trail for him, I doubt the benefit of doing so. The Ruphiri plow through paths that do not exist. Valor would lose precious days tracking them up and down mountainsides.

Since Zavaan is still moving westward toward the Ascent, that information must sustain Valor.

Imagining Valor's response to the ransom letter Zavaan must have sent drips sweat down the back of my neck. Did Erianna's will prevail when it came to plotting Leelah's rescue or were Valor and King Lorennt successful in restraining the queen? Having seen the perverse lust with which Zavaan and others regard Leelah, if Valor appears without the queen, Zavaan would allow the Wolves to devour Leelah out of spite.

The thought is abhorrent. I must not wait to learn what Valor's plan will be. I must wrest her from the Ruphiri before the exchange, and for that, I need her cooperation.

CHAPTER TWENTY-FOUR

TRENT

February 2nd

The means to speak with Leelah is presented in a base manner that makes me thirst for Ruphiri blood. Zavaan gives the silent order to make camp for the night. It is the loathsome Orjek who claims the task of lifting the captive from her saddle. I lose sight of her behind the horse when he lowers her to the ground. Whatever offensive touch he forces upon her causes Zavaan to laugh and strike upon an idea.

"Mistress Tareth, how good of you to provide viands for my famished men." Zavaan pulls Leelah to the center of the camp where the men who were laying the fire have paused their work. "Besides Orjek who is never sated, who else hungers for what this woman offers?"

A wave of fear crests and crashes upon Leelah's face when the Ruphiri encircle her. I add myself to their number, bloodlust burning fire through my veins.

The villains around me loosen belts and shrug off cloaks. Leelah's hands drop to her womb, shielding her babe. Her eyes close, but her lips move on mute words. When Leelah's body quakes despite her bravery, Zavaan smiles and draws close to whisper in her ear. Her flinch at his proximity whets his vile hunger. What he says to her I cannot discern, nor can I comprehend the directive that he voices aloud to his Wolves, but I glean the meaning when they grumble and fasten their weapons belts about their hips.

Leelah's stiff shoulders relax. A deep breath fills her lungs and mine. He means only to torment her with fear.

Zavaan's keen eyes burn red in the night. "I suppose my queen's bait will survive being nibbled…"

Leelah's head jerks around. Zavaan pounces, banding her arms at her sides and crushing his mouth against hers. She fights to free herself which makes his fingers bite into her tender flesh.

My baleful growl is drowned by the jeers of the Ruphiri. Intuiting that Zavaan is the sort of monster who takes pleasure in her pain, Leelah makes herself rigid and unyielding as stone. At her impassivity, Zavaan shoves Leelah into the arms of a waiting dog who paws at her and forces kisses upon her closed mouth before passing her down the circle.

The tearing of my restraint must be audible when the Ruphiri next to me strokes the swell of Leelah's belly, mocking that which is sacred. My hands are forced to jam my sword back into its scabbard when Leelah is thrust into my arms.

Every instinct demands I hold her tenderly with my off hand while wielding my sword to keep her safe, though if I did, her life would be forfeit. Instead, I do what repulses but will ultimately protect her. To make a good show, I pull her body flush against mine, yank Brynjar's cowl below my chin, and bury my face in her hair just behind her ear. I hope the days of beard growth and indifferent moonlight conceal my identity.

"Do not react," I hiss then rein my anger that is not for her. "Tis Trent, Leelah. I have come for you."

Despite my warning, she gasps and tries to pull her face back to see mine. I sink my hand into her hair and arch her neck to hide her reaction behind mine, hoping the Ruphiri do not notice.

"Sorry," she says through clenched teeth, feigning to be a pillar once more.

With mere moments to convey what must both prepare and sustain her, I murmur, "Be ready for me to free you. Do not provoke Zavaan. Remain stalwart. I stand between you and ravishment. I am sorry I could not prevent this. I knew of no way—"

The Ruphiri next to me complains. I press my mouth to Leelah's throat, reluctant to release her but not in the way I purport. "I sent for Valor. Tirzah is with your children."

I feel a sigh of relief move her chest.

"Brynjar!" A Ruphiri snaps.

I run my hands down her arms offering comfort and vowing safety as she is pulled away from me.

❖ ❖ ❖

February 4th

Frustration eats at me, becoming an enemy equal to the one I watch. As if told secrets by some foul wind, Zavaan's grip on Leelah becomes unrelenting. He goes so far as to tie a leash to her bound feet while she sleeps—a leash which he holds.

I do not believe Leelah has given any indication that she has the means to flee. She has paid me no more notice than any of the other Ruphiri which attests to an impressive amount of will on her part. People cannot help but give away their intentions, be it ever so subtly, unless they are a masterful deceiver like Zavaan. And Silla.

I know that we have reached our destination when the outstretched arms of Aspen Canyon greet us. It is unnerving that Zavaan knows the body of Malesiir so intimately that he chose a perfect place to lay an ambush. I hope that Valor will discern this scheme before it is too late to undermine it.

As expected, we are sent into the forested walls of the canyon to scout. My inability to understand the Limban tongue grows deadly. Nodding and grunting my agreement has sufficed for a short while, but if specific or unique orders are given me, I will be unable to reply or comply.

With the scent of battle on the air, taunting Leelah is no longer Zavaan's concern. His rapt attention is fixed eastward, awaiting Erianna. Leelah is reminded of her status with daily mistreatment that takes the form of slaps and shoves. I bide my time, marking for death those who rough her.

For two nights, we camp on the rim of the canyon. It is not a frequented road, leastwise this time of year, but those who do traverse it have no notion of the predators observing them.

CHAPTER TWENTY-FIVE

TIRZAH

February 6th

Micah slams his bowl on the table, splattering porridge on Lois and Ivy who begin to scream. "This is awful! I hate your food!"

"Micah, that's rude! You can't say that." Karris jumps to correct him.

I try to head off the fight before it boils. "Karris, it is alright."

Micha's retort rings my ears. "You can't tell me what to do! You aren't Mother!"

"Micah, calm down," I urge to no avail.

"She isn't here!" Karris snaps, "So you have to do what I say!"

"No, I don't!" Micah hurls the wooden bowl at Karris. It strikes her cheek and covers me in what remained of the porridge. Karris bursts into tears and lunges at Micah who darts under the table and flees into the garden.

Before I can attend to Karris's swelling cheek, little Fialla finishes what Micah began and knocks her unattended bowl onto my lap. Deciding she is more angry than hurt, Karris shrieks and chases after Micah. My head throbs as my own frustration surges.

"Enough, girls!" I bark at Lois and Ivy who are still fussing. "Clean yourselves and finish your meal."

I set Fialla in her play bed in the corner to contain her then follow the two brawlers outdoors, hoping I find Micah before Karris does.

Since there is no place to hide in the barren garden, I go toward the barn but am waylaid by a call from the gate.

"Tirzah!" Lourna waves. "I have a letter."

Hope pours cool relief over my frayed nerves. "You could not have come at a better time." I reach my hands through the iron bars to clasp hers and accept the crisp paper.

"Oh, dear," Lourna says, glancing at my porridge covered self. "I saw Karris and Micah tearing across the courtyard. Looks to be one of those days."

"I am beginning to think there are no other kinds." My wry response makes her chuckle.

"You are doing good by these children, Tirzah. Never doubt it." Her encouragement is salve to my worried heart.

I break the wax stamped with a nondescript seal. The familiar writing and Nev's initial tell who wrote the letter.

Tirzah,

I am relieved you are with the children and that you are all safe. We received the letter from T over a week past. The three most concerned set off immediately. My husband is with me, away from the danger, and none pleased by it.

Thus far, we have learned nothing of consequence, but we are hopeful for a decisive resolution. Forgive me for not being more informative. My husband fears our letters being intercepted. Expect to hear from me a week hence with favorable news.

Your friend,

N

I clutch the letter to my chest, taking hold of Nev's optimism as my own.

"Has she been rescued?" Lourna's anxious question draws open my eyes.

"Not yet, or, perhaps by now. But Nev believes all will turn out right," I assure her. "I expect another letter in a week."

"I shall watch for it. Do you need—"

Banging and screaming echo from within the barn, interrupting Lourna.

I hasten that direction while calling over my shoulder, "Prayer only, Lourna! Much prayer!"

TRENT

February 6th

The scouts return early this day and hasten toward the center of the camp. I feel the thrum of excitement on the air as the *zars* confer with Zavaan. Amidst the dissonance of words I do not know, I pluck names.

Ironforge.

Tareth.

Královna—one of the few Limban words I have come to recognize. Queen.

Erianna has come. The queen's will conquered her commander's.

For Leelah's sake, I am grateful. For Erianna's, I fear.

I notice the warlords marking their faces with stripes of charred wood from the dying fire. Several other Ruphiri stripe their faces as well, but the pattern is different. This may be a form of warpaint. Since not everyone is marked, I feel safer in keeping my face clean and cowled than potentially giving myself away by wearing the wrong marks.

Zavaan's warlords break from the circle to issue commands that launch the Ruphiri into motion. I keep my ear attuned for my assumed name while watching Zavaan reach for Leelah, saying, "Come, Bait. Your time to enjoy my hospitality has ended. Tis time you serve your purpose."

I hear my name called amid a stream of others by the hated Orjek. A few of those names I have matched to faces for the purpose of being able to follow them and mimic their response to orders to hide my ignorance of the language.

We break camp, make ready our horses, and lead them onto the canyon road. All of the Ruphiri in my group possess laden quivers and additional sheafs of arrows. Bows ride our chests, ready to be drawn into action. When Zavaan comes to stand in the center of our ranks, I determine that we have been chosen to be his personal guard.

It serves me well to be near Leelah to protect her and close to Zavaan to make his body my new quiver.

Like Brynjar's fellow Ruphiri, I ready my bow and nock an arrow. Those Ruphiri that are not stationed on the road hide in the trees, waiting to ambush Malesiir's soldiers.

A chill dread sits in my stomach like a stone. Blood will soon be shed. Men on both sides will soon fall. For the villainous Ruphiri, the thought brings satisfaction, but it is overshadowed by the impending deaths of Malesiirians.

A dust cloud heralds the approach of warriors I had wished to subvert by rescuing Leelah. In that, I have failed. I shall not fail, however, in ensuring she and Erianna escape the jaws of this snare.

The river of Malesiirian soldiers that is of such number I cannot see its end is forced to narrow into a trickle just four horsemen wide. At the fore are Valor and Kragorn who flank Erianna in full war armor. They are a sight to behold, our Warrior Queen most of all upon her ill-tempered destrier. Excitement radiates from Zavaan. Long has he plotted and planned how to manifest this opportunity. If he knew Erianna better or possessed a beating, red-blooded heart, it would not have taken so long for him to find this weakness in her defenses—a weakness that shows itself evident as Zavaan orders Valor to halt their advance, but Erianna charges her stamping destrier several lengths past, holy fury twisting her cold features into a snarl. Her eyes are fixed on Leelah, her best friend who is colored with the hues of bruises, fresh black to sickly yellow.

"Anxious to greet me, Wife?" Zavaan's sharp tone forbids her obvious desire to trample him beneath the shod hooves of her mount, Reaper. For some strange reason, she wears the same stripes of coal upon her cheeks and brow as the Ruphiri *zars*. Is it a custom native to Limba? If so, why then has she never worn this warpaint in prior battles?

Wasting no time on posturing as a man might have, Erianna swings to the ground and squares off against the villain who murdered her husband—our king.

"You do not need your weapons," Zavaan says in a conversational tone, but the order is clear. "After all, you are among family."

As Erianna divests herself of glaive, sword, and daggers, Valor demands, "Send Leelah to us then Erianna will come to you."

Amusement colors Zavaan's reply. "I think not. They will proceed simultaneously."

When Erianna takes a step toward the Ruphiri line, Zavaan shakes Leelah, loosing a whimper of pain that she bites in half. I repress the jerk of my reaction. It is nothing compared to Kragorn's rage that burns across the demarcation line.

Baring her teeth, Erianna turns back to her destrier and slips the pair of small throwing knives from her vambraces into her saddle bag. She spreads her arms wide to show she is unarmed and advances.

Shifting my gaze back to Kragorn, his eyes lock with mine. Seeing only the garb and weapons of the enemy, he promises me a bloody death at his skillful hands. I harken back to when he attempted to temper my vengeful thoughts toward Zavaan and all Ruphiri. Will the death he deals this day be of the righteous sort, as he called it, or will it be of the vengeful, excruciating kind? I do not doubt his wife's bruised face and musings of what the Ruphiri may have inflicted upon her have pushed him past the place of restrain.

As our queen steps from safety into the enemy camp, Zavaan matches her pace while using Leelah as both bait and shield.

Fire burns in my veins to see my sovereign queen near her greatest foe. The harsh, forbidding set of Valor's jaw displays that same anger, but he conceals a storm of calamitous wrath for the one who has violated his beloved Erianna.

Even though Leelah's life is in the balance, only a plan that ensures Erianna's safe return to him could have convinced Valor to move forward with this trade. I flex my fingers upon the grip of my bow, anticipating the moment when Erianna's plan is revealed. Peering over the shoulders of the foremost Malesiirian soldiers, I search for the hulking shape of Anders but cannot find him. Grim delight moves in my chest. There is no mug of ale so deep nor wench so pretty that Anders would miss this battle. His absence portends ruin for the Ruphiri.

After days of tethering her to himself, Zavaan releases Leelah to cross the middle ground. When the women reach each other, Leelah catches Erianna in a fierce hug. They exchange whispered words until Zavaan interjects, "Touching. Had I only known that the life of one means more to you than the lives of hundreds…"

Erianna squeezes her friend's shoulder and nods toward the Malesiirian force, urging her toward them, while she enters the maw of the Wolf. Leelah watches Erianna take slow but unfaltering steps. The queen is all steel and defiance as she gazes upon Zavaan. He leans toward her, arms slightly bent and fingers spread wide, a predator crouching to pounce upon his prey.

The animal can wait no longer and lunges across the last two strides that separate them. It snaps Erianna's restraint. She thrusts her elbow up to fend him off while retreating from his grasp, but it is too late. She is thoroughly snared. The fear in her eyes shoots through me. Without thought, I bend my bow to its full draw and hear Ruphiri do the same around me, though their target is the Malesiirian line.

Zavaan produces a cord to bind Erianna's hands behind her back and pulls her spine to his chest. She thrashes in his grip, enhancing his perverse pleasure, as he sinks his face into her neck.

"Leelah, move!" Valor bellows over the outrage of Malesiir.

Standing not much farther than where Erianna passed her on the line between the two armies is one livid Leelah, watching Zavaan violate her friend.

Kragorn also beckons to his wife, but it is Erianna's desperate cry telling Leelah to run that decides her.

Taking a step backward, Leelah says to her husband, "It is like we always say, Kragorn. If only we had been there…"

"No!" Kragorn barks. "Do not! Leelah!"

But Leelah turns on her heel and runs toward Erianna, momentarily diverting Zavaan from his assault of our queen.

Despite the roars of Valor and her husband, Leelah declares to Zavaan, "Where Erianna goes, I go."

Genuine amusement draws laughter from the murderous villain. "Far be it from me to force a woman to do what she does not want to do."

"Leelah!" Erianna pleads once more to no avail.

"Sorry, Majie," Leelah says as she strides into the midst of the Ruphiri. "This is not going to go your way today."

Zavaan shoves Erianna after her as Zavaan's horse is brought toward him. The war cry of Valor cracks the air. Orjek's arm falls, ordering a volley of arrows. I loose mine into the middle ground where it will do no harm. When Zavaan drags Erianna onto the fore of his saddle, I gamble that Orjek will be too busy directing the attack against Malesiir and safeguarding Zavaan's escape to be Leelah's keeper. I urge my horse toward Leelah and hoist her up before me. I wrap an arm around her and spur after Zavaan who gallops away with our queen.

"You're a fool, Leelah Tareth," I hiss into her ear.

She startles, not realizing who held her, then retorts, "No matter their plans, Zavaan will not lose Erianna this day."

The same fear burns a hole in my gut, but still, "You should have gone with them."

"Tell me I am wrong," she contends. "Tell me their plan will succeed and Zavaan will be careless enough to lose her."

I shake my head alongside hers.

"As I thought. If Erianna is to survive this, it will take both of us."

"She allowed herself to be captured so that you could be free!" I snarl.

Leelah huffs. "I will not claim freedom at that price."

I growl but say no more, hearing the approach of riders behind us. A glance confirms they are Ruphiri.

Miles fall away, bringing us ever closer to the Ascent—Malesiir's natural border of shale and elevation. However, Zavaan cuts northward down a near invisible path, deeper into the heart of Malesiir.

CHAPTER TWENTY-SIX

TRENT

February 7th

The slivered moon fights a feeble battle with the night when Zavaan rides into a copse of evergreens. Within their shroud, bodies become silhouettes, one looking much like another, excepting Zavaan's diminutive prize which he drops to the ground, heedless of the way she crumples.

A terse string of commands spills from his vile tongue while I lower Leelah to the ground. She flies to Erianna, speaking overtop Zavaan. "Cut her hands loose, you Barbarian!"

He wheels on her. "As you are once more a recipient of my hospitality, I will do you the courtesy of reminding you what you seem to have so quickly forgotten." The strike of his hand against her cheek knocks her to the ground. "You do not give me orders, Leelah Tareth!"

With his prey bound at his feet, the bait is no longer necessary—a fact Leelah does not seem to recognize as she continues to dictate to the ruthless Wolf. "She needs water! You will have a very dead queen on your hands if you do not allow me to attend to her. That would make you a greater fool than I know you to be!"

In the black of night, I struggle to see Zavaan's response. The shadow of him doubles as Leelah comes to her feet. A gurgling noise explains what I cannot see—Zavaan has Leelah by the throat.

I draw a dagger and hasten toward them, still leading my horse. If I take Zavaan by surprise, I may be able to cut *his* throat, allowing the women to flee atop my mount while I hinder the rest of the Ruphiri.

"Stop!" My queen's command stalls my steps though she does not speak to me. "Zavaan!"

Leelah collapses atop Erianna, gasping then cursing Zavaan. "Villainous spawn of a frog! You milk-sop! Slimy trout!" A rasping cough interrupts her. "Horse apples!"

Erianna, who is well-versed and oft utilizes real profanity, laughs. I sheath my dagger and feign tending my horse, waiting for an opening. Erianna's laughter sounds painful and uncontrolled. I doubt she can hear Leelah's calming words as she falls to wheezing. "Cannot... breathe..."

Zavaan crouches over her, hauling her to her knees. "Stop this!"

Her hysteria is unchecked by the threat in his voice. I tense in the shadows, twitching with a vengeful need to gut her enemy. Erianna can only be settled with gentleness, time, and assurance of her safety. My inability to protect my queen shreds me.

Leelah's steady voice requests what I cannot. "Give her over to me and pass me a water skin?"

He thrusts Erianna into Leelah and barks a command, his arm outstretched. I untie my water skin from my horse and give it to Zavaan. As he takes it, I consider yanking it back to off-balance him, then thrusting my knife deep into his side beneath his cuirass. Instead, I let him pass the water skin to the women. Were the night not so dark and Erianna in full command of herself, I would dare.

As Leelah settles the queen with sips of water and whispered words, Zavaan stalks away. I follow his path with my eyes as the shadows embrace him.

One chance. I will have but one chance to free them.

I cannot waste it.

February 8th

I stay near the women through what remains of the night, as does Zavaan. Near dawn, Orjek arrives with the Ruphiri that survived Valor's forces. Nigh to half of those that fought must have been killed or captured. I hope Valor managed to take some alive, for he would not think to follow the Ruphiri deeper into Malesiir. He would have ridden to the Ascent.

Zavaan rouses from Erianna's side, drawing his sword. I do likewise and take a position alongside him. This is not the manner I imagined he would kill Leelah. Death by the sword is far too kind. Thus, he must suspect an enemy.

He slides his strange russet eyes toward me. *"Brynjar, ravat. Bránjit jim."*

I nod my head and acknowledge what I hope is a command. *"Kyzar."* My voice is gruff from disuse. It aids in making the guttural consonants of the Ruphiri dialect.

I hold my drawn sword at the ready as Zavaan advances on his newly arrived men. A bared sword in the hand of the *Kyzar* has an immediate effect on the Ruphiri. They still their movements, shifting their focus to him.

"Orjek," Zavaan calls on his apparent second in command. That Ruphiri dismounts, his single braid bouncing on his shorn head.

"Kyzar," Orjek bows his head without taking his eyes from Zavaan.

The languid taunting cadence with which Zavaan addresses the women is absent. In its place is a tone that is harsh and direct. Zavaan gestures toward myself and his prisoners who have stirred awake. My heart pounds faster, knowing that the discussion concerns us. Thankfully, Erianna whispers a quiet translation to Leelah. "He believes Orjek has betrayed him because Torvarik marked me as a *zar*."

"The Ruphiri warlord whom Valor captured?"

"Aye."

"Why does—"

"Hush!"

Leelah holds her questions while Erianna listens.

"They are kin—brothers, I think—though Orjek claims no allegiance to Torvarik. There is enmity there."

With no forewarning, the edge of Zavaan's sword lands at Orjek's throat, cutting a thin river of red into his flesh. I jut my chin against that phantom pain. His cunning, his speed, the accuracy displayed in that one motion put to death the illusions I held about besting Zavaan with blades. At most, I might slow him and grant the women a chance at escape, but I will not survive the confrontation.

"Zavaan has named Torvarik a renegade. His land, his wives, and his children are forfeit." A tremor runs through Erianna's words. "If Orjek wishes to live, he must vow to kill Torvarik and seize his tribe."

Orjek wraps his hand around the blade at his throat then raises his bleeding palm.

"He swears it," Erianna whispers, though this action needs no translation.

Zavaan lowers his sword and clasps Orjek's bloody hand then dismisses him. Only once Orjek is engaged with refreshing his horse and his men does Zavaan turn his attention back to the women.

My fingers tighten on the leather-bound sword hilt. The balance of it is different than my own. It is also shorter. With Zavaan coming ever closer, I feel the lack of my friendly weapons all the more. Should he speak to me again, how ought I to respond? Surely nodding will not suffice for a second exchange.

Zavaan extends his sword over the heads of the seated women. He swipes at the blood gleaming on the edge, rubbing it between his fingers, then inhales the odor. Erianna shudders. Her response pleases the vile Wolf. Using the hem of her cloak, he cleans his blade. Inwardly, I consider where I can bury my sword in him. Outwardly, I do nothing —not shift my weight to my back foot, draw a full breath, nor tense my muscles. The predator would notice and wonder.

As if conversing about nothing more pressing than the weather, Zavaan says, "It seems a waste to use you up quickly, Mistress Tareth. My wife is quite fond of you. Thus, a change of your guard is needed. Orjek feels entitled to what you offer. Though I am certain you would be happy to entertain him, his duties lie in protecting his *kyzar*."

Zavaan flicks his burnt eyes to me and rattles a question in that accursed foreign tongue. Given the context he presented Leelah, I hope he is asking if I will take responsibility for her. I nod my head.

He asks something else of me. I intend to nod again, but a weight unfurls in my chest and a quiet voice not my own seems to speak directly into my being. *No.*

Compelled, I shake my head in the negative. "*Na, Kyzar.*"

He peers into my cowled face. "*Deh?*"

"*Deh,*" I reply.

His sword returns to its scabbard.

I exhale and likewise cover my blade. A pleased twitch moves Zavaan's mouth at that. He enjoys evoking fear, even among his own men.

"Mistress Tareth, meet your new caretaker, Brynjar, though you ought to give him leave to use your given name after kissing him so wantonly."

Leelah's dismissive response is perfect. "One of you Ruphiri is much the same as another."

"I am glad to accommodate you." Zavaan bows then seizes Erianna's arm, causing her to flinch. "Come, Wife. You have denied me your company far too long."

While Zavaan leads Erianna about the camp, displaying his prize by the looks of it, I take Leelah by the arm and guide her to the edge of the woods for her privacy.

"Did you have any notion what he said to you?" She whispers without moving her lips.

"None."

She sighs. "Praise You, Almighty, for answered prayers."

Remembrance of that voice makes me ask, "You prayed I would answer rightly?"

"Aye."

Beyond any doubt, I know two things that interfere with my entrenched way of thinking.

One, the Creator exists.

Two, He has taken an interest in what happens to Leelah and Erianna, else I would be dead.

CHAPTER TWENTY-SEVEN

TRENT

February 12th

With every mile Zavaan puts between Valor's forces and us, I worry. My duty ensuring Leelah is fed and tended—though blessed is the opportunity to remain near her—prevents me from laying the promised trail for Valor. If he has not tracked us thus far, my efforts will likely be in vain. Especially because I cannot fathom where Zavaan is taking us.

There is no other way down the Ascent that is known to us Malesiirians. Yet he is driving us parallel to the Ascent. Could he have discovered an ancient corridor that grants passage on that shale slide? There is naught ahead of us besides insignificant towns and the incomplete port city of Halden. Were he to have a ship waiting in the harbor—which is impossible—the seas are too rough during the winter to sail. We are locked inside a natural fortress. But onward we ride, skirting mountainsides and weaving through snow dressed forests.

At the midday respite, I unbind Leelah's hands from the saddle and grip her beneath her arms. As she swings her leg over the saddle, she grimaces and falls into me. I catch her and drag her away from the horse that shies at her awkward dismount.

Leelah's ashen coloring sends a bolt of fear through me. "What's wrong?"

She fists my sleeves while the color seeps back into her face with her each measured breath.

"*Leelah,*" I press.

"Cramp," she grunts.

"What can I—"

"Trent!" She gasps looking past my shoulder as a scuffle breaks out. I follow her gaze. Erianna is battling Zavaan over control of a dagger.

"Do something!" she urges.

Supporting Leelah, I close the distance to Erianna. Her defiant expression and fearless attack on Zavaan is the first genuine showing of our Warrior Queen since she was captured.

Blood flecks the air, but it is not from the gleaming dagger shearing the leather laces of Erianna's cuirass. It is spat from Zavaan's mouth. Whether from the scent of first blood or the theft of the armor that Zavaan rips from her grasp, Erianna turns feral. Snarls rip from her mouth matched to the jabs and thrusts of fists, elbows, knees, and feet. When Zavaan locks one of her arms beneath his stealing her vambrace and glove, he unleashes her claws. She gouges his flesh with her fingernails while thrusting a knee that narrowly misses its sensitive target. Zavaan's growl layers her animalistic sounds as he jabs an elbow toward her face. She jerks to the side, diminishing the blow, but still her lip splits at the force.

Leelah foolishly lunges toward her friend. I catch her back against me and seize that excuse to draw my sword, angling it toward her throat in what appears a threat. "Be still," I put the words in her ear. "The queen holds her own. Look to the Ruphiri." Her gaze runs around the clearing noting what I also did. They are entranced by the vicious battle. The woman they helped capture is not the weak little queen Zavaan claims.

The brawl over possession of Erianna's greaves causes both to yield blood. Though Erianna is the loser of the contest, she has gained something of greater value. Breaths puffing both of their chests, Erianna views the crimson decorating her enemy and laughs. The Ruphiri shoot looks of astonishment to each other. Zavaan notes the murmurs resulting from Erianna's mockery. His fist hooks beneath her jaw, dropping her to the ground in an unconscious heap, but the damage is done. The Warrior Queen has earned the reluctant respect of her captors.

Zavaan shouts the order to break camp and stalks away.

"Now," I urge Leelah forward, allowing her to lower alongside Erianna and take the queen's head in her lap. My sword guards the backs of the women, but to the enemy, it appears a threat for the women to behave.

Leelah dabs the blood on Erianna's chin while she waits for her to rouse. Pain stabs my chest to see my queen laid out, though pride in her is a balm to the ache.

Across the camp, a knot of Ruphiri argue amongst themselves, inciting many to nod or disagree with a shake of the head. Leelah casts me a look of rampant curiosity. I quirk a brow, sharing her interest. A low moan issues from Erianna followed by the flutter of lashes on her cheeks and slitted eyes. A deep breath causes her to moan again. The pain masked by her battle fever must be thrashing her now.

Leelah bends over her, murmuring. Erianna grows still once more, feigning sleep, though her lips move, putting forth words too soft for me to overhear. When her eyes open again, they skim the exposed steel in my hands, then raise to glare into my eyes. I hold steady with her until recognition blazes, driving back the ice.

"Trent." She forms my name on her swollen lips, causing blood to trickle into the corner of her mouth.

Now! Fight! Raze the camp! My heart roars. Again, I stymie the desire. If I do not temper the fiery rage of the warrior with the cold logic of the spymaster, it will mean the loss of the women that cause me to stand here disguised as the enemy.

With peripheral awareness of the movements of the Ruphiri, I dare a wink at Erianna, offering the barest of comfort to her. My mind flashes back to the anger that blazed in me for her deception regarding Silla. I condemned her for doing whatever she felt necessary to unmask the traitor thereby preventing Zavaan from capturing her. Seeing her laid on her back, beaten and bloodied at my feet, I curse myself. The price she remitted without asking I would willingly pay tenfold to have prevented this. However, Erianna's love for her friends as witnessed by what was meant to be her sacrifice for Leelah proves her a greater friend—a greater warrior—than I have ever been. She knew this and more could be the cost. She chose to pay it.

Encroaching upon our position is the cause of all this evil. I shift my attention to him, reminding myself I must not give him any cause to question my loyalty. Or my identity.

"We ride," he tells the queen, towering over her prone form.

"To Halden?" She challenges. "You are daft to sail at this time of year!"

Surprise shoots through me, both at this plan and Erianna's knowledge of it.

Zavaan's ire grows like a cloud. "You test my patience, Wife."

The queen's defiance is untamed. "Try harder, little *Zar*. You are no *král* that can make me kneel."

Zavaan bends over her, spitting his vile intent into her ear. "Do hold on to that reckless spirit until we reach the ship. I want you at your best when I lock you in my cabin and take a week to bring you to your knees before me. Again."

A tremor runs through the sword in my hand. Could I impale the Wolf upon it before he rises?

"Never again," the queen snarls.

I angle back a step to ensure the hand Zavaan closes around my queen's neck does not further trespass. Fury pounds a drum through my veins as his fingers slide beneath the collar of her tunic.

He muses, "It has been so long since I have had such a spirited woman as my wife. Thayas, my first wife, also possessed such spirit. Not surprising since she was the younger sister of Torvarik."

My mind presents an image of the Ruphiri warlord Valor took captive. Did Torvarik sacrifice his sister to this monster? Perhaps to advance his rank?

Zavaan chuckles. "Torvarik likes his secrets." The hand he clamps around her throat belies his amusement as he hauls her to her feet then to her toes, choking away her breath.

Leelah scrabbles upright. I use the flat of my sword to push her away from Zavaan. Hot ire flashes from her eyes, but I do not care about her indignation as long as she is safe.

Zavaan threatens Erianna with the story as her face turns red. "She broke quickly in my house. Too quickly. I cast her body upon the Spires for my wolves. But I have learned since then. I will not use you up so quickly, Little Queen. I will take much pleasure in making your days of torment stretch into years. Then, when you are unrecognizable, once I have all of the Continent at my feet, what is left of you will fill the bellies of my wolves."

Erianna's eyes fill with fog as her mind fades into darkness, soon to be followed by her life if he does not release her. In my thoughts, I plot the exact swipe of my blade to bring down Zavaan. Two strikes—one across the back of his legs, severing tendon and sinew to ensure he cannot escape while Erianna collapses to the ground; the second, a stab to his throat to spill his lifeblood upon the thirsty Malesiirian ground.

With a shove, Zavaan drops Erianna in a heap. She gulps the cold air, wincing from pain, as she rises to her knees, ever mindful that a warrior never leaves her back exposed. Leelah pushes at my restraining arm, but I look to Zavaan for permission. He grants it with a nod. I recenter myself behind Erianna, loathing myself as each of her breaths wheeze through her abused throat.

Leelah wraps her arms around Erianna while growling her unintelligible wrath at Zavaan. A wicked smile turns up the corners of his mouth, and a sound of pleasure hums from his chest. "You, however, I will not be so deliberate with. I will feast on you. And once I have had my fill, I will give you to my men. You, Leelah Tareth, will not last a single night."

My vision blurs at the edges. The middle hones upon the villain. Despite his forewarning, these women cannot imagine the evil he intends to work upon them. But I can. I have seen the effects of it. The bruises. The blood. The death.

Staring purest evil in the eye, Leelah drags Erianna to her feet and declares, *"Make your plans, but they will come to nothing. Speak your words, but they will not stand. For the Almighty is with us."*

Power spears through her words, straight into the confidence of Zavaan.

He rallies quickly. "Is He? I do not see Him. No, you are quite at my disposal, Leelah. Make no mistake," Zavaan croons, "I will dispose of you. Far sooner than the woman for whom you relinquished your freedom." His eyes fall to the babe in her belly. "Very foolish." He angles his head toward our queen. "How many have died for you, Erianna? Even I do not know the number."

Erianna's grip tightens around Leelah, her glare promising death.

Steam from Zavaan's breath wraps around the women when he orders, "Mount up."

When Leelah and Erianna hold their ground, I shift my weight, readying for a fight. Too many Ruphiri are watching. If the women do not yield, Zavaan will obtain their submission by force.

Thrice I see their breath fog the air before Leelah speaks for the both of them. *"In the Almighty, whose words I praise, in the Almighty I trust. I shall not be afraid. For what can mortal man do to me? Though all his thoughts against me are for evil, though he watches my steps and seeks to steal my life... in the Almighty I trust. I shall not be afraid. For the Almighty has delivered my soul from death and has kept my feet from falling that I may walk before Him in the light of life."*

An image overlays my vision. I imagine I see light flaring outward from Leelah, and the darkness shrouding the Ruphiri trembles in response. The light exposes a deep, hidden darkness in my own heart. It is made of hate, selfishness, vengeance, lust, and murder. When I am forced to acknowledge its existence, it rattles with a sound like chains.

I want to duck my head, hiding from what abides in me, but movement jerks my gaze to Zavaan. Confusion, even fear, drives him back from Leelah. Abruptly he grabs for his horse and shouts orders in Limban, one I recognize means to move out.

As Orjek comes forward to claim Erianna, I set my hand on Leelah's arm to guide her away. She ignores my touch, taking hold of Erianna's hands. "You see, Erianna. The lies of the enemy crumble against the power of the Almighty."

"If only I knew more," Erianna whispers her regret. "I cannot recall the words of Truth to fight him like you do."

"Of course, you can!" Leelah insists, that indomitable fire in her blazing brighter. "Even my little girls could. You need only sing. Our songs of praise are verses taken directly from the Holy Texts. It is why we teach them to our children. Those songs are the first verses from the Texts that they learn."

Leelah wraps Erianna in a hug until Orjek pulls Erianna away.

"Come, Leelah," I murmur from behind my shroud. My voice rasps from disuse, but the quiver that runs through it I can only attribute to the exposed darkness, now snuggling inside the caves in my heart. Knowing it exists frightens me. What if I cannot control it? What if it surges out when I am unprepared to restrain it?

As if hearing my own fears, Leelah shouts, "Sing! Sing to fight the darkness, Erianna! Sing through the night!"

I grip Leelah's upper arm, assisting her over the uneven ground, though her steps do not falter. Perhaps it is she who guides me toward her horse, my mind grappling with the enemy around me and the black hate within me. I assist Leelah to the saddle then bind her hands, looping the excess rope around the pommel. I ensure her feet are seated in the stirrups before taking hold of her reins and mounting my dun gelding.

A sweet voice shivers on the air. "*I lift up my eyes to the hills, from where comes my help?*"

My head turns to the bruised queen. Her chin tucked to her chest in fear, slowly rises with the tune. "*My help comes from the Creator, the Maker of heaven and earth. He will not allow my feet to be moved. He who keeps me neither slumbers nor sleeps... The Almighty will keep me from all evil. It is He who holds my life.*" Her gleaming faith blasts the shadowed evil of Reuel Zavaan. He tucks into himself to withstand the light in her smile, a light that shoves against the darkness in my heart, making room for hope. I cling to it, determined to not let the darkness smother it.

I nudge my horse into line behind Erianna's, admiring her confidence, the straightness of her back in the saddle though her hands are bound.

Zavaan stops the procession, looking at the ground. I track his gaze to the pile of Erianna's armor. "Brynjar," Zavaan drawls, then spews a string of Limban that I do not comprehend.

Erianna's head jerks to Zavaan then to me. "You mean for him to dispose of my armor?"

The translation of his order protects my identity, but it costs Erianna some of the high ground she gained by allowing Zavaan to believe he riled her. "You have no need of it."

A Ruphiri rides toward me to take charge of Leelah. I transfer her reins to him then collect Erianna's armor, mastering my expression as I seize upon this long awaited opportunity.

Zavaan issues another command to me. Erianna must not think it one of importance for she remains silent.

"Deh, Kyzar," I reply, stacking Erianna's armor into a bundle and mounting the dun.

I spur into the forest in the opposite direction of the advancing Ruphiri. When I have gained enough distance to not be seen by the scouts, I spur toward the nearest road. It is one of the paths that lead toward Halden. I break the tips of a series of branches at chest height leading from the edge of the road into the forest, too deep for a casual passerby to discover the bundle. I arrange Erianna's armor beneath the drooping boughs of an evergreen save for one of her vambraces. From my saddlebag, I withdraw a piece of paper and tear it into a small scrap. I press it against my thigh, my pen poised as I debate what to inscribe. There is much Valor will want to know, much I wish to convey, but I have little time and less room if the scrap is to fit in the empty slot of the vambrace where a slender throwing knife ought to be. It also must not be discernible should the message be found by someone other than Valor.

The dun snorts his impatience as I jot information that will reassure and inform Valor when he finds it. *If* he finds it.

E drew first blood from Z. L and E are whole. Their singing scares the R.
    Fly to Halden. They sail.
    February 12th

I wave the paper in the air to dry the ink then fold it and slip it into the vambrace, leaving the edge of the paper sticking out. With shaking hands, I place it atop the pile of armor. To increase its chances of being discovered, I break the tips of the branches of the tree concealing the armor. *Almighty, let it be enough. Let Valor find it. Let them not be too late.*

The prayer forms a refrain as I mount the dun and weave back to the game trail through the forest, digging my heels into the animal's sides.

CHAPTER TWENTY-EIGHT

TRENT

February 19th

The second watch of the night suits me. In the dark hours when most men have settled into a deep sleep, the Wolves with a wicked bent stalk close to the women, testing the strength of the shadows surrounding their prey.

Prey. The word weighs my shoulders like a doe my arrow pierced.

For unknowable reasons, Tirzah presses upon my mind. Her insistence on crossing the valley at night burns behind my sternum. *"I do not want to shatter your naivety, but men, even the ones here, could do you unspeakable harm."*

"I am not naive, Cuyler."

She was naive. Sakes, despite my many encounters with despicable men, even *I* had some naivety lingering about me. But not anymore. Not after another week of watching these wolves with their whetted appetites making prey of my women. Had I not drawn my sword and laid it across my thighs where I crouched at the edge of camp, Orjek would have stolen away with Leelah, no one the wiser. Thereafter, I have only found sleep with my hand encircling Leelah's, the other on my sword. Zavaan was amused by this and gave an order to me the next morning, one Erianna did not translate but with a slight dip of her head, told me to agree to. *"Deh, Kyzar."* It seems the only thing I say anymore.

Erianna has continued to hold her own against Zavaan's increasing intimacy. The proximity that displays his possession, the lingering touches upon her body, the way he devours her with his eyes—it all compounds to stoke my fury.

Despite the danger that keeps me in a state of constant vigilance, my eyes droop. I have pushed my body past its uttermost limits and must soon sleep and eat my fill. If I do not, my body will collapse without my permission. One way or another, I will fall soon.

We reached Halden late today, bringing an end to my search for an opportunity to free them both. Either I will make a way to free the women or I will die in the attempt on the morrow. I desperately hope Valor and our soldiers have reached the town. Avoiding roads slowed the Ruphiri when we found deep snow in the mountain passes. Perhaps Valor managed to overtake our lead. I fix my weary eyes on Leelah, studying the rise and fall of her shoulders in sleep. She has begun to eat little and sleep much these past days, seeding worry in my gut. It cannot be good for her or her babe to be dragged across the kingdom at this destructive pace. Still, in sleep, she appears at peace.

My vision shimmies, replacing Leelah's prone form with Tirzah's. *She exits a house, radiant after successfully delivering a babe into the world. Tree bark bites into my fingers where I watch her from the shadows of an oak, drinking in the beauty of her unbound hair, then stalking closer. "Cuyler." My name drips like honey from her lips. Sweetness. Admiration. Love. But she is prey to me. I herd her toward her cottage. From outside my body, I see Orjek locked in the single room with her, removing her dress, pushing her toward the bed. I rage and scream at him to stop, but no sound leaves my mouth. "Don't sham me, Cuyler," Tirzah pleads, trusting herself to me. To him. To the predator in me.*

With a jerk I fall backward in the snow. I shake my head to dislodge the dream, the burn behind my sternum increasing tenfold. *I am not Orjek! I am not!* While I scramble out of the snow amid the cloak of dense evergreens and regain my balance on the balls of my feet to keep myself awake, I repeat the chant to stifle the burn before it eats a hole in my chest. *I am not Orjek. I am not.*

Sounds of a scuffle penetrate my haze. I trace the outline a sleeping Leelah before seeking my queen lying on the other side of the camp. Zavaan shoves her away, vilely cursing her. In the wash of moonlight, Zavaan retreats from Erianna. A relieved breath has barely parted my lips when he seizes Leelah. Dragging her to her feet, he lands a punch to her face, folding her in half. Erianna screams when his fist flies again, this time into Leelah's belly with a sickening thud.

An arrow is nocked to my bow, feathers tickling my nose. It flies through the night, a half foot from Zavaan's head. Again, I nock and loose another, this time splitting the throat of a Ruphiri nearby. A target draws his sword. My bowstring stretches, bending the limbs toward my body. The force enters the arrow, whistling across the night, sinking into the face of the enemy. My shots are not pretty. My aim is to fell Ruphiri, not make clean kills.

Bound hand and foot, my queen crawls like a worm in the mud, screaming curses at Zavaan. Enraged, I think I loose a scream as well. Zavaan grabs Leelah by her hair then stills, hearing my arrows and seeing his men drop. I long to riddle his body with arrows, but he is too close to Leelah. In the fickle moonlight with both of them moving, I might hit her instead of Zavaan. Two more arrows sing, spraying black ink into the night before I match an inhale of breath to my next draw. The arrow flies wide, thunking into a tree, spitting bark.

"They have found us! Here! Here!" Erianna shouts, drawing Zavaan away from Leelah. I cannot slay him before he has dragged my queen upright, using her as a shield against my onslaught.

"Run, Leelah!" She screams. "Run!"

The spine of an arrow settles on the riser, I take aim on Zavaan, dragging Erianna away from the battle deep into the closing Ruphiri ranks. His head peeks over her shoulder scanning the forest for the Malesiirian forces Erianna has made him believe are closing in. The shot isn't there. I could just as easily kill Erianna as Zavaan. The divisiveness written upon her face is the same she wore a few nights past, when Orjek stalked Leelah. Though Leelah slept through it, Erianna saw. Erianna knew. When her eyes met mine over my drawn sword, her expressive eyes communicated the choice she had already made. *Free her and leave me.*

I shook my head then as I do now. *No, my Queen.*

Free her! "Run, Leelah!" She commands.

Arms clutching her belly, Leelah stumbles toward me, into the rain of arrows.

I shift the tip of my arrow to aim at a Ruphiri pursing her. I flex my fingers, loosing the string. The arrow flies straight into his unarmored chest. Before he drops to the ground, I nock another arrow, feeling the burn in my neck and shoulder muscles as I fell another of Leelah's pursuers. She enters the forest several yards past me, beginning to run. I pelt arrows into the Ruphiri camp without taking aim, hoping my barrage convinces them that there is, indeed, a contingent of Malesiirian soldiers bearing down upon them.

Ducking behind trees and branches rather than giving chase, I continue firing until I reach behind my head for another arrow and grasp only air. I sprint after Leelah, seizing her from behind.

She screams, fighting my arms wrapped around her. I let her thrash against me, her arms pinned helplessly beneath mine. Within moments, the Ruphiri dash past us toward the horses. To their eyes, Leelah has been captured before she could escape to the Malesiirian forces waiting in ambush. *Let them not notice my empty quiver,* I plead with the Almighty.

I drag Leelah, still yowling and clawing my forearms, toward my dun horse. Zavaan is already galloping into the night with Erianna seated on the fore of his saddle. My heart tries to follow my queen, loathing myself for abandoning her to the enemy with this deception. A cadre follows Zavaan while the rest mount up to fight the Malesiirians, unaware the only Malesiirian they need fear wears the skin of one of their own.

"Leelah, I have you," I put the words into her ear then lift her to the fore of my saddle. Her agonized expression flays me as I swing up behind her. She falls against my chest, groaning, her head landing in the crook of my neck. One arm banded around her body, the other gripping the reins, I follow Zavaan's party at a measured pace until they draw out of sight.

Cradling her head with mine, I guide the dun through the dense evergreen forest till his hooves hit the snow packed road. I kick my heels into his sides, sprinting him into the fledging town of Halden.

TIRZAH

I bolt upright in bed, gasping and reaching for the little ones curled at my sides. Slipping from the bed, I set my hand on each of their heads, ensuring they are all well, breathing, and sleeping soundly. I even check on Karris in her room. She rustles in the sheets but settles.

Going to the stairs, I creep down to the great room. The fire is banked for the night, but I could no more go back to bed than I could fly. Fear clogs my throat, a certainty that something is gravely wrong. A discarded blanket lies on the arm of a chair. I cast it about my shoulders and drop to my knees, shaking.

"Almighty, hear me. Please be with Leelah and Erianna. Protect them. Guard their lives from the wicked Ruphiri. Protect Leelah's babe, preserve it, please. Almighty, cover them with your hand, rescue them, hide them. Help Trent find them. Grant him the skills to rescue them. Please, please, be near. Save Leelah. Save Erianna. Preserve their lives."

Tears prick my eyes. An urgency fills my spirit, making my prayers echo in gasps and moans in the cavernous room. Long past the time my knees ache and my legs are numb, I huddle on the floor, praying as if their lives depend upon it.

CHAPTER TWENTY-NINE

TRENT

February 19th

"Breathe, Leelah!" I urge as I deposit her on the thin, lumpy mattress.

She groans and curls around her belly. I dart back into the night, glancing up and down Halden's empty street—its only street. I lead the dun inside the vacant cabin lest any Ruphiri search the town and recognize the beast tied outside. I bolt the door then use a broken, overturned table to make a visual barrier to relegate the horse to one corner of the single room.

Leelah's pain scrapes against my skull as I pull packs off the horse, searching for my tinderbox to lay a fire in the fireplace. I break a chair into pieces. The horse skitters in the corner at the destruction and noise. Thankfully, enough charred bits of wood remain on the hearth to use as kindling. After plunking the pieces of the chair into the fireplace and arranging the kindling beneath it, I open my tinderbox. I pinch out the char cloth but the striker steel tumbles from my trembling fingers, sparking on the hearth. I retrieve it then hold it steady against the char cloth while I flick the blade of my dagger on the striker steel, catching the sparks on the char cloth. When it burns, I set the cloth on the kindling, blowing gently to set the kindling ablaze.

Whimpers sound from the bed, drawing me to Leelah's side. Grabbing the rough cut edges of the bed, I drag it across the room to be nearer the heat of fire and the scant light. A swollen, dark splotch mars Leelah's cheek. Zavaan struck her without restraint. My breath lodges in my chest hearing the thump of his fist against her abdomen. He might have cracked her ribs. Or worse, struck her babe.

180

"Leelah, I need to see your side."

She holds her breath, stoppering her pain behind pinched lips.

"Do you understand? That means—"

With an impatient grunt she fists her skirt, hiking it up her legs.

Not my friend's wife. Just a soldier. A patient, I tell myself, helping her work the dress higher. *Aye, a patient.*

One I wish Tirzah were here to tend. My stomach roils at the spots of blood on her inner thighs. Not from the blood itself, but the knowledge that I have no notion how to help her. Her left side is discolored, the uneven edges reaching across her lowest ribs onto the swell of her belly. I gently prod her ribs, causing her to groan. They seem to be in place, not giving too much. "Your ribs don't seem to be broken, only—"

Her stomach tightens suddenly. I touch the top of her rounded belly, feeling that the muscles are taut across the whole. Leelah holds her breath, leaning into the pain. Flashes of aiding my father's livestock to deliver their young surge from the past.

Labor pains. Leelah is in labor. Prematurely. I shake my head, trying to dislodge the fear.

With the release of the pain, air gusts out of her, and she drops onto the pathetic mattress. I cannot bind her ribs, leastwise I do not know how to with a babe inside. Her possibly cracked ribs must wait. I tuck her dress down but not all the way, fearing I may have to deliver her of her babe. My cloak acts as a blanket providing her additional warmth and a shade of modesty in this horrible situation.

My fingertips knead my brow as another pain seizes Leelah, and she bears into it.

"How can I help? What can we do to stop this?" I ask.

She grabs hold of my hand, shaking her head. "Can't." Tears catch the light in the corners of her eyes then stream down her temples.

Please, no. I drop to my knees at her side. Touching my head to her hand. The accursed shroud still covers the lower half of my face. I rip it away with a snarl, cursing Zavaan and his Ruphiri. A sob shakes Leelah's chest between labor pains.

How can I explain to Kragorn that I did not protect his wife? That my negligence cost him his child?

Almighty, I know You care naught for me, but You must care for Leelah. Please, please help. Save her and the babe.

I feel my own tears drop to our clasped hands. There must be something…

Stealing across my writhing thoughts comes Tirzah's soothing voice describing how she aided the young woman laboring before her time. *Her labor pains finally went away after I made her lie down and drink copious amounts of water.*

Could the same help Leelah? I bind my hopes to Tirzah's superior knowledge and dash for my water skin. I unstopper it and fit the spout to Leelah's lips. She jerks her head aside.

"You must drink. It might stop the pains."

I slide my arm beneath her head, supporting her and encouraging her to drink. She manages a few mouthfuls before another pain takes hold, curling her inward.

"Don't, Leelah. Breathe through it. Relax."

She shakes her head, stubborn to her marrow.

"Help me stop this! Help me save your babe," I demand, needing her to yield though I feel a brute at hearing my own words and tone.

Her lips part, sipping a long, narrow breath then exhaling it in the same way. I pounce when the pain subsides, wielding the water skin. She drinks until the next pain comes. In this manner, we pass interminable minutes. When the water skin is empty, I leave her to melt snow in a shallow bowl. Once it turns into warm water, I compel her to drink it also. Tirzah said *copious amounts* of water. I treat her words that may be an exaggeration as an oath and continue plying Leelah with water.

Though I have no way of knowing, her pains seem to be decreasing in intensity and frequency. When she is distracted by breathing through one of the pains, I lift the cloak and her hem. There does not appear to be fresh blood.

I tuck the cloak tightly about her, trapping her body heat. She extends her hand to me. I take it, returning to her side. Leelah looks worn through. There is pain in her eyes and shadows beneath them. Lines of worry take residence on her brow. Her mouth appears to have never known a smile.

Nevertheless, Leelah fares better with each infrequent pain. What had folded her in half now produces a mere grunt of acknowledgement. Her grip on my hand slackens till it is only I holding to her as she slumbers.

Have we done it? Did we truly stop her labor?

I set my hand on her belly, waiting for any contracting of the muscles while I watch her sleep and count her breaths. When they number in the hundreds and still her muscles are relaxed, I find room to breathe through the noose of my fear, though it still hangs around my neck.

There is still much to be done to ensure her safety.

After laying her hand on her belly, I come to my feet, assessing the cabin beyond my prior cursory glance to decide it was unoccupied and habitable. Perhaps it was a transient house used by the master mason during the warmer months. My discarded shroud laying in the middle of the floor swings my thoughts a darker direction, the direction of the Ruphiri. The house could have belonged to one of the casualties of the Ruphiri attacks this past autumn.

I rough my hands over my face, returning to the inescapable fact that I abandoned my queen to the monsters who haunt her nightmares. Unlatching the shutter of the single window, I ease it open two finger widths. I stare into the night through the sliver of space, formulating a plan to free my queen or at least give her a chance at escape. Snow collects in drifts around the houses along the street, but most have a shoveled path to the door, indicative of habitation. This house did not. Verily, the shutter of the window would scrape the top of a drift if I attempted to open it wide.

A cloud skitters before the moon, casting all below in shadow. I tug the shutter closed and latch it, returning to my vigil at Leelah's side. Should her health not deteriorate, at dawn I will search for a trustworthy soul to look after her while I attempt to rescue Erianna.

Getting close to my queen will undoubtedly prove difficult. I'll not be able to disguise myself as Brynjar again. By now, they will have noticed that the arrows that felled their men were both Malesiirian and Ruphiri made. Leelah and my absence is all the remaining proof needed to point to Brynjar's betrayal. I hope Zavaan does not question Erianna about this. Without me to watch over her and prevent him from acting on his vile compulsions...

I drop my head in my hands, sick with worry for my queen.

TRENT

February 20th

"Why are you still here?"

Leelah's croaked words rouse me from a half-sleep. My gaze sweeps the room, noting the dawn light sneaking around the cracks of the window shutter, before landing on her. "You're awake."

"Aye. My babe woke me." She presses her palm to the side of her belly. A smile fills her countenance with relief.

My hope, however, struggles to rise through the ashes. "Is he well?"

She takes my hand and guides my fingertips to her side. Fearful moments pass. Too many. Not once in the hour I sat with my hand on her belly last night did I feel the babe move. I doubt very much it will now.

Guilt overwhelms my soul. If she loses the babe, it will be my fault for not acting sooner, for failing her and Erianna both. I try to pull away.

"Just wait," she insists.

I shut my eyes, unable to bear her expectant hope. A flutter that could have been her breath moves my fingers.

"Did you feel that?" Even her voice is hopeful.

I gentle the stiffness in my fingers and wait. An uneven beat thumps beneath her skin then pushes against my fingertips.

A quiet laugh bubbles from her joy. "You see?"

Leelah's hope was not in vain. It has been realized.

Wonder makes me spread my whole hand on her side, perhaps more liberty than I ought to take.

The little thumps grow into a full movement that bulges her belly as the babe rolls within her.

"*Ah!*" Leelah exclaims, sitting partway up, grimacing. "How much water did you make me drink?"

My brow pinches. "I cannot be sure, but it—" Realization smacks me. "Oh!" *Copious amounts of water* need somewhere to go.

Leelah is unsteady on her feet and requires my assistance more than either of us like. Tirzah would think it amusing that this overqualified spymaster makes a rotten midwife.

"How did you know what to do?" Leelah asks as I help her return to the sagging mattress. "Without you, my babe would have perished."

Thoughts of Tirzah assail me. Her teasing smile. The easy banter we shared. The sight of her covered in wood curls and straddling the shavehorse. Also her determination. Working hard with me all day then dragging herself home in the middle of the night after tending her patient. I want to evade a truthful answer to Leelah's question that will inevitably stir up more questions, but I cannot bring myself to steal any glory from Tirzah. "Your thanks is owed to Tirzah. I heard her describe stopping an early labor to Salome Brighton."

"What? When did you have occasion to be in their company?" Leelah's sharp mind clicks into action. "Why were you in Parse Kítaran when Karris found you?"

I look straight into her piercing amber eyes, hoping she does not sense what I hold back. "Tirzah's roof collapsed. I stayed in Parse to help her repair it."

Leelah's eyes melt to honey. "You cannot stop yourself from helping a woman in need, can you?"

What I cannot do is bear her esteem. Part of me wants to tell her what I did to erase it, but I will not expose Tirzah to make myself feel better. Not again.

"I had the time and skills to help. It was no more than anyone else would have done." I retrieve the water skin and pass it to Leelah then rummage in my saddle bag for food. Only a crumbling bit of hardtack and an inedible strip of smoked venison remain. "Could you eat?" I extend the rations to Leelah.

She declines with a grimace. Knowing that I must soon battle the Ruphiri, I grind the food between my molars. It settles like a lump in my stomach, even less appetizing on the inside than the outside.

"When do you leave to rescue Erianna?" The question poorly conceals what she means as a demand. *Go rescue her. Now.*

"I must first find a villager to look after you." The dun horse is restless in his corner of the room. I offer him a drink of melted snow.

"That seems unnecessary. You will rescue Erianna then both return to me ere long," Leelah declares, allowing no contradiction.

Arguing with her would be a waste of time—time that she needs to rest, I need to prepare, and Erianna cannot afford to lose. "So be it."

I add more broken furniture to the fire. "Is there any comfort I can give you before I go?"

She shakes her head. "The Almighty be with you, Trent. This day, Erianna will be rescued."

A prayer that I echo, though I do not doubt it will require my life to answer it.

I push the door against the weight of snow that shifted to block it in the meager hours of rest we found. The day is farther past dawn than I believed. As the wind's voice carries into the town, its cadence is all wrong. Atop the drum of the breakers on the coast comes the shrill argument of steel.

My boots chomp through the snow, pounding a rhythm to the plea rising from my gut. *Please, please be our soldiers!*

I reach the crest of the hill that descends to the harbor and sweep my gaze, trying to make sense of the chaos below. A battle rages upon the shore, fought between the black clad bodies of the Ruphiri and the forces of Malesiir. It spills onto the lone pier where a Malesiirian ship is docked. I shade my eyes that seem tricked, but it is as it seems. Ruphiri are manning the vessel and descending on the dock, hampered from advancing by the vicious contest between... Zavaan and Valor!

My breath lodges in my throat. If Valor is pitted against Zavaan, then... At Valor's back stemming the advance of the Ruphiri from the shore are a lanky Ruphiri and my glaive wielding queen. I watch open-mouthed as the enemy bodies they fell grow into a barricade the Ruphiri cannot circumvent. It allows the flanking Malesiirian soldiers time to crush the Ruphiri between them.

As the tide of the battle begins to turn, a fraction of the Ruphiri seem to change sides. It is that demoralizing action that marks the death throes of the Ruphiri incursion into Malesiir. I move down the sloping path to enter the fray until the retreat of a cloaked figure up a distant slope draws my notice. His black garb and spider-like ascent of the steep rock face mark him as a Ruphiri. The single braid dangling from his shorn scalp identifies him.

"Orjek," I snarl, charging after him.

I run along the ridge that drops to the shore, hurrying my steps as he nears the cliff's edge. Had I not used all my arrows, I would riddle his body with them till he grew too heavy to drag himself higher. Watching his body plummet to the earth would be a welcome sight. But maybe this way is better. Drenching my hands in his blood appeals mightily.

He swings onto firm ground as I close on his position. Hearing the pounding of my boots, his head jerks around.

"Orjek!" I hurl curses at him in Ruphiri, having heard them often enough to intuit their meaning. I would ensure he knows death comes for him.

He falters over the face that does not belong to Brynjar. Furry snaps between us. He goes for his sword as I draw mine, then he stops. In an instant, he is sprinting away on the ice slicked ground.

"Coward!" I roar, returning my sword to its scabbard as I try to overtake him. In Ruphiri and Malesiirian I curse him, but he does not slow. On winged feet he increases the distance between us. He vaults over an outcropping and skids into a ravine, running away from the coast. How I long for my bow! I skid to a halt, my mind tripping over

Leelah's prone body. Though I do not doubt our fighters will win the day, how are they to find her if I do not lead them to her? She is too weak to stand.

Raging, I watch Orjek disappear from sight. Claiming his life could mean sacrificing Leelah's. That I cannot do.

Hastening back to the edge of the cliff, I track my eyes along the coast to the pier and see Erianna turn from her defensive position. The lanky Ruphiri guards her back as she closes upon Valor and Zavaan. Theirs is a bloody contest that will likely mean the death of both warriors without a deciding force. My warrior queen is that force. I have witnessed Valor feint then insert Erianna into a battle to gain a decisive victory. Her glaive is at the ready if only Valor will allow her to take the life of Zavaan which he has cursed and claimed over and again.

"Yield, Valor," I say into the wind coming off the ocean. "Let her end this."

Still Valor clings to his bloodlust though I know she pleads with him.

"Fool! Yield!"

All those days of Zavaan's taunts, his descriptions of what he would do to her, how he would make her suffer... The nights of him touching her to disturb her sleep, to remind her that she was his prisoner, tormenting her...

"It is her due! Yield, Valor!"

With a bellow that echoes to the top of this rise, Valor throws his full weight into his sword, following it to the ground to pin Zavaan's sword. Before Zavaan can open Valor's throat with the knife he draws, my Warrior Queen's glaive is wetted with Zavaan's blood. Erianna's long taunted threat that she would behead her enemies upon the steel of her glaive is no longer a taunt. Zavaan's head thumps to the dock. His body follows it.

Somehow, from this distance, Erianna has also taken me out at my knees. They land in the sodden ground, my palms pressed against the earth as my breath heaves out of me. I lose sight of the dying fray between Malesiir's soldiers and the Ruphiri as Erianna is reunited with Valor.

She is safe.

My queen is free.

I drag my sleeve across my eyes, scrubbing away the moisture that stole my vision. Taking prisoners and dealing death blows in the last pocket of fighting is the hulking shape of Kragorn. I push to my feet, sprinting back to the abandoned house. My task will soon be done.

"Leelah!" I bark, shoving into the house. She startles on the cot, groaning at the sudden motion. "They're here! Malesiir! Kragorn! Zavaan is dead! Erianna slew him!"

Though my words are a jumble, she discerns the parts of import. "Take me to him."

I pull the dun horse around and lead him outside. Leelah has pushed to a sitting position when I return to lift her from the cot. She wobbles in the saddle, thus, I quickly follow her up and steady her in my arms. I restrain the dun to a slow walk till again I crest the hill.

"There," I point to Kragorn on the shore. "And there is your friend, the one whom you love." I point to Erianna, gently held by Valor.

"Praise You, Almighty," she breathes the words then puts the tips of two fingers in her mouth. Her piercing whistle calls the attention of all to our position atop the hill. With a shout, Kragorn claims a horse and flies the mount toward his wife. Not bothering to fully stop the animal, he leaps to the ground and reaches for Leelah. His tortured expression as he takes in her battered face keeps my warning to be careful with her behind my teeth. Kragorn lowers his wife into his arms with a gentleness he reserves for his family. He holds her close and kisses her mouth then her bruises. What drives me back from the reunion is when the unfaltering warrior begins to weep.

"Never again, Leelah. Never again will I leave your side," he vows.

CHAPTER THIRTY

TRENT

February 24th

From the shadows, I watch my queen grip the railing of the Malesiirian ship as it is tossed upon the winter sea. For the sake of expediency, it was decided to risk the diffident sea for the few days necessary to land us in Port Veritae instead of the weeks of slogging through the mountains. It was a decision with which I heartily agreed. However, with her next decision, the queen shoved a fiery coal down my throat where it has burned for five days and is the reason I cannot abandon my guard over her, despite her assertions of her relative safety.

Her fine boned face turns in profile toward me, silhouetted by the setting sun. Her acknowledgement of my presence is an unspoken order to come to her. I rid myself of the shadows and set my back against the railing while my eyes continue roving the deck. Words in the grating Ruphiri tongue burn in my ears, fanning the coal in my gut. The guilty men that spoke them stroll the deck freely. No shackles bind their hands or feet.

Erianna tracks my baleful gaze. "They were as much a prisoner as —"

"As you? As Leelah?" I nearly spit upon the deck from the foul remembrance. "I didn't see their shackles when they were beating you, humiliating you, planning to violate—"

"Stop."

Too late her soft word silences me. The raw memories I abraded begin to bleed. Erianna's sniffle makes me feel heartless.

"Forgive me."

She shakes her head. "It's merely this accursed cold wind. It itches my nose and…" The tremble in her voice belies her words.

When her fingers dash tears from her cheeks, I cannot withstand her pain a moment longer. Gently, I tug her toward me.

One glance at the misery writ on my face that reflects her own causes her to relent. She wraps her arms about my waist and allows me to surround her with the protection of my presence as I wanted to do every hour of the past benighted month.

Erianna's dam breaks. Between her sobs that scald me, she growls out, "I cannot seem to stop crying. That wretched Valor won't let me keep my emotions locked up. It is much easier not to feel them."

"I'm sorry. If I had freed you, you would not have a month's worth of crying to do. I should have helped you escape."

Her reddened, tear-streaked face peers up at me. "It was impossible. Even so, you stayed with us. Protected us. Leelah would never have survived without you."

The bruises marring her skin dig shards of guilt deep into mine. "I should have found a way."

"There wasn't one," she asserts in her queen voice. "But knowing you would not allow Zavaan or any of the Ruphiri to defile us gave me the courage to endure."

"I let them beat you."

"We all did what we must to survive and defeat the *Vragh*. Let it be done, Trent."

I clench my teeth on another retort. If she can forget what happened, at least dull the memories, I will not force the horror of what I saw upon her. The sight of Valor and the tame Ruphiri warlord, Torvarik, makes the burning coal of my outrage unbearable. Sensing my fleeing control, Erianna returns to her place gripping the rail, and I leave her in Valor's care.

Apart from learning to balance on the heaving vessel, the novelty of traveling on the merchant ship escapes my notice. Heading toward the Malesiirian bunk room, I descend into the dark belly of the ship while gripping the stair rail to avoid being jounced against the walls. Thankfully, the motion of the ship does not make me ill as it does the queen and many of our soldiers. Oddly, none of the Ruphiri suffer from seasickness. How are they accustomed to it? The maps I have seen show no vast lakes in the middle of the Spire Mountains. Perhaps it is some heathen magic. They are the sort to sacrifice children in exchange for immunity to common ailments.

"Atokt vohun!"

My feet are pulled from beneath me by hands reaching over the side of the stairs. Pain blasts my shoulder as I fall then roll the rest of the way to the landing.

A pair of Ruphiri are upon me before I can draw a weapon. Their fists thunder against my body, giving me no opening to rise. I fight from the ground, blocking my head and kicking at any part of them within reach. In their growling, grunting language, they spew curses and accusations that I do not understand, though well I can imagine the hatred they harbor for me after infiltrating their ranks, slaying their men, and rescuing Leelah.

A well aimed kick causes one to stumble, but the other fills his place. My heel strikes his thigh, though he does not retreat. Finding that I fight well from the ground, they slide the advantage their direction by bringing wickedly sharp dirks into the fray. Pinned by their attack with no room to maneuver between the close walls and stairs, I focus on blocking their blows before they land, because each punch now carries the ability to skewer me. How I miss my hardened cuirass! The Ruphiri scale armor is excellent at allowing freedom of movement, but it lacks the same ability to turn away a blade.

I parry the first thrust of the dirk on my vambrace, but it is followed by another that catches my upper arm, drawing blood. They seem as ghouls towering above me on the dim landing with their hoods drawn and black garb. I focus on the flash of those blades, anticipating where the next will strike. After another parry, I reach for one of my daggers, but as if waiting for such an opportunity, the Ruphiri lunge, aiming for my ill protected body. Bringing my arm up, I know my defense will be too late.

A pounding echoes on the stairs at seemingly the same moment a dark blur launches across my field of vision, knocking a Ruphiri into the wall with a crunch. Shock slows the other Ruphiri's response. I swipe my legs toward him, taking his feet from beneath him. As he falls, my rescuer lands a kick to his chest that shoots him down the corridor. His head bounces on the planked floor, then he is still.

I push to my feet, extending a hand to thank the vicious warrior till I recognize him. "Torvarik."

He ignores my proffered hand that I quickly drop. "Will you live, Brynjar?"

My lip curls at the name. "Trent."

The scant light turns his crooked toothed smile menacing. "I see

Brynjar, as did they. Continue flaunting that you were a spy and they will continue to take revenge."

"Yet you will not?" Insults flow from my silver tongue as easily as compliments. "No, you will not. My queen gelded you after taming you."

His chuffed laugh sounds a threat as he stalks down the corridor, not sparing a glance for the unconscious—possibly dead—Ruphiri.

"*Královna* offers you Malesiirian clothes," he says over his shoulder, "not that you will accept."

He is right. It galls me that my motives are known by this faithless Ruphiri.

I *want* his people to know that I infiltrated them and felled their best warriors. Thus, I will wear what I killed Brynjar to gain.

Blood soaking my sleeve warns that I ought to be more alert for the coming fights. Which I shall, after I stitch this wound.

February 25th

I can feel my teeth cracking. If our queen continues to dismiss the crimes of these Ruphiri, I will not have any serviceable molars. Pain pounds in my temples from the restraint I have shown while she interviews then excuses one guilty man after another. They all should be groveling on their faces at her feet for causing her harm, through their fists or by their idleness. Her current subject changes his tone from pleading to accusatory as he gestures toward me, his Limban words tumbling over themselves. My hands hover over the hilts of dagger and sword, hoping he gifts me with a reason to end him.

The queen must sense my control eroding with the swiftness of a turbulent sea, for she ventures to my off side as she speaks and takes my twitching hand between her small cold ones. I can accept the gesture as one borne from her concern for me, not a deliberate action to shackle my sword hand, for she left it free to defend her.

Calming as Erianna's presence usually is, I find no peace watching her play at conversation with her mortal enemies, even once she dismisses this one. Tension runs up my arms, lodging in the tendons knitting my shoulders to my neck.

The ship drops suddenly into the valley between waves, unbalancing Erianna. I steady her, noting the pallor of her skin as Valor voices it. "Time to go above deck?"

I take a step back as he takes charge of her, but the entrance of her pet warlord firms my feet for battle.

"Indeed. *Královna* looks pale." He speaks without an accent, except the native way Ruphiri words roll off his tongue.

"It seems everyone has their sea legs but I," she complains.

Disrespecting the queen, the ship pitches upon the waves. But for our hands that reach to steady her, she would have landed on the planked floor. Hers ball into fists at the embarrassment, and she pushes between us to sit on the edge of the bed, waving us back. I then catch the defensiveness of her posture, the way her eyes dart between us. "Thank you, but stay over there."

Intimate with her wounds that brought upon her sudden panic, Valor crouches over his heels, making himself smaller and less threatening. I go to the door, granting her more space to breathe, and affect a casual stance though my eyes track the warlord who takes a seat in a chair and stretches his long legs before him.

Erianna's struggle to control the fear that leaks from behind her queenly aura fans that coal in my gut. Would her fears not be assuaged by seeing all her tormentors diced and fed to the monsters of the sea?

"Better?" Valor asks.

Her smile is feeble. "Aye."

Guilt pours through me. Had I known what would transpire at the outset, I would have riddled the Ruphiri camp with arrows a month past when I first discovered Leelah. Perhaps then my queen, my friend —though I doubt she would name me that now—would have been spared much torment.

Her weary eyes find mine. "It is not your fault, Trent. You were there when I needed you, when Leelah needed you. I am so grateful to you."

"Don't," I snap. "I should have rescued you."

"It was impossible to free us both. You acted as Leelah's protector and cared for her—"

"Stop, Erianna." I hate this dead assertion she resurrects. "Stop."

Valor, *her betrothed*, sides with her. "She speaks true. You were precisely where the Creator wanted you to be. Had you not been in Parse and available to track the Ruphiri and infiltrate their ranks…"

Tirzah's tear ravaged face shoves to the fore of my mind, damning me. "You have no idea of what you speak, so don't blame that on the Creator!" The Creator that Tirzah loves protected her crops from hail. Surely it was not His fault I was in Parse ravishing her heart and future.

Erianna's voice steals over my anger, calm and inquisitive. "Trent, why did your plans change? What kept you in Parse?"

After what I allowed her to endure, learning that I have ill-used her friend would destroy her illusions of gratitude. She would know how much I have failed those I took under my care. Skirting her gaze, I back out of the room. "I'm going below to check on the prisoners."

Despite my intent, my boots trod up the stairs and carry me to the stern of the ship, watching the forked tail of the ship's wake spear across the sea. One thought clangs through my mind. *I did not die.* Though I thought my life was forfeit, I am still standing. It would be simpler if I had died. For I must now contend with the consequences of my misdeeds.

Day becomes night as I weigh my sins. For all my honorable intentions when I decided to help Tirzah and ensure her brother was not neglecting or mistreating her, it would have been better for her had I left her to fend for herself. Capable as she is, she would have managed. All my kindness toward her became tinder for my lust to ignite. She was nothing more than a means to escape confronting my family and a beautiful woman with which to pass my time. To her, my kindness was the start of a relationship between us, our night of passion the mark of its permanence.

My father's voice booms in my memory. Though not a man of great faith, he wielded the Holy Texts to instill morality in his family. The passage he used to bludgeon his skirt-chasing second-born effectively clubs my bowed head in the present. *"If a man seduces a virgin who is not pledged to be married and sleeps with her, he must pay the bride-price, and she shall be his wife."*

Even from his sick-bed, my father attempted to impress the gravity of my actions upon me. He saw the way my eyes turned my whole body when an attractive woman passed before me. That would not have given him such concern had I not been an adept flirt. "If you continue on this path, Son, it will be the death of your character and the ruin of an innocent young woman."

My blithe response was always the same. "If I find myself in that position, then I'll not mind taking such a beauty to wife."

Witnessing my foolish arrogance burned my father. *"'If her father absolutely refuses to give her to him, he must still pay the bride-price for virgins.'* Do not think you can behave in this manner and escape suffering! In one form or another, it will cost you."

He was right. I hurt Tirzah, and the guilt I could not fathom feeling in my youth plagues my conscience. When I realized beyond a doubt that I had spoiled her, horror overrode my last bastion of honor. It is why I fled. Thus, I shall do what I must. I will wed Tirzah.

CHAPTER THIRTY-ONE

TRENT

March 6th

With nothing less than glee, I unshackle and shove the last of the Ruphiri into their jail cell. The door clangs shut. I give it a tug to ensure it will remain closed until King Lorennt holds a trial for all the Ruphiri including those that switched sides when their demise was certain. The wrath of the High King will override the merciful intentions of Queen Erianna. I shall ensure he knows what happened to her so that none escape the noose.

I pass the handful of shackles to the warden. Lest any attempted to flee, once we arrived in Port Veritae, all the Ruphiri were shackled. "Trust none of them," I instruct.

"I'll not, Sergeant Trent," he assures me with a loathing glance in their direction.

I urge the dun horse through the streets filled shoulder to shoulder with the city's rejoicing inhabitants till I come upon the rear of our returning company on our way to the castle. Our victorious entrance into Malsihra signals the last leg of the journey. I will see our queen safely ensconced in her domain then join the contingent that will return Leelah and Kragorn to their children and me to… to my bride.

I exhale, forcing the thought to settle. Tirzah will be my wife. That decision has relaxed the stranglehold of my guilt, though now my nerves run rampant. I have spent the past days recalling the restful time I spent in her company, the delicious meals she prepared to nourish me, even the night of pleasure we shared. Such thinking has been a balm to my nerves. A man could do far worse than Tirzah.

I understand vividly why Erianna hid in Parse Kítaran following her first capture and escape from Zavaan. Being a witness, nay, a passive participant in her and Leelah's trauma has scraped the peace from my life. My sleep has been disturbed with horrific scenes, and my waking hours are spent with my hand gripping my weapon, certain an attack is imminent.

Aye, sleeping under the safety of the roof I built in the soothing company of my favorite healer is exactly what I need.

Our company spills into the lower bailey of the castle where stable hands are ready to receive our horses. I turn the dun over to a groom. Despite the grueling trek he has endured, the gelding has maintained his condition looking as healthy as the day I claimed him from Brynjar. I feel oddly sentimental toward him though I still regret the loss of my own bay. "Give him a thorough rub-down, feed and water him, then make him ready for travel. I leave within two hours."

"Aye, Sergeant," the groom takes the reins and walks briskly into the stable.

I traverse the fringes of the celebration, aiming for a side entrance to the castle. Though I do not own a second set of armor, I can claim a change of clothes and a few familiar weapons from my room in the castle. A furrow opens in the press of bodies, offering safe passage. I shift into a trot before it can close.

The cry of my name and blur of motion give me little warning to prepare myself for an ambush. A slender woman collides with me, wraps me in her arms, and hooks a hand behind my neck. Her lips are upon mine in the same breath, overwhelming my senses with the familiar taste of her mouth and feel of her body.

Silla.

With an arm around the small of her back, I stumble toward the closing gap in the throng. My traitorous body responds to her with enthusiasm, meeting her kisses and holding her close. Walking blindly backward till I strike the wall of the castle, I savor what she gives. When the press of her body on mine draws shrill whistles of encouragement from some in the gathered crowd, I set her back and try to find my breath. Her kisses continue in a trail along my unshaven jaw, down my neck and back up.

"Steady, Silla," I catch her hands, unlinking them from my neck and gently pushing her away.

Emotion pools in her eyes, lining them in unshed tears. It startles me. Never has she shown me her feelings with such unveiled clarity.

"I feared for you, Cuyler. Everyday was a torment. When your letter came that you were tracking the Ruphiri," her voice cracks, and she lowers her head, "I was so worried."

Her admission churns convoluted feelings. Lingering attachment to her, sympathy, but also indignation. It is the last that takes hold of my tongue. "You had so little faith in me?"

Grief creases her smooth, fair skin. "You were one soldier against so many. Of course, I was worried!"

In a rush, I am flooded with the pain of her betrayal that grew out of her doubts in me. It contrasts sharply with the blind faith Tirzah placed in me even to the point of her detriment.

Reading my anger, Silla attempts to erase it. "It does not matter anymore. You are home, and we are together."

"No, we are not." I drop my restraining grip on her hands. "There is no reconciling what you did, Silla. Nor what I have done as a result."

"I will not believe that. Must you hear me say it? Very well. I am sorry, Cuyler. I am sorry for the things I did and the ways I hurt you. What must I do to prove myself earnest? Truly, I am sorry. Cuyler, you must believe me."

I lean my head against the wall, closing my eyes under the weight. Why could she not have felt this way before I left? It is what I wanted though it seemed beyond her capability. Regret is a bitter tonic. "I believe you. But I am now bound by my own actions."

"Cuyler," she sets her hand on my arm, her voice careful. "I know your weakness, but you needn't punish yourself for behaving as a man and acting upon the needs of your body."

My head snaps forward. "What do you know of it?"

She cants her head. "You were aggrieved with me. Even if you spent that pain upon another woman or an entire brothel in Chishelm, I will not hold it against you, nor must you explain yourself to me. Let us move on."

I cannot decide if her statement is absolution or condemnation of my character. She knows my regrets with women in broad strokes and my commitment to do better. How can she be so dismissive of what I did? I feel myself shaking my head. There is no way to dismiss what I have done. I owe Tirzah the commitment I implied by laying with her. "No, Silla. I cannot move on. Not with you. I am bound to another."

She stares at me for long moments then chuckles derisively. "I did not think she had it in her to snare you."

She cannot know. Unless Tirzah communicated it to Nev. "Who?"

Silla rolls her eyes. "Tirzah. The woman who came to court

determined to catch a husband. I knew she was determined, but I did not know she would be so calculating."

"What do you mean?"

Her eyes fill with sympathy. "Cuyler. You are a good man. If you lay with a chaste woman, of course you would feel honor-bound to take her to wife. Many women have caught a husband that way. It is a cruel trick to play, one you should not condone."

"That is not what happened." Even as I deny it, my heart pounds in my ears. Tirzah *was* determined to make a match, even one of convenience, but she would not entrap me. She would not entrap anyone. Would she?

Silla bobs one shoulder. "Only she knows that for certain."

I back toward the side entrance of the castle.

"Make what restitution you feel is necessary, but do not allow her to manipulate you."

"My path is set."

"Or you could come back to me."

Her plaintive suggestion follows me up the stairs as does her apology. Why could she not have recognized her mistakes sooner? I would never have gone to Parse Kítaran, never would have been with Tirzah.

I bang through my trunks, tossing clothing and weapons upon the bed. When a maid delivers the wash basin I forgot to request, I make use of it. Silla must have had it sent.

"*Agh!*" My fist pounds the desk. Why now? Why become attentive when it is too late?

I trade Brynjar's weapons for mine. The sword I affix to my weapons belt is of inferior quality—being the one I was given when I joined the army—to the Ruphiri short sword and my purchased longsword. I draw it from its scabbard, feeling its heft and balance. Familiar and serviceable is preferable to anything forged by the accursed Ruphiri. I must make time to retrieve my weapons and armor from where I stashed them in the woods, assuming I can both recall their location and they have not been claimed by a fortunate passerby. After I settle things with Tirzah, I shall seek them.

A bitter taste forms on my tongue, curdling my sweet remembrance of her. Would she entrap me? Though the greater portion of me denies it, I cannot erase all doubt. Huffing, I stow the Ruphiri weapons and refresh my other supplies. No matter her intentions, I am responsible for my actions that night. Jerking open my desk drawer, a brass key slides to the front. For a moment, I am stymied. Searching backward, I recall my extravagant purchase. An utter waste. One I must now attempt to sell.

Or...

Restitution. I roll the word around then sweep the key into my pocket.

CHAPTER THIRTY-TWO

TIRZAH

March 8th

Ever since the arrival of the couriered letter from King Lorennt telling of Leelah and Erianna's rescue, the children have been pressed to the windows and front gate at all hours of the day awaiting the safe return of their mother. Witnessing Leelah being beaten and taken captive has caused deep wounds in each of them. The month of waiting for some definitive word has been an agony. As days climbed into weeks then into a month, my own fears for her became unmanageable. Knowing that Kragorn had set after her, in the dark stretches of the night I wondered what would become of the children if their parents were both killed.

Dragging my burdened heart to the Creator in prayer became too much for me. All that I could ask was, *Almighty, please. Please bring them home.* Surviving the days with the aggrieved, frightened children was often more than I could manage. Leelah has always been an inspiration to me, but I never comprehended the load she bears being the mother and queen of this domain until I had to carry it. However, I have come to love her children more each day. They have sunk into my heart, and had the unthinkable happened and their parents perished, I would have done whatever was necessary to keep them as my own. Mercifully, that is not the path we must walk.

"I see a horse and rider!" Micah shouts.

"Is it Father or Uncle?" Karris shouts back, dashing into the courtyard.

I run after her, heading for the wall-walk while searching the road between the iron bars of the gate.

"No, I don't know him, but there's a whole bunch more coming behind, and a covered wagon!"

Only just now catching sight of the rider—could it be Trent?—I follow the sound of Micah's voice to discover what vantage he has found where he can see more than me.

"I see Father!" He crows from his perch.

Oh, heavens above! He's atop the steeply angled roof! How did he manage to get up there?

"Micah! You must come down! Carefully!"

He attempts to obey, but slips in his descent. Without pause, I rush to his aid, spying the ladder he used to make his ascent. "Karris, come work the gate!"

The ladder is perched on the corner of the wall-walk that connects to the back of the house. He must have kicked it when he climbed because the legs are anything but stable. I right it and tuck the front of my skirt into my belt. "Do not move, Micah! I shall come to you."

"Tirzah, I'm scared!" His frightened little voice usually so full of mischief sends pangs into my heart.

The tall ladder wobbles near the top, I hold my breath, willing it to still. In the background, I hear the heavy gears of the gate clanking as Karris raises it. The clomp of horses and rejoicing of the children is a happy sound that is momentarily lost upon me. My head peeks over the slate tiles. Micah whimpers pitifully, frozen upon the corner of the roof he must cross to come back to this side.

"Help, Tirzah! I'm ever so sorry I climbed up here even though Mother's told me to never ever never climb on the roof." Though he tries to brace himself, his little body slips closer to the edge. His shrill scream pierces my heart from one side to the other.

I climb from the ladder to the roof. Planting my backside firmly upon the tiles, I use my hands to shift myself closer to Micah. "Just stay still, Darling, I'll be to you in a moment."

A shout from the ground steals my attention to the courtyard milling with soldiers and horses ever so far below me. I close my eyes, breathing through my nose to clear the whirling sensation from my head. I turn my head toward Micah then open my eyes. The sight of his small, shaking body floods me with determination. I scoot the last few feet. Swiftly, I clutch his arm and feel relief I have no reason to feel. The difficult part has only begun.

"Micah, I'm going to pull you across to sit in my lap. Try to help me if you can. Alright?"

He nods.

"On three then." I plant my feet wide, but the worn leather soles of my shoes slip. Keeping one hand around Micah, I use the other to unlace then toss my shoes over the edge of the roof. Hanging modesty on the gallows of safety, I untie and tug off my stockings as well, though I stuff them down the front of my dress, not having the courage to rain them upon the soldiers. With the length of my dress tucked into my belt, it would be a mercy and a wonder if every soldier in the courtyard hasn't seen a shameful amount of me. Irony pricks my heart. Pretending I possess a scrap of modesty to preserve is laughable in my fallen state.

Secured by my bare feet, I use both hands to take hold of Micah. "One...two...three!"

When I pull, Micah pushes hard, landing me on my side with my arms wrapped around him, but my planted feet keep us from sliding from a neck-breaking height. With Micah in my lap, I work slowly across the roof to the ladder where a bearded soldier waits to receive the boy. Micah repents over and again his mistake in climbing the roof.

"All will be forgiven, sweet boy," I vow, silently adding, *As long as we survive this latest mischief.*

One more push sees us in reach of the soldier who says, "I have him."

A raucous cheer rises from those watching from the courtyard as the boy is passed safely to the soldier. But my hands flail back while I suck in a breath, recognizing the soldier's voice.

Trent braces me with his free arm, unsettling me more than the horrid height. His unshaven beard, the lean angles, and the grim look in his once warm, brown eyes all conspired to disguise him.

"Are you steady?" The exacting edge to his voice makes me want to agree no matter the truth.

I can only nod.

"Stay here."

Again, a nod is all I manage.

Wrapping a strong arm around Micah's chest, Trent pins the boy's back to his side and descends the ladder with one hand.

"Aye! I have him." The broad reassurance of Kragorn's voice makes me want to weep for Micah who has landed safe in his father's arms.

If only the eyes that meet mine over the edge of the roof held such kind regard. Trent's gaze skims the coast of irate. "Come to me. Slowly."

Incrementally, I crawl on my hands and feet. Falling off the roof seems a mercy compared to what I shall face with him.

His hand locks around my calf. "Stop there. Now, roll to your belly."

I flop flat on my back, sliding forward with the quick movement.

Trent arrests my fall. "Carefully!"

More cautiously, I roll to my side then belly, Trent's hands bracing me around my bare thighs.

Oh, aye. My modesty is a vapor on the wind.

"Push with only your hands," he instructs. "I'll direct your feet."

The same as he has done once before, he guides my feet to the second rung of the ladder. Unlike the last time, he wraps an arm round my waist, his chest firm to my back as we descend. The tickle of his breath on my ear unearths a host of poorly buried memories.

I can barely breathe when his boots land on the stone wall-walk, and he lifts me from the ladder that Kragorn braces.

"Are you well?" The genuine inquiry from Kragorn causes my lip to wobble. I nod vehemently.

He claps me on the shoulder. "Thank you for saving my boy. For…" He ducks his head and turns away abruptly. Kragorn does not allow his softer emotions to be displayed.

A gusty exhale behind me sends shivers down my arms.

"Why is it always ladders with you?" Trent walks around to face me.

Aye, Trent not *Cuyler*. I used the month to train myself out of thinking his given name.

"I have a mind to ban you from even touching the cursed things." He sweeps his gaze down my person then tugs my skirt free from my belt in an oddly proprietary gesture. What business has he to adjust my clothing?

I step back under the guise of smoothing my skirt. "How could you possibly ban me from ladders?" I ask as if he was not speaking in hyperbole.

I receive a long, enigmatic look in answer. It reminds me of the look of disgust I recall him wearing the morning after he bedded me. I cross my arms, shifting my gaze to the courtyard. Kragorn is carrying Leelah from the covered wagon up the steps of the vestibule.

"She needs you," Trent murmurs.

Worry binds my heart in knots. I waste only the time to collect my shoes from the mud of the courtyard.

By the time I complete Leelah's exam, the courtyard has cleared of soldiers, and the borrowed covered wagon used to transport Leelah is returning to the castle. My pulse is given permission to return to a normal rate with Trent gone. Seeing him was woefully unsettling, never mind the way he held me on that miserable ladder.

I press my hands to either side of my face. No, I will not think of him anymore. It is done. He is gone.

I sift through my healer's basket to find the restorative tisane blend and note what supplies I will need to replenish. Despite the demand for bandages following all the children's mishaps and one event that required sutures, the only other supply I depleted was my tisane to combat sleeplessness. It has been a trial unto its own being mentally and physically exhausted simultaneously yet unable to sleep at night owing to my constant worry for Leelah and Erianna.

I set water to boil and hear one of the children exit the bathing room attached to the kitchen. "Your mother is ready to see you. I'll be up with tea for her in a moment."

The utter silence behind me causes a prickle of unease. Children are never silent.

"How is Leelah?" Trent asks.

Chaos, instant and thorough, explodes in my mind.

"Is she badly injured? What of her babe?"

Hearing the way she was beaten after riding hard across the breadth of Malesiir, I understand the fear stitching his words together.

Turning to face him, I will myself to speak factually. "The babe is moving well, and his heart is strong. I doubt very much he sustained injury, but we cannot know for certain until he is born." I take a breath, making my words that of a healer—precise and dimmed of emotion. "Leelah is in worse condition. She has lost weight, is badly fatigued, has two cracked ribs, and her body was preparing to deliver the babe." The last gave me the greatest concern, considering how far she is from the babe's due arrival and the intensity of labor pains and bleeding she suffered following being beaten. "Had you not worked to stop her laboring..." My voice wavers. I shake my head, trying to find a healer's resolve. "It would have meant the life of her babe, possibly her own."

Trent's guilt is rancid as he says, "I should have never allowed her to be captive so long."

I wondered at that myself, but I was not there. It is not my place to judge what was or was not possible. Leelah is home now, and she is under my charge. The sooner Trent is on his way, the better. "Thank you for bringing her home. I shall ensure she recovers." *Go away.* I drop the sachet of tisane into a mug and pour boiling water over it.

"There is still the matter between us. I desire to have it resolved as soon as possible."

I stomp my foot, wishing beyond anything to never speak of it again. "There is nothing more to say. It was a mistake." A terrible, heartrending, life-altering mistake.

"Aye. It was. Thus, I shall pay for it. Do you prefer to have it done here, or will you come with me to Malsihra?"

I turned around while he was speaking in an attempt to make sense of his words, but I am at a loss. "Have what done?"

"The marriage."

"What marriage? Who is marrying?"

Rancor exudes from him. "Do not play at being coy, Tirzah. You are too candid a woman for it to be believable."

"What marriage?" I near shout, knowing I will hate his next words.

His mouth twists into a bitter curve. "The one between you and I. That *is* what you wanted. A marriage of convenience."

I feel cold then flushed in rapid succession. "Are you accusing me of entrapping you?"

He derides, "What could be more convenient?"

Never in my whole life have I wanted to inflict bodily harm upon my fellow man, but in this moment, I truly wish for claws and fangs so I could remove the limbs from his body. "You would use my words spoken in honesty and confidence to accuse me of ruining *your* life? How dare you! You who can walk away from me without the least consequence for your actions? It is *my* life that has been altered, *my* path that has been forever changed!"

"Aye, it has!" He closes the distance between us, using his height to impose upon me. With the stove at my back, I have nowhere to go. "Knowing me to be a man of honor, you preyed upon my weakness to gain the husband you've been hunting."

"The husband I want would never pretend to court a woman then sard her!"

Trent clamps a hand over my mouth. "Never again use that vile word," he growls then lowers his hand. "That is a base action men do to harlots. What happened between us was nothing like that."

A chasm opens in my heart. I hug my arms across my chest, trying to hold myself together. Defiantly, tears puddle in my eyes as the truth forms on my lips. "Then why do I feel like a whore?"

Trent is struck dumb. For agonizing moments, I cry into my hand while he watches. Shock erases his bitterness. Guilt rewrites his expression and tone.

"Tirzah, I'm sorry."

I cry harder, hating that we have come back to this. At least his accusations gave me something to fight. I can do nothing to defend myself from his guilt and the way it makes me feel.

"Let me make this right," he pleads. "We will wed. You can continue being a healer, here or in Malsihra." Reaching into his pocket, he offers me a bronze key. "I have a house there. A large, beautiful house with a terrace. I can provide for you. I will look after you. Let me do this."

His words form a beautiful painting. Had he presented me with such an offer at court this winter, I would not have hesitated to accept him. But there is no color in the painting. He cannot promise me the thing I want most. He has already told me so. How could he wed me while loving Silla?

"No, Trent. I cannot allow you to marry me."

"I know I have hurt and offended you, but this is for the best."

I swipe my fingers across my cheeks, sniffling. "It is not the best for either of us. You've no interest in my being your wife beyond assuaging your guilt and maybe the marriage bed. Nor have I any interest in what you offer."

He shakes his head, again irritated. "Do not be difficult. This is the same as when I persuaded you to allow me to repair your roof."

"That is exactly why I am saying no! I do not want this!" Even my plans for a marriage of convenience included some amount of mutual affection in addition to respect and benefit. A union with Trent would destroy me every day.

Trent appears genuinely surprised. "Marriage would provide—"

"No! Can you not hear me saying 'No'?" I shout. Hastily, I tuck my supplies into my basket.

He drops the key on the table. "So be it. If you are absolutely refusing me, allow me to make restitution by giving you the house."

My whole body stills. Bitterness takes root in my heart. "At least I am a well-compensated whore."

The rancorous version of Trent returns in force. He flings the key across the kitchen. It ricochets off the wall. "Foolish woman!"

"I am going home." I hook my basket on my arm and gather Leelah's tisane.

"Is there nothing I can say to change your mind?"

"Nothing." Clearly the man I held in affection does not exist.

"Very well." He glares at me. "As long as I did not get you with child."

He waits for my assurance, which is absurd. We were together but one night. "I am not with child."

"Fine." He reaches beneath the table to locate his key.

I recall the last time I cycled which was…

My palms grow sweaty. No… It is not possible…

Yet no matter how I count the weeks, I know for certain, I have not cycled in the month that I have been caring for the children. "No. No, no, no…" Dizziness washes over me.

A hand at my elbow steadies me. He moves the mug of tisane from my shaking hand to the table. "Tirzah?"

I cannot delay this forever. Though I wish to deny it, though I would rather ignore the truth and make excuses, I meet Trent's gaze and reveal the fear in mine.

TRENT

Profane curses overflow my mouth. Tirzah covers her ears. My father was right. I will pay for using women. I stopper the curses that could continue unbroken for hours. Curses at myself. My foolishness. Her stubborn pride.

I pull her hands from her ears, shackling her wrists. "We shall marry in Chishelm tomorrow, then return to Malsihra for a time—"

"No."

I close my mouth. After accusing her of entrapment, I ought to be accommodating. "I understand if you do not want to leave Parse Kítaran, but I—"

"No," she interrupts, pulling against my hold. "I meant, 'No, I will not marry you.'"

I release her, but hold my ground. "Enough, Tirzah! We are past that. Your objections no longer matter."

"They very much matter!"

"You are with child!"

"We do not know that, not for certain." She lowers her eyes when she says it, revealing the lie.

"I may not be a healer, but even I know that it has been more than a month since I laid with you and therein the proof."

"There could be another explanation."

"I await it!" Her futile denial angers me.

She bolsters herself, belligerent in her choices. "Even *if* I am with child, I will not marry you. I shall make my own way."

"I will not allow my child to be born a bastard! Nor will I abandon his mother! Think of me how you will, but I shall not allow it!"

"The choice is not yours."

"Benighted woman! It is mine! If you continue to refuse me, I shall bring the matter to your brother. I am certain he would see things my way."

Tirzah's complexion pales causing the smattering of freckles to stand prominent. Even in my anger, I recognize my folly in accusing her of being so cunning that she could entrap me. She is not capable of it.

"Please do not involve Mather. I need more time."

I muzzle my anger and gentle my tone. "What will more time prove?"

Nothing. I read it in her fearful eyes. But if time will bend her, then I will not break her to my will. "Write to me and keep me apprised, else I will come for you. And I shall appeal to Mather if I must."

She shoves against my chest. I yield a step, allowing her to collect her healer's basket and flee the kitchen. I scrub my hands down my face. This was not at all how I intended our conversation to end. It should have ended with her acceptance—gratitude would not have been unreasonable—and a warm meal and soft body to curl against for me.

Even when I try to make amends, I somehow make things worse. I push through the kitchen door and nearly collide with a wide-eyed Karris.

"I… I… came for Mother's tisane."

Perfect. She overheard us.

"It is on the table."

I pass Kragorn coming down the stairs on my way to the door. I tell him, "I'm for Malsihra. Lorennt requires a full account of my time with the Ruphiri."

He clasps my arm and slaps my shoulder. "Thank you, Trent. Safe travels."

I jerk my head and stride for the door.

Over my shoulder, Kragorn asks, "Karris, were you not fetching the tisane? And where is Tirzah?"

I hasten my steps.

The girl stammers, "She... left."

I close myself into the vestibule and open the exterior door. Unfortunately, it does not silence Karris's voice. "Father, what does 'sard' mean?"

I close the door and break into a sprint for the stables, ducking my beating like the knave I am.

My dun is still saddled in anticipation of ferrying Tirzah home. I am mounted and spurring through the gate when I hear the door of the house bang open.

"Trent!"

Instead of heading straight and overtaking Tirzah, I veer into the woods, following game trails toward the lake.

The night is old when I approach Tirzah's cottage. Light spills from her curtains and splashes the muddy ground, assuring me she is still awake. I dismount, looping the dun's reins around a post of the lean-to. Tirzah's stack of firewood is still full from when I replenished it after repairing her roof. I knock on her door, not expecting her to answer. "Tirzah, it is Trent. I have hunted a young boar for you. I took it from near the lake, so you will owe none of it to someone else. I strung it from the tree nearest your cottage to protect it from the bears. It will keep till morning. You should have no difficulty lowering it and preserving it on your own."

I want to leave her the sack of coin I brought from Malsihra, but I know she would take offense. The wild game was the only way I could provide for her that she cannot refuse. She will not let the boar go to waste. If she tries to gift it to a neighbor, they will insist on compensating her. I feel secure in knowing the mother of my child is provided for until I return in a few weeks time or until her letter summons me.

CHAPTER THIRTY-THREE

TIRZAH

March 10th

For a solid day, I work to preserve the boar between bouts of fretting my state and reliving every exchange with Trent. Of the three, only the scent of smoked game provides me comfort.

This day, I mean to track down Mamey, visit Lourna to say thank you for her regular visits, then check on as many of the elder members of our community as possible, beginning with Elder Eloham, after I tend the smokehouse.

My plans go awry when the broad shoulders of Kragorn crest my hill atop his destrier. He leads Leelah's stout pony bearing sacks of provisions. "Why must he be here?" I groan.

I take charge of the pony while he dismounts. "Good morning, Kragorn. How fares Leelah?"

"She is well and resting. I am seeing to her errands to keep her abed." He unfastens several smaller sacks. "These are for you."

"Thank you." It is not difficult to accept the needed provisions graciously knowing he feels beholden to me.

He sets the sacks at my doorstep. "Thank you for all that you have done for my family."

"They are dear to me. I could not have done otherwise."

"Karris said they did not make your task easy."

"I have untold depths of respect for Leelah after setting my hand to her tasks."

Kragorn hums his agreement. While I shift uncomfortably, Kragorn watches me over his crossed arms, appearing at his ease. It is one of his favored tricks to provoke people into expelling their innermost secrets.

I look across the field that is mucky with melting snow, hoping to wait him out, futile hope though it be. By the agape look Karris gave me when I fled their home, I know she heard some of what was said. The anticipation of wondering how much she overheard is worse than not knowing.

"Karris is not one for keeping secrets," I say without looking at him.

"She is not."

Kragorn's succinct answers could drive a woman mad. "I would like to know what she heard."

He studies me, but does not give a direct answer. "What happened to your roof? Much of it has been repaired."

Letting my eyes settle on the freshly split shingles evokes a river of emotion. "The front corner was collapsed when I returned home from court. Trent refused to leave until he knew how I meant to have it repaired. Then he wanted to know why I would not send for Mather."

Kragorn nods. "That would have piqued him."

"I told him enough but not everything. I could not."

"What happened, Tirzah?" The gentle question from the man who knows my full and undiluted past wraps me in shame. Kragorn was integral in helping me recover and reforming my opinion of men after Leelah brought me out of Chishelm to protect me from the travelers, the soldiers, and the bawd who daily tried to persuade me to earn money in her brothel.

"He moved me to Salome's house and slept in Valor's barn. I could not convince him to leave. We worked for two weeks to repair my roof. He would only allow me to pay him with food. It was all so honorable." I hang my head, ashamed of my stupidity. "But he was kind. And winsome. And I am so easy to lead astray."

I cover my eyes, wishing away my foolishness. Kragorn allows me to continue at my own pace. Leelah would have had the whole of it from me by now. I appreciate the time to consider my words. "He objected to my walking home alone at night. The day he was to leave, I was called away to a birth. He gained directions from Salome and was waiting to walk me home."

Kragorn's eyes are pinched at the corners, his mouth a taut line. I push through to the end. "He told me what I wanted to hear and allowed me to make more of it. The next morning, he was guilt ridden and disgusted. With himself. With me. It was horrible. He couldn't get away from me quickly enough."

"Then Karris intercepted him on the road," Kragorn concludes.

I nod. "Trent had been so kind to me. Clearly, that could not last."

Kragorn takes my shoulders in his large hands. "Tirzah, we have already slain and buried that lie. You are a modest woman. The coarse way men speak to you, the indecent way they look at you is not your fault."

"It was that night," I whisper.

"Perhaps." He says it as if there is an alternative.

Bitterness curdles my voice. My heart. "Trent has vehemently explained that he has no affection for me."

Kragorn levels me with a look of gravitas. I brace myself. He does not mince words.

"That night, your insecurity collided with his weakness. He was compelled to rescue you from it, and you could do naught but heal his pain. The culmination of both your strengths and weaknesses proved your undoing."

I tuck away his words, needing to let them steep before drinking them. Of a certain, there is something to them. However, my recollections of the man that laughed with me and repaired my roof contrast sharply with the harsh man that returned.

"You refused his offer of marriage though you carry his child."

His statement invites me to reconsider my actions, but incessantly reliving our exchange has a quick defense upon my lips. "He accused me of entrapment while making it perfectly clear how little he desired the arrangement but felt he ought to compensate me for what he took. I could not accept him!"

Kragorn shakes his head, anger slipping past his ever present restraint. "I could thrash that fool." Always Kragorn has sided with the women in his charge even when dishonor colors our actions.

Though I agree, it does not make me feel better. Perhaps answers will. "There was so little of the man I knew in him. He is much changed." So much it affected his very appearance. "What happened to him, Kragorn?"

Shadows cloud Kragorn's immovable features. "You know of the way trauma can affect a person's mind? Recall the state of each of my children when we found them."

I was not present for those instances, but I recall Leelah's tales. The way poor Ivy could not speak. How Lois still hides in corners at times. Karris's longstanding fear of abandonment.

"A similar thing can happen to soldiers. The violence of battle can harden them. Fear can unseat their emotions. They can become unrecognizable as the men they once were. Or they may seem themselves one moment, the next a different man."

Does this explain the changes in Trent? But why? He is already battle hardened.

Kragorn lets me mull what he has said before stating, "We all have noticed marked changes in Trent. The queen is particularly concerned for him."

Ache blooms in my chest. "Why? What happened?"

"In order to protect Leelah and Erianna, Trent disguised himself as a Ruphiri and became one of their captors. He holds himself accountable for each wrong done them."

Understanding alights with fierce pain. Trent's time as spymaster revealed the darkness of mankind, darkness that haunted him despite all his levity. To then be unable to protect those he went to save would destroy him. Add to that the guilt he feels for bedding me.

Could that be why he accused me of entrapment? Was the guilt too much for him to bear? Is that why he tried to relieve some of his burden by making it my fault?

"Oh, Cuyler," I sigh, moved by his pain though it cannot erase mine.

"Is there aught I can do for you?" Kragorn asks.

I shake my head. My foolishness and consequences are mine alone. "Keep Leelah abed. Assure her I will come to her in a few days. I must be about the valley."

"Aye. Be well, Tirzah." Kragorn's benediction follows me inside, echoing in my mind.

Be well. How can I do that?

"Replaced?" The word clangs, discordant with my every plan. After finding Mamey cutting across the valley in her little two-wheeled pony cart, I expected her to be pleased to see me and eager for my help. I was wrong on both counts. Mamey's chiding tone is so utterly unexpected that I falter over her words, disbelieving her. "I don't understand Mamey. What do you mean you replaced me?"

She drops her chin, eyeing me beneath an arched, scolding brow. "You ran off to court for two months, had been returned for days, then disappeared again without a word."

"Did Lourna not explain I was watching Leelah's children? I had reason—"

"A healer has a responsibility to her community. You abandoned yours and left me with more work than I could manage. A woman arrived at the end of harvest season, an experienced healer who has trained with an apothecary, and offered her help. But I turned her away believing you were dedicated to becoming a healer in full. After struggling without you this winter, I had no choice but to replace you. I need someone I can depend upon. That is not you, Tirzah."

The burn in my throat prevents me from answering. I can but stare.

Seeing my hurt, Mamey huffs. "I may be able to purchase some of your salves come summer, but naught else. Good day, Tirzah." She snaps the reins, setting her pony into a fast trot.

I stumble along the path to Lourna's home, feeling little beyond righteous indignation at Mamey's decision. How could she replace me? She makes it sound as if I ran off on a whim. I was caring for the Tareth children under dire circumstances!

Lourna's farm comes into view. Her boys scamper in the pasture under the direction of their father, Thad. I offer a wave to him. Lourna is bidding farewell to a woman of fair looks and middle years when I approach her door. Lourna's eyes go a little wide and her voice squeaks unnaturally. "Oh, Tirzah! So good to see you. Kragorn was by earlier to collect oats and winter wheat. I was relieved to hear Leelah will be well."

"She shall, I hope. Though she needs help managing till the babe is born."

"Mamey, plans to visit Leelah this eve," the woman informs Lourna whose eyes dart between us.

Mention of Mamey burns me anew. How dare she replace me without word or warning!

I wait for the woman to take her leave before expressing my grievances to Lourna, but she lingers into a period of awkwardness. To dispel it, I force a smile and offer pleasantries. "Good day, I'm Tirzah. Are you new to the valley?"

She returns my smile and bobs her head. "We arrived several months past, though I am still making acquaintances with all my neighbors. I'm Nell, Mamey's assistant healer."

My smile crashes. I look at Lourna, whose wide-eyed guilt reveals she knows full well how I feel about her guest.

"Wait," Nell, catches my arm, "are you the Tirzah who apprenticed with Mamey for a time?"

For a time? No, I am her assistant, *you usurper!* "Aye. There's not another Tirzah in the valley."

"Everyone speaks highly of you," Nell says. "I have much to prove before they will trust my tisanes and salves as they have yours."

Upon my life, I have no notion why I came to see Lourna. All I want to do is run. I make my excuses quickly. "It was nice to meet you, Nell." I glance at Lourna. "I only came to say hello. I'm for Elder Eloham's to see how he fares before…"

At the miserable look Lourna offers, my words wander off.

"Tirzah," she says gently, "Elder Eloham passed. I did not want to tell you knowing you were much burdened with the children and worries for Leelah."

"He was a dear man," Nell says. "Bless him, so confused at the end. It is a shame when the mind fades before the body."

"You tended him?" I manage to ask around my shock.

"*Mhm*," Nell hums her reply. "There was little I could do beyond making him comfortable. He was quite distressed and kept asking for Mirande."

Me. He wanted me. Grief douses my grievances. I cross my arms, unable to form an answer. Where has all my healer's resolve gone? Men grow old and die. Life gives way to death. Not any tisane or remedy will prevent it.

My cottage welcomes me atop the knoll, but I've no memory of the walk home or bidding Lourna farewell. I add wood to the smokehouse in a daze.

Once inside, I unlace my homespun dress, letting it fall to the floor. My chemise is an embarrassment, patched and stained. More than all else, it displays my poverty. I can hide it beneath my two dresses, but it is there all the same, reminding me whenever I see it.

I climb into bed, pulling the worn blanket over my head, hiding from the world and myself.

CHAPTER THIRTY-FOUR

TRENT

March 10th

Torches flicker in the twilight causing the upper bailey to writhe. My heated breaths gust into the air as I tromp the stairs. The porter swings open the doors to the vestibule. I give word to a guard to notify King Lorennt I have returned. Though I do not expect to be summoned, I wait while the message is delivered, thus, my surprise when the guard says, "The king bids you refresh yourself then meet him in his office."

I look to the dais. Lorennt's gaze awaits mine. I bow to him, and he resumes his conversation with Valor. I wonder at the urgency of the meeting but can only guess that he wants his suspense resolved concerning what transpired between the Ruphiri and Queen Erianna. Her tendency to withhold information frustrates him. I find a seat at a low table and fill a plate with game and roasted potatoes while sifting the conversations surrounding me. There is naught of particular importance. Though I would like to dull the edges of my mind with wine, I abstain to remain sharp for my meeting with the king. My hunger sated, I excuse myself as servants bearing the dessert course enter the hall.

Maids and manservants scurry in the corridors, refreshing the rooms of guests and emptying chamber pots while the nobility take their dinner. As I come off the stairs to my wing of the castle, a flaxen head steps out of a room holding a pewter basin. The sight of her untethers the control I spent two days fighting to regain. I want to slam the basin from her hands. Instead, I fist mine at my sides and snarl, "You viper!"

Silla startles then goes still.

I close the distance between us and yell into her face. "What have I done to you that makes you hate me? Was it not enough to destroy what was between us? Why did you put poison in my mind?" I jab my temple.

Silla remains quiet. She is far too skilled a manipulator to be ignorant of what I speak. Never would I have considered Tirzah capable of entrapment, not without Silla's prodding and the evidence she produced. However, it did occur to me that Silla herself tried to snare me with the same.

"*Now* you have nothing to say? No defense? Not when you tried to preserve your own hide by claiming my name before the king learned of your betrayal?"

Her placid expression does not shift. But her hands do, subtly gripping the sides of the basin. Defensively.

The threats that bred mile after mile form on my tongue. I could ruin her. Have her ejected from the castle. A well placed word to Lorennt could see it done. My eyes fix upon her white knuckled grip on the basin. Instead of enacting my plot to destroy her as she has done me, a groan of defeat falls from my mouth. "You know me so little?"

I turn away from her. Exhaustion sweeps over me. I brace an arm on the wall. Threatening Silla? Accusing Tirzah? I feel not myself. How have I fallen so far? This woman bears some of the blame, but the brunt of the blame is mine.

I know Tirzah. I should not have believed ill of her. Though Silla has manipulated me time and again, I am the spymaster. I should have been unmoved by her schemes.

"Trouble me no more, Silla. Please. Grant me that much peace."

Her reply is sedately given. "Unless you will it, our paths shall not cross again. Farewell, Cuyler."

March 11th

After hours scraping my memory and spreading all the filth therein upon the ears of the king, I can well imagine the cause of this day's summons. Made aware of the ways I have failed, the king will demand my sword and expel me from the army. It is the least of what I owe.

The guard admits me to his office. Expecting King Lorennt and perhaps a brace of guards, it surprises that Queen Erianna and Commander Ironforge are to be the witnesses to my expulsion.

"Sergeant Trent, be seated." Lorennt motions to the vacant seat before his desk adjacent Erianna. "How long have you served in our army?"

"Nigh to ten years," I reply. Long enough to know how mightily I failed my queen.

"Of those, nearly five have been served as Valor's spymaster?" He confirms.

"Aye, Majesty."

"Valor has made me aware that for several months last year, you fulfilled his duties as Hand of the King when he was incapable."

Erianna flicks an annoyed glare at the king for his bald speech, though it is the truth.

"I did."

Valor perches behind Erianna on the edge of her desk, unfazed by the conversation. Why would he reveal such to the king? Did he wield the information in an attempt to mitigate my punishment?

"How did you find the work?"

Lorennt's question is unexpected, thus, I answer it truthfully. "The work is necessary and honorable."

"You enjoyed it?" He presses.

I incline my head. Tirzah's words come to mind unbidden, but I repeat them nonetheless. "I enjoyed working in the light for a change and taking affirmative actions to better our kingdom."

Valor crosses his arms, settling back with a proud smile for me. He shifts it to the king with a touch more arrogance. Lorennt ignores him, which is a change. The commander enjoys baiting the king, and the king does not usually disappoint him.

Lorennt observes, "You have learned much of the court and the machinations of the nobility as you sought to rout the traitor from our midst."

"A mark against me since I was courting the traitor," I grumble.

Lorennt's mood darkens. The mercy he extended to Silla was begrudging at best. "With that I cannot argue."

"Yet were we not all thoroughly duped by her?" Erianna interjects.

As Valor nods, Lorennt snaps, "Not all of us."

The king never liked nor trusted Silla. Nor did he trust Reuel Zavaan when he was disguised and living at court. "You have better judgment than most, Majesty."

"Or he dislikes most people thereby trusting few," Erianna shoots off the rejoinder.

"That is ironic, coming from you," Lorennt parries.

Valor seeks to refocus them. "We are losing sight of the point with much yet to do."

The king's gaze slides away from the queen and back to me. "Then we come to your insertion with the Ruphiri and rescue of Leelah."

"And failed rescue of the queen," I tag on.

Erianna says, "Had General Kannik lent you immediate use of a company, I do not doubt you would have rescued Leelah within a day of her capture."

"Perhaps," I allow. "But it matters not when you both remained captive nearly a month."

"There was naught you could have done differently," Erianna argues.

I meet her argument with derisive certainty. "There is always something to do differently, always a path unexplored. I should have found it."

The king hums his agreement. "My sister would have you be at peace, but I respect you for requiring much of yourself."

Respect me? This is not leading any direction I anticipated. Why admit respect before demanding my sword?

"When I asked Valor for recommendations on whom I should consider naming Commander and Hand of the King, yours was the only name he presented."

Hand of the King? The space between my ears turns into a cavern, echoing silence. Far from demanding my sword and expelling me from his army, Lorennt is offering to make me... His Hand? I cannot reconcile that with what I know. "How can there be two Commanders? Or two Hands? There must be one clear commander of the military, one man doing the bidding of the crown in the sight of the people."

Valor diverts the question to the king who does not hesitate in his answer, knowing the question would arise. "This information has not left the walls of this room nor can it, but the decision has been made to sieze the Limban throne from King Arcto and crown his daughter Queen of Limba. We yet plot Limba's conquest, but be assured, the queen's consort shall be at her side."

Erianna fills her lungs and sits straight-backed in her chair. Valor rests a hand on her shoulder, supporting the twice royal queen. Soberly, he says, "We are to wed in a month's time."

Lorennt's weighty revelations continue. "Further, we shall aid the warlord Torvarik in becoming the next king—"

"*Kyzar*," Erianna interrupts. "It means overlord. The Ruphiri have no king."

Lorennt spears a withering look at her. "The next *king* of the Ruphiri."

I huff a breath, trying to swallow the deluge of information.

"With the conquest of Limba upon the horizon, I must install my own Hand and a new commander for my armies to free Valor and Erianna to prepare for their war."

War. The word silences the room. There has not been a full scale war between kingdoms for generations. Though Malesiir did not instigate it, there can be no other response to the Ruphiri attack sponsored by Limba. I scrub my hand across my mouth. "Aye. Malesiir must give answer to the Ruphiri and Limban assassination of King Grandileer and capture of Queen Erianna."

"I must strengthen Malesiir for the upcoming war on the heels of our own civil unrest. The governance problems within our cities and provinces must also be righted. For that I need a Hand and Commander of Malesiir that will hold himself to the highest standards. I will require more of him than any man in Malesiir. As I shall work tirelessly for this kingdom, he must do the same."

The magnitude of what Lorennt offers becomes real as he speaks. Valor and Erianna are leaving Malesiir. My time as the commander's spymaster has come to an end. But I have the opportunity to become the next Hand of the King.

Lorennt rises as he speaks. "My Hand will answer directly to me. He shall advance my will for this kingdom, be my mouthpiece and my arbiter. He shall also be the instrument of my wrath for those that defy our laws or seek to undermine my rule. As the Commander of the King's Army, the meanest soldiers to the highest generals will answer to him. He must ensure that every garrison does its duty. He will orchestrate the movements of troops and wield my army to protect our kingdom from within and without. In all of Malesiir, only I shall be greater than my Hand or bear more responsibility."

The king stands magnanimous, allowing the enormity of the task to take shape. For silent minutes, he waits. There can be only one answer for what he is asking of me.

Rising to my feet and moving to stand before the king, I cross my arm over my chest, fisting my hand over my heart in salute. "Sire." On bended knee, I bow before my king.

The king draws his sword and sets the flat of his blade upon my head. "Sergeant Cuyler Trent of Gistin, do you accept the position as the Hand of the King and the Commander of the King's Army?"

"Aye, Your Majesty. I shall serve you with my life and my sword. May only death break my vow."

The flat of the sword touches each of my shoulders. "I, King Lorennt Rodiharian of Malesiir, do hereby name you Commander Cuyler Trent, Hand of the King."

March 13th

Two days pass in a blur. Between being presented to the kingdom as Lorennt's Hand and scarcely leaving the king's side as he made me aware of every plan in motion and those he still plots, my mind is numb with fatigue when I lay my head on my pillow to sleep. When I awake, it spins with the details of all that must be accomplished. Nevertheless, I feel as if I am returning to myself after the heat of battle. My thoughts are becoming clearer. The grip of anger that has dulled most other emotions is subsiding.

Somehow the claws of winter have yielded to the spring melt leaving our kingdom in the season of mud. Yet we must have a war in motion by summer. Already, letters are making the journey to the generals of Grevnhold and Farreach, our outposts upon the Continent. Lorennt has also sent letters to Twin Lakes and Seaport requesting the ruling body of the Midlands and Lowlands, collectively the People's Commonwealth, to allow Malesiirian warships into their waters for an extended voyage to Limba. It was vociferously debated whether or not to make the Commonwealth aware of our intentions to overthrow King Arcto, the conclusion of which being we must not or we risk Limba learning of our plot. Arcto must not be given time to prepare for war more than he already has with his own machinations. Let him assume we come for the Ruphiri, not his throne.

I clench my right hand, feeling the thick band of the king's signet ring grip my middle finger. How long before I am accustomed to the weight of it? The fine black cloth of my new, formal over-tunic edged in red and gold announces my station as the Commander of His Majesty's Army. Never again will an order of mine be met with less than absolute obedience. If anyone in the kingdom dares, I am to meet defiance with swift violence.

There is also the matter of choosing my own spymaster and aide.

That will take time. I must find someone willing to swear loyalty to me above all others. In this, not even King Lorennt's orders will take precedence over mine to my aide in the same way that I served Valor's will above King Grandileer or Queen Erianna.

Still wishing I had my best sword, I adjust the straps binding this one to my weapons belt. Though the elements have very likely ruined my light armor, I am hopeful that my sword, daggers, and bow may yet be saved. Thus, I marked on a map where I thought them likely to be and tasked a pair of soldiers with retrieving them. It will take time for me to become accustomed to delegating.

This day, however, I shall relish being the one responsible for the task ahead. After personally retrieving the frozen box containing the most despicable thing in all of Malesiir, I join the royal procession leaving the castle proper.

Lorennt's desirous glance at the box as I situate it on the fore of my saddle makes me chuckle. "Do you want to hold his head one last time, Majesty?"

He nudges his fidgeting horse into line. "If not for my wife and sister's delicate natures, I would have it displayed in my office."

"You are all perverse," Erianna derides from her place in line behind the king. "This day cannot be over soon enough."

At her side, I know Valor disagrees, but he consoles her instead. "What say you to a detour to Mari's shop before returning to the castle. I imagine she has spent days baking queen's cookies in your honor."

Lorennt's accompanying mockery of Valor for that remark is entirely feigned. I have come to realize that he is deeply grateful to Valor for the care he gives his sister.

Throughout the city, Malesiirians line the streets, cheering for their royals. Shouts of "Warrior Queen" rise up and echo in Erianna's wake. Children have even fashioned sticks into miniature glaives to match the one across the queen's back.

I smirk at her over my shoulder, feeling a levity that has been long absent. "Wait till Kragorn hears of the children proudly wielding glaives." Initially, the queen disparaged having to use a "sword on a stick." Kragorn finally moved her to his way of thinking in his favored manner—brute force.

"If you tell him of this," she says with lethal quiet, "your neck will be the next one Violet severs."

Lorennt grumbles under his breath. Only Valor truly appreciates the humorous name she bestowed on her glaive.

Our banter carries us across the city till our horses' hooves touch the cobbles of the square. Sobriety descends upon us with an implacable grip as the crowd of commoners, nobility, and soldiers cheer our arrival. In full battle armor, we ascend the platform surrounding the gallows. I set the box on the platform. A pry bar awaits my gruesome, anticipated task.

The king does not waste time. He spreads his arms and silences the throng. "We come to you today to honor the promise made you. Today, Malesiir shall have her justice!"

A shout answers his words as I wedge the bar between the wood slats. The crack of wood and fetid smell of decay greet me. The face I once feared is grey and inanimate. The eyes that burned with malice are milky and collapsing into their sockets. Perhaps it is perverse, as the queen claims, but I feel a dark satisfaction when I use both hands to hoist Reuel Zavaan's head into the air and declare, "Here is King Grandileer's murderer, fought and beheaded by your Warrior Queen!"

A roar answers my declaration. The stomping of thousands of feet pound the stones, drowning out the squelch of flesh when I affix the murderer's head to a pike where it will remain till it is picked clean by crows and the bones bleached white in the sun.

The king shouts over the noise. "Today, I shall deliver justice to the rest of the Ruphiri, but let us remember—" He raises a hand to quiet them when another cheer goes up. "Let us remember that there is a difference between revenge and justice. Revenge takes our pain and forces it back upon the wrongdoers—and not in equal measure. Justice holds men accountable for their crimes, yes. But justice leaves room for mercy."

He gives the crowd a moment to measure his words, but not long enough to breed concern.

"Thus, I have evidence to present to you before we dispense judgement." Lorennt unrolls a parchment inscribed by Torvarik and begins to read the laws that govern the Ruphiri in the Spire Mountains. "According to the clan law of the Ruphiri, any man who has compromised a woman becomes responsible for that woman. He is to wed her and provide for her. If he refuses to do so, he is to be held accountable for his crimes by his clan's warlord and put to death. If the aggression was committed against a child, the punishment is death. According to the clan law…"

Ringing supplants the words of the king in my ears. Even by Ruphiri standards, I stand condemned for what I have done to Tirzah.

How could I have put her from my mind these past days? The sick feeling roiling through me nearly drives me from the platform. Movement in my periphery jerks my attention to the king in time to grasp the scroll of Ruphiri laws he slaps into my hand with a sharp look. Though the reprimand is for my wandering attention, it feels like condemnation.

While pacing along the platform toward the queen, Lorennt explains to his people, "I could continue reading, but as you can see, the laws of the Ruphiri are just and harsher than our own Malesiirian laws. Over and again, Queen Erianna and I heard from several of the Ruphiri that no true Ruphiri would ever harm a woman. They found the abuse of her contemptible and offensive. Then why do stories abound in the kingdom of theft, murder, and ravishment at the hands of the Ruphiri? Because those men willingly served the murderer Reuel Zavaan, the former Chief of the Ruphiri." Lorennt points to Zavaan's spiked head. "But what of the several Ruphiri who detested Zavaan and his treatment of Malesiir's people?"

Playing my part, I return the scroll to my king who reads, "According to the clan law of the Ruphiri, every clan must remit one man for every fifty clan members to serve at the behest of the *kyzar* in whatever way he requires." He lowers the parchment. "Conscription. That is why some of the Ruphiri are in Malesiir against their conscience and against their honor. *Zar* Torvarik, step forward." On his cue, the fully armored warlord ascends the platform. "Here is the first of several Ruphiri to fight at our side, to turn against the corruption of Zavaan that polluted his people, and aid us in routing the enemy from our kingdom." In a show of royal approval, Lorennt claps Torvarik on the shoulder. "He led the charge on that day of battle in Halden Harbor alongside Commander Ironforge and convinced many of his fellow Ruphiri to renounce Zavaan and fight on the side of Malesiir. This man is honorable. This man is just. This man is the man that Malesiir recognizes as the next *Kyzar* of the Ruphiri. *Kyzar* Torvarik." The rehearsed Ruphiri words roll off Lorennt's tongue.

The crowd assesses the warlord with distrust. Like a practiced leader, Torvarik addresses them and quickly sways their opinion. "Malesiir has suffered at the hands of Reuel Zavaan. The Ruphiri have as well. But no more!" He shouts, pointing to the pike and inciting a raucous cheer from the people. "To honor the Ruphiri law and the laws of the great kingdom of Malesiir, I shall ensure that Malesiir is recompensed for all that was stolen plus fifty percent interest. Until my true Ruphiri and I return to the Spire Mountains, we shall begin working to pay our nation's debt to Malesiir. This day, I swear it to you. The Ruphiri will no longer be a threat to Malesiir. We shall be allies, working together for our mutual good. But first, the wicked must be brought to justice!"

King Lorennt does not wait for the roar of the crowd to quiet this time but adds to it. "Bring forth the prisoners!"

There is grim anticipation in the warlord's eyes as I lead Zavaan's Ruphiri to the gallows. He aids me in slipping the nooses round their necks.

"You despise your clan men," I observe as he bares his crooked teeth in a lupine smile at one of the men while tightening the noose.

He stands my side while I grip the lever to release the bar supporting the trapdoor of the gallows. The crowd becomes strangely silent. At the king's order, I shove the lever. The pounding and shouts in the square threaten to burst my ears. Still it does not conceal the sharp sound of five spine-breaking cracks. The great height of the prison gallows ensures the drop is lethal—mostly. For that, soldiers stand beneath the platform to pull the legs of the hanged ensuring a quick execution. Swords are a last resort.

Torvarik and I ready the next Ruphiri for execution. He asks, "Did you feel mercy for the brigands—your fellow Malesiirians—who wrought evil in your land?"

I look across my shoulder at him. His question needs no answer.

"These gladly served the man who murdered my sister. The atrocities they committed are innumerable." He slides the noose taut against the back of a Ruphiri's neck. "My only regret," he murmurs, "is that my brother Orjek is not among them."

Despite attempting to locate that villain following the battle at Halden Harbor, Orjek's tracks disappeared, leaving us to wonder if he is hiding within our borders, yet Torvarik firmly believes he is making his way toward the Spire Mountains.

We shove the bound men into place on the trap door. Soldiers slide into position, the points of their swords keeping the Ruphiri from attempting to evade the noose.

I slam my weight against the lever. The sound of justice meted at the end of a rope is seared into my mind like a brand.

CHAPTER THIRTY-FIVE

TRENT

March 13th

"Commander Trent!" Anders bellows.

"Huzzah!" With a dull clunk, ale sloshes over the sides of tankards, and the men—soldiers mostly—in the packed alehouse chug till the bottoms of their cups are facing the roof. Froth gathers under my nose. I thumb it away and plunk into the chair, grinning at my companions who roused what seems a battalion to celebrate my appointment to Commander and King's Hand.

Maids flit around with pitchers, refilling tankards raised aloft.

"To the Gnarled Oak!" I toast. "Where the pours are full, the maids are pretty, and the brewster serves the finest ale in the city!"

The stout proprietress tips her head in thanks while men echo, "The Gnarled Oak!"

Anders slaps his palm on the table and raises his tankard for another pour. "Speaking of pretty maids, here comes your favorite waggle-tail."

A young woman with dishwater curls piled atop her head weaves through the outstretched hands, ignoring the raised tankards though she carries a pitcher.

"Kierie," I say in greeting.

She sets a hand on my shoulder as she fills my tankard. "From the brewster for the commander."

I sip the stronger, finer ale then raise it with thanks to the watching brewster.

"You got a hearty one there, Kierie?" Anders asks, passing his tankard.

"Specially for the commander's table." She flashes a coy smile then pours for the soldiers seated with me, her hand lingering on the back of my neck.

"You need aught?" She asks me, a mischievous light in her eyes.

I shake my head, trying to gently turn her aside. Up to my ears in trouble with women, I won't dive into more.

Braun, a soldier from Anders's company, watches her swish through the alehouse. "She a trull?"

"Nah," Anders says, then toasts his cup to me. "But she knows Commander Trent."

"One conquest of many," Regold boasts. "We laid siege to the capital after returning from the Continent."

"That we did!" Anders slaps Regold's back, sloshing his ale. "Handled more skirts than a dressmaker!"

I swill the ale in my tankard, not recalling anything worth bragging about in my conduct. For some reason, I imagine having to confess to Tirzah about those days. I can well imagine the candid healer covering her ears at my debauched tale.

"Now that you're not occupied with the little traitor, what hens will you pluck first?" Anders's eyebrows jig with the question that he did not intend to sting. Courting Silla while she betrayed us is a strong mark against my intelligence and honor.

Unwilling to grab for Valor's soon to be abdicated title of *vestal*, I say, "None tonight. I mean to swim home." I drain my tankard to the sound of cheers.

"Cards or bones?" Regold asks.

"If the brewster keeps pouring from her good stock, best make it bones." Anders chuckles. "My purse is too light to play at cards."

Diverted from stalking the maids with his eyes, Braun produces a handful of dice.

Anders jerks his chin. "Pass those to the commander so he can tell if they're heavy."

"You don't trust me?" Braun growls, dropping the dice in my open palm.

I roll them around, then drop them on the table repeatedly. When they turn up random faces each toss, I determine they are not weighted.

"Know you too well to trust you," Anders jibes.

Braun begins the game. We make our bets with coppers, quickly becoming too deep in our cups to gamble high since Kierie keeps our tankards overflowing.

She sidles onto my knee between tosses. I hold my hand up for her to blow on the dice before I roll them. She obliges. When my dice land favorably, Kierie claps, but Braun objects.

"S'not fair to keep all the luck for yourself." He tugs on her skirt beneath the table, but she swats his hand away then leans into me.

"Leave off, Braun. You're drowned," I scoff. In Kierie's ear, I advise, "Water his next pour."

"Let Amee pour. I'd rather sit with you a spell," she whispers back, setting her arms around my neck. "Brewster will post me a room once your men leave."

Though the scent of ale sloshed on her clothes and a long day's work taint her skin, it is not that which makes me unwind her arms. "I have a woman, Kierie. I will not betray her."

She pouts. "Is she pretty?"

I nod.

"Beautiful?"

"A beauty inside and out."

"Will you take her to wife?" She presses.

"Aye." Though I must convince her to have me first.

Kierie huffs. "I suppose I'm not a marriageable woman."

"You are a fine woman," I say, though I would not consider taking to wife a woman with a known wandering eye. "But my heart is elsewhere." An exaggeration used to avoid paining Kierie, but it is a pair of accusing violet eyes that pain me. *Gah!* To have a chance to make right what I ruined, to profess some feeling for her and convince her to wed straightaway. But then I would not be in this alehouse.

I push Kierie to her feet. "Dance quickly tonight. These soldiers are full on bloodshed and ale. All they want now is a skirt."

"I'll be sure to invoke your name if I come to trouble," she acknowledges with a saucy smile.

Practiced at her trade, she twists through the crowd, dodging the grasping hands.

When my pile of coppers dwindles to a sad pair, Regold taunts, "Anyone seen Kierie? Commander's bout to lose his purse if she doesn't come turn his luck."

"He's well beyond help," Anders argues.

Braun nudges a few coppers my way. "Beg for mercy, Commander, and I'll buy you out of your shame."

I laugh at their raillery and rub my two coppers together. "I've company enough to not need your alms."

"Company! That's what we need." Braun forgets the dice in his hand. "Someone spy me a lush jade."

Never liking that term, I shoot a look at Anders who also thinks better of women than that, even joy women. "You'll not find one here. Brewster keeps a respectable alehouse. Toss your dice, man, afore my beard turns grey."

Regold laughs. "You've not looked in a mirror lately, have you, Brigadier?"

Anders scoffs, "What would I want to do that for when the Almighty made fairer things for my eyes to behold?"

Braun shakes and spills the dice across the table. "Whatever became of Commander Ironforge's companion?"

The hair on my neck bristles.

"Who?" Regold wonders.

"That strumpet he brought to court. The one that caused trouble for the queen." Braun lifts his tankard in a silent toast to her majesty before taking a pull.

"Tirzah," Anders intones—half derision, half admiration. "She's a termagant to be sure, but oh, her hills and valleys."

"*Ah*! That woman." Regold grins. "I would've had her, but her claiming Ironforge and Tareth as protectors put me off the hunt."

Heat builds under my skin. No man ought to speak of her like this. If I could beat the very memory of her from their minds, I would.

Braun leans into the table, a predatory gleam in his eye. "They did not stop me from trying, not when she was prancing and panting like a salted mare. Every time I saw her, I offered to—"

I flip the table as I launch over it, landing a punch that sprays blood from Braun's nose before we hit the ground. "Filthy knave!" My fist cuts under his jaw, snapping back his head. He shoves and throws uncoordinated punches that miss the mark. With my knee in his gut, I pummel him from both sides. "Never speak of her again!"

Hands clamp on my arms, but I shove them off, flipping around to cut Anders across his flapping jaw. Catching him by surprise, he takes the blow full in the face. He careens into a nearby card game, knocking the table and coins to the floor. Outraged curses add to the din of my violence. Regold tackles me off Braun, rolling us into a crowd. Ale showers down on us. I drive an elbow into his side.

He groans, throwing himself at me again. "Smite you, Trent!"

"Get hold of yourself!" Anders leaps back into the fray as I drop

Regold who stays down.

"Canting fool!" I roar. "You know naught!"

Ready for my attack, Anders dodges and retaliates. I step into the blow, throwing my left fist into his kidney. He howls, but I don't slow. Other soldiers are caught in the melee until the alehouse is launched into a full brawl.

March 14th

The door to the king's office bangs closed, shuddering in its frame. "Assaulting a brigadier! Assaulting a subordinate—nearly beating the life out of him! Destruction of an alehouse! Inciting a brawl among my soldiers that spilled into the street and had to be quelled by the city guard!"

I stand at silent attention as the king bellows in my swollen, bruised face.

"Explain why was I dragged out of the Gathering in the chapel to hear the charges being brought against my Hand!"

I open my mouth but snap it shut when the king continues his tirade. "I made you my Hand against the recommendation of my core generals, and three days later you make me question not only my decision but if I should allow you to remain in my army!"

When the silence stretches, I reply, "It was a matter of honor."

Lorennt's red face splotches with purple. "I do not care if someone names you a polled milksop! Your honor—"

"Not mine!" I snarl then moderate my voice. "It was not my honor."

Rather than drawing his sword to behead me for daring to interrupt him, Lorennt scratches his piqued interest. "Whose, then?"

I work my jaw, still furious with Braun for what he said. "My woman's."

Lorennt's irritation climbs. "Silla is not worth—"

"Not her," I bite out.

"Who?"

Willing to risk fanning the king's wrath by dodging a direct answer, I say, "Recall when you laid Anders on his back for how he spoke of your lady?"

The flame in Lorennt's eye tells that he well remembers.

"That was mild compared to what Braun and Anders said of mine."
I would do it again, I do not need to add. The king infers it. "Inciting the

brawl and wrecking the alehouse was unintentional and regrettable. I shall make amends with the brewster and pay for the repairs or do them myself, if I must." Unquenchable ire burns in my chest. "But I will knock the face off the next man who compares my woman to a mare in heat and propositions her."

Tirzah did not exaggerate her claim in the slightest that men wanted her for only a night. Embarrassed, she chose not to reveal the full extent of their vulgarity. Then I bedded her and fled, only to return and accuse her of entrapment. Her tears and wretched admission of feeling like a whore have been a scourge upon my conscience. If a man treated one of my sisters the way I treated Tirzah, I would begin by splitting him chin to navel.

Lorennt crosses his arms, glaring at me. I hold the line I have drawn. If the king flogs and banishes me, so be it. I will sooner be at Tirzah's door and righting my grave mistakes.

Lorennt comes to a decision. "Herein lies the problem. When you pull back your fist, you pull back mine. When you draw your sword, you are drawing mine. When you take just action, it is with my power that justice is served. And when you demolish an alehouse," he bellows, "I have demolished an alehouse! You are my Hand, an extension of my throne and my very body! What you do tells more of my reign than what my wife does. If you cannot conduct yourself with justice and restraint, then you will not suit as my Hand!"

I bow my head, feeling the weight of the burden I did not comprehend. Imagining the king tossing tables in an alehouse brawl, while not out of the realm of possibility being personally acquainted with his volatile temper, causes me to regret the ensuing chaos from my actions. "Aye, Your Majesty. I see my error. In the future, I will remember that I act in your name, in all things."

"If you must knock someone's head off, then do it and be done. Do not involve an entire company. But if there is another way, one that preserves honor and satisfies justice, take it. Wearing my signet does not give you liberty to act upon your whims. You are the law. You cannot be above it."

The rebuke is well placed and not soon forgotten. "Aye, Sire."

Lorennt sits on his desk, pinching the bridge of his nose. "For the sake of expediency, remit payment to the brewster from the royal treasury. I will have our treasurer dock the cost of the damages from your earnings."

"Aye, Your Majesty. I shall see it done immediately." With a bow, I turn to leave. The king lets me gain the door before stopping me.

"You did not answer my question. To whom was the insult paid?"

I grimace. There is no straight way of answering that question that does not beget more.

"Sit, Trent. If you are courting a woman, I will have the full of it known, especially one who causes such chaos among my soldiers."

I tap the side of my fist on the closed door. Curse it all.

CHAPTER THIRTY-SIX

TIRZAH

March 16th

I soak my dirt-blackened hands in warm saltwater, whimpering at the pain that spikes from my fingertips. Pulling weeds and prying rocks from the earth are ruinous on a woman's hands. Using a stiff bristled brush, I attack the dirt crusting my fingertips.

With relatively few skills to recommend me, I gladly accepted the tedious task of preparing my neighbor's garden in exchange for the basket of chicks now cheeping next to the warmth of my hearth. With a good flock, I can provide meat and eggs for myself and have enough manure to maintain my own garden. Day after next, I will earn the seeds for my garden in exchange for helping Lourna do the spring airing of her home. I am grateful for the work, but it gals my pride knowing Lourna and her girls could manage the thing without me. Charity is good as long as I am not the one receiving it. Unfortunately, Sow the bear left me no choice when she destroyed the seeds I carefully preserved from last year's garden.

Setting aside the wash water, I straighten and feel a throb of pain in my lower back. It seems as if each day brings a new symptom that my life has irrevocably changed. I keep an ongoing tally of symptoms in my head, becoming obsessively aware of every twinge and ache within my body, comparing them to what I usually feel before the onset of my cycle. To my great frustration, I learn firsthand the truth of what Mamey tells newly wed young women who badger her about such things—wait and see.

Of its own accord, my hand drifts across the table and catches hold of Trent's letter. I must have read it a hundred times. Even so, I unfold it again.

Tirzah,

I beg your forgiveness. The anger and accusations I brought against you were unfounded. Instead, I should have come to you with promises of protection, provision, and regard. I shall endeavor to be a good husband to you, esteeming and respecting you as you deserve.

You are a beautiful woman, filled with compassion. With your strong character, I have no doubt you will make an excellent mother to our child.

Recall what good partners we made while working to repair your home, and let your fears be silenced. Send me word quickly. I shall come for you.

Humbly yours,

Trent

Though my heart longs to know the love of a husband, perhaps camaraderie with a good man and mutual love for our child could be enough. In time, he might come to feel something beyond respect for me.

"Why could you not have made such a speech when you were here?" I complain to his letter. "Don't you know I would have run into your arms?"

If Kragorn is to be believed, which I've no doubt he should, the man that slandered me was not the man I came to know. He was as one of my injured patients, hurling insults and cursing me because of their own pain. The Trent inscribed upon this paper is the one I came to know, the one that stole my heart with his winsome smile. But what of his heart? Does it still ache for Silla, to have mended what she tore?

I spread the letter flat before me. The twinge of pain low in my belly may steal the choice from me. Hard as I am willing to work to earn my living, I am not so great a fool as to believe that I will be able to sustain myself when I am round with Trent's child. Coin is rare in this community built on bartering. I will need Trent's help.

"Would you resent me forever if I claim the name that you offered me? One that we will share with our child?"

His letter seems to indicate he would not. My fertile imagination needs no help to cultivate our future. The dreams bloom sequentially in my mind. A small wedding with only our dearest friends bearing witness... Coming together again, but this time as husband and wife... Making a way to blend our lives... Might we again discover that place of happy companionship that existed between us? He has written that we shall. Finally, that joyous moment when I present Cuyler with our first child. He is the sort of man I have prayed would father my children. Kind. Diligent at work. Loyal. Unwaveringly protective of those in his care.

I will wait a little longer—just a little while longer—to be absolutely certain. Then I will send my letter to him. I do not doubt that he will come for me. He would not shirk his duty to our babe.

Unbidden hopes take root. Of a babe deeply loved by his mother and father. Tiny hands and feet. The joy of caring for a life so precious and small.

Aye, a few more days then I will write to him.

March 17th

I wake in the dark hours of morning. The sheets feel sticky against my skin. My body aches in an all too familiar way. What I expect to find, I find. My strained heart ought to be relieved.

Numbly, I go about my morning ritual. There are no words of prayer or praise to lift to the Creator as I draw water from the dusky river. There have not been for a while. There is only a hollowness where my hope should be.

The monotony of routine guides me through all the menial tasks without demanding anything of me until I clasp chilled fingers around my mug of tea and settle into my chair. Through the steam warming my face, my gaze lands upon Trent's letter.

A frown tugs my mouth down at the corners. It is unfair that with the receipt of my letter, Trent might escape without a moment's more turmoil when I am still aching. The tendrils of a vindictive thought uncurl.

What if I wait a little longer to tell him?

I nurture the plot for a moment, imagining the uncertainty that would nag him for days. The guilt. Perhaps some worry? My conscience gets hold of me and squashes the plot. If Trent has felt anything near the angst that I have over the possibility of there being a child tying us together, then it seems wrong to deliberately leave him in suspense. Especially if what he truly wants is to mend what is broken between him and Silla.

I ache as I tear away the blank half of the page. Paper is a rarity I cannot afford to waste. Taking my pen, I deliberate long over my reply only to resign myself to the simplest of sentences. I do not sign it since I fear it being read by anyone else. Unless Trent is a secret lech, he will know the note is from me.

Unwilling to waste even a drop of my precious beeswax which I need to make salves, I dab the edge of the page with heated resin. After inscribing his direction upon the back of the letter, I abandon my cooling tea to sooner have done with this task.

Cuyler Trent will undoubtedly be a fine father, but I will not be his child's mother. The sooner he knows he is free of his obligation to me, the better.

I deposit my note into the letter box at the chapel. It flutters into the dark interior, that scrap of paper conveying weightier matters than its neighboring thickly inscribed letters.

Unsure of what to do with myself, my feet lead me on a churned path through the woods to a safe harbor. I pick my way along its edges until the fortified house comes into view. In the courtyard, a child so muddy he resembles frog spawn hurls himself at my skirt. I wrap my arms around him nonetheless.

"Tirzah! It's been forever since you were here and Father's made me do all Lois and Ivy's chores for climbing on the roof and nearly killing you even though it was to protect our keep from attack."

Finally, he takes a breath. "Hello, my Darling Boy." The words I might never say to my own son come out on a choked laugh.

"But I got muddy," he shout whispers, "so's I can't go in the house to do their work 'cause Mother won't let me. It's my best plan!"

I chuckle as I catch sight of Kragorn rounding the corner from the garden. "Best scurry. Here comes your father."

Micah looks over his shoulder in wide eyed horror then darts toward the barn, leaving mud splotched across my skirt and arms, a price I'm willing to pay for his exuberant hug.

Kragorn plants his hands on his belt, scowling. "That scamp is nothing but bones and mischief." Eyeing my skirt, he asks, "Is he covered in mud?"

"Aye, his best plan to avoid consequences." I grin.

"I ought to dunk him in the freezing creek." Exasperation blends with wry amusement, something both Micah and his mother excel at evoking in people.

"How fare—"

I step on Kragorn's question. "Is Leelah inside? I thought to check on her."

He nods, letting me pass. "In the kitchen."

Chaos reigns within, as usual, but I am greeted with a hug, as always. I return it. "Didn't I tell you to stay abed?"

"I am feeling stronger," Leelah exclaims, setting a hand to her rounded belly. The hollowness in my center echoes like a stone cast into an empty well. How can I miss something that never was? "Besides, Karris cannot manage—no, Fialla!" Leelah dives for the toddling infant who has seized a rather tolerant cat by its tail and is attempting to drag the animal from its hiding spot beneath the table.

Before Leelah can straighten from rescuing babe and cat from each other, Lois and Ivy burst into the kitchen.

"Mother, Ivy took my pillow cover!"

"I did not! This is mine that I took from the laundry line."

Lois's retort tags Ivy's denial. "Is not! My cover has a hole in the corner where I accidentally cut it."

Leelah steps around the bickering girls to poke her head outside. "Kragorn!"

I reach for the pillow cover in danger of being rent between the girls. "Let me see if there is—"

"*Ah, ah!*" Leelah interrupts me. "Do not engage them."

Moments later, Kragorn appears, breathless. "What is wrong?"

"Oversee this please," Leelah instructs the man whose eyes sweep his wife top to toes, toes to top, assuring himself she is well. Leelah pushes me into the great room, closing the door on Kragorn's authoritative voice sorting out his children. Micah will escape his dunking and chores a bit longer. I follow Leelah above stairs to her room that is the one tidy corner of the lived-in home.

"There now!" She exhales, dropping to the bench at the end of her bed. "It has been such a help to have Kragorn about, though I do not doubt we shall soon begin to chafe each other." Being a self-sufficient woman has made Leelah a perfect match for Kragorn, a man who is constantly moving about the kingdom as one of the foremost generals in the army. Since her capture, however, Kragorn has made good on his vow to never again leave her side. What that means for his future in the army is yet to be seen.

"How fare you?" Leelah's broad question directly strikes my conflicted heart.

I delay my answer. "It is I who came to ask you that. Have you had any more labor pains?"

She dismisses my concern with a wave. "Tell me of yourself."

"You are a terrible patient."

Leelah fixes me with a look of annoyed tolerance that only mothers have mastered. "I've had a few brief spells of discomfort that quickly subsided with rest."

"You must rest more, Leelah. Let Kragorn and Karris tend the house. I will also come by as oft as I can."

"Has Mamey apologized and asked you to work with her again? It was wrong of her to replace you. I ensured she knew it and that you are the only midwife I will accept."

Leelah's loyalty is unwavering. "She has not, but I have found work elsewhere."

"How long can you continue doing the menial things no one else wants to do? You chided me, but what of yourself? Ought you not take care, especially in the early months—"

"It seems that shall not be a problem for me. There will be no babe."

She blinks at me, speechless for a rare moment. "Did you lose…?"

"No. I have no reason to think that. It is a more common occurrence among brides than you might believe." I smile wryly. "Not that I can claim that respectable state. Trent will be glad to be rid of his obligation to me."

"Will he?" Leelah disagrees. "Kragorn and I have discussed your situation at length, and I think Trent holds you in affection."

The humiliation of my sin being discussed between my friends nearly chases me from the room. "I assure you, Leelah. He feels naught."

"Then why is it that he came back to you that night?"

"I imagine the same reason he pursued you when you were captured. He was compelled to help. It is an inexorable part of his character, one my foolish heart did not understand." Though my past should have prepared me to rebuff his attention.

Leelah bobs a shoulder. "Perhaps. But he also stayed and loved you."

I hide my face with my hand. "That was not love, Leelah. He admitted as much."

She dismisses my claim with a sniff. "He is a man. He would not own to his feelings except under duress."

"Not so. He admitted his affection for Silla. He revealed much of it to me."

"Truly?" Leelah perks at the thought. "Men do not confide in women or, for that matter, anyone without great trust."

I frown, wanting her to be right, though I misdoubt her opinion. "Is Kragorn in agreement with you?"

She scoffs. "He is biased against any man who loves a woman without first taking her to wife."

I am inclined to believe Kragorn has the right of it and decide not to waste time arguing with Leelah. "No matter. When Trent receives this letter, it shall be done."

"Or," Leelah drawls. "He will return to you nonetheless."

"Do not give me false hope. My heart cannot survive it."

Leelah smiles. Oddly, it is the same look of mischief Micah wore while scheming to dodge his chores. "This is the best situation. With no babe to force a marriage, Trent's true feelings may now be seen. Either he will pursue you, which I believe he will, or you shall not see him again. If he turns from you without a fight, then you will know he was only motivated by lust and guilt. But if not, if he pursues you… Well. Then you will have a love match."

My heart wants it so badly that I lean into what she says. "You truly think it is possible that he has a care for me?"

"I am certain he does. You did not see him moping aboard the ship. If he didn't care for you, he would not have been so troubled."

I find myself clinging to Leelah's confidence. With fragile hope, I find a smile to offer her.

"There." She rises, hooking my arm with hers. "Now that's settled, you'll spend the day with me, won't you?"

CHAPTER THIRTY-SEVEN

TIRZAH

March 26th

Through concerted effort, I have found new ways to earn coin that give me reason to be quite proud of myself. The foremost of which being the loyalty of some of my neighbors. Leelah's sharp tongued rebuke of Mamey has traveled by foot about the valley. As it happens, not everyone is pleased with the healer for replacing me, especially given the circumstances of Leelah's capture that required me to ensconce myself at the Tareth's home. What Mamey views as inconstancy, others view as loyalty and sacrifice. Thus, Leelah's choice to name me her midwife has inspired others to do the same. Though they are few, it has done my dejected heart immeasurable good to be respected as a healer.

Their patronage has not, however, entirely satisfied my needed income. That has been arranged by my continued menial labor for my neighbors and a creative application of my herbal knowledge.

Squatting over my heels, I work my small hoe in a circle, careful to go wide of the roots. Thrusting both hands into the soil, I loosen the long thin tubers from the ground. I set them on top of the soil and slice the tip of a root. Red sap ekes from the wound. "You are precisely what I am looking for," I tell the humble plant. Dusting much of the dirt from the tubers, I tuck the whole bloodroot plant into my basket, careful not to displace my respectable pile of several kinds of lichens.

I emerge from the woods with a heaping basket of foraged gold. Processing these plants into salable dye will require much work, but I hope to turn a tidy profit for my trouble. In addition to the dye I will sell in Chishelm, I shall take the bricks of soap enriched with herbs and beeswax curing beneath my bed. Gathering herbs from the wilds around the mountain lake is arduous and sometimes yields little, but I have found enough.

Dipping into the chapel, I search the box of letters waiting to be collected. There are few present since yesterday was Gathering and most would have been retrieved then. Foraging in the wilds has prevented me from attending, and my guilty conscience did not mind the reprieve.

A crisp letter sealed with wax and stamped with the royal crest awaits me. Thinking it is from Nev or perhaps Erianna, I break the seal, but it is Trent's signature across the bottom.

A quick perusal reveals it is a repetition of what he already wrote with an additional plea that I will at least reply and let him know I am well even if I need more time before marrying.

My note must have crossed his along its way. His inquiry after my wellbeing heartens me. Leelah might yet be proved right.

I fold the letter and tuck it into my pocket. The niggle of unease I feel for putting all my hopes in Trent's reaction is made worse by the tome sitting upon a lectern at the head of the chapel. I do not need to page through the Text to know that my actions of late contradict what is written. Salome's gentle reproof is reiterated. *You are placing more significance on the love of a husband than on the love you have already been given.*

I close the door to the chapel, trilling down the hill toward the path to my cottage, attempting to outrun the Spirit of Truth's convicting pressure. With mixed success, I put it from the fore of my mind.

The clomp and jingle of metal turns me around. My hackles rise at the approach of a woman in her little cart. Hoping to avoid the encounter, I step to the side allowing her to pass when she overtakes me. Instead, she draws on the reins.

"Tirzah, I was coming to see you." Mamey leans in her seat to peer into my basket. Her lips purse with disapproval. "I know some apothecaries use bloodroot in their tisanes, but it is dangerous—"

"I know this," I snap, then deliberately gentle my tone. "I am making dye not tisane."

"Ah. Good." The tightness in her face is mirrored in her grip on the horse's reins that cause her knuckles to stand in white peaks. "After speaking with Leelah and considering what she told, I believe I spoke too harshly with you. You were not being flippant toward your duties, rather you chose to support your friend in her time of need. I apologize."

"Thank you for recognizing that. You have my forgiveness." Had Mamey come down from her cart or conveyed her apology with a different tone, I might have hope that all will be made right between us. Yet I intuit the censure still remaining. I also note that she said nothing of her decision to replace me.

"Being an influential woman, Leelah's decision to name you her midwife has made dangerous ripples in our community."

"Dangerous?" I scoff. "To whom?"

"To the people who have chosen to follow her path and named you as their healer."

Oh, to be possessed of Leelah's sharp tongue or Erianna's quick wit when it comes to defending myself. My shock leaves me scrabbling for an appropriate response. "How am I a danger to them? I was not a danger when I was training with you."

"Indeed, because I was directing you and overseeing all that you did. My experience was the cushion to your missteps while learning."

"I am no longer a novice, Mamey," I blurt, affronted at her belittlement. "I have been tending patients and even a birth without your intervention for quite some time."

"But still I followed your ministrations, ensuring you did not miss something an experienced healer would recognize. You are an apprentice, Tirzah. Without my oversight, someone could be badly hurt or killed from your negligence. What would you do if you encounter something you do not know how to treat?"

"I would send for you as I have always done! I would not hesitate to seek help when it is needed, I care too much for those who have placed their trust in me."

Her reserve blunted by frustration, Mamey declares, "Their trust is misguided by Leelah's stubbornness. I am disappointed in you, Tirzah. A healer thinks first of those in her care."

Bitter tears burn my eyes. Rather than listen to more of her disparagement, I retreat onto the hillside where she cannot follow in her cart.

Her voice breaches the distance. "I pray that I am wrong, and your arrogance does not cost someone their life."

TRENT

March 27th

The courier's appearance at dinner holds no import since the king receives a steady stream of letters. Then he bows and extends the scrap of paper to me.

"Forgive me, Commander Trent. This missive ought to have been delivered some days ago, but owing to its size, it was misplaced. As such, I brought it to you straightaway."

I accept the paper that is folded and torn along one edge. Could this be from her? The script is unfamiliar, but precise, and none but someone of poor means would use resin instead of wax to create a seal. Surely, it is from Tirzah. "Thank you."

Wanting to devour the contents more than I want the lavish repast upon the high table, I excuse myself with a bow to King Lorennt. Though Valor's commands rarely sent me where I did not want to go, it pleases me greatly that I need not justify my comings and goings. In an abandoned parlor, I unstick the edge.

My every fibre is coiled, prepared to launch into action. Though I am certain she will want to continue being a healer in Parse for a time, I hope she will be convinced to join me in Malsihra. I would have her near so that—

I am not with child.

The single sentence does not make sense. I flip the page looking for more script. There is nothing but my direction. I read it again, still not comprehending. It does not fit within my plans. I look at the back of the page. How could she not include more?

I can well imagine the quirk of Tirzah's mouth as she says, *What more do you need to know?*

Much! Did you lose the babe? How fare you? After all this, do you truly believe I will abandon you?

I crumple the paper in my fist. Aye. That is what she believes. Having no babe compelling me to take her to wife, she sees this as the end and is perhaps glad of it. Her adamant refusals made it clear that she would rather continue alone than tie her life to mine, even were she with child.

I stumble over that thought. Would my candid healer have lied?

It goes against her character, but I did threaten to invoke her brother's help to force her to marry.

I need time to weigh this possibility. Wandering out to the upper bailey, I come upon Regold leading a sortie. With feigned lightheartedness, I ask, "What's the rabble plotting this night?"

The men salute. I remind myself not to look over my shoulder for a superior officer to whom I should also salute. "Good eve, Commander. We're for the Cold Stag Tavern. The merchants have just arrived with heavy purses. We mean to lighten their burden then row home. Care to lead the charge?"

"Another time. Leave the merchants some dignity, will you? I don't want to hear of this come morning."

They chuckle and shove off.

When I am intercepted with similar offers from other soldiers and even a band of nobles, I seek a place I won't be interrupted on this lively night.

The quietude of the chapel offers such a place for meditation though I usually avoid its heavy doors and uncomfortable benches as one avoids the pox.

Braces of candles provide subdued light nearest the Holy Text at the head of the nearly empty room. An aged man with bowed head dozes in the corner. His presence will not intrude on me.

I trod down the central aisle and drop into the second row. I open my fist around the balled paper. Smoothing its creases against my thigh, I stare at the words. Raising the paper in the dim light, I recognize it as one of the fine sheets used by King Lorennt and now me. She must have torn this from the first letter I sent. *How dire are your needs, Tirzah, that you cannot spare a scrap of paper or a few drops of wax?* I rub my thumb across the curves and lines. *How am I to convince you to do what is in your best interest without a babe between us?*

The straight backs of these benches do not allow a reclined position. They seem designed for prostration. I brace my forearms on the back before me, hands linked as if in prayer. Candlelight undulates on the walls transfixing my gaze. A presence seems to fill the room making the air heavy. I look over my shoulder, but the dotard has not moved.

The presence presses down upon me, seeming to surround me, making itself… Known.

I bow my head between my arms. The longer I sit here, the more exposed I feel. It is as if a light is illuminating my heart, revealing my every failure and rotten motive. He knows me and that is terrifying. Remaining silent while in the presence of such otherness becomes a struggle. He seems to demand something of me. Burning fills my eyes and squeezes my throat till I cannot remain quiet. On a halting gasp, I question, "What do you want from me?"

"Curse the Almighty and die!"

I leap to my feet at the venomous shout.

The man chuckles. "Or so says Job's wife when he was in great turmoil."

My pulse rams my neck. I pry my fingers away from their involuntary grip on my sword.

We consider each other for a long moment before the man speaks. "You are Lorennt's Hand. Trent."

Being that I am near the braces of candles while he is enveloped in shadow, all I can do is acknowledge, "I am."

Pressing palms to his knees, the aged man pushes to his feet then draws near with a fluidity of movement that does not match his years. When the candlelight welcomes him, I know why.

"King Boldizar." I bow deeply. Humiliation lights a forge within me. "Forgive me for disturbing you."

He lowers to the bench I occupied. "I returned the favor in greater measure."

Inferring he means to keep company with me, I reclaim my seat.

For one with few years left to waste, he does not rush his words. Or perhaps time seems a vast quantity owing to the many years he has conquered, causing him not to feel its press.

When finally he speaks, his observation falls short of the grand pronouncement I expect. "Tis a place of quietude amid much noise."

"Aye, Your Majesty."

Boldizar's attention is drawn to the crunching noise from the paper in my fist, but he does not comment. My vivid plans to atone for the pain I have caused her are more ruined than the paper.

With his gaze on my hand, Boldizar says, "'I have the desire to do what is good, but I cannot carry it out. For I do not do the good I want to do, but the evil I hate—this I keep on doing.'"

I squeeze my fist, feeling the paper tear. Did the king somehow see what is writ? His statement seems plucked from my inmost resolutions. Have I not resolved to abstain from ill-using women? Yet lust makes a liar of me. How can he know this?

He expounds, "The Apostle Paul wrote those words a thousand years ago, yet they perfectly match my intents and misdeeds. I was contemplating that dichotomy ere you entered."

"You, Majesty?"

He looks sidelong at me. "Think you that I have mastered self-control because of my many years practicing?"

I admit, "I cannot imagine you landing yourself in my trouble, Majesty."

"Though our predicaments are likely different, I find myself in a ceaseless battle between acting on the right intentions of my heart and my sinful being asserting its will."

That does not sound very different from me. "I am the king's Hand, in word and deed. I embody the law of Malesiir, yet I cannot keep the standards I set for myself."

"The burden is greater for those charged with authority, but it does not change the fact that all of us have fallen short of the standards set for us, and will fall again." A contradictory peace abides in the king though he admits that he has betrayed the laws which he wrote. It begins to anger me. Boldizar is touted as one of the greatest king's of Malesiir. How can he own his failures with a smile? Guilt should be a scourge to him for the mistakes of his past, not this cloak of peace.

"The Almighty set laws in place for man to obey. It should have been possible for many of us to obey them if we bent our will to it. *'Do not murder. Do not steal. Do not commit adultery.'* Not so difficult those. Malesiir's laws reflect them. But as the list continues, perfect obedience becomes more difficult. *'Honor your father and mother'*? I disrespected my father more than once. *'Do not covet'*? Hardly possible. It was not until the Almighty sent His Saving Son, the embodiment of His word and His law, that we learned how far we had fallen from the laws given us. The Son told, *'Anyone who is angry with his fellow man shall be subject to judgment, and those that hate shall be judged guilty enough to be condemned.'* Which of us have not harbored anger or hatred in our hearts? As for adultery, the Son explained, *'If a man even looks at a woman lustfully, he has already committed adultery with her in his heart.'*" Boldizar scoffs, "Present to me a man who has not broken that law and I shall give him my kingdom."

"Why amplify the strictures of the laws if the original ones were impossible to obey?" Already I can guess. The vengeful being that inhabits the heavens would of course do something like that.

Boldizar replies, "The Son was the embodiment of the word and the law of His Almighty Father. He did not amplify the laws; He interpreted them."

"No one can obey those laws. They require perfection."

"Indeed. The law condemns each of us. Mercifully, I am not subject to the law." He explains, "The Saving Son lived a flawless life in perfect obedience to the law, but He was reviled and crucified as though the wickedest of men. In so doing, He took the judgment for all our trespasses upon Himself, and *'He blotted out the charge of our legal indebtedness, nailing it to the cross.'* He died to pay the ransom for our debt."

"Why? Why would anyone do that for someone who is guilty?" I certainly felt no hesitation to hang the Ruphiri for their crimes. It is unfathomable that someone would step into the noose in the place of a guilty man.

"Our wickedness separated us from the Father that loved us. He would not be satisfied until He freed us from our damnation, though it cost Him everything."

The picture Boldizar describes is not that of the aloof Creator I thought I knew nor is it the wrathful diety whom my father warned would hold me accountable for each of my failures. This depiction matches Tirzah's near and loving Heavenly Father who attended to her prayers.

"While the Deceiver yet rejoiced that he had slain the Saving Son, the Almighty's power was at work. Death could not hold the Son. He carried our guilt into the grave and left it there, defeating death, and rising victorious from the grave. His glorious resurrection ensures ours when we place all our hope in Him, repenting all our wrongdoing, and believing fully that with His death He paid our ransom."

Admitting my wrongs is not difficult. They are many. However, something makes me uncomfortable with the turn of our conversation. I seek a respectful way to extricate myself. "You have given me much to think on, Majesty."

"I do not doubt it. However, I shall leave you with one more morsel. The only way to find peace on the other side of the guilt that drives you is to seek forgiveness and fall on the mercy of the Saving Son. Only then will you know the grace of a redeemed life."

This is no morsel. It is Tirzah's recipe for peace.

Forgiveness. Grace.

It seems too simple. Verily, no amount of apologizing to Tirzah has budged my rancid guilt. How could asking the Creator for forgiveness feel different? If He is keeping account of each of His laws that I have broken, I have not enough breath left in my lifetime to confess all my wrongs. I am drowning in my guilt.

CHAPTER THIRTY-EIGHT

TRENT

April 1st

Tirzah whistles one of her cheerful melodies as she makes her way home late in the night. Her glowing smile tells that she aided the midwife in another successful birth. Moonlight glitters on the water of the river where she crosses the slippery weir that serves as a bridge near her home. She pauses on the bank to scoop a handful of water to her mouth and, in so doing, shifts her basket of supplies away from her full waist rounded with child. My child.

She straightens with a hand to her belly then swishes her way up the path to her cottage, circling around the little copse of trees. A throaty chuff breaks her whistled tune. She whips her head toward the trees and comes face to face with a black bear. Tirzah freezes, violet eyes wide in fright.

The bear sniffs at her and at the basket on her arm. She sets it down with slow, steady movements. The bear noses into the basket of medicinals while Tirzah backs away, inching toward her house. She quickens her pace but stumbles upon a pair of cubs who squeal at her sudden appearance. The mother bear growls, charging the woman standing between her and her cubs. Tirzah gathers her skirts and sprints toward her door, but she cannot outrun the bear. I watch in horror as the mother of my babe is mauled.

Cold sweat trickles down my back as I jerk upright in bed, not for the first time this night. The terrors that disturb my sleep have lessened in frequency since returning to Malesiir, but when they occur, they are always slathered with blood and violence. At times the dreams reoccur as the first one did this night. Again I saw myself as Orjek, preying upon Tirzah. I can persuade myself that was conjured entirely within my mind. But the bear attacking her...

I hold my eyes open until they blur with the need to blink. The

249

moment I let my lids fall, Tirzah's mauled body awaits. It has been torture to honor her wish to be left alone. Doubt still niggles at me regarding the veracity of her note. The missive I received from Anders has increased my worry tenfold.

I launch into motion, laying out a plan. My pack lands on top of the incomplete draft of my third letter to Tirzah. I cannot continue without hearing the truth of the matter from her lips and gaining her word that she will cease leaving her house after dark. Her pride can suffer my bridling if it means she will be safe. Then, perhaps, I can sleep.

While leading his company through Chishelm, Anders spotted Tirzah walking down the street alone with a pack upon her shoulders. Having learned that I have a care for her, though not the full, sordid truth, he tried to intercept her but lost her in the crowd. Still, I am grateful he thought it unusual and made me aware of her movements. Nothing good will come of her being alone in that bustling city with its garrison of soldiers.

Boots and greaves in place, I tug the buckles of my vambraces snug then don my leather gauntlets. My new armor, though far better than what I could previously purchase, feels foreign. I jounce my shoulders, learning the fit of the hardened leather cuirass. I adjust a few laces till it feels comfortably secure. Though I could not afford the purchase of one before, I consider adding my new shirt of chainmail hanging on its wooden cross-tree. Since I may need to track Tirzah to Chishelm, I decide it best I appear in full armor when I first enter the fort. Impressing Tirzah is also a consideration. The chainmail sings as it settles on my shoulders. Of all the fine armor and weaponry I now possess, it is the welcome grip of my own sword that most pleases me. As expected, the soldiers found my armor and weapons in disrepair, but the daggers, sword, and bow were salvageable. I loop and knot the weapons belt then sling quiver and bow across my shoulders.

My footfalls are silent as I cross the dim great hall, but the ring of chainmail announces my presence to the guards positioned at the base of the stairs to the royal wing. They salute as I pass. I give them a stiff nod, my focus riveted on the woman two day's ride distant.

"Trent."

Valor's softly spoken call spins me around with my sword half drawn. What is he doing awake at this hour?

I return my sword to the depths of its scabbard. Valor sits concealed in shadow near the glowing hearth. Drawing closer, I notice the possessive way he holds what appears to be a bundle of blankets.

"Where are you off to?" He asks quietly.

I mimic his whisper. "There is something I must attend to in Chishelm. I will be gone about a week."

"Is it anything I can help with?"

"No. I must see to it."

"I am leaving in two days for the high valley. If you can wait, I will travel with you," Valor offers.

"I'm afraid I cannot wait."

"Then safe travels," Valor bids, dipping his head.

"You should leave on the morrow instead," the bundle of blankets suggests.

"So bored with me already?" Valor teases his betrothed.

"You have pestered me nigh unto madness," Erianna replies then softer says, "I would rather you two not travel alone."

"Can you wait till morning?" Valor asks, altering his plans at the mildest request from Erianna.

My feet say no, itching to be moving. But I have a care for that pile of blankets too. "I can wait till morning."

"Good." Valor rubs a circle on Erianna's back. I wonder how often they meet like this in the middle of the night, abiding together when her sleep is shattered with nightmares. It would be better for her if they shared a bed, but Valor is an honorable man. He will not be with his betrothed until she is his wife. Unlike me who took a woman to whom I had no claim.

"Trent," Erianna interrupts my inner castigation without shifting from her place on Valor's lap. "Do not neglect to take a gift with you. I like when Valor brings me little gifts and notes. It shows he has been thinking of me when we are apart."

My brows shoot up. How does she know of my plan to see Tirzah? Lorennt is no teller of tales. The back of my neck burns when I deduce that Leelah, however, is. "You think a gift would smooth my path?"

"Especially if the gift is a book. Perhaps a medical text?"

I decide to trust my queen's insight since I likely need every help available to sway my woman. "I shall."

"And Trent," she adds, halting me as I walk away, "You need to stay clear of the Tareths until you have settled matters."

Aye, that is the sure path of her information. "Thank you for the warning."

"You sneaky little imp," Valor scolds her. "What do you know that I do not?"

"Much too much to tell." She sighs dramatically. "Poor oaf. Your simple mind is not up to the task."

Valor's head disappears into the blankets causing Erianna to giggle. My presence is forgotten.

I head from the great hall to the kitchens, packing food for Valor and I for the next three days.

❖ ❖ ❖

TRENT

April 4th

Valor offers no parting words as I keep pace with him into Parse Kítaran nor does he comment as I deviate from the path toward his house to cross over the bridge that will lead me to Tirzah's. It is uncomfortable knowing that all my friends are in possession of details that I would prefer to hold close, as I am certain would Tirzah. Thus, I appreciate Valor's choice to speak around my reason for venturing to Parse, conversing only of the kingdom's affairs.

Tirzah's cottage glows brightly against the failing day. A lazy curl of smoke winds upward from the chimney, carrying the scent of one of her delicious meals. That woman can do more over an open fire than most can do with a cookstove.

I lead my mount to the lean-to, but it is already occupied. And not by a farmer's horse. A large destrier stands alert at my approach with his military tack slung over the fence. He is bedded down. His master must be staying for the night. Hot ire courses beneath my skin.

Tirzah has company. Long-legged company, judging by the length of the stirrups. Why would a soldier be here? Her taunt about turning trade as a harlot like her mother leaps across my mind, but I strike it down. She has too much honor. Had I to guess, she would rather starve than ply her body in trade for food.

Then why is a soldier here? And why was Tirzah in Chishelm? Did she meet this man at the fort? The notion of Tirzah in that fort filled with men like Braun bathes me in fury. If a man of that sort is with her, I shall speed him on his way.

What does she mean by this? Is she being courted by this soldier?

The thought of another man courting her, holding her, knowing her, makes me want to draw my sword. I loop the dun's reins around the fence seeing only a haze of murderous red as I stomp up the steps. I nearly break through the door, but some residual reason bids me knock.

"Who's that at this hour?" A male voice demands.

"Likely someone in need of a healer," Tirzah replies.

"Turn them away. I'll not allow you out at night."

Blood roars in my ears. This lout has no authority to order about my woman!

Tirzah opens the door only enough to poke her head out. She startles at seeing me and steps into the night, closing the door behind her. "What are you doing here?" She hisses, shooing me away from the cottage.

"Who is he, Tirzah?" I ask, sliding my eyes down her modest dress. If she lied and there is a babe hiding beneath the homespun fabric, I cannot discern it.

"You must leave," she snaps.

"No. I am going to drive away this carp, then you and I shall speak."

"If you received my letter, there is naught else I have to say." Her arms are extended as if herding a stray animal. That she so badly wants to keep me away from the soldier makes me determined to have words with him.

I sidestep Tirzah, but she moves with me, blocking my way with her palm pressed to my chest. Stilled, I gaze into her upturned face. Wisps of hair fly loose from her braid. The fatigue of a long, hard day makes little lines on her brow. "Why are you here, Trent?"

The violence of the moment is displaced, though blood continues to pound in my ears. I catch her hand by the wrist, keeping her close. The panic leaves her eyes, replaced by something akin to longing. Forgetting the usurper in her cottage, my mind and body come into agreement that I ought to scoop up Tirzah and make off with her into the night. The look in her eyes says she might not object.

Of all the questions bludgeoning my skull, only one seems to matter. "Are you well, Tirzah?"

She nods, leaning into me. I catch her other hand in mine, tugging her closer.

"Tirzah!" A man barks from the doorway, jerking her away from me. "Who is out there?"

The lout blocks most of the light from inside with his broad frame. My bloodlust returns with fury.

"A friend come to look in on me," she calls back, voice quivering. "I will be but a moment."

"You must leave," she begs me in a whisper. "We can speak tomorrow, at the river."

"Who is he, Tirzah?" I snarl, allowing my displeasure to be clearly heard by the usurper.

"Bring him inside," the gruff soldier demands. "I will meet him."

With a final plea, Tirzah says, "Leave, Trent."

Her persistent use of my surname when once she spoke my given name like a song provokes me. She places distance between us while another man occupies her home like his private domain. I glare into her pleading eyes before stepping around her.

The man backs out of the threshold, allowing me to enter. He is a large brute with a crooked nose and judgmental countenance. He looks ready to beat his ham sized fists into my face until he takes stock of me. Noting the colors of my tunic that identify my rank, he glances at the signet on my hand.

Curse Lorennt! This has naught to do with him! But his presence looms over my shoulder, nonetheless. My personal affairs now involve the king. I'll not be allowed to pound the life out of this man or put another bend in his nose.

Tirzah closes the door behind her, leaning against it. With a resigned look at me, she makes the introductions. "This is Sergeant Trent. He serves Commander Ironforge. Trent, this is Captain Mather. My brother." She shivers with the pronouncement, fearful of my claim that I would invoke his power over her.

My ire at the thought of a soldier bedding down in my woman's house shifts to feelings of intrigue and protectiveness of a different sort. This is the brother who holds no affection for his sister and whose aid she refused to seek. I look closer upon this notorious man, searching for a resemblance to Tirzah. Apart from their nut brown hair, there is none. I could sooner believe him a relation of Anders.

"You have it wrong, Tirzah," Mather says, changing the course of my plans. "This is Commander Trent, the Hand of King Lorennt."

TIRZAH

The Hand of the King? The pronouncement rattles inside while Mather eyes me, trying to pick apart the secrets he now knows I keep, but I cannot move past the information Trent neglected to include in his letters. Hand of the King! Clad in chainmail and covered in armor and weapons as if he is going to war, I cannot argue that he looks like the Hand of the King. It is difficult to imagine this imposing warrior splitting shingles with a mallet and froe.

Mather, too, is affected by the introduction. Had Trent been a mere sergeant, I've no doubt Mather would have demanded answers straight away or simply called him to swords for the impropriety of coming to my door alone and at night. Instead, he says, "Join us for dinner, Commander. Tirzah, fetch another bowl."

Trent removes his bow and quiver then hangs his cloak on the hook by the door. He tugs off his gauntlets and drops them in the middle of the table. I hope Mather does not notice Trent's easy familiarity with my home. The men sit while I serve Trent. My shaking hands fumble the mug of water as I set it before him, clicking it against the bowl. His eyes hit mine before returning to Mather. Silently, they partake of the stew made from venison, foraged greens, and morels. Mather tears a hank of bread from the loaf then offers it to Trent who sops it in his stew.

It is a mercy that I have sparingly used the winter wheat Kragorn brought and was able to set the loaf of dark bread in the center of the table. The bread and my shelves overflowing with foraged herbs, sacks of seeds, drying lichens and bloodroot give the impression of abundance. I doubt either of them—even Trent with all his investigative prowess—will question my ability to provide for myself.

I would rather they not learn I am living on a knife's edge. The dyes, soaps, and salves I sold in Chishelm did not fetch the price I had hoped. Verily, had I other options, I would not be planning another venture there. I left for the journey in the dark before dawn and returned in the dark after sundown. But coin is coin. I will not be ungrateful.

Trent is the first to break the silence. "This is excellent, Tirzah. Thank you."

The compliment wraps warmth around me. I continue looking at him after he has returned his attention to his meal. Before Mather's interruption, had Trent intended to hold me? The disproportionate longing I feel for his touch is embarrassing. Since that morning I woke held warm and safe...

Do not think there! I chide myself. Mather's probing gaze bores into me. I attend to my stew, chasing the bits of venison in the bowl.

"You are most welcome." It amazes me Trent is able to eat heartily. Being in the same room as Trent and Mather has stolen my appetite.

Why did Trent pick tonight to come see me! Mather, too. He visits no more than twice a year. Why today? Their meeting bodes ill for my future and my freedom.

Trent sates himself by asking Mather the questions I previously dodged. Where is he stationed? To whom does he report? How long has he served? Trent is quite intrigued to learn Mather spent his early years serving in Grevnhold under General Tergehn.

"What brought you back to Malesiir?" Trent inquires.

"Family." Mather pushes back his bowl then belches. I wince, hating his uncouth manners. He wipes his mouth on his sleeve then settles his forearms on the table, eyeing Trent. "How came you to know my sister, Commander?"

I stare hard at Trent. *Lie! Don't tell him I was at court!*

Trent ignores my silent plea, but Mather studies my expression. I drop my gaze on the instant.

Trent swallows his last bite of stew and slides his bowl forward. I jump to my feet, collecting the bowls and dumping my uneaten stew back in the pot. Trent's chair squeaks as he reclines from the table. I collect his mug, refilling it from the dipper.

"Last summer, I was in Parse guarding Lady Nev and Queen Erianna. The queen introduced me to Tirzah after Gathering."

Surprise thrums a pleasant chord in me. "I had forgotten."

Trent accepts the mug, his fingertips brushing mine. "I could not."

I press down on the smile that teases my lips and regain my seat. My heart is hopelessly malleable. Pray he does not smile at me. I might swoon.

My scolding helps me find center.

Trent meets Mather's glower without flinching. "Tirzah is a particular friend of the queen, thus, she bid me inquire after her wellbeing while on my way to Chishelm."

I hear in the quality of his answer that it is not entirely true, but where is the lie?

Mather's brows lower over his eyes in disbelief. He cuts his gaze to me. "You did not mention such a notable thing as befriending the queen."

In this I do not need to lie. "The queen being here was a great secret."

"For her safety, it could not be made known," Trent reinforces.

Mather grunts. "If the queen has a care for Tirzah, a letter would have served. Does the queen care so little for being an honorable woman that she would ruin my sister's reputation as she has done—"

"Do not finish that sentence." Trent's each word cuts. "I will not tolerate any disrespect of my queen."

Though his tone sets my nerves trembling, I love Trent all the better for defending Erianna. I love him less for his next statement.

"The queen has a great care for those entrusted to her. She does not send infrequent letters when a visit better serves."

Mather recognizes Trent's disparagement at the minimal care he gives me and jabs back, "Here I thought you *served* the king."

"Mather!" I gasp.

Trent maintains his control and that of the conversation. "King Lorennt feels indebted to Tirzah for the many services she has rendered the queen, Lady Nev, and the Tareth family. And I have taken an interest in Tirzah's wellbeing." He levels the threat with a glower.

I tense. Mather is a despot. He answers threats with violence, and I have never seen him lose a fight. Despite the way Mather's hands curl into fists, Trent does not cushion his declaration. He leans into the table, willing to enforce it.

Mather unfolds, pushing slowly to his feet. Trent remains seated, assured in his dominance.

My cottage is too small for the tension billowing from the men. If they come to blows...

I shudder, fearing the destruction. Perhaps, I also ought to fear for Trent, but his firm confidence while staring down my menacing brother gives me faith that he can hold his own.

Mather stalks around the table, still Trent remains seated, though it is with a taut energy that could launch him into a fight. Trent refuses my pleading gaze, cocking his head to track Mather by sound.

Mather raps a knuckle against the lowest purlin, one that Trent replaced. My heart drops into my stomach.

"I spoke with Brick today," Mather announces, making me want to crawl under the table. "He has a memory for names. Said a soldier named Trent repaired the roof. Strange since Tirzah did not tell me the roof was damaged. But I can see it was."

Mather turns to Trent, wrath boiling between his gruff words. "Makes me wonder how my sister paid for the work, and what I owe the man on her behalf."

Fear, guilt, and humiliation brew a potent tisane that burns my insides. It is exactly as Mather claimed. Perhaps he will keep his vow to sell me to a bawd for finding me compromised. Again.

Trent works his gauntlets back onto his hands—the motions restrained and deliberate. "I have two sisters, Captain. If someone danced that close to maligning their honor, I'd call him out. Since I cannot imagine it was your intent to taint your sister's honor, I must assume you misspoke."

Trent slings his quiver and bow across his shoulder then takes his cloak from the hook, draping it over his arm. His presence looms larger than Mather's despite his average height. "On the chance that you misspeak again, we'd best continue this conversation out of doors."

Trent opens the door, waiting for Mather to exit. The look of detest Mather hurls at me bows my head. He did not misspeak, rather, he restrained the amount of vitriol he wanted to deliver.

Trent lingers in the threshold, his attention upon me, but I cannot look at him. "Thank you for the meal, Tirzah. We shall meet again soon."

He closes the door softly behind him.

I go to the window and crack the shutter. Fickle moonlight illuminates the confrontation of the two men. I hear Trent relate in an abbreviated, impersonal manner how he came to repair my roof. Mather's terse reply is too quiet to discern, but after a moment, he salutes Trent who collects his horse and rides away behind the dense copse as I have seen him so often do. Only when he is gone from sight does Mather return. I latch the shutter.

"What have you done, Tirzah?" Mather growls, dropping the bar across the door.

"Not what you assume."

"Benighted woman! Do not lie to me!"

I pinch my lips together.

"Though you be a fool, I am not. I can see the roof that was repaired. The coin you have acquired. The venison and salt pork you stored." Mather jabs the air in the direction of each evidence that someone has helped me. Except the coin. That I earned, not that he would believe my word should I argue.

"Women do not hunt. Never before have you had stores of meat." He crosses the room to better rant and rage in my ear. "Yet Commander Trent arrives with bow and quiver on his back. Tales of his superior skill with that weapon abound."

I quirk up a corner of my mouth, unable to resist prodding him. "Trent is so newly appointed that news has not reached us in the valley, yet tales abound of his skill with a bow? I thought he was little known."

"Rumors travel on wings! While rescuing the queen, he felled twenty Ruphiri in the span of a minute with his bow! His skill and cunning earned his place as Commander of all Malesiir!" Spittle flecks my cheek as he yells the last.

Knowing what truly happened that night from one who was there, I know Mather's statement to be exaggeration, though perhaps not as amplified as exaggerations usually are. I could correct him, but a part of me is glad that Trent has earned renown. He *is* skilled and *is* worthy of being Lorennt's Hand. It gladdens me that he will no longer work in shadow, wrecking himself while serving as spymaster. I wonder if that prior occupation of his has been made known.

"You are wicked, Tirzah! Despite all my efforts, you have become your mother—a kept woman."

I shake my head, hating how accurate that description feels. Mather interprets it as dissent.

"You think not? Did he tell you he loves you? That he will marry you? It is a lie! You are a harlot's daughter. It is in your nature. No man can love you."

I try to stopper my ears from drinking his poison, as Kragorn has told me to do, but I cannot. His words strike at my deep fear, making me ill.

"You even look like a whore, formed to tempt a man to sin. The same as your wretched mother."

She was your mother too! I want to scream it, to batter him with the truth, but I know better than to remind him. He wishes to disassociate from the woman that loved him, that protected him, that sold her soul to provide for him when his father—her beloved husband—died. All that she got for her trouble was his hatred and me—another burden from someone who used and discarded her. My sire could have been any of the men who entered her hovel, lay with her, left coin, then fled.

Shame twists my heart. My story is beginning to sound so much like hers. Too much.

"What was your plan? For me to find him with you, call him out, and force him to marry you? Fool! It has come to nothing! Had he still been a sergeant, I might have tried. Far better for me to be rid of you than to be forced to provide for you. But you are a fallen woman, and I cannot call him out without proof that he ruined you, which he did not. You spent your virtue in Juniper, if a harlot's daughter is born with virtue."

Of all the things he could dredge from our past to make me miserable, that is one I dearly wish to forget, not that he will let me.

"I should have left you there. Had I known you would sard the *accursed Commander of Malesiir*, I would have never saved your whoring hide!"

I flinch away, but in this cottage, there is no where to go. I cross the room to the bucket with the dirty bowls from dinner. Mather could carry on all night if I let him. He has a deep well of hurt and anger stored up at our mother which he pours out on me—if I believe Leelah's explanation of his behavior. I scrub the dishes with a rag while he tells me how much he hates me.

"You have smeared my honor with your vile nature. Now the commander knows we are related, a captain and a harlot. I cannot force a marriage between you, nor can I make good on my vow to you. Have you forgotten what I swore?"

I drop a bowl into the bucket and pick up the next one, scrubbing the rag on its surface.

"Give answer!"

"Never have I forgotten," I say quietly. When a brother vows to break all connection with his sister then sell her to a bawd if he again finds her compromised, it is not something she forgets.

"Then why have you made this arrangement?"

Though it is a lie, I must protect myself from Mather's vow, and I will not feel ashamed for it. Dropping the bowl and rag, I turn to face him, selling my lie by staring brazenly into his angry, mottled face. "If you take me away from Commander Trent, he will be furious. He will strip you of your captaincy and cast you out of the military. As you have heard, he is a cunning, tireless adversary. If you sell me to a bawd, he may even kill you. So leave me be, Mather. Go and trouble yourself with me no more. I have found a provider."

CHAPTER THIRTY-NINE

TRENT

April 5th

Tirzah does not alter her morning routine. As the blue predawn light surrenders to the gold of the sun's first rays, Tirzah descends the hill coming toward the river. No cheerful tune sounds on the breeze, nor do her skirts swish merrily with her steps. Instead, she plods around the trees without a thought to her surroundings, her eyes fixed on the ground before her feet. The water bucket dangles from the limply clasped rope handle.

I am unsure whether to intervene or if I ought to run before she sees me. Each time I help seems to make her life worse. When first we met, she was full of optimism and joy that overflowed. The sight of her broken spirit flays me. I take a step toward the edge of the forest, but doubt over the veracity of her letter stays me. Before deciding how to proceed, I must know if she lied about the babe.

Leaning into the desire to help, I slowly close the distance between us. At the soft jingle of my chainmail, Tirzah's eyes dart upward, and she stalls. I do not hesitate to take the bucket.

With a long sigh, she follows me to the bank of the river then settles upon her preferred fallen log. Pebbles crunch beneath my boots as I bend to fill the bucket with frigid water. The spring melt has swollen the river, causing it to rush and cover the stone weir. "You do not try to cross the river when it is like this, do you?"

"That would be foolish, and I am not..."

I glance over my shoulder. Tirzah winces, letting her words trail, undoubtedly recalling the dozens of ways Mather named her a fool and worse.

Gritting my teeth, I set the bucket on the bank. After working Mather into a froth, I knew it unwise to leave Tirzah defenseless against anger. However, doubling back to ensure her safety nearly incited me to murder when I heard the things he said to her. It was nigh unavoidable when he saddled his horse and spurred away into the night. No one would have known what became of him. Somehow, I restrained myself.

I crouch at her knees, the river ebbing around my leather soles. "You are not a fool. Nor a kept woman. Nor a whore."

She tucks her chin to her chest. "Why did you come back?"

"I feared for you, and rightly so. Mather is a—"

Tirzah's fingers cover my mouth. It startles her as much as it does me. But does it make her heart pound? My full attention homes to the feel of her fingers on my lips. They rasp against the unshaven bristles around my mouth as she pulls away.

"Please," she says on a breath. "If you overheard what he said, you know I have been fed more course language than I can stomach."

My eyes are fixed on her calloused fingers knotted in her lap. I regret not catching hold of her when she was within reach. "Forgive me. I feel the cause of that."

"You were only partly to blame," she replies with her beautiful candor. "Mostly he hates me and was looking for a reason to withdraw his support. Earlier, he told me he had taken a wife—poor woman— and said I must join them in Klaptin till he could arrange a marriage for me."

But that was not what I heard him threaten, what nearly drove me into the cottage and made my brawl in the alehouse seem a friendly tussle. "Would he have sold you to a bawd?"

Her eyes meet mine. The longstanding ache she reveals is answer aplenty. Though I know her claiming me as provider was a bluff to protect herself from Mather's wrath, I felt as if she lifted the words from my mind. "I would do it. If he sold you to a bawd, I would kill him. All that you spoke and more I would do if he hurt you."

She searches my face, testing my veracity. I hold her gaze with ease. *Look long, Tirzah. You will find no lie.*

Softly, she queries, "Why are you here, Trent?"

Kneeling before her, the answer seems more complex than what I told myself at the castle. More than anything, I want to restore the joy that once flowed from her like water from a spring. I want the camaraderie between us that was so easy that I took it for granted. I want her to whistle. I want her skirt to swish when she walks. I want to touch her hair.

I want her note to have been a lie.

"You were rightly angered with me when I asked to take you to wife. It was wrong of me to accuse you of something you would never do."

Tirzah takes a breath to speak, but I quickly continue. "Thus, when I received your letter, I wondered if the thought of marriage to me was so abhorrent that it led you to lie."

She stares blankly at me. "You thought…"

Sudden emotion contorts her face. With a shriek, she shoves both palms into my shoulders, knocking me onto my backside in the water. Stumbling, she flees up the path.

"Tirzah!" I call after her, baffled by her outburst. Pushing to my feet, I try to follow but trip over the bucket, sloshing the water up my leg. Grumbling, I refill it and tote it to her door.

Rapping my knuckles on the wood, I plead with her. "Please talk with me, Tirzah. I do not understand why you are upset."

Over and again, I call to no avail. "Tirzah, please."

Desperate, I try to open the door, but she has barred it. I consider the latched shutter on the window. It would not be difficult to break. "Tirzah, I will not leave this time."

I hear her muffled, frustrated howl. "Aye, you will. You have no obligation to me. I am not with child, so you are rid of me."

I lean my forehead against the door, feeling something inside me wilt. "That is not what I want."

"Nor I, so please leave."

"What do you want, Tirzah?"

Silence is my answer. Despite, my pleas, she does not open the door. I sit on her stoop, unwilling to surrender. Propped against her door, the hours of the morning pass without her answering my intermittent knocks. I listen to Tirzah chopping then the repetitive tap of her mortar and pestle. I let my mind wander to the moment I have visited so often that it is a wonder I am still asking her this question.

What do you want from me, Tirzah? Her answer was so candid that I did not understand it. *I want you to love me.*

Why can she not see that is what I am offering? I could grow to love her. It would be effortless, like the camaraderie we shared and those talks at Salome's table that carried late into the night.

"Mather is a lying—" I stop myself from cursing him and cut to the point. "He was wrong. When I see you, I do not see a temptress. I see an admirable woman. A healer. Kind. Beautiful. Honorable."

The tapping has stopped. She is listening.

I push to my feet. "Allow me to show you."

"Is she not at home?" A man hollers.

Brick from whom she lets the cottage trudges across the field. Seeing my opportunity to gain entrance, I nearly grasp it, but I want Tirzah to come to me by choice. Nor do I want to dishonor her with the questions that would arise from me laying siege to her door in the sight of her neighbor and landlord.

"No, she is not. I thought to wait for her, but I must be on my way. I shall return another time. When next you see her, could you tell her that Commander Trent called?" I tell Brick, stopping his advance.

"Aye, Commander."

"Much thanks, Brick."

CHAPTER FORTY

TIRZAH

April 6th

Guilt is a powerful motivator. Upon that, I can agree with Trent.

I shift on the bench in the chapel, seated next to Salome. It is what brought me here this morning though there are many present whom I wish to avoid. My attention wanders while the elder speaks. The passage on unity and generosity from which he reads seems to justify the pointy looks I shoot at the back of Mamey's head. And that woman with whom she replaced me.

I sigh, staring out the window into the sunny day that darkens suddenly beneath a scuttling cloud. My guilt has only carried me this far. I struggle to breach the wall I built between myself and the Almighty. For certain, had my sin with Trent yielded a different result —namely his love and the promise of a marriage of the heart between us—I doubt very much I would feel guilty. Which makes me wonder, is what I feel guilt or regret?

True, I loathe feeling like a slattern, but would I feel like this if Trent had returned my love in full measure? I doubt it. My actions also instigated a series of unfortunate events that led me to be ruined by Trent yet still aching for him, ousted from my role as healer, abandoned by my brother, and living upon the precipice of destitution. Guilt, regret, guilt, regret—it is difficult to delineate them.

I tug the skirt of my dress, ensuring the hem is as long as it can be. With her sitting next to me as is usual, my nervous motion comes to Salome's notice. I take a bracing breath and still myself. From the corner of my eye, I watch her cloudy eyes watching me.

Salome pats my hand. "Walk me home after Gathering."

I am shaking my head before her last whispered word. "I cannot. Perhaps I can come visit you later in the week."

My noncommittal reply reveals my true feelings.

Instead of chastising me, Salome squeezes my hand. "When you are ready, Dear One."

Her unconditional love makes me squirm. I do not want to admit how badly I have failed.

When the last prayer is prayed, I slip out of the chapel during the final song. There is no one I want to speak with this day, but my wishes are immaterial.

"Tirzah," Brick hails, pursuing me across the meadow.

The most childish urge to run trickles into my feet, skipping them along faster for a few paces. But I cannot outrun the misfortune hounding my steps. I plant my feet and turn with a smile. "Good morn, Brick. How fare you?"

His long stride eats the ground between us in a few bites. "Tirzah." He neglects the customary greetings and responses to get to the meat. "I trust Mather spoke with you?"

"He did."

"When is he returning to collect you?"

I pull my spine straight. "He is not. I will be responsible for the payment to let the cottage."

His face betrays his disapproval. "That won't be possible with your means."

I project confidence in my calm, reasonable tone. "I assure you, I am capable of remitting the cost, though I will need to pay you each month instead of seasonally."

Brick rolls his lips inward, chewing on his answer.

"Verily, I have most of the payment set aside. I expect to have the rest by the end of the month."

He jerks his head. "Mather has not paid for you to let the cottage this month. I cannot afford you to live there without paying the month in advance."

Afford it? How utterly ridiculous! He already owns the property. It is purely income without expense. But I will compromise if it keeps me housed. "Then I shall bring you the payment for the two weeks ahead and the rest in two more weeks."

I can tell he is still not pleased with the arrangement, but I cannot fathom why. "Brick, you know me. I have never neglected to care for the cottage. You have commented before how well I have tended it and improved the gardens."

"You neglected it this winter and the roof caved in."

Me? I neglected it? Had it been in his care through the winter, the entire roof would be sitting on the cottage floor! But shouting at my landlord will not smooth my path. "I was told the roof was rotting and the purlins insufficient in number to hold the burden of snow. It would have collapsed whether I was there or not. Nevertheless, it is repaired and improved."

Brick shifts his weight from one foot to the other then back again. "Commander Trent came to call on you yesterday. Said to tell you he'd soon return."

Is Brick stalling? Why? "Very well. The commander may do as he likes."

He fixes me with a squinted stare, waiting for something more, but I am at a loss.

"I do not see his relevance to our conversation, Brick. Will you allow me to let the cottage?"

Uncomfortable of a sudden, he scratches his chin before meeting my gaze. "Will you have the remainder of the payment after Trent returns?"

My mouth falls open. I sputter for a moment till heat floods my veins. I advance a step. "Are you accusing me of being a harlot?"

His face turns red as he backtracks, embarrassed by my candor. "That is not what I said. Maybe Trent pities you or means to court you properly. I can't know. Either way, I do not feel right about accepting his money."

I should have never let Trent repair that miserable roof! His kindness has ruined my reputation. Or perhaps it is as Mather said. Whenever a man looks at me, he sees a harlot. "The coin I have is my own! I earned it with honest work as I always have!" I shove my reddened, scraped palms toward him. "See the evidence. Making soap and climbing through brambles to forage a meal is not soft work."

Brick does not spare my hands a glance. "Very well, Tirzah. If you bring the first payment today and the remainder in two weeks, you may let the cottage."

"Thank you." I fairly spit my parting words.

Stomping and fuming all the way home does not carry me across the breadth of my feelings, but there is no time to wallow. I must rally. If I am to make good on my word to Brick, I must venture to Chishelm sooner than I anticipated. Thankfully, I have more salves ready to sell as well as dyes.

All my plots come to a halt when downy feathers blow across my path. Horrified, I scan the garden for my young chickens. Instead of finding the pullets happily scratching for insects, downy feathers blow in flurries like snow. Perched on the edge of the lean-to, a large hawk bends his head below his golden shoulders to rip a strip of flesh from the mangled chicken gripped in its talon.

I screech and wave my arms at the bird who cocks his head to view me through his merciless eye, deciding if I pose a threat to his meal. He stretches his wings that spread farther than my arms and flaps them thrice then folds them back into place and returns to his meal.

A frustrated scream tears from my throat. I search the lean-to, the garden, and the edge of the forest for any of my chickens that might have escaped the slaughter but find none. If they do not return of their own accord before nightfall, they won't survive the night. All the effort and feed I have invested into raising my flock is wasted. I fist a rock in my hand and hurl it at the hawk, but my aim is wide. It scolds me with a piercing shriek.

I turn my back on it, flinging my accusations at the sky, where they belong. "The birds of the ground are mine! Could You not have protected them from the birds of the air that are Yours? Or is this to be the punishment for my sin? Do you now withhold Your hand of blessing and apply Your hand of chastisement? I cannot sustain myself if You continue to foil my efforts!"

My rant goes unanswered. I feel bereft of the peace and assurance I once held dear. I am no longer confident in the outcome of my situation because my plans are slipping through my hands like sand. Unlocking the door to the cottage, I collect the precious few coins I have saved, hoping that Brick does not count them till I leave. It is only a third of what I owe him.

CHAPTER FORTY-ONE

TIRZAH

April 8th

Wisps from my tightly plaited hair cling to the back of my neck despite the pleasant temperature of late afternoon. I tug the collar of my dress and blow air against my sticky skin. My discomfort is more than worth the result. While I sold few of my salves, I sold all of my soaps and dye. There was a great demand for the expertly harvested and dried material. It gives me hope that the coin I earned today will not be the last I shall see.

I head out of Chishelm at a brisk walk, making plans for a lengthy foraging venture to the lake. With the sun aligned for its nightly descent, realizing that I might still be on the road after nightfall does not please me. Briefly I consider spending a bit of coin at a reputable tavern for a hot meal and a bed for the night. I have enough, but I cannot be sure I won't be in the same or worse need of it to pay Brick for next month's rent. I tug the hood of my cloak up to cover my hair and fall in with the other travelers leaving the city. If I stay in a group, I will be safe enough. Blessedly, a patrol of soldiers exits the fort as I am passing by. They bring up the rear of the procession.

As the miles crawl by, keeping apace with the wagons and mounted soldiers proves difficult on my exhausted feet. I feel each barbed stick through my thin soles. Though I have a bit of food in my satchel, I cannot stop to partake or I risk falling too far behind my traveling companions. By listening to their talk, I learn the wagon folk ate at the Foxtail Tavern before leaving Chishelm. It makes me wish I had done the same.

The soldiers turn north at an intersecting road to complete their wide circuit around Chishelm leaving me to trail the wagons as twilight descends in earnest. With another mile separating me from the river that will lead me into Parse Kítaran, the wagons veer off the road at a glen where they will make camp for the night. After listening to the coarse talk of the men in the wagons, I dare not attempt to make protectors of men who may wish for something in exchange for a space at their fire.

The drone of crickets fills the cooling air. Fireflies flit through the brush at the edges of the road, seeming to disappear then reappear in a distant spot with the flicker of their green lights. I hurry onward despite the creeping feeling that settles between my shoulder blades. Though I want it to be naught but my imagination, intuition warns that I am not alone on this road.

With night's shadows close at my sides and my hood making a bowl of my field of vision, I cannot know for certain without stopping to look behind me. Something whispers looking over my shoulder would make me seem like prey.

Keep steady. March like you are unafraid, I order myself, but my body is not listening. So focused am I on what is behind me that I neglect to attend to what is before me. My feet stumble on a sharp stone, sending me into a sprawl in the middle of the road. With an involuntary cry, I push myself from the ground.

A jerk on my satchel pulls me backward onto my rear. Grasping hands rip the straps from my shoulders. I scream and whirl at the thief with clawing nails, but a rank body hooks my arms behind me with little effort.

I kick my heels back trying to connect with his shins.

"Enough!" He jerks my back flush against his chest with my arms pinned between us. Fire shoots through my upper arms to race across my shoulders. I bleat from the pain, tugging away, but am held fast.

The wiry man who snatched my pack lifts it in the air near his ear and shakes it. My clay jars of salve clink against each other, but it is the jingle of coins that causes an open-mouth smile to part his lips.

"Well! The wench is prime for plucking!" He chases the jingle until he finds my purse then drops the pack. The clay pots break with a dull clank.

"No! You're ruining everything!" I protest.

With a mean smile, he kicks my pack. More jars break and some of my belongings roll across the ground. I snap my mouth shut. Expecting fairness or mercy from villains is the height of folly. He dumps the contents of my purse into his hand. "Look here! This is a fine little catch. What have you been doing to come out of Chishelm with such shine?"

"I'm a healer!" I spit the words. "Unlike you, I earned every copper by working to help people!"

He cackles. "Then you won't mind helping us through your generosity." My coins disappear into his pocket. "She have aught else worth taking?"

The man at my back sniffs my hair. "Mayhap."

I jerk my head away from his sour breath.

"Search her," the wiry one orders.

Manacling my arms in one of his, he roves my belt and skirt seeking more coin then makes a leisurely, intimate perusal of my body. I thrash at his touch that scalds through my garments till the wiry one tells him to cease.

"Let her go. We have what we want."

The foul man obeys but argues. "Not all. I want her."

"Nah, you don't." Wiry jingles his pocket filled with my coin. "You can buy three of her with your lot, and they'll be accommodating."

Without a spare glance for me, they head toward Chishelm, plotting the ill spending of my coin. I burn at the injustice of them brazenly walking down the middle of the road without a fear of consequence and me without recourse. I cannot fight them for the return of my money. I doubt I can report them without the ability to match their faces seen in the dark of night to someone I might pass in the city in the bright of day. Frustrated tears stream from the corners of my eyes. It is not fair. Were I a man, this would not have happened. No one would dare steal from Trent or Kragorn or even Brick.

Brick...

I begin to cry in earnest. There is no way for me to pay for the lease of my cottage.

Light shines in Salome's windows as I wearily trudge toward home. It beckons me up the steps to her door. She pulls the door open once I announce myself.

"Tirzah! The hour is late, why are you about?"

She guides me into the house where I drop onto the bench by the door. Sweat, dirt, and the opposing scents of my broken jars of salves waft from me.

Salome brings a lantern close to my face, illuminating me for her failing eyes. She nearly drops the lantern. "What has happened to you? My dear girl!"

I suppose I truly look the sullied woman I feel. Beneath the dirt, my skin stings where I fell in the road. My cheek also hurts though I cannot recall how I injured it.

"The Almighty is against me. I sinned, and He has chastised me in every way. I am now without work, without a home, without friends, and ruined. I should never have trusted Trent. He trampled my heart and left me nothing but his guilt and my misery."

A mug of tea appears in my hands.

In muddled fits and whimpers, the whole of the story comes out. Salome washes the grime from my hands and face while I speak. "I have tried my best to live honorably, but the Almighty has crushed me for my mistake. It is just as you said. I scorned the love He gave me by pursing the empty dream of a husband's love. Now I have lost everything because the Almighty has rejected me."

I drain the mug of tea. Salome urges me into a chair by the fire and places the refilled mug back into my hands. "I am disappointed, Tirzah."

My chin droops to my chest. "I know."

"No, clearly you do not." She lowers herself into her plush chair. "I am disappointed that you have such a narrow view of the Almighty's love and grace that you believe you have used it all up. He is not a fickle patron who only answers prayers and shows favor to those that have obeyed Him perfectly. You have lost sight of Him in the midst of your trials. Recall what he said to His chosen people, though they were repeatedly unfaithful to Him. He said to them, *'I have loved you with an everlasting love, I have drawn you to me with lovingkindness.'* He never stopped loving His people though they turned away from Him, nor did He change His plans to rebuild them and restore them to their homeland. This is the same everlasting love with which He loves you, Tirzah."

My heart aches to believe Salome, but these horrible things did not happen to me until I gave myself to Trent. "The truth of the Holy Texts conflicts with what I am experiencing. How can it be that all was well with me until I went astray?"

"Is your faith in the Almighty contingent upon your circumstances?" She speaks with placidity though her words cast me into turmoil.

I mumble my reply into my mug of tea. "I did not believe my faith was so weak, but perhaps it is so."

"No, Tirzah. Look back. You know the trials through which the Almighty has brought you. They did not overturn you, nor did you believe they were a result of His chastisement. He has made a way for you before. He will make a way for you again."

Her words salve my wounds, but they do not erase the weight of guilt that leads me to believe this is the recompense for falling into the pattern of my mother.

"Do you know why the Almighty tells His people to abstain from sexual sin?"

"Because we are to remain pure, holy, and set apart. Relations between man and woman are only to be enjoyed within the sanctity of marriage." I answer without needing to consider it.

"If it is enjoyable, why would He withhold something that is good from us?"

I recall Trent's love that was bliss incarnate followed by his rejection that cut me to my soul. When I keep my thoughts inside, Salome gently explains, "There is nothing more intimate between a man and woman. It was a gift from the Almighty to seal the marital union, the binding together of one man and one woman into one new being. It is as sacred as the marriage itself. But the Deceiver has planted a lie that men and women can enjoy the pleasure without the commitment. What is left is a cheap substitute that leaves the participants bereft. They become one but not truly. After the pleasure, there is emptiness. That is why the men return again and again to the brothels. They are not satisfied. That is why women pursue one lover after another, seeking one who will truly be theirs and make them feel complete."

"The Deceiver kills, steals, and destroys," I murmur.

"Aye. Your Holy Father loves you, and this is why He warns you, *'All other sins are committed outside the body, but sexual sin is a sin against one's own body.'* The pain is deeper, and the consequences can be grave. The Almighty would never give a bad gift to his children, but this gift can do much damage if it is separated from the safety of the marital union."

The answer I could not discern comes with a wave of surety. Even had Trent loved me with his heart and taken me to wife, still our misuse of the Almighty's gift of intimacy would have had consequences, and I would have regretted what we did. "Aye. Much damage," I agree.

"Are you ready to begin healing?"

I nod. This surrender feels like a long awaited release of my guilt and pain. All along, the Almighty has been waiting to show me His forgiveness. I pour out my heart to Him telling him how sorry I am, how I doubted that His love was enough. Again, I put my hope in who He is.

Salome also prays over me asking the Almighty to heal my wounded heart.

In the peaceful quiet that follows, I untuck Kragorn's explanation of that night. *Your insecurity collided with his weakness. He was compelled to rescue you from it, and you could do nothing but heal his pain. The culmination of both your strengths and weaknesses proved your undoing.*

The gentle prompt of the Spirit of Truth builds in me. Long have I placed the blame solely on Trent's shoulders for deceiving me. It was easier than taking ownership of my own mistakes. Though he has apologized to me innumerable times, I have not forgiven him, nor have I sought his forgiveness.

TIRZAH

April 10th

Standing upon the knoll overlooking the cottage I can no longer claim, I feel like a leaf ripped from its tree in the wind. Untethered. Tossed. Without control of its direction.

The sun crests the peak of a cloud to fall across my shoulders, warming me in that remarkable fullness that can only come from above. I fill my lungs to bursting, letting the sunshine warm even my breath before I release it. It is no small thing to let go, to trust that there are better plans than mine. If I do not believe with my whole heart that the Almighty loves me, being thrust from the safety and friendship I have found within the arms of this valley will crush me.

As I watch a wagon crawl along the packed valley road toward the bridge where I will meet it, words that will mortar my future well up from the depths of my being to be caught in the air.

"I have tried to mold my life into the shape that best pleases me. I'm letting go now. Do with my life what You will."

The first steps toward that bridge feel like leaping from a mountain peak. All my illusions of control have vanished. I am walking in realms of grace.

CHAPTER FORTY-TWO

TIRZAH

April 10th

I bump into Chishelm atop a cushiony pile of raw wool fleeces from the spring shearing at Lourna's farm. The sale of their fleeces coincided perfectly with my decision to leave Parse Kítaran. Thad was generous to offer his protection by allowing me to ride with them into the city, sparing me a long walk on a stretch of road that frightens me now that Trent's dire predictions have proved true.

Thad sets the brake on the wagon then disappears into the warehouse in Chishelm's trade district situated on the largest and most level roads in the city. Nate, Thad's grown son, leaps from his seat to help me descend from the wagon. He holds my pack while I fit the straps across my shoulders. "You sure about moving here, Tirzah?"

"I know I cannot stay in Parse, and I have peace with my decision." The words are more a spoken reassurance for me than him. It is unnerving to return to this city that proved a harsh landing place years past.

Nate tugs me close to the side of the wagon when a grizzled tinker nearly pushes his cart overtop us. "Mind your step, fellow!" Nate objects.

The tinker aims a stream of spit at our feet in passing.

Disgust curls Nate's upper lip. His hand remains on my elbow to keep me from being swallowed by the confused bustle.

I note, "The king's improved roads seem to have already had an impact on trade. Twas not this busy when I lived here years past. Nor this large." The original city square of Chishelm was little more than a crossroads laid at a gap between the mountains sending travelers onward to the capital and the port cities in the west, south to the farmland, or north to the wilds. As the crossroads grew into a village and now a respectable city, it entirely filled the gap between the mountains and rambled up the gentle slopes creating a web of streets that appear to have been designed by a drunken spider.

With another wary look at the crowded streets and little offshoots that branch in every direction, Nate offers, "Would you like me to walk with you till you find a place to stay?"

When I first came to the valley, Nate was a blushing youth who made paltry excuses to speak with me at every chance. He has grown into a confident young man in the passing years that also swept away his infatuation.

"Your father cannot spare you. Do not fret for me." I smile up at Nate then wedge myself into the flow of people moving toward the intersection that leads to the street lined with shops and taverns.

"Farewell, Healer!" He shouts above the voices bartering their trades.

Although the manner in which Mamey warned me that I have not enough training to call myself a healer still hurts, I feel there is truth in what she said. Thus, I enter the most respectable physician's storefront to pursue the knowledge I lack.

The physician of middle years is speaking with another man when I enter. I surreptitiously attend to their conversation while looking around the shallow front of the shop. A few rows of shelves are neatly lined with common medicinals. A wall separates the front of the building from the greater portion comprised of a workshop and rooms for patients. Physician Breckett gave me a tour of his workroom the first time he bought salves from me. I found him knowledgable and kind.

When the man leaves, the physician motions me forward. "Good day, Tirzah. Tis surprising to see you this soon. I'm not yet ready for more salves."

"Good day. I am here on another matter. Have you need of a physician's assistant?" I ask boldly.

"Well, if the man can provide good references and demonstrate his knowledge..." He trails off at my confused look.

"I must not have been clear," I say, though a lack of candor is not something of which I have ever been accused. "*I* am seeking a position as a physician's assistant."

He stares at me a moment then laughs. At my indignant expression, he poorly conceals his laughter with a cough.

Breckett tilts his head to a patronizing angle, his voice gentle and slow. "Tirzah, while you make fine salves, there is much more to being a physician than blending a few herbs."

Intuition tells me this exchange will not go my way and I would do best not to waste my time, but a tenacious disposition makes me defend my authority on the subject. "I am not uninitiated in the profession. I have spent the past two years training beneath a healer and midwife. I intend to further my education."

Breckett dismisses my claim. "Assisting a midwife is not the same as assisting a physician. Healing the body is a complex endeavor that takes a strong mind and virile nature to withstand the rigors of attending to patients. Illness is unpleasant. It is why the fairer sex cannot become physicians."

A hot choler gathers under my skin at his condescending arrogance. Having met his brand of idiocy before, I give him my candid thoughts on the matter. "I would argue that attending a birth that lasts all the hours of a day and night is more rigorous than healing a cough. It is also impossible for a cough to be more unpleasant than a woman's bowels loosing on your hands as she pushes her child into the world."

The physician snaps straight as a pole, his nostrils flaring. Before he can summon an indignant rant, I back toward the door. "But of course you are right, Physician. If this is your opinion on the art of healing, I must look for someone truly competent to instruct me."

I resist the compulsion to slam the door on my way out, but I do not bother to stifle my tongue as my feet march me down the street. "Condescending fool! I'd not train with you if you begged me! I shall simply find a healer who appreciates my skills. And then—"

I seal my lips at the askance looks of passersby and turn my scolding inward. *You are not in your cottage! Don't be caught speaking to yourself lest you become known as a madwoman, you loon!*

"Sound advice," I mutter.

It proves difficult to obey as each physician and healer turn me away with excuses or a scoffing dismissal. The reputable sections of town give way to the less reputable. Disheartened after speaking with every healer in the city, I begin seeking a position in apothecary shops, but those, too, turn me away.

Salome's parting wisdom has bolstered me through these trying hours. She vowed that the Almighty's ordering of our steps does not always look like open doors and fair skies. It can look like foiled plans and unfair circumstances. He is perfectly capable of using both to direct our path. If our hope is rooted in our plans or the outcome, we will be disappointed. But if our hope is found in Him, we will not be shaken.

"My hope is in You alone, not my best laid plans. I know Your way is better. Guide me, please." After the whispered prayer leaves my lips, it is answered with a kernel of peace. In the midst of all the uncertainty, it is better than a pound of false self-confidence.

Late in the afternoon, I rest in the shade of the looming stone wall of the new fort. Chewing a strip of salt pork, I wonder if the fort has been given a name. I have only heard it called 'New Fort' which seems unfitting for the grand structure that occupies the northwest corner of the town. Atop the wall soldiers make their round, appearing and disappearing behind the crenelations of the battlements. The grinding of the man sized gears that control the gate jolt me from my repose. The iron bars of the portcullis rise upward into the gatehouse with the clinking of chains. The rumbling of the ground steals my attention from the ordered movements on the walls toward the dust cloud rising in the wake of an approaching mounted patrol. The crowded streets part before the double line of riders.

As the soldiers draw even with me, I come to realize the shouting atop the battlement is directed at me. I crane my neck back to see the guard whom I can barely hear over the noise of dozens of pounding hooves.

"Aye! You cannot be there! None of you allowed in the fort. Go on back across the city."

What could he possibly mean? I have not done anything nor tried to enter the fort. "I do not want to enter the fort. I am only resting, but I will leave if you wish."

The soldier points across the city. "Go on with you! General Kannik won't allow your kind here."

Beginning to understand his inference, I shove my meal into my pack and rise, dusting my skirt. It was foolish of me to rest here. Few women travel alone. Fewer still would linger outside the fort with innocent intentions.

A rider has stopped before me, probably to ensure that I leave. I attempt to ignore him till he shouts, "You have it wrong, Smithe! This woman is a respectable healer not common baggage."

My gaze jerks up past the massive, armored body to the familiar, bearded face. If not for his bright eyes crinkled at the corners in merriment, the soldier would be terrifying.

The guard shouts down, "Apologies, Brigadier Anders. You know how the general feels about baggage."

"Well I know it!" Anders laughs and the guard joins in the shared jest. Anders swings to the ground, keeping a firm hold of his champing destrier. "Sergeant Smithe, tell the general I will be late giving my report. I have orders from the commander."

"Which commander?" Smithe questions.

"The one the general doesn't like," Anders replies making Smithe guffaw as he continues his patrol.

"Which one is that?" I ask.

Anders grins. "Both!"

Though I have always found Anders to be coarse beyond bearing, something in his demeanor softens me toward him, and I smile in answer.

"Sit. Finish your meal," he urges, but I shake my head. "What brings you to Chishelm, Healer?"

"I live here." The words are chased with my huffed sigh. "Rather, I will once I find work. And a place to live." Reminding myself that Anders did not interrupt his soldiering to listen to me complain, I say, "Thank you for intervening, but do not let me keep you from your important orders."

Anders gives me a long quizzical look.

I return it, waiting for him to elaborate.

He jounces his eyebrows, again grinning. "Perhaps I can help you get settled, and you can help me with my orders."

Glancing at the sun's descent, I cannot argue that I could use help if only to find a safe place to sleep tonight. "I would be grateful for your help, Brigadier."

He takes my pack from the ground then loops the straps around his saddle's pommel while I collect my basket. Puffing out his chest, he offers me his arm which I cannot refuse without being rude. As he leads me toward the center of the city, I tell of the places I have already inquired after a position. "I also have experience as a laundress, but I am not yet that desperate."

"Not a healer such as yourself." He assures me, "There is a position doing what you love if you'll give me a turn at finding it."

I must admit that the simple act of crossing the city is not half as exhausting at his side. The crowds part before him with looks of awe infused deference.

"Have you coin to let a room?" He asks.

I tell him the sum I possess down to the last copper. After hearing that I had twice journeyed to Chishelm to earn the money to pay him and been robbed the second time, Brick felt badly for pressuring me. Because of that, when I cleared out the cottage, he gave me the coins I had already paid him in exchange for the rest of the smoked venison, pork, and my other goods that I could not bring with me.

Anders's mobile eyebrows reveal his concern over the sum that feels a goodly amount to me. He pauses in the middle of the street, scrunching his face in thought. Like a rock in the river, people alter their course to accommodate Anders's presence.

I watch as he slowly formulates an idea. Turning me and his horse in the opposite direction without a thought to the people he knocks aside to do so, he guides me with a purpose to a skinny building of three stories squished between a tavern and a merchant's house. A midwife's shingle hangs above the door.

"You! Lad!" Anders hollers at a boy loitering in the alley by the tavern. The boy's eyes flare wide as if he's been caught in some mischief. "Come here."

Not daring to disobey, the boy approaches. "Aye?"

Anders drops his destrier's reins into the boy's hands. "Mind my horse."

The horse lowers his head, seeming to weigh whether or not he will allow the boy that privilege.

"Was that wise?" I worry as Anders opens the door and waves me inside the shop.

"Aye. Now the lad will be too occupied to put his sticky fingers into my saddlebags."

Startled, I glance over my shoulder to view the boy with a different mind. He and the horse are still appraising one another. Anders closes us inside the tiny shop. It is a dim, cluttered jumble of medicinals, crates, and all manner of items. With surprising agility, Anders weaves between the heaps. I attempt to follow his path without deviation.

"Hulloo!" Anders sings out. "I'm in need of a wife!"

I gape at him. Of all the ways he could help, this is not one I imagined.

"Midwife!" Comes a cattish correction from the depths of the mess.

"Having one would create a need for the other," he replies, catching me when I stumble upon something in my path.

"Seems that's not the way of it with you, you philandering

philistine!"

Anders grins. "A worthy woman could fence my affections."

She barks a laugh.

"You aren't holding the kisses of that little light skirt against me are you, my Tildy?"

Provoked past enduring, a wild golden head pops up from behind a teetering stack of crates. "Hie yourself out my door! The bawdy house is that way!" Flinging her arm knocks a trio of vessels from the top of the crates. She shrieks, vanishing behind the stack to gather the sherds.

It is not hard to imagine Anders's actions that led to their present discord. Though the state of this midwife's shop clearly begs for an assistant, I wonder at his brazenness for coming within earshot of the woman he scorned.

"If you want me to leave, tell me plain, my Tildy."

"Stop naming me that!" She screeches.

"Then I may stay?" He prods.

In a flurry of yellow skirts that clash terribly with her gold hair, the woman flies from behind her crates. Anders tucks me behind him, but I cannot help staring around his bulk at the strange woman.

"Get out! I want you out! I told you never to speak to me again!"

He pats the air between them. "Steady, Matilda."

Catching sight of me, she caws like a bird, her arms flapping outward and upsetting stacks of miscellany. "You wanton wastrel! Did you get this poor chit with child?"

"It is Brigadier Wanton Wastrel these days, Tildy. And like you, this woman is far too honorable to align herself with me." His puffed beginning ends on a note of what sounds like genuine regret. "Will you allow me to introduce her?"

She bobs her head side to side then folds her arms and stares across her left shoulder toward the door. "I suppose you will leave faster if you tell me why you dared darken my door."

I want to laugh at how Matilda makes a rhyme of her words, but I fear she would think I mock her.

Anders shuffles me forward. "Midwife Matilda, this is Healer Tirzah. She arrived in Chishelm just this day seeking work. She has trained beneath Healer Mamey and is well respected in her community. The Warrior Queen herself sought Tirzah's help to tend the battle injuries of Commander Ironforge and a foreign warlord. Tirzah is also a talented apothecary. She has come to Chishelm to advance her skills and gain more experience than her little community will afford."

Midwife Matilda considers me in the silence following Anders's high commendation. Her golden hair is mostly unbound from what was probably a knot atop her head this morn. Though she could give Leelah stiff competition for being the liveliest woman I have ever encountered, the fine lines framing her ordinary brown eyes whisper that she is nearing her fortieth year.

"Well? Are you as competent as he makes you sound?"

Sensing brutal honesty will curry me more favor with this woman than decorated truths, I say, "I have done all he claims, though my accomplishments sound better strung together on the same thread than they have a right to."

A smile tweaks the corners of her mouth, but it is not permitted freedom. "How so?"

"I was the queen's second choice to tend the injuries of her commander. The castle's physician was occupied with grave injuries at the time."

"Did you heal the commander?" She interjects her question.

"I did, though I believe the Almighty is the ultimate healer, and I am but his instrument. Cleansing the wound and applying a daily poultice drew out the commander's infection. The warlord had a finger severed, but the injury was several days old when I saw it. I treated his mild infection and ensured the finger remained clean while skin grew over the stump."

"To make a potent poultice you must be competent with apothecary," she notes.

Without bravado I state, "Apothecary is my strongest skill."

Matilda inquires in great detail after my other strengths and weaknesses as well as the amount of practice I have with midwifery. It comes to my notice that while we speak, Anders is absolutely silent. Judging by the way he voraciously stares at Matilda, perhaps he is hoping that she will forget to banish him from her presence if he does not draw her attention away from me.

His brief feast is brought to a resolute end when the midwife announces, "I can pay you little for your apprenticeship; however, I can offer you a place to live and twice daily meals if you are not particular. I surmise you will need both."

A weighty burden floats upward from my shoulders with her declaration. "I would be too grateful to be particular, Midwife Matilda."

"Very well. Have you brought belongings?"

"They are with Anders's horse."

I sense him cringe at my routing her attention back to him, but she has already moved past the turmoil his entrance caused. "You had best go retrieve them, because he will not be permitted to enter my door ever again."

The raw longing writ on Anders's face, even in the way he leans toward her as she walks away, makes me sad. But this seems a love past the point of reviving, else why would the ferocious warrior yield without drawing a weapon?

He leads me back through the mountains of clutter to the door. With a deep inhale, he steps out the door and retrieves his irreverent persona on the bustling street. His destrier tosses its head at Anders's approach, lifting the waif clear off his feet. From his purse, Anders pinches a silver piece between his fingers. My surprise nearly matches that of the miniature thief. Anders flicks the coin into the boy's palm. "Honest work pays far better than thievery if you are persistent."

My experience is contrary to that, but I do not relate my story to Anders till the impressionable pair of ears have disappeared down the tangle of alleys.

Anders becomes sober, appearing the hardened man he rarely shows. "You were more than fortunate, Tirzah. Believe me when I tell that I am astonished you escaped unharmed and alive from those thieves." He makes a woofing sound, shaking his head. "Why must foolhardiness walk hand in hand with worthy women?"

I bristle. "Pardon?" Already I know my folly. He needn't slap me with it.

"Naught. I shall inform General Kannik, but there is little chance we'll find the curs." He pats my shoulder. "Be safe, Tirzah. Be smart, eh?"

"Aye, Brigadier." I back away as he mounts. "Thank you for arranging this. Truly." I motion to the shop, then remember with a start that I did not keep my bargain. I chase after him as he sets heels to his horse. "Anders! What of your orders from the commander? I was to help you."

He chuckles. "You have. Commander Trent will be most pleased that I looked after you."

"What has he to do with this?" I squawk, sounding like the eccentric midwife.

Anders restrains his stomping mount. "Trent cares for you, so I aided you."

My heart jigs to an uneven beat. "He told you he cares for me?"

Anders's booming laugh turns most of the heads in this part of the street. "Aye. His fists were hollering his affection when we got too specific in our compliments of you while swimming in our pints."

Before I can comprehend his meaning, he lets out the reins and trots down the street.

Matilda is hovering inside the door awaiting my return, but as she prattles a list of my responsibilities and guides me above stairs to the second floor workroom then up again to the third floor residence, the vast majority of my attention is bent around the idea that Trent's closest friends believe he has a care for me, a care so great that he would not tolerate lewd comments my direction.

CHAPTER FORTY-THREE

TRENT

April 12th

Solitude is expensive. Yet the view of a thousand stars in this tame quarter of the city tempers the sting of the cost.

I tug the letter from my pocket, again wondering how it is that Tirzah's words can act like a solid wall sprung up in my path. If she could see the way her words linger with me or the way I must find solitude to be alone with her letters, she would no longer think she has no place in my affections.

Woe's sakes, when did it happen? Her beauty captivated me from our introduction as did her teasing manner with my friends. How different might events have been had I pursued Tirzah in earnest and not been distracted by a flirtation with Silla that snared my heart? The candid healer would not have manipulated me for her gain. Verily, I believe she has been more concerned with my wellbeing than I have hers.

Commander Trent,

I rejoice to pair that title with your name. Forgive me for my selfishness in not offering my congratulations from the first. You shall serve the king better than any other. It pleases me to hear tales of your prowess flying across the kingdom. Most, I am happy that you shall no longer work in shadow to your detriment.

I write to you to confess that I have wronged you and seek your forgiveness. Repeatedly, I have taken the kindness that you offered me without restraint and made of it what I wanted then faulted you for it. Far easier for me to blame you alone for the events of that regretful night than to own that I was an instigator and wholehearted participant. I have been angry with you and refused to accept your sincere apologies because I wanted something different from you. I have been unfair.

A friend offered me insight that has been a revelation, though it makes me uncomfortable knowing that very intimate moment between us has been discussed openly among our friends. Do you also feel embarrassed?

We are strong in similar ways. You are compelled to rescue others and I must heal them. It allowed us to get along well, you helping me with my tangible difficulties and I attempting to heal your inner pain. But our weaknesses did not pair so well. You have a weakness for women. I struggle to see myself as other than a harlot's daughter. Though you did not know the cause, you sensed my insecurity and tried to rescue me from it by making more of our friendship than you felt. I wanted to heal your broken heart by claiming it, selfish and humiliating as that is to admit, but you know every inch of me, you may as well know the truth. I ask your forgiveness for acting so selfishly, then and till now.

I have wrongly withheld my forgiveness from you. Because the Almighty has forgiven me much, so I must also forgive. Please know that I hold no animosity or ill feeling in my heart toward you. I pray that the Almighty would bless you and be the antidote to your guilt as He has been for mine. His forgiveness is immediate. His mercy is depthless. His grace is life abundant.

Be well,

Tirzah

Were it possible to traverse the distance between us ere dawn, I would set out immediately. I would assure her that I do not fault her. How can she seek my forgiveness when I am the one clearly at fault? Furthermore, how can she forgive me without allowing me to make any recompense?

"It is not fair, Tirzah. You who hates unfairness must see that your grace is unfair."

Her letter cannot give answer. She told that grace speaks of the heart of the one forgiving the offense. Truly, I can see her generous heart that owns her mistakes and forgives those of others. How can it be? With every reason to hold me in contempt, she wishes me well.

I cast my eyes up to the stars, past them to their Creator. "If You love her, why have You not protected her? Her brother reviles her. I used her. Men slander her. How can You allow it to continue if You love her?"

The answer is silent, but implacably resonant. *The Thief comes to steal, to kill, and to destroy. I have come that they may have life, and that they may have it more abundantly.*

The darkness hiding in the caves of my heart bucks at the Voice.

Is that what I see in Tirzah, abundant life overflowing from the fountains of her heart with kindness and unmerited grace despite her circumstances?

I recall Leelah's courage as she stared into the visage of evil incarnate and declared with unwavering faith that the enemy would not prevail, how light seemed to shine forth from her, causing the darkness to quake and retreat. Even I felt exposed by that glory.

And our beloved queen, who though stained with bruises, showed compassion to the men that raised their fists to her out of fear for their own lives. I could not see their bondage. I could only hear the bellowing of my own bloodthirsty vengeance.

More contrasts come to mind when I think of Valor and Kragorn compared to Anders and me. Though far from flawless, Valor and Kragorn do not allow the desires of the flesh to override their principles while Anders and I have glutted our lust to the detriment of others.

My father's strictures could not curb me. I merely obeyed from a fear of punishment. Yet in my friends, I sense no fear. They obey joyously.

I feel a rumbling from the caves in my heart. Arguments waft like smoke. *I am but a man. My lusts for vengeance and for women are my nature. I am no more selfish than some and better than most. Have I not sought to uphold the Malesiirian oath to protect the defenseless, aid the hurting, and see justice satisfied?*

Again the guilt of my failures harangue me. I have not upheld those oaths.

I cannot find contentment in myself.

I want more.

I want life abundant.

CHAPTER FORTY-FOUR

TIRZAH

April 20th

Besides being an eccentric, Midwife Matilda's shop abides in a state of disarray because she is in such demand as a midwife that she cannot manage her storefront. She barely maintains her workroom. I deduce that her popularity is partly because of her skill and partly because she charges little compared to the other healers in Chishelm. It endears her to me for I understand the burden of paying for a healer when one is too sick to work.

I spend most of my days creating order in her shop then assisting her in the workroom. It is not long before she trusts me to blend the tisanes she most often uses and assist the patrons who require an apothecary while she is away.

Despite my gratitude for the position, I find myself missing the opportunity to tend the sick. I especially wish she would permit me to attend births with her, but she is too pleased to have me managing her shop. I also intuit Matilda is slow to trust and that I must prove myself to her before she invests time instructing me.

The tinkle of the bell above the door turns me from the shelf I am loading with medicinals. A woman enters dragging her sick friend who can barely stand.

"Bring her here," I urge and hasten to clear the space around the sick chair I have gently suggested Matilda not clutter.

"Please can you help her? She's been plagued with a cough and fever many days," the woman frets.

I help her lower the sick woman to the chair which is when the stench of illness mixed with perfumed oil invades my nose. Other details quickly pile on. The dinginess of their bodies. The revealing cut of their tattered dresses. The rouge stain on their cheeks and lips.

"Please," the harlot whispers.

Within her desperate plea, the woman I might have been collides with the woman I am. Far from the Almighty being against me, He has led me around every pit and loosed my feet from snares. My mother never forgot the good of her life before, and she instilled hope in me for the same. When a wicked man tried to bind me with the circumstances of my birth, the Almighty sent Mather to pluck me from disaster. He then sent Leelah to lead me toward Himself. He gave me abundant life. Perhaps, as Salome thought, the small disasters that combined to propel me to Chishelm were not His chastisement, they were His guidance. Staring into the world weary eyes of the woman I might have been, a surety of purpose takes root in me, quickly blooming like the first flush of spring. No one is willing to see past the depravity of this woman's circumstances. But I can. And I have the skills to help her.

It is not difficult to surmise that they have been shunned at every turn, if not for their status, then for their lack of coin. The sick harlot is listless, muttering in her delirium. Compassion rushes through me. "What's her name?"

"Lolly. My name's Clara."

Likely not their given names, their assumed names. It makes no difference. They were made in the image of their Creator the same as I.

"I'm Tirzah. How long has Lolly been like this?"

"It came on slow-like, with a cough and an ache in her head. Then the fever. She's been like this nigh three days."

I touch the back of my hand to her forehead then cheek. Her skin is aflame. I find the pulse in her wrist. It is rapid and weak. Her breath rattles in shallow gasps. "Of utmost import is the fever. If we cannot bring it down, she will not survive long enough to treat her cough."

Clara braces Lolly else she would slump from the chair while I blend a tisane for the fever. While it steeps, I set a bowl of water alongside her. I instruct Clara in how to cool her face and neck. The cloth absorbs the heat from Clara's skin seemingly the moment it touches her.

I spoon tisane into her mouth, praying she is cognizant enough to swallow.

"Good girl, Loll," Clara cheers when she gulps the liquid.

Matilda's tread sounds on the stairs. Relief loosens my tension. In such a grave instance, I am glad for Matilda's years of experience. "Midwife, the patient suffers from cough, fever, delirium—"

"What are you doing!" Matilda shouts.

I jerk around as she stomps off the stairs. Matilda's face is mottled with rage. "Those are whores!"

Clara whole demeanor hardens. I rise to protest Matilda's anger. "Midwife, she is ill. If we do not give aid she will die."

"Good! One less louse to plague the city." She points at the door. "Get out! Do not dare come here again."

"Matilda!" I gasp. "You cannot mean that. She is a person."

"No, she is not! She is part of a perverse pestilence infesting Chishelm and the whole of Malesiir!"

Clara has already hoisted Lolly upright. "A pox on you, fishwife!" Clara spits on the floor.

Matilda grabs a broom and swings it at Clara. Aghast at her malice, I can only stare as Matilda bangs the door closed and slams the bolt of the lock while the bell sounds its glad note.

"Clean this shop. They've undoubtedly left lice in their wake."

Though I know the way Matilda responded is no different than what most would do, I am astonished for I believed her a different sort and tell her so.

"You hail from a small village, Tirzah. You cannot know the misery brought to me by those strumpets."

I feel I know very well the dark bearded source of her misery. "You cannot hang all those women from the rope of one man's failure. Tis unjust!"

"Unjust?" She rounds on me. "When your future has been stolen by corrupt women who plied your man with drink and taunted him with their wares for the pittance of a few coppers, then you may tell me I am unjust! Until then we will never speak of this again!" Matilda tromps up the stairs but halts midway to glare at me. "If you aid those vermin, you'd best pack your belongings. You'll have no place with me."

My shock must be the desired assurance that I'll not circumvent her mandate.

As day plods toward night, my worry for Lolly will not leave me be. It feels wrong to disobey Matilda, but I know that the Almighty does not approve of her hatred toward those women. "What would You have me do? You know that I am living on a thread. If I help them and she learns, I'll have no where to go. I cannot return to living upon the generosity of Salome and Leelah. You must make a way for me."

Shame overtakes me for even considering my wellbeing when weighed against the certain death of Lolly. But how can I find her? There is one large brothel in Chishelm, but nearly every alehouse has its own set of women for hire. Beyond their names, I am not certain I could describe them well, so focused was I on Lolly's illness.

The stirring in my heart will not let me alone. I feel the Spirit of Truth prompting me toward action, but I cannot imagine how to help them.

"Almighty, You must direct my steps. How will I find them? Whom could I ask?"

Marching up to the bawd and asking if any of her women are ill hardly seems wise. But who else might know such women?

The thought hits with a swiftness that makes me giddy. "Anders!"

I clap my hands over my mouth and listen at the stairs. Thankfully, Matilda must not have heard. Rushing to the back of the store I dash off a note. A pounding at the door startles me, making me scrawl an ink line on the page. I flip the paper over and go to the door.

"Midwife! I need... the midwife." The man puffs air as though he has run across the city.

"Come inside, I'll fetch her." But Matilda is already descending the stairs, her pack across her shoulders.

"I am here. Remember, Tirzah. If someone else should call for the midwife while I am away, leave a note with your direction so I may find you when I return."

Part of Matilda's eccentricity is reminding me of the same things each time she is called away. I assure her that I will not forget. Of a sudden, I find myself with the privacy to execute my plan.

After drafting my missive, I enter the tavern adjacent Matilda's shop which I discover becomes less reputable with the falling of night. My plan to find a waif to relay my message loses viability since there are no waifs in sight. There are, however, soldiers. I gather up my courage and walk toward the nearest table occupied by His Majesty's Army.

"Forgive my intrusion," I begin then talk quickly, not allowing them an opportunity to comment. "Do you know if Brigadier Anders is at the fort or about the city? I must get a message to him."

My regret is instantaneous as whistles and brazen suggestions ensue. One of the soldiers who looks vaguely familiar offers me a smile and speaks over the others. "The Brigadier is not at the fort, but I can ferry your message to him if you wish it, Healer Tirzah." The lewd comments cease. With fresh eyes the soldiers appraise me.

His certain use of my name startles me. "Forgive me, soldier, you look familiar to me, but I do not recall your name."

"Regold. I serve with Brigadier Anders."

"Thank you, Regold."

The midwife returns long after Anders has come and gone. Thankfully, he did know of the women and where to find them to deliver the sachets of tisane, though it was a surprise for him to think of harlots being ill. Twas as if he had never considered the life they lead beyond the time he spends in their company.

I fill a mug with tea and pass it to Matilda. She murmurs her thanks and drops into a chair at the large oaken table that serves as her workbench. Despite the chaos in the shop below, Matilda's workroom is fastidiously kept.

While she drinks her tea, I make my pallet near the fire. There is a heaviness clinging to the midwife. I let her get to the bottom of the mug, then I refill it before asking, "What happened?"

She sips the steaming tea without waiting for it to cool. I join her at the table. After working to the bottom of that mug, she sits in leaden silence, staring through the table. I clasp her hand, offering solidarity. Matilda finally intones, "Birth progressed rapidly. Mother was well and strong, but the babe was stillborn. Cord was wrapped round its neck. Twas her second failed birth."

I squeeze her hand. There was naught she could have done.

She says, "Tis a heavy burden, being a healer. We do all that we can, but it is not within our power to undo death. When all that we can offer is comfort in the face of grief, it does not feel like enough. Be certain tis the path you are made to walk, Tirzah."

I do not want to disrespect this misery Matilda must bear—that all healers must bear—with an exuberant answer. Thus, I collect my words until I can reply with sobriety. "I feel a surety of my path in those quiet moments between the joys and the sorrows. This is my calling."

She motions to the kettle. I pour what is left into her mug.

"I regret my harshness with you earlier, about the harlots," she says. "There are many people, more than we can possibly attend, that need our aid, many of whom are impoverished. It does no good wasting our time and our resources upon those who spread disease and destruction when we can put that to better use upon those who will not waste our assistance."

She searches my face for my understanding but finds my silent disagreement. She addresses it with no small amount of honesty. "I know that I am bitter because I was betrayed, but that does not invalidate my choice. You have a generous heart, Tirzah. Do not let it be deceived by those who would prey upon it."

Matilda carries the rest of her tea above stairs to her room. As I lay upon my pallet, her words rattle like a loose wheel on a wagon. It is not for me or her to decide who is deserving of aid. Did the queen not call upon me to tend to both men involved in a vicious fight, one of whom was in shackles? As healers, we are called to heal. It is for magistrates and the king to decide where justice will fall. We are ministers of aid.

It was wrong of all the other healers to turn away the harlots for being unable to pay just as it was wrong for Matilda to turn them away on moral grounds. Better than most, I know that a woman may find herself in bondage to a life she abhors. How dare we judge her for something which she may not be able to escape?

Though I respect Matilda and find much in her worthy of admiration, in this, I must hold to my convictions, even if that means circumventing her instructions and risking my position as her apprentice. Who will help these women if I do not?

CHAPTER FORTY-FIVE

TRENT

April 30th

I stalk the outskirts of the wedding feast, keeping watch over the guests and royal family that now includes Valor as the queen's consort. The rolling hills of the valley are lush with spring grass and dotted with blossoms. The vantage from the chapel sweeps the length and breadth of the valley, proving assurance that none can ambush the wedding. Still, I struggle to find the warrior's blend of vigilance at rest.

I pick apart the crowd to find the diminutive bride which is not hard with her imposing husband never far from her side. Twas on this very hillside when I witnessed her freedom after being redeemed that I began to question if such was possible for me. Her transformation was not fleeting but has grown more evident with time. I pray that mine is likewise evident, particularly to the woman who has strayed from Leelah's side and been steadily approaching me for several minutes. When Tirzah is distracted by yet another wedding guest asking how she has fared since moving to Chishelm, I am tempted to intervene, but I resist. Perhaps she is not coming to speak with me. Perhaps she is merely making her rounds as women are wont to do. I do not wish to appear overeager by stealing her attention from her friends.

Though I fought the realization that my feelings toward her were not rooted in guilt or simple physical attraction, acknowledge them I finally did.

I am in love with her.

I catch myself clenching a fist around the hilt of my sword, perhaps wishing to slay the feelings that are a distraction from my duty to the king. Admitting it to myself is still difficult. While I have been attracted to her from our first introduction, it did not grow into infatuation, as did my attraction to Silla.

Grow is not the correct word to describe the shift from attraction to infatuation, for infatuation is a shallow feeling, lacking depth. It is thrilling at the time, but it can die suddenly. No, my attraction to Tirzah did grow. It grew into respect. Admiration. An overwhelming desire to protect her, care for her. A consuming guilt when I hurt her. It is why I had no paltry words to excuse what I did. I care far too much to make light of it. *Benighted fool!* I made her one with me in body but did not wed her first nor did I recognize the bond already forged between our hearts.

I draw my sword only enough to slam it back into the sheath. It does little to abate the tide of anger. Somehow, I must rebuild the foundations of what I tore down, though I wonder if I have a right to try. With the encompassing claim my position holds on my time, how will I manage to woo Tirzah? On the morrow, I escort the royals to Chishelm then make a circuitous route back to the castle where we shall stay for a short time. I am then to ride with Valor and Erianna on a tour of the kingdom allowing Valor to formally introduce me to his contacts throughout Malesiir. Such a journey will claim much of the summer.

As the crowd around Tirzah thickens, I shift impatiently. She will be in Chishelm near the second largest fort in all of Malesiir encountering hundreds of soldiers and tradesmen of all sorts who would be willing to overlook her lack of virtue for the chance at taking such a beauty to wife.

Over the heads of the guests, Anders tracks my gaze then cuts me a wicked smile and moves in Tirzah's direction. My feet are striding with the purpose of outpacing Anders before he can say or do something to incite me into adding blood to the queen's wedding, a sin for which she might behead me.

I flank Tirzah, ensuring her companions take note of me. They budge over, granting me room to say, "Would you care to dance, Tirzah?" a moment before Anders can interfere. Her breath hitches as she turns to me, but her eyes are uncertain. Anders throws an exaggerated grin at me, reminding me I am neither on the hunt nor the battlefield, though my demeanor suggests it.

I shift into my winsome skin, righting my intense expression with a smile and relaxing my posture. I extend my hand toward her, putting her in a position of accepting or being extremely rude for refusing.

Tirzah smiles at her friends and says, "Excuse me." Then her fingers alight in my palm. Such a simple touch should not be scorching, yet I feel branded by this woman. I realized how untenable freeing myself of my attachment to her would be when she arrived late yesterday with Anders's company and I lifted her from the saddle of her mount. Her hands upon my shoulders, mine upon her waist was like a spark to kindling. The regal amount of restraint I showed in releasing her then maintaining a few minutes of polite conversation proved I am worthy to wear the king's signet. Having witnessed my struggle, Anders has been laughing at me ever since.

As I pull her into my arms for the dance, I recall my objectives. Tirzah is not materialistic like Silla. The key to securing Tirzah's affection will be convincing her that she has an indelible grip on mine. To do so, I will ensure she notices that she holds my attention. I will also attempt to revive that effortless camaraderie between us. I also need her to learn that I have received grace but in a natural manner so that she will see it is genuine. All of which would be easier done if I were not so accursed distracted by her presence!

"You are fearful for the royal family?" Tirzah asks.

I meet her gaze which further befuddles my mind. "No."

"I can see your tension, Commander." Her smile is teasing. "The only incursion you need to be alert to is a four-legged, white, and wooly sort." Her fingers flick from my arm toward the distant flock languidly grazing the slopes.

"They don't seem intrepid." My tone sounds strained to my ears. I must do better.

Tirzah archly confides, "One would think that, but if you had seen their invasion of the fellowship meal while the rest of us were at Gathering, you would amend your opinion."

Her description of all the matrons shewing the flock away from their meal while the children stirred the animals into a frenzy infuses levity into my stilted mind. I chuckle and spin Tirzah fluidly in the steps of the folk dance.

Tirzah carries the conversation from one dance to the next, letting me adjust to the pleasure of her company. I ask after her apprenticeship with the midwife in Chishelm and guide her away from the dance when the effort of talking and dancing makes her pant. I loop her hand around my arm as we walk the perimeter of the wedding feast. I regret being bound to watch over the royal family when I would rather walk along the riverbank with Tirzah.

She stops abruptly, pressing her fingers to her lips when I again sweep my gaze across the feast, ensuring all my charges are safe and accounted for. "I have been chattering at you without ceasing."

I tug her hand away from her mouth. "Forgive my divided attention. I must guard the Rodiharians at all times, though I find the task irritating when I would rather give you the whole of my attention."

She tries to make sense of my comment but dismisses it. I must be more pointed in my regard.

"I am certain you feel especially alert given Nev's delicate state."

Lorennt's wife bounces their infant son in her arms and kisses his fuzzy head. She appears well to me. "What do you mean?"

She taunts, "Have you set aside your spymaster's skills along with the title?"

"If she is ill, Tirzah, I would have you tell me."

She laughs at me. "Only insomuch as any woman in her state would be."

Chasing the crumbs she drops, I lean close and ask lowly, "You cannot mean she is with child?"

Her chin tips up, a coy smile creating a fissure in my mind between thoughts of kissing her once eager mouth and our conversation about the king's consort.

"Why can I not mean that?"

"She has recently given the king a babe. Tis too soon for another to follow."

The amusement in her eyes warns of the coming candor which is sure to test my restrain. "Is it so inconceivable that they are in love and act on such?"

My restraint groans, threatening to crack. Oh, to be alone with her, away from the eyes of those who would scorn her if I close the distance between us. I unwind her hand from my arm and raise it to my lips. Lightly, I kiss her fingertips then press her palm over my drumming heart. "It is not inconceivable."

There is wonder in her eyes, begging for an explanation. I brush back the wisps of hair fanning her temple. Her eyes flutter closed. I feel my restraint fall to the memory of her soft skin. The pad of my thumb traces the curve of her chin, following it back to her jaw. My fingers cradle the nape of her neck. Perhaps no one will notice one kiss...

Tirzah jerks away, crossing her arms defensively. "Do not mock me."

"Mock you?"

"Aye!" She closes the distance between us and hisses, "You must think me credulous to believe you acted on love."

I won't let her resurrect that argument again, not when it is not the real battlegrounds. "It frightens you to think my feelings for you might be genuine, doesn't it? Or is the thought of being anything like your mother so horrifying to you that you are willing to sacrifice a future with me because we made a mistake?"

The wounded noise she makes tells my arrow struck true, but it hurts me to have caused her pain. I try to salvage the moment. "Please give me another chance. Tell me your forgiveness reaches that far."

"I *do* forgive you, Trent, but," she shakes her head, "I only want to be your friend."

My hope burgeons on a swift tide. "That is the first time I have heard you lie."

Fear muddies her wide eyes. She retreats into the crowd, and I let her go. For now.

Rapidly closing on my position is Anders. I see our exchange did not go unnoticed. "You besotted loggerhead," he derides. "Where's your sense? I've ne're seen you bungle a skirt."

I cut a glare at him, piqued by his ribbing. "What's it to you?"

He shoves my shoulder. "You rushed her and cost me ten silvers, that's what!"

"To whom?"

"Regold. He wagered you were too twisted up by the healer to snare her in a day. I stood by your unblemished record. Then you go and muck it!"

My ire spikes as I stare him down. Then his beard wags with his restrained mirth. I chuckle and scrub my hands over my face, feeling the tension leave me. My ideal of convincing Tirzah to let me court her in a single day is entirely ill conceived.

"To my thinking, you owe me coin, Commander Trent. But I'm a generous knave. I'll wager you for it."

"Speak it," I agree, needing a distraction from the healer presently dancing with that youth, Nate.

Anders points with his chin toward the bridegroom. "How long will the vestal wait till he disappears with his bride? I wager he's gone afore the golden hour."

"That's not a fair wager," I argue. The day before our departure from the castle, Lorennt and I were late to meet Erianna and Valor in their office. The ardor in which we discovered them had Lorennt gripping his sword. I restrained his hand, reminding him they were betrothed. However, the sight of his sister's well-kissed mouth proved too irritating a distraction for Lorennt and too enticing a distraction for Valor. I recommended she keep company with Lady Nev and let us attend to the final details of the travel plans, to which she agreed with flush stained cheeks.

"Then hand over the silvers now and forget the wager," Anders taunts.

Grumbling, I compromise. "I wager they leave at dusk. That is the best odds I'll give you."

Anders slaps my hand. "Done."

TIRZAH

I spend much of the wedding feast avoiding Trent, though I sense his persistent attention. Is he trying to upend me? It was everything in me to speak to him like a friend not the man that stole my heart and body. What could he mean by kissing me again? The vaguest thought that direction causes my pulse to rush like a river in the spring melt. Why is he attempting to fabricate feelings toward me? Is it a way to cope with his guilt? Surely he cannot be genuine.

Again, Trent's eyes find mine through the crowd. His smile snares me. My foolish heart is far too easy to capture. I must keep it away from him. His attention shifts to someone behind me which should have warned me to turn about but watching Trent is far too engrossing.

A deep voice over my shoulder startles me. "Loving you has been good for him."

"What?" I gasp, feeling the warm flush of embarrassment.

Valor smirks. "*Being* in love with you. What did you think I meant?"

I retort, "Groom or no, I'll not explain myself. Nor does Trent love me."

Valor's smile remains despite my pronouncement, but there is sobriety behind it. "For years I have prayed for him. It was the grace you have extended him that cleared the path for him to accept the grace of the Almighty."

"Then?" I ask, unwilling to infer something so important.

"Aye, Tirzah," Valor replies. "Trent is redeemed. He's been at

Gathering these past weeks, and I hear that King Boldizar has become a mentor to him."

Regardless of the valley between us, my heart soars for Trent. He has carried the burdens of his guilt and the shadows of this world's darkest pits far too long. I am pleased beyond speaking.

"You have naught to fear from him, Tirzah," Valor murmurs as Erianna joins us.

The radiant bride pokes his side. "We agreed not to meddle. Or was I speaking with a different churl?"

He catches her hand. "We did agree, thus, I spoke only of facts."

Erianna delivers her rebuke with a single arched brow. Valor receives it with a smile that scorches the air between them.

Mercy! I cast my eyes downward.

"Although," Valor says, "if someone were to meddle, it ought to be you, my Queen. Your plans go sideways far less often than others. Like Leelah's."

Erianna groans at the mention of Leelah's failed schemes. She touches my arm. "Forgive us for interfering, Tirzah. You need no one to tell you what you already know."

Valor chuckles as he tugs his bride back toward the dancers.

Trent moves into my line of sight once more, evenly dividing his attention between me and the Rodiharians.

What is it that the queen presumes I know?

Later in the day, I look for her to ask her, but cannot find her. I sense Trent steal upon me in the crowd.

From behind me, he murmurs in my ear. "The bridegroom wearied of sharing his bride. Look across the river."

I do as bid and see them walking hand in hand toward Valor's home. Their home. A tiny sigh skips across my lips. "They deserve all happiness."

The warmth from Trent's body glances across my skin as he whispers, "You do too." I feel the gentlest brush of a kiss against the shell of my ear. It is so light it might have been unintentional, but the wild flutter of my heart argues it was not. His fingers lacing with mine for a brief moment answer resoundingly that Trent is pursuing me.

Erianna's statement then becomes clear. No one needs convince me of what I know and want. I must simply acknowledge it to myself.

CHAPTER FORTY-SIX

TIRZAH

May 1st

"Plans have changed," Anders informs me as he tromps into Leelah's kitchen in the dark of the morning following the wedding.

I continue stirring the porridge while watching him pour a mug of tea. "How so?"

"Lady Nev and Queen Celiea have decided to remain with Leelah while their men go to Chishelm. I'll be staying here to look after them."

I set the spoon down. "Will I still be able to return? I told Matilda I would be gone only a day."

He drinks deeply of his tea then slurps the moisture from his mustache with his lower lip. "O'course. Commander Trent will escort you."

If he speaks true, then I will be the only woman among the large company of soldiers and the kings. "Is there anything the matter with the women?"

His shoulders jounce. "Not that I was told."

I take up the spoon and stir the porridge vigorously.

"If you still mean to return, I'll saddle your horse," Anders says.

"Of course I mean to return. I must."

He sneaks alongside me and dips a finger in the pot. I shout and smack his hand away. He waggles his brows at me as he pops his finger in his mouth on his way out the door.

My flustered thoughts do not find a perch though I busy myself filling bowls with porridge and mugs of tea. Karris arrives to carry the breakfast above stairs to the women and to feed her siblings. She assures me that everyone is well, but Lady Nev is particularly tired from the days of travel and the wedding.

Leelah is in a similar condition after orchestrating the wedding. Though Mamey believes her fully recovered from what she endured at the hands of the Wolves, her time is nigh. Hoping to give her a full morning of rest, I assured her I was capable of preparing breakfast for her family and the royal guests to keep her abed. Thankfully, the large company milling about the courtyard and camped outside the Tareth's walls are able to feed themselves from their rations.

When King Lorennt and King Boldizar enter with packs over their shoulders, I quietly serve them while they converse. Trent enters but a moment later. Though I try to ignore him, a nervous energy courses through my limbs. It banishes my lingering fatigue from rising early.

The men discuss all manner of things, most of which I know nothing, until they discuss the reoccurring thefts along the road. "Tirzah was one of the victims," I hear Trent say. "Thankfully, all they stole was her coin."

I pause scrubbing a dish to agree with him. Though I knew he would be disturbed that such had happened after his many warnings, the taut violence, like that of a drawn bow, limbing his motionless body is frightening, even knowing it is not directed at me. *This is a death-dealing warrior*, I remind myself, lest I forget again.

The kings are equally grave, but Boldizar expresses compassion. "That must have been frightful for you. Then to have to continue on in the dark after being set upon... I am sorry you suffered that."

He described it quite accurately. It was horrifying. "Thank you, Your Majesty."

"Were you injured?" He asks.

"Not badly," I say, but Trent must not have known I sustained any injury for his gaze darts anxiously around my face and person.

Kragorn's enters the kitchen and sets a stack of bowls in the washbasin. "Thank you for breakfast, Tirzah. Leave these for the girls. Leelah wishes to say farewell."

"Is that all she has to say?" I tease.

Creases about Kragorn's eyes form his answering smile.

Leelah does eventually say farewell, but only after extracting every detail of what passed between Trent and I at the wedding. She is happy as can be plotting our courtship and perhaps more happy to have proved Kragorn wrong for once. She, after all, knew that Trent held me in regard. I am taken to task for being unable to stay to deliver her of her babe, an event that could take place any day. Her one consolation is that Trent and I will be in Chishelm together.

The men are in the courtyard when I descend. I hand off my pack to Anders whom I assume tended to my borrowed horse. It seems something has gone awry.

"Sorry, Healer," Anders shrugs his brows. "Your horse has thrown a shoe. No time to set it."

"Truly?" I query.

"Truly," Trent answers, striding from the stables. "I sought the truth myself."

There's an amount of reproach in his tone directed at Anders who only grins. "There is not another palfrey."

"What am I to do?"

"Toss me her pack," Lorennt orders. "You will ride with, Trent."

Since I cannot argue with the king, I follow Trent toward his dun horse. "I feel maneuvered," I confess as he tightens the girth of the saddle.

"As do I." He slides his fingers between the horse's belly and the strap. Satisfied, he pats its flank. Motioning me forward, he sets his hands upon my waist. With a mischievous grin he hoists me to the fore of his saddle. "But I will not complain."

Along the road, Trent asks me to point out where I was set upon. I do my best but it was very dark.

The soldiers are alert to danger, but surrounded with this large company, they are surely the greatest danger on the road. None would dare test them.

I try not to shift too often, but this military trot is uncomfortable. Trent takes notice. "Would it help to turn in to me?"

"Probably," I admit. "But how would that look to your men?"

"Like you are my woman."

The bald statement startles me. He meets my eyes for a moment, nothing of teasing in them. What has changed that he is now pursuing me as a man in love? Can I trust it? If I do, will he interfere with my learning to be a healer? What would he think of my call to help the harlots against the wishes of the midwife? With the press of soldiers around us, I do not dare ask. Nor do I dare turn and wrap my arms around him.

Rather than going straight to the fort, the company advances through the streets of Chishelm behind the king's standard bearers. A joyous shout rides the dust of the streets high into the air. Trent's arm around my waist is implacable against the rises and twists of the street.

When we near the side street leading to the midwife's shop, the king passes my bag to Trent, and we break from the company parading the streets. I do not recall telling him precisely where the shop is, but he stops outside its door without any direction.

"How?" I question as he swings to the ground.

I go into his arms that lower me easily. There is a strength in him that is not obvious, but I feel it beneath my hands braced on his chainmail clad shoulders and in the strength of his answer. "Anders, Regold, and many others have been watching over you since you entered Chishelm. They know I care for you."

Hidden between Trent and his horse, the bustle of the streets fades. I forget to move away from him, not that he releases me. His hands made bulky with his gauntlets are snug in the curve of my waist. All those questions I wanted to ask bubble then subside, excepting one.

"Are you earnest, Trent?"

"I hate that I gave you reason to doubt me. I should not have plunged ahead with you without knowing my heart. What Kragorn said was true. Our strengths and weaknesses did coalesce into something that should not have been, incredible as it was."

The memory does not embarrass him as it does me. It sits boldly in his thoughts as he stares at me. I realize, "You are no longer overcome by guilt."

He shakes his head with a half smile. "I have your forgiveness and that of the Almighty."

Truth resounds like a clear bell in his words. Before the resonance of it ends, he says, "I am in love with you, Tirzah. I wish to court you and make you rightly mine. Will you let me prove myself to you?"

TRENT

I canter up to the fort, clinging to Tirzah's answer. Had that eccentric midwife not burst through the door to steal Tirzah from me without acknowledging my presence, I choose to believe she would have answered with more enthusiasm. Instead, as she was pulled into the shop, Tirzah offered me a reserved nod. Unlike nearly every man and woman I have met, I can trust the veracity of such a simple gesture from Tirzah. I wonder how soon my obligations will permit me to call upon her. As the fort breaks over the heads of the lesser buildings, I fold up those soft thoughts and tuck them away. Today is a day for swords.

I receive a volley of salutes as I enter the fort and pass my mount into the hands of the stable lads. In the great hall, General Kannik is reporting on the completion of the fort to King Lorennt and King Boldizar. Kragorn, however, stands far to the flank of Kannik, eyeing him like a ravenous bear. The uncontrollable twitch in Kannik's sword hand is telling.

I salute Lorennt and fall in with him. Kannik grudgingly acknowledges me with a bow of his head as he speaks. My appointment to commander has been a bitter gall he must drink at our every meeting. I do not doubt that it has occurred to him that his refusal to aid Leelah and thereby the queen made it possible for me to prove my capability and gain the king's notice. He must have wondered what he could have earned by being the one to claim the glory of rescuing Leelah and subduing the Ruphiri from the outset of Leelah's capture. It will never be known. After today, he will know nothing more unless Kragorn is in a merciful mood. I glance past Kannik to Kragorn and smirk. No mercy to be found there.

Lorennt wearies of Kannik's stalling. "Have you all the information you need to take control of the fort, Commander?"

"Aye, Sire."

Kannik grabs for a thread of hope. "Am I to receive a new appointment, Majesty?"

Lorennt belittles the condemned general with a grunt of laughter. "Did you think your incompetent handling of the capture of Mistress Tareth would go unanswered? You were tasked with guarding Chishelm and hunting the Ruphiri. Because of a petty rivalry, you willfully neglected your duty. Any general of sense would have personally cast a net for the enemy swimming directly under his nose. You, however, let them pass despite having been pointed in their direction."

Lorennt's indictment is delivered in the hearing of all those who paused their duties to listen. Since Kannik's disregard of the law was within sight of those he commanded, his punishment will be equally public.

"Moreover," Lorennt continues, "you have egregiously slandered Queen Erianna. If what Zar Torvarik tells is true, your words to the queen were utterly treasonous. I do wonder, was that your hope in refusing to aid Mistress Tareth? Knowing our queen would ride to her aid, were you hoping to avenge yourself on the queen and Commander Ironforge by seeing her... What was it Torvarik said?" The king asks of me though I know of a certain he has not forgotten. Lorennt burned with rage as did we all when Torvarik relayed Kannik's words. Only under duress did Erianna confirm he spoke true.

I relate, "When Kannik crossed paths with our queen as she was riding to save Mistress Tareth, he said to her, 'Soon the Limban whore will writhe beneath the Ruphiri dog and rid our kingdom of two great evils.'"

The statement has the silencing effect of thunder on the murmuring soldiers. It also leaches the color from the ignominious general's face.

"I have been much occupied of late," Lorennt says, "far too engrossed in the affairs of kingdom and family to attend to you. Until today."

Kannik holds steady and silent under the king's discipline, however, the vengeful gaze of the usually contemplative Boldizar causes him to flinch.

"Today, Kannik, your accounts have come due. There is one to whom you owe an outstanding debt of honor. Alongside that debt, you shall feel my judgment."

No longer can Kannik resist looking over his shoulder at the menacing general behind him.

"Ready him for a trial by sword, Commander," Lorennt orders and strides with his father toward the outdoor training rings.

I motion Regold to my side. "Fetch a scribe and join me in the general's room."

In silence, I observe Kannik don his armor, ensuring he does not secret any weapons upon his person. He is only permitted those items of a warrior worn upon his weapons belt. The scribe documents Kannik's final wishes regarding his body and the distribution of his possessions and property to his family.

I add, "The queen wishes you to name the harlot and your bastard son among your beneficiaries."

Kannik's disdain is powerful, but he knows the "wish" of the queen is a requirement, thus, he complies.

All the occupants of the fort surround a training ring in the fort's bailey. I can see that it was chosen for the superior vantage afforded from the walls and roofs of the outbuildings which overflow with bodies.

Regold and I follow Kannik through the hole in the wall of soldiers pressed shoulder to shoulder. Boldizar and Lorennt await on the far side of the ring. Kragorn kneels in its center, head bowed. He looks up as Kannik enters. His righteous vengeance blazes like an unquenchable fire. Did Kannik not feel death at his heels, he feels it now.

King Lorennt throws his voice to the far corners of the bailey. "A trial by sword has been demanded of General Arne Kannik by General Kragorn Tareth. General Kragorn, state your validation for the claim."

"I call his honor as a man and a soldier of Malesiir to account. Because of his insolent pride, he rejected our vows of conduct by refusing to aid my defenseless, injured wife who was taken captive by the Ruphiri from our home in the sight of my children. My wife who is with child protected our home and children like the warrior she is, but like a petty child, Kannik refused to give aid and prevented the then Sergeant Trent from leading a company to her rescue. Kannik is not worthy of the title of general, not even that of a man."

An enraged murmur flies from the gathered soldiers. That Kannik refused to protect the wife of a fellow soldier, who was with child no less, is despicable. Add to that the respect Kragorn has earned from his decades of service to the crown, and their ire toward Kannik doubles.

Lorennt then foments their ire into bloodlust. "To that charge, I add those of the crown and name General Kragorn the instrument of my judgement. General Kannik, I charge you with three counts of dereliction of duty, two counts of slander of Queen Erianna, and one count of treasonous speech. To all these charges, I demand you give answer. What say you in your defense?"

Kannik holds his head high. "I stand by my actions. My sword shall speak my defense."

Having satisfied the legal verbiage of the trial, Lorennt raises his hands to the generals, signaling the onset of Kannik's demise. They raise their swords in response. Lorennt commands, "For honor! To the death!"

The rhythmic stomp of soldiers becomes a drum beat for the oncoming clash. A bestial roar rips from Kragorn's throat as he charges Kannik who parries the first downward hew, but the rapid twist and upward second cut unbalances him. Kragorn thrusts, drawing first blood. There is unparalleled ferocity in his attack that makes Kannik fend off the cuts but not all despite being an accomplished swordsman. Rage pours from Kragorn in howled blasts. It is unsettling to watch. Never have I seen him release control of his emotions in a battle. Kannik sees his death in that fury. Terror flashes across his face.

Kragorn swipes his legs. Kannik stumbles. Before he can raise his defense, Kragorn drives his sword down through Kannik's neck. The soldiers fall silent. Kannik sputters. Still Kragorn yells. He shoves Kannik's body from his sword with a booted foot then ends his suffering. His shoulders heave as he towers over the slain general.

The silence is impenetrable. Even the king does not say anything, forgetting his duty to name the victor. Kragorn stalks from the ring, his sword gleaming crimson. The soldiers part a wide path for him. Once he rounds the corner into the keep, Regold murmurs, "That was no trial. It was an execution."

In stilted action, Lorennt takes control of the scene, naming Kragorn the victor and ordering the body removed to the city for burial. I turn to follow my friend.

I overtake him on the stairs. He is limping heavily, though Kannik never dealt a single cut. He enters the room where his belongings were set. He wipes a cloth over his blade, removing the worst of the gore then sheaths it.

"The king wants to give you command of the fort," I say. "Will you accept it?"

He intones, "If Leelah survives the birth."

All for her. His rage. The ferocity. It was recompense for Kannik's refusal to protect Leelah, for the month Kragorn endured fearing he would lose his wife and the fear still gripping him.

"You felled him quickly. Honorably."

Kragorn drinks from his water skin then stows it. He swings his pack over his shoulder. "The temptation to make him suffer was too great to do other. The Almighty takes no pleasure in the death of the wicked. Neither should I."

Lorennt waits in the great hall. Kragorn salutes him and leaves for Parse Kítaran without a word.

"Will he accept it?" Lorennt asks.

"Indeed." I claim the position for Kragorn, believing in the happy outcome he struggles to see.

"Until then, Fort Dead Wolf is yours, Commander."

CHAPTER FORTY-SEVEN

TRENT

May 3rd

Wax puddles on the folded edge of the page. I press my signet into it and add it to a small pile as the expected knock sounds on my door.

"Come."

"Commander," the soldier salutes then proffers several letters.

Recognizing the handwriting upon the topmost, I flip it and break the wax seal while the soldier waits.

Trent,

It pleases me to tell that Leelah has been delivered of our babe and is recovering well. She has given me a beautiful, healthy daughter. It is our wish to honor you by naming her Cuylah. We shall ever be grateful for the aid you gave her and Leelah. Unless you object to the name, Cuylah her name shall be.

Please convey the news to Tirzah and inform her a letter from Leelah is forthcoming with all the details of the delivery that are the purview of womenfolk. I shall spare you such. Leelah recounts the birth with all the grim delight that we recount a favorite battle.

Kragorn

Leelah wishes me to add that Cuylah shall be her name even do you object.

I chuckle, feeling nearly as amused by Leelah as I am honored by my friends' choice in name. Releasing the guilt that consumed me over not sooner freeing her has been a process. I have come to a place of trusting that the Almighty provided the opportunity when He wished it, and the matter was beyond my control. Though Leelah and Erianna bear emotional scars from their captivity, seeing them thrive on this side of the trauma has been a balm to me. Their earnest insistence that I did help them amid their trial has also penetrated the barrier of my self recrimination allowing me to view my actions from their perspective. The aid I gave will always be less than what I desired, but I can see that the Almighty used me to protect them from greater harm.

I tuck Kragorn's letter atop mine beneath the string wrapped around the book I selected as a gift for Tirzah. Having noted her tattered few volumes on healing and apothecary, I sought a medical text to augment her collection, as Erianna suggested. This is not the sort of book a woman would typically be allowed, but I know my healer will appreciate the recently printed anatomy text that goes into much detail with accompanying illustrations to describe the workings of the human body. To prevent a scandal, I ensured it was wrapped in muslin when I purchased it.

"Have Regold deliver this to Healer Tirzah." I extend the book and accompanying letters. "These," I present the letters for the king and those dealing with other martial matters atop the personal stack of letters identical but for their direction, "are for the courier."

Anticipation rolls over me in the wake of his departure. Much I have set in motion this day to prove my love for Tirzah. With her determination to care for the harlots and outcasts of society, Tirzah is choosing to forfeit her apprenticeship with Midwife Matilda. So much do I admire her determination that I have set out to support her by inquiring after a new apprenticeship on her behalf from all the best healers, midwives, and physicians in Malsihra. I envision her surprised delight when I present her with a stack of requests from those talented healers asking her to employ with them.

The clanging of the bell in the training yard summons me back to my demanding schedule though my thoughts linger on my beautiful healer.

TIRZAH

May 10th

"There's another here," Matilda huffs her way into the workroom.

I grin and push to my feet, batting the wood ash from my skirt. She follows me below stairs to air her grievances. "Had I known accepting you as an apprentice would daily bring soldiers sallying into my shop,

I should have sent you elsewhere."

Despite my tacit acceptance, Trent has been persistent in his suit. Though his responsibilities have kept him away, he has sent a letter to me nearly every day ferried by one of his soldiers which irks Matilda, likely because it brings Anders to the fore of her mind. Thus, her complaint does not ruffle me. "You do not mean that. I am an excellent apprentice."

"You are an apt apprentice and an excellent apothecary, but your beau is bothersome."

The amused brown eyes set over a winsome smile awaiting my appearance make my heart cartwheel. "I can make other arrangements to deliver my letters if you would prefer it, Midwife."

My feet do a slow dance, swishing my skirt across the floor. "Commander Trent, this is Midwife Matilda."

I force myself to look away from him to make the introduction. At this time of day, Matilda's hair is springing in all directions from the knot atop her head. She looks Trent top to toe then shakes her head. "Silly sot."

"Matilda!" I hiss, but Trent laughs.

"Anders sends his regards," he says to her.

Matilda snaps upright with a glare that she fixes on me. "Take him to task or turn tail."

I open my mouth to do so, but she interrupts, "Not here. I have not patience for the nonsense of ninnies."

"Fetch your basket," Trent whispers. "I shall escort you on your rounds."

I squeeze his arm in thanks and dart up the stairs, an immovable smile curving my lips. Rather than tucking away all those questions that have been stacking up, I have been asking them of Trent in my replies to his letters. To my surprise, he has attempted to match my candor in answers. In regards to healing, he heartily supports my endeavors to aid the harlots, but he was concerned by my venturing into the disreputable parts of the city. Thus, he sent Regold to deliver one of his letters and play escort.

Realizing my dress is coated in a layer of ash from cleaning the fireplace and attached brick cookstove, I spare a moment to strip it from my body and don my clean dress. My fingers fly to ladder the laces across the bodice—fingers that have ash crusting the nails. I scrub them in the washbasin and take a rag to my face which is probably also grimy. I glance into the hazy looking glass, grateful my hair is still contained in the tight, intricate plait I wove this morn. I take a breath to quell my nervous energy. It does not help.

I descend the stairs as if unhurried. Trent bows to Matilda whom I can tell is mildly flustered by the handsome commander. He catches my hand, tugging me out the door and into the adjoining alley.

"I have missed you," he murmurs, setting his lips to my knuckles.

"Surely not, Commander," I banter. "There must be hundreds of soldiers demanding your attention."

"You think they are a substitute?" Still holding my hand, he opens it, kissing my fingertips one at a time. It is excessively romantic until I recall them covered in soot. It makes me snicker. Tis a good thing I scrubbed them.

He lowers my hand. "My kisses are amusing to you?"

His faintly insulted tone makes me laugh harder. Then his gaze dips to my mouth. My laughter immediately dries up. I dodge his gaze and tug him back into the street.

Being with him makes me slightly lightheaded, as when I imbibed wine at court. His letters have the same effect on me, but his presence is much worse. Or better. Certainly more intense. But I like it, this dizzy feeling he inspires. And the way he looks at me with his full attention. Especially that.

"You are talking to yourself," he says.

I gasp. "Not aloud?"

He leaves me wondering for a long moment that increases my worry. "No. Not entirely."

I dip my chin to my chest, relief whooshing out of me.

"You hum and bob your head as if having a conversation with yourself," he explains.

I groan. "That is nearly as bad!" Nearly. But not entirely. He could have heard my silly commentary.

"Where to first?" He asks.

"The Pike's Belly."

Conversation flows like a stream between us, merry and refreshing. He guides me into the alehouse then greets the proprietor. "Your girls above stairs?"

"In the brewhouse," he says. "Hard to believe a respectable healer wants aught to do with those strumpets."

Trent motions me through the door to the back. He stands in the threshold giving me space to tend to the women while he speaks amicably with the proprietor.

The three women that serve as maids and companions for hire are busy cleaning the brewery and boiling the malted grain for the next batch of ale. I talk with them in turns. The youngest woman, a girl of no more than sixteen, has a blistered burn on her arm. I give her a jar of salve and leave behind tisanes for all of them to hinder them getting with child. They are sincerely appreciative, although hardened and brash.

Trent praises me as we return to the street. "You are doing a good thing for them, Tirzah. Most people would not consider them worthy of help."

"True. The same men who disdain them are the ones who use them, and no women are willing to associate with them lest some of their ill repute attaches itself to them. It seems I am uniquely suited to help."

Though Trent escorts me without hesitation into two more alehouses and a tavern, our conversation is stilted. Perhaps I have been affected by the plight of the women, but it seems he bears a tension of his own. Outside the Corked Raven, Trent halts me, guiding me into an alcove where the alehouse ties into the adjacent building.

"Is there something wrong?" Of all the places we have ventured, this one is cleaner and the proprietor was the most welcoming of my aid to the five women that work here. However, there is a chance that one of them is with child. I am most determined to speak with her and ensure she is well.

Trent stares at the wall over my head, working his jaw. He swipes a hand over his face then looks at me, a frightening amount of resolve in his expression. I feel myself responding with apprehension. "This place is an old haunt of mine. I know the women here."

The tension in me loosens. "That is sad, unfortunately many women find themselves—"

"Tirzah," he snaps, jamming a rod in my spine with his tone. "I *know* them."

A slow pour of icy water flows across my skin. "You know them… Like you know me."

He cups my chin, leveling his eyes with mine. "Not like I know you. You might not understand the difference, but please try."

I feel dizzy again but not with giddiness. I feel struck.

"Which of them?" I hear myself ask.

"All."

I whimper.

"Oh, Tirzah." His thumb strokes my cheek. "I feared you would

314

learn of it from someone other than me. I did not want you to find out that way."

"When."

"Over a year ago."

"Were there..." I clamp my foolish mouth shut. Truly, I would prefer ignorance.

He takes that shield away from me. "Aye. There were others. It is something I deeply regret, as much for being one of the men to visit misery on them as for the pain it has caused you. When we found Ivy being peddled in that tavern, I learned of the horror that claimed so many of those women at a tender age. Since then, I have been at war with my lust. I have not won every battle, but I vow to you, it is a past life to which I shall never return."

When my mute stupor drags into uncomfortable minutes, he lowers his hand from my face. "Shall I take you back to the midwife's?"

I want to say yes. I want to be alone. But I cannot. Thoughts of the young woman who may be with child swoop at me with claws. "You are certain it was a year ago?"

"More than," he vows.

I nod and push away from him toward the door.

In a haze, I enter the Corked Raven. The proprietor is as boisterous as he was the time past. Trent greets him as he has done with the others, smoothing the way for me to tend to the women. They share telling glances after seeing me enter with Trent. When it proves a barrier between us, I answer what they are asking themselves. "He told me."

One of the older women with life-hardened eyes says, "Then why are you helping us?"

I meet her gaze. "Because it is not your fault for being with him more than any other man."

Trent and I exit the alehouse, progressing to Main Street as though strangers. Though the thought of parting ways and never speaking to him again does cross my mind, I need his help. "The youngest woman, Aiyla, is with child. It is not safe for her or the babe to continue working there."

"What must be done?"

"I believe Salome would take her in and that Aiyla would be amenable to the arrangement."

"Then she needs only transportation?"

I draw my basket in front of me and loop my other arm through it.

"Not only. The difficulty is that her family was in dire straights for coin. She was the second oldest daughter and the prettiest. They sold her to the proprietor. If she leaves, he will go after her family, perhaps claim one of her sisters. If she is to be free..."

My thought trails off when I realize Trent is no longer next to me. I look back to see him frozen several paces back. Then he darts into an alley.

"Trent?" I call, following him.

One hand braced on the wall, he is bent over a midden heap, heaving.

I draw near, but he waves me back. I wait.

He stumbles to the other side of the alley and collapses on the ground, his back against the filthy wall.

"Almighty!" He gasps. "Will I never escape my sin?"

I consider walking away, even look into the street, numbering the minutes it would take to deliver me to Matilda's door. I could find someone else to help me. Kragorn would certainly intervene.

However, as much as I loathe what Trent did, his visceral reaction proves he hates it more.

Like the whisper of wind across my heart, I feel the urging of the Spirit of Truth. *Grace.*

Are you sure? I argue. *It is not my place.*

The answer does not change.

Very well, I relent. *But I will not continue this courtship.*

Trent covers his eyes with his hand, the look of a man defeated.

At the sound of my footfalls, he drops his hand, squinting up at me. "You do not have to stay."

My accursed soft heart twists into knots. "I do."

He cannot look at me. "I thought admitting my mistakes to you would be the worst of today." His disgust with himself shades his tone with ugly colors. "I should have known... I should have never..." He bangs his head back against the bricks. "I should have never!"

Words take hold of my tongue. I crouch before him, setting my hand on his arm crossed over his knee. "The longer you belong to the Almighty, the greater you realize your need of his grace. The wonder of being redeemed and receiving grace you could never have earned does not fade. It intensifies. Which is why you will find those who are redeemed holding onto their new life with both hands, pursuing a righteous life with everything they have, and telling others of the miracle of being redeemed. It is not because we believe we are better than anyone else. It is because we know how greatly we need grace."

Tears streak his cheeks. "I hate who I was."

"Doesn't that make it all the more wondrous that the Saving Son called us while we were yet gripped by our sin? Twas nothing good found in us. It was only Him."

He nods, wiping his face against his shoulder. I slide my hand down to his, waiting.

He flips his palm up, clasping my hand with a grip that suggests I am dragging him out of a miry pit.

Trent guides me down Main Street, as sober a man as I have ever seen, yet his hand clinging to mine is telling of his shuddering grasp on control. "I am not certain of the legal recourse available to Aiyla. Kragorn will know."

"She has none." I explain, "In the eyes of the law, she has become property. She was sold to the proprietor. If he chooses, he may sell her or keep her until her death."

"Slavery is illegal in Malesiir!" Trent fumes. "How has this escaped legal redress?"

I shrug. "They are harlots. No one cares."

He rounds on me. "I care! This will not endure."

A flicker of understanding passes through me. Has the Almighty set Trent in his position of power to fight for the cause of those who cannot defend themselves?

A horn blasts above the noise. "Make way! Make way!" A soldier shouts then blasts thrice more on the horn.

Trent positions me behind him in the press of the crowd. I grab hold of the back of his tunic when the crowd jostles me, though his hold on me is steadfast. "Hold, Norte!" He waves to one of the men who immediately draws even with us while the rest continue to the fort.

"What trouble?" Trent asks.

"Commander," he salutes. "We were on patrol. Found two travelers waylaid, robbed, and left for dead. The man is barely alive. The woman," he spits in the dirt, "she probably wishes she was dead. We're bringing them to ole Therig."

"The poor woman…" I murmur.

I feel the spasm of Trent's hand on mine.

"Give me your horse," Trent demands. Norte obeys without

hesitation. I release Trent and back away as he swings to the saddle, expecting him to ask Norte to escort me back to Matilda's.

"Tirzah, make haste," Trent urges, reaching for me.

I lurch forward, fitting my foot in the stirrup and allowing him to haul me upward. The horse shies, but Trent reins him around, setting heels to him.

We follow in the closing gap left by the patrol. The organized chaos inside the indomitable stone walls is like that of a small castle. Stablelads take control of destriers, and men rush out of an outbuilding with a litter. The unconscious traveler draped across a saddle is carefully lowered to it. A second bundle is passed from a mounted soldier to another on his feet. I spy a dirty face peering from the bundle.

A stocky lad appears, taking charge of Trent's borrowed horse.

"Come," the commander orders, leading me toward the injured. A wizened man with tufts of gray hair sprouting above his ears and growing in a cape round the back of his head bends over the wounded man, checking his pulse and peeling back his eyelids.

"Physician Therig," Trent says, "I have brought you an assistant. This is Healer Tirzah."

The physician glances up at me and bobs his head in acknowledgement. "Healer. See the woman settled then attend me. My assistant is ill, untimely as it is."

"Tis always untimely when a healer is ill."

"Indeed."

Trent halts me with a gentle tug on my hand. "Stay with Therig. I must pursue the villains."

My heart squeezes when Trent spares a moment to press a kiss to my knuckles before taking control of the company rallying to hunt the wicked men.

A shrill scream whips me around. The woman is writhing inside the blankets while the soldier tries to carry her into the infirmary. I rush to her side. "It's all right! It's all right. You are safe."

She cannot hear me over her wails.

"Set her down and back away," I instruct the soldier, who does so with slow motions to keep from dropping the thrashing woman. I kneel at her side. "It's all right. I vow you are safe. No one will hurt you."

She fixes her gaze upon me and settles. "I am Healer Tirzah. I will look after you. What's your name?"

"Delwyn," she croaks, her voice shattered from screaming.

"Can you walk, Delwyn?"

Unsteadily, she pushes to her feet, clutching the blanket. I reach to help her but give her a chance to refuse. Instead she nods.

The soldier that was given charge of her waits near the door to the infirmary. He holds it open for us to enter then leads the way down the hall, quietly explaining the layout of the building for my benefit. He guides us into a convalescent room with a cot, pitcher and washbasin set atop a small stand, chamber pot, and a stack of blankets.

I help Delwyn to the cot.

"Is there aught you need, Healer?" The soldier asks.

"Bring a boiling kettle, two mugs, and a robe."

"Aye, Healer."

I unwrap the blanket from Delwyn revealing long flaxen hair and a tattered dress ill-covering her scraped, bruised body. I help her out of it, replacing it with blankets. While I wait for the soldier's return, I use the provided basin to cleanse the abrasions on her body. A tap at the door interrupts the soothing stream of words I speak over her as I apply salve to her injuries. I answer it and accept the items with gratitude.

"Name's Edric, Healer. I'll await your instructions in the corridor." He dips his head and exits, closing the door.

I blend a tisane for pain with another to induce sleep and set it to steep. I dump honey crystals into the mug in advance.

Once Delwyn is dressed in the robe and wrapped in layers of blankets, I strain the tisane and put the finished mug in her hands. As she sips it, I ask what Trent needs to know. "I know this will be difficult, but can you tell me what happened?"

The story falls piecemeal from her memory. "We—my brother and I —were traveling to visit our sister. On the way, we were set upon." Her eyes are distant. "Two men came from the wood. They demanded all our coin. When we told them we had nothing, they did not believe us. They attacked Crishoff. I couldn't stop them. When they saw he had nothing of value, they grew angry. They..."

She stops speaking as the tears that gathered while she spoke of her brother begin to fall. I take her hand, hoping to prevent her to succumbing to the torrent in her mind. "Can you describe the men to me?"

She shakes her head.

"I know it is difficult, but it will help the commander find them and

319

hold them accountable for what they have done."

"It was dark," she says. "I did not see their faces. One man, the one who spoke most often, was average height but very thin. Like a willow branch…"

Icy dread rushes over me. I want to add to her description, but I make myself listen acutely.

"The other was brutish. Gruff. Large. So mean." A sob shakes free of her. "He… he was the one who…"

"It's alright. You're safe now. You're safe."

"But, Crishoff!"

"I will go help with him after you finish your tisane."

At that, the young woman who must have a great deal of pluck gulps it down to the last drop. "Go to him."

I help her lay down and tuck the blankets securely around her. "Will your sister be worrying for you?"

"She'll be very worried," Delwyn murmurs against the pillow.

"I can have word sent to her. Where does she live?"

She casts an anxious glance at me. "In a high valley."

I startle. "She lives in Parse Kítaran?"

"Aye."

"Until recently, I lived there as well. Who is she?"

"My sister is Nell. She is the assistant healer. Her husband is Auld. Know you of them?"

The hateful thoughts I harbored against Nell turn acrid and accusing. "I do. I vow to get word to them. Rest. You are safe here."

I write a note for Trent telling him what I learned before leaving Delwyn to her rest.

I hand it off to Edric who waits in the corridor as he said. "Deliver this to the commander with all haste."

In a larger treatment room, Physician Therig is still working to save Crishoff. I wash my hands in a basin. "Tell me how I can assist."

"He has been stabbed several times and beat about the head."

I insert myself into the battle for the young man's life, praying over him as I assist Therig.

Once his wounds are cleansed, the bleeding staunched, and sutures in place, little more can be done. To give him the best chance, I spoon tisane into his mouth while Therig massages his throat to force him to swallow.

The remainder of the day passes in a blur. Delwyn sleeps through most of it, aided by my tisanes. I stay at her side when she is awake then help Therig work more Tisane into Crishoff's body.

Edric deposits a tray of food for Therig and I at some point. Near middle night, he fetches me from Crishoff's side. I find Trent waiting outside the infirmary. A knot behind my sternum loosens at the sight of him. Armored and plastered with reddish dust from a day's hard riding and likely traipsing through the wood trying to scare out the thieves makes him no less appealing. There is comfort in his assuredness, in the warmth that softens his commanding presence when I appear.

"How do they fare?" He asks.

I lean against the wall of the building. "Outwardly, Delwyn will be fine. But she has endured a horrific ordeal. Those marks are indelible."

Trent joins me against the wall, staring up at the glowing moon hidden behind a thick veil of cloud. The moon seems to wear a white halo.

He utters the thought that I have beaten back repeatedly. "It was nearly you my patrols found on the side of the road."

"It was. But we cannot dwell on that."

His silence is loud.

"We are doing all that we can for Crishoff, but it is too soon to form a conclusion."

Trent hums his understanding. "I sent a contingent to fetch their sister. She should arrive by morning. I am also devising other means of netting these thieves."

I roll my head toward him, tracing his profile in moonlight. It is still entrancing.

Stop. I check the softness of my heart. Did I not agree with myself that our courtship was at an end?

Trent says, "Though there are only two thieves stirring up this trouble, I am determined to make an example of them. 'Twill hopefully deter other such crimes."

"Good."

He folds his arms across his chest, clinging to these scant moments of repose. "I sent word to Matilda that you were still safe in my keeping."

"My matronly master midwife Matilda?"

He chuckles.

"Can you imagine Anders courting her?"

Trent smiles at the picture. "He would have loved every torturous second."

I frown, feeling something inside me tumble downward. *What if, in a moment of ale-soused weakness, Trent made such a mistake?*

"It would never happen," Trent murmurs.

I assure myself I did not speak that thought aloud then say, "What would not?"

He has turned toward me, leaning one shoulder against the wall. Reaching across me, his fingers trail fire down my arm till he catches my hand, lacing our fingers together. "I will not betray you. Not ever."

Perhaps it is unfair of me to harbor such a fear after witnessing his soul deep pain over his past decisions, but it gnaws at me like a louse. "Matilda probably believed that of Anders."

"Probably. But there are several differences. Anders is a happy libertine. If he has any guilt, I have never seen it. He may have restrained himself for a time to be with her, but it could not last." Trent's thumb draws circles on the inside of my wrist. "If you determine you will not have me, still I shall not go back to that life. It is not who I want to be. King Boldizar has told me that although grace is free to receive, it was costly to purchase. I will not spit upon what the Saving Son did by treating grace like it is cheap."

Almighty, protect me. I love this man. Please don't let our story be Matilda's. Peace floods me in response.

I rest my head on his shoulder, letting myself trust him, trust what is happening between us.

"You will stay in the room with Delwyn?" He asks, gently stepping back. "Edric can bring a cot for you."

"*Mhm,*" I agree.

"Good. Send word if there is any change," he instructs.

He stands watch until I return inside the infirmary.

The physician informs me there is no change in Crishoff, which could mean his body is beginning to knit itself back together, or it could mean it is taking all that he has to cling to life.

I rest in a chair in Delwyn's room, not wanting to sleep so deeply that I will not be alert to her needs. A hand rests on my shoulder, bringing me full awake. The blue light creeping through the window tells it is near dawn. I follow the hand up to the pained smile of Nell. So as not to disturb Delwyn, we remove to the corridor where I give Nell a full account of what befell her siblings.

Afterward, she hugs me tightly. "I am so grateful the Almighty placed you here to help them. Thank you, Tirzah. Over and again, thank you."

It is strange to see good come from my being thrust into Chishelm, where I wholeheartedly did not want to go. I feel the pinch of regret at having been bitter toward Nell, though she probably had no knowledge of my dislike. It seems we are both where we ought to be.

"Have you seen Leelah recently?"

Nell indicates she has. "She and the babe are well. Mamey has no cause to believe she suffered any lasting ill affects, and I agree. However, if you do not visit her soon, I am afraid she will march all the way to Chishelm to see you."

After collecting my basket, I leave Delwyn to Nell's care. Physician Therig's report is grave. Crishoff's color has worsened, and his eyes are no longer responding when his eyelids are pried open. Therig does not speak of the worst, but I infer his meaning. Crishoff is likely to die. The charges against the thieves will be raised to the hanging offense of murder.

I wander out of doors in pursuit of air not tainted by the stench of death. Though the sun has not yet rolled away the shroud of night, the bailey is thrumming with soldiers like ants in a hill. Officers shout orders that are answered with quick action. The dawn patrol makes ready to depart even as the call comes to open the gate for the night patrol. I close my eyes to the scene, letting the thrum blanket my senses.

The needs of the ill call to me. Is there another blend of medicinals that would infuse Crishoff with the strength to heal? Surely between Therig, Nell, and I, we can think of something else to try.

But his unresponsive eyes...

I rub my chest, wishing I could massage away the bruise on my heart. *Healers do not admit defeat.* I prod myself to action. *Go back and—*

Pain jerks me off my feet. I throw my arms out to arrest my fall, but my knees slam into the ground. I cry out.

"Get up!" A man barks. He fists my arm, hauling me upward before I can collect my feet beneath me.

Fingers take a deeper bite of my tender flesh.

"Stop! Please!" I pull at his wrist, but his grip is implacable.

"Silence!"

I still at the voice, praying, pleading with the Almighty that my ears are wrong.

When I dare look, I cannot argue with my eyes.

"Mather."

CHAPTER FORTY-EIGHT

TRENT

May 11th

Shouting in the bailey attempts to disrupt my meeting in the war room with the officers and city guard. I ignore it. "Tis all too easy for two men to leap into a den when our patrols pass. Increasing our presence will deter more thefts, but it will likely not net us the thieves. We must find their berth. They will be spending the stolen coin. If we plant soldiers at all the taverns and alehouses in Chishelm—"

"All of them?" A brigadier objects. "That seems a waste of swords."

"We plant soldiers dressed as common folk. Tis where they will be when not on duty regardless. I may as well buy their drinks in exchange for them tuning their ears to anyone boasting about thefts or spending inordinate amounts of coin. It is worth the effort."

"Who would be so foolish as to boast about ill gotten coin?" A captain argues, raising his voice to be heard above the clamor in the bailey.

"Thieves are fools above all and—"

Pounding on the door to the war room interrupts me.

"*Gah!*" I slam my fist on the table. "Enter!"

Edric pushes into the room. "Commander, you're needed at once."

I precede him out of doors to discover the source of the commotion. The soldiers have ceased all activity. The dawn patrol has not yet departed while the night patrol clogs the gate. I shoulder into their midst.

At the center of the throng I glimpse Regold standing beneath the portcullis with drawn sword, shouting, "I say you'll not take her anywhere without the commander's permission!"

The soldiers jeer and shout their own opinions, most supporting him it sounds.

"What goes here!" I roar, shoving aside the men in my path. A hole opens in the press of bodies. At its center is Tirzah, her arm held in the grip of a giant of a man that is none other than her brother. The same one who disowned her.

Why is he here? This is not his post.

Wrath boils beneath my skin as I straddle the line between the men. Tirzah's eyes plead with me, fear marring them.

"Commander." Mather inclines his head with respect he does not feel. He is a cross word from swinging those meaty fists. "This soldier is preventing me from escorting my sister home."

"I'll not go with you," Tirzah insists.

"Healer Tirzah is tending an injured woman at my request, Captain. Release her."

"You have no claim on her to make that request. If I say she goes, she goes." Mather marches her past me toward the gate, inciting the crowd with his disrespect. Regold still blocks his path.

Tirzah drags her heels, throwing a last look at me over her shoulder. "Cuyler, please!"

The woman knows how to move me.

I vowed to her, if this moment ever came, I would intervene. However, when I imagined this moment, it was private, not before two hundred soldiers all watching how their commander will act and wondering what history has given birth to this moment. My impulses urge me to cast off Lorennt's signet. To settle this with fists for every hateful thing Mather has heaped upon Tirzah.

Instead, I order, "Captain, Healer, join me in the war room."

Mather considers me. Obey the order to an uncertain outcome, or disobey the Hand of the King to certain punishment.

He pushes Tirzah ahead of him toward the keep. I motion Regold to my side.

Halfway across the bailey, I round on the soldiers protesting the end of their entertainment. "Have you caught the thieves? Are they swinging from the gallows? No? Then, move!" I bellow.

They snap into action, returning to their duties before the interruption.

"What happened?" I ask quietly of Regold.

"The healer came out of the infirmary, seemed to be getting some air. She was keeping to herself. Next I look back, Captain Mather is dragging her to the gate. It was obvious they were acquainted, but the way she was fighting him and begging anyone who would listen to fetch you, I knew something was amiss."

"She called for me?"

"Was in a right panic till she heard your voice."

An emotion fierce and hot fills my chest. "When you saw that, you stopped them."

"Aye. Then Mather's contingent fell in with him, but the rest argued Tirzah was yours."

I clap him on the back.

In the war room, the officers have begun demanding an account from Mather. I bang the door closed, silencing them. We do not have time to waste with the thieves running unchained, but Tirzah's fate is of greater importance to me.

"What goes in here, shall never be spoken of, understood?"

At the murmurs of assent, I turn to Mather. "Remove your hand from Tirzah or I shall sever it."

He complies.

She rubs her arm, crossing it in front of her body, and puts distance between them.

To the officers, I say, "Without the presence of the king or a magistrate to arbitrate, I must ask you all to decide between us on a personal matter. If you do not wish to do so, please leave and you will be summoned when we resume discussion of military matters."

No one does.

"We haven't time to pander, thus, I will be candid. Mather, you disowned and abandoned your sister. You have forfeited your rights as her guardian and cannot make her go anywhere."

Mather balls his fists. "I did so only because she claimed you as her provider."

It is a claim weighted with ramifications. If I am her provider, then she is my mistress. Though many of the men in this room keep women besides their wives, a kept woman loses her societal honor in exchange for provision and protection.

Tirzah is not willing to make that exchange. "'Twas a lie told to make you leave me be."

"Commander?" General Harkerse, the most seasoned officer, asks.

I confirm, "I am courting Tirzah, but she is not my mistress."

"Then legally, if Captain Mather wishes to remove her, you cannot intervene."

Tirzah bristles. "What of my will? Does that not matter?"

The general remains impassive. "Unless you can prove abandonment or that he has inflicted great harm on you, no, Healer. You are under his guardianship."

The injustice presses upon her. Again, she looks at me, asking me to find a way.

I consider the likely outcomes of this meeting. Mather could make good on his threat to sell her to a bawd, which is her greatest fear though I believe it unlikely. Of greater probability now that the entire fort knows of their kinship is his relocating her to his home in Klaptin till he can marry her off, something I cannot abide. Even if I do manage to free her from Mather, her position with Midwife Matilda will come to a swift end once the midwife inevitably learns that Tirzah is tending the harlots against her wishes. Tirzah will again find herself in this same untenable position until she is given a foundation of permanence.

"Send for an elder."

"What say you?" Mather demands.

"I will marry Tirzah."

General Harkerse's brows jut upward. "You mean to marry this day?"

"I mean this moment." With my attention demanded by the matter of the thieves, I cannot afford for it to be divided with worry for Tirzah. I will not allow her future to be uncertain or bleak.

Regret twangs a discordant note. Tis not how I planned. I wanted to spend months wooing her and giving her time to become certain of my affection. I hope she understands.

The general asks Mather, "Will you allow it?"

Mather glowers at me, making me await his answer. It is a petty maneuver but not nearly as petty as eventually saying, "If the commander agrees to the bride price."

The corner of my mouth quirks up in a smile that is not a smile. "Name it."

"That is not fair!" Tirzah objects. "I have no dowry, you cannot ask it of him."

Mather names an exorbitant sum. The officers object. Regold says, "Be reasonable, man!"

I extend my hand to Mather, palm up. Tirzah steps between us. "Do not do this, Trent."

"Regold, fetch my coin purse and the elder," I order then address my intended. "Is your only objection that it is unfair because you have no dowry?"

"Not my only, but—"

I bend close to her, lowering my voice. "You are a healer. An apothecary. An accomplished cook. An incomparable beauty. A farmer. A decent roof maker. An overqualified wife. Tirzah, you are your own dowry. And besides all that, you are the woman I love."

She is stymied. Mather slaps my palm.

I move Tirzah closer to me, away from Mather. That gentle touch on her arm causes her to flinch.

Black smoke billows from my smoldering anger. If he harmed her...

A knock at the door keeps me from enacting on my long restrained desire to fell this brute. Edric, the guard assigned to the infirmary, enters with grim news. "The man we rescued has succumbed to his wounds."

A chill makes a pass through the men, but it smites the healer who wears spots of Crishoff's blood on her dress from her efforts to save him.

Regold arrives on Edric's heels with my coin purse. It is good that I carry extra from the royal treasury, for I must borrow against my future earnings. Since Lorennt told me to take Tirzah to wife, I know the king would approve my decision. From the purse, I count out the gold and drop it into Mather's fist.

He jangles it then says, "When you learn she is not chaste, will you come for your coin?"

Lorennt's words flash through my mind. *Do it and be done.*

I cut my left fist into Mather's gut, folding him. My right rocks his jaw, dropping him in a heap. Gold flies from his fist and sings as it scatters across the flagstones.

Those are the last words you will ever speak to her, I vow, standing over his crumpled body.

"Come, Tirzah," I reach for my bride. "Your brother will not be permitted to see you marry."

My bride is best described as reluctant as I lead her above stairs to my room. Dutifully, quietly, she repeated her vows before the Almighty and the soldiers breakfasting in the great hall. Following the succinct ceremony when Mather entered the hall, General Harkerse approached me with advice while the applause still sounded. "Go make her fully yours lest he cause you more trouble."

Sound advice considering the malice wafting from Mather. Would my bride understand? It is not as though we must consumate our union. We must only stay in my room long enough to give the impression of having done so.

The general assured me, "We shall select the spies to plant as you ordered. They will be ready for your instructions when you return."

Before deciding, I appraised my bride. Having endured one shocking blow after another, her fragile expression could not withstand the scrutiny of sharing a meal in the great hall.

Standing in my room alone with her, I am not entirely sure this is for the best either. She looks disoriented, like a person coming to after being thrown from a horse. Her words prove it.

"Trent. Are... Are we married?"

"Aye, Tirzah."

I am not sure which is more piteous—the shock hazing her eyes or the way she holds her arm close to her body, unconsciously wincing when she tries to rub it to soothe the pain.

I guide her to a seat on the edge of my bed and kneel before her. "Tirzah, your arm is injured. Will you allow me to see it?"

She nods absently. Watchful of a shift in her mood, I unlace the bodice of her gown then the drawstring of her chemise, sliding the neck of the dress off her right shoulder and working the sleeve down to expose her upper arm. It is striped with angry red lines from Mather's fingers. She lets me help her fully out of her dress and slide her injured arm from the chemise. Her inner arm is dotted with large, red circles where his fingertips dug into the tender flesh.

When I look up, her eyes are in mine. If she can see my intent to murder him, she does not shy from it.

Regold's knock draws me to the door. I swipe her dress from the ground. I ensure he'll not see her, then open the door partway. He extends Tirzah's basket. The handle is broken, and the sides are collapsed as if trodden by hooves or boots. "Sorry, Commander. I found it in the bailey. She must have lost it when Mather grabbed her."

It is the final insult to all that Mather has done to her. It must be the last. He'll not survive another. "Why has he come? He is stationed at Klaptin."

"His brigadier sent him to give the martial report for their district."

Of all the days for him to arrive... "Tell General Harkerse to hear

Mather's report then remove him far from my reach."

"She is injured," Regold intuits. "Have you need of the physician?"

I shake my head, passing him her dress. "Have that laundered straightaway."

He dips his chin. "Sergeant Deben is informing the midwife and collecting the healer's belongings. Brigadier Anders has also arrived with his company. I wager he'd be happy to remove Mather to a grave."

"Tempting. Inform him what has transpired."

"Aye, Commander."

I close the door and hazard a glance inside the basket. The small clay pots of salve are smashed. Her carefully blended herbs float freely in the mess. It all looks ruined. An impulse tells me to hide it behind my back, to not let her see. This has been her livelihood. Her most treasured belongings are within.

"Trent?" The plaintive question stabs like a dagger.

I carry the basket to her, a tattered offering on a day I should have given her gifts, at least a wedding ring. I have nothing.

"Is there a salve or some remedy in here for your bruises?"

Tentatively, she opens the lid. Her chin quivers at the sight of the destruction.

"Tirzah?"

She crumbles inward and weeps.

"Oh, Tirzah," I murmur, setting the basket aside and drawing her into my arms.

That which she has dammed can be contained no longer. Sobs wrack her body. I know she cries for a hundred reasons, probably including our hasty marriage. But she clings to me, accepting my comfort, which I count as good. "It will all be alright. I have you. You are safe. I promise."

CHAPTER FORTY-NINE

TIRZAH

I wake incrementally, tucked into an unfamiliar bed. Golden light shines through the window. It must be late afternoon.

I prop myself upright and regret it. "*Ah!*" My right arm throbs. It feels hot and stiff.

Vague recollections firm into remembrance. Mather finding me... Attempting to remove me... Trent intervening... A room filled with judgmental men... Then...

I gasp and leap from the bed, looking round the room—Trent's room —with fresh eyes. The memories assail me faster. Speaking vows. Crying in his arms. Trent dropping Mather with only two blows. Gold scattering. Oh, so much gold...

I burry my face in my hands, spinning with the rush of feelings. Ashamed of what Mather did. Aghast at Trent's decision. Appalled at myself for being so helpless.

"What have you done? After all your hard work, you still find yourself right here! How?"

But I have no answers for myself. Hence, my current predicament— standing in my chemise in Trent's room.

"Where is my dress?" It has vanished, but my stockings are neatly folded atop my shoes. Did I do that? My memories are hollow between crying and waking.

Next to my shoes is my pack. I know that was not my doing. It should be in Matilda's workroom. Trent must have retrieved it. What did he tell her? Am I no longer to apprentice with her?

I want to sit on the floor and scream my frustration at the questions that peck me like birds, but sitting on the ground will not solve a thing.

I dig out a dress from my pack and make myself decent. There is not a looking glass in the room, but my fingers tell me the mess my hair has become. I last plaited it yesterday morn before Trent called on me at the midwife's. Heavens, but that was an eternity ago!

A cooled platter of food sits on a desk. When did that come to be there?

"*Bah*! No more questions! Answers only!"

I try to exit Trent's room, but the door is locked. Did he lock me in? I stomp my foot. Surely there is a key hidden somewhere.

I begin opening drawers only to find a key sitting in a prominent position next to the food. "Oh." He did not lock me *in*. He locked others *out*.

Not until I am upon the stairs near the landing do I pause to consider if I ought to have left the safety of the room. What if Mather is about? Surely he would not dare take me from Trent, not now.

A caress floats across my mind in Trent's voice. *It will all be alright. I have you. You are safe. I promise.*

"Mistress Trent, can I be of assistance?"

The soldier startles me from my reverie, causing me to look behind me. Mistress Trent?

He stares, waiting on my answer.

"Almighty," I whisper, slapping a hand to the wall to steady my weak knees. *I am Mistress Trent.*

The soldier braces me beneath my elbow, guiding me to a nearby bench. I immediately feel foolish for my overreaction. "That is not necessary. Is the commander... my husband," Oh, but that is strange! "Is he... *Where* is he?"

"In the war room, I believe. Do you wish me to deliver a message or... deliver you to him?" His voice inflects an additional question at the end, as if uncertain if he is permitted to do such.

"No, he is much occupied. I will visit the infirmary."

"Do you require assistance?"

I wave him aside. "Not necessary. I am well."

As he walks away, I think to call him back to inquire Mather's whereabouts so I can go the opposite direction, but I don't. I shall keep watch for him myself. What miserable timing for Mather to have found me in the bailey, appearing to his eyes like the worst moment of his life repeating itself. Miserable, miserable timing.

There is naught for me to do in the infirmary. With Crishoff's passing, Nell attends fully to her sister. She tells that they have plans to leave for the valley on the morrow, if the soldiers can be spared for the escort.

I remove to the bailey, watching the comings and goings of the soldiers, but I leave with the feeling I am not supposed to be there. I have become an object of speculation to the men. It sends a crawling feeling across my shoulders to be observed by them.

Back in Trent's room, I find my ruined basket hidden in a corner. He likely was worried I might come undone at seeing it again. However, his concern is unwarranted. The basket was merely the last drop that caused my bucket to overflow.

I pick at the food on the platter while setting to rights what I can. Sadly, it is not much. Provided with new pots, I might be able to preserve some of the salves, but there is much that is rubbish.

Consumed with my task, I do not look up until a key scrapes in the lock. Trent pushes into the room. His concern eases into a smile as he looks me over. "My room smells of you."

"Like medicinals?" I guess.

"Never quite the same, but always fresh. Like my mother's herb garden."

The description pleases me. "Is hers a large garden?"

"Not as large as the one you planted at the cottage."

My dear little cottage. Without that garden, I shall be hard pressed to restock my medicinals. I must forage for more soon.

"Did you sleep long?" He asks.

"Until late afternoon."

"Good. Did you tend your arm?"

"I applied a salve." I point to the broken pot separate from the rest. He nods.

Uncertain of what else to say, I return to my task.

"I am sorry it happened like this."

"The basket? It is a loss, but—"

"No." He motions between us. "You and I. Married like this."

I stare at him. Does he mean practically being forced into taking me to wife? Or the cost? But he did not fight it. Perhaps I should have objected more strongly.

Uncertain, I offer a noncommittal reply. "Tis not ideal."

"No. It is not what I planned."

His words dig into me like briars. Was it the embarrassment Mather dealt him?

"It will be difficult," he continues, "to begin like this. I must attend to the fort till Kragorn can take command. Then I must accompany Valor and Erianna on a tour of the kingdom. Afterward, Lorennt has plans that will keep me in motion for at least a year..."

I do not realize I am crying until tears splat on the desk. I brush my cheeks. This day has been a disappointment to us both.

"We will make the most of the time afforded," he resigns. "I must go into the city tonight, but would you like to join me for dinner first?"

"What of Mather? Will he not object to my presence?"

"You are mine. You may do as you please. No one will dare object."

I repeat his words to myself, shoring myself up with his vehemence. Protected. Provided for. It counts for much.

Trent crouches at my side, seeing the tear streaks upon my cheeks. "He is gone Tirzah. I had him sent away. You are safe."

"He had his reasons for acting as he did."

Trent's mood darkens. "There is no reason, not ever, to mishandle a woman."

For all his faults, in this, I can grant Mather a heap of compassion. "Mather told you that he returned from his post at Grevnhold because of family. I was the reason. There had been several... Unpleasant encounters with men who thought being a harlot was hereditary."

"They made advances on you."

"Aye."

"How old were you?"

"Sixteen when my mother began sending letters to Mather pleading for him to return to take charge of me. He sent us a portion of his earnings, but his wages could not support us. My mother took to locking me in our hovel when she ventured into nearby cities to sell herself. The most lucrative places were the military camps. When they were occupied, she could support us for several months afterward. It was two years later that Mather returned to Malesiir. Unfortunately, he did not warn us of his arrival. He also did not know that Mother no longer allowed men to come to her."

"She went to his camp."

That Trent has bent his attention entirely to listening and understanding makes the telling easier.

"He saw his mother exiting the tent of his friend and other friends soliciting her."

Trent shakes his head, trying to reckon the horror.

"When he followed her home later... That was the worst fight I have ever witnessed. He never raised a hand to her, but seeing them screaming and crying, both of them..." I trace swirls in the herbs that fell onto Trent's desk. His hand upon my knee, helps me continue. "Mather took charge of me that day. I have not seen my mother since."

"Is that when you moved to Juniper?"

"Aye." I brush the herbs into my cupped hand and rise, running from the memory. I toss them into the fire and tidy his desk.

"You never speak of living in Juniper."

The spymaster has paid close attention. "Because I want to forget it."

"Who was he, Tirzah?"

I continue tidying. How could I have forgotten to make the bed? Clearly the past day has addled me.

"You know I never believed you when you said no one courted you."

Almighty, please spare me this!

A knock at the door makes me sigh my relief.

After answering the door Trent follows the soldier into the corridor.

I ease to the edge of the bed, staring out the window. Night is tearing at the seams of day. Soon it will yield, the vibrant threads upon the horizon rent by midnight hues.

"Thank you, truly," I tell the Almighty. "It is better this way."

The door opens. "We are finishing this."

TRENT

My wife glares out the window. "Shall I assume you disagree?"

"Disagree?"

She flicks her hand at the sky. "The Almighty. I asked… Never mind. You wished to go to dinner?" She crosses the room, fleeing.

Never has she been so recalcitrant. It makes me all the more determined to know what she is hiding. "We are taking our meal here."

Her eyes dart to the door then back to me. "Then you are going into the city?"

It is what Regold came to ask. The soldiers dressed simply and with minimal weaponry are leaving in pairs and small groups to infiltrate the taverns and ale houses. I planned to be among them, but a deep unease held me back from leaving Tirzah.

I tease, "Does it bode ill that the bride is already anxious to send her groom away?"

Hurt slides her gaze to the corner.

What have I trod upon?

I drag the chair opposite where she sat and make myself comfortable. Reluctantly, she regains her seat on the bed. I parse what she has said of Juniper and the insults Mather hurled at her. He believed she had a lover there. I know she has only been with me, though she had some experience with kisses. The thought pulls my attention to her lips, recalling their softness. Her willingness. That she now sits on my bed…

I corral my thoughts. "Mather settled you in Juniper. Where you worked as a laundress?"

She affirms it.

"Did you have any connections there?"

"No one."

"Until…" I prompt.

Her shoulders droop, conceding defeat to herself. "I made a few friends, but it was the potter's son whom most often kept company with me. He was near my age and had some qualities which attracted me to him, I suppose. We had a lengthy flirtation.

"Before settling me in Juniper, Mather made me swear to never speak of our mother or from where I hailed. 'We were orphans of a respectable family,' I was to say. Mather even allowed me to use his surname. But I was stupid with love. When the lad spoke of marriage to me, I thought he deserved my honesty. Thus, I told him everything. He was shocked but said it did not matter to him. However, it was shortly thereafter that he sought my favors. He wanted kisses, which I gave, and more than kisses, which I did not."

She shifts uncomfortably and looks for my judgment. I reach for her hand, stroking her wrist with my thumb. My wife. I want to take away this pain from her. The surest way I know to do that is to dig out the source of her hurt.

"Mather was suspicious. He did not trust the lad's intentions and came to discover the truth of it. When he arrived he found me compromised. He hauled the lad off to his father and had the full story. When the potter learned who my mother was, he forbade his son from marrying me, but he encouraged him to…" She shudders, catching her breath. Determination cinches her features. She fixes her gaze on me. "He meant to take all that he wanted from me then sell me to a bawd."

My curse flays the air, though I would rather flay the men. "I hope Mather beat them into the dust."

"He did." The thought does not seem to please her as it does me. "Mather relocated me to Chishelm thereafter, but it was too much to forgive. Believing I had done as our mother, giving myself to a man who promised much but never intended—"

She cuts herself off with a hard swallow, but the blow lands in my gut. What that youth did not take from her, I did.

"Mather vowed that if ever again I compromised myself, he would follow through on what the potter planned and sell me to a bawd."

Which explains everything. Her fear of Mather, but not of his fists. Why she was desperate to marry. Why the mistake we made whispers that my love for her is not genuine. She has been slandered and devalued by those who should have told her of her worth.

"How did you come to be in Parse Kítaran?"

"Leelah. The Spirit of Truth laid me on her heart, and she brought me home with her the day we met. I thought for sure she was a bawd. I almost did not care if she was."

"Because being Mather's ward was unbearable."

She shrugs.

I brace my elbows on my knees, considering how my wife's past has brought her to me. "Leelah rescued you."

"'Tis what she does. What you do." Her smile is sad. "Even when it is not what you want."

Her statement knocks me askew. "Not what I want?"

"I am glad to be free of Mather, but sorry to have become your burden and at such a tremendous cost."

Irritation bolts through me. Does nothing I say matter? In how many ways must I show her I love her before she will take it to heart?

Instead of arguing with her, I pray. Boldizar assures me that the number of words do not matter, simply that I do it earnestly.

Almighty, give me the words. What must I say?

I take her hands in mine. Not the soft, delicate hands of a noblewoman who has known nothing more taxing than needlepoint, but the strong, work calloused hands of a woman who has dedicated her life to the care of others. How greatly I admire her! What I told her was true. She is her own dowry, far more valuable than gold.

Far more valuable…

"May I tell you how I view the cost? At Gathering, I heard a parable that explains it perfectly…

"There once was a man working in a field. It was a beautiful field, as beautiful as any he had ever seen. To his surprise, he found a treasure buried there. He greatly admired that treasure. He even held it in his hand, though it did not belong to him." I cup her face, grazing her lips with my thumb. "But the man was not a dishonest sort. He knew the treasure was not his, so he returned it to the ground and went away.

The man knew he was not deserving of such treasure, however, he could not stop thinking of it."

"You are telling the story wrong," she softly objects.

"I am telling it exactly as it happened," I reply. "The man loved that treasure, and he settled it in his mind that he would do whatever was necessary to have it. Though the cost to purchase the field was steep, how great was his joy when the day came that he sold all his belongings to purchase the field. The treasure was finally his."

Tirzah's wide eyes are luminous, reflecting her hope. I aim to make it realized.

"You are beautiful, Tirzah, far more than any field. Your heart is my great treasure. I told you once that a man would count himself the most fortunate of all men to claim you as his wife. And I do, Tirzah. I am."

She throws herself into my arms so suddenly that the chair beneath me rocks. I pull her close, balancing the chair on all four legs. Before I can speak caution, her soft lips are on mine, leveling my coherency.

Her sweet kisses unlock my ardor. My fingers trace the line of her neck. The crossings of her plaited hair. She answers with a little sigh that has me chasing her responses to my touch. The fullness of what I feel for her overwhelms me. Knowing she is mine makes my eyes burn.

I cradle her, lifting, then lowering her to the bed, letting our kisses coalesce. Time falls away, at once fast and slow. Here. Here is where I want to be.

Caution taps my shoulder. I want this to be wholly her desire, too, not only when her senses are dulled with passion. Not so long ago, she confessed her belief that my motivation for wedding her might be to gain a bedmate. Never do I want her to have reason to believe that. I want her to know my heart.

I retrace ground that we covered, slowing our kisses, banking this fire till it smolders. I lay next to her, watching the long, slow blinks that lay her lashes against the dust of freckles on her cheeks.

"I love you, Tirzah Trent. That is why I shall not go farther with you this night. Tis too soon."

She curls into me and lays her head on my chest with a reluctant sight. "You are probably right."

As if responding to her own thoughts, she hums and sighs in bursts. Her limbs become pliant though her arm still drapes my waist. I trace her hairline, following it from her brow, around her temple, behind her ear.

My feelings for her surprise me for their intensity. Never has a woman so captivated me. This is utterly new.

Going into the city to ferret out the thieves seems a very good idea for how unappealing it is compared to staying in the arms of my wife. I ease my arm from beneath her head and settle hers on the bed. She stirs from her sound sleep.

I kiss her cheek. "I'll return ere dawn."

"Love you," she murmurs, halting me.

This feeling is a near ache for how it fills me. "And I you."

CHAPTER FIFTY

TRENT

May 14th

I have set myself the ambitious aims of solving my need for an aide and catching the thieves in one evening. Too much has this pair of thieves occupied both my mind and time, as King Lorennt reminded me in his letter this day. Though it is the duty of both the fort's general and the captain of Chishelm's guard to keep order and arrest any criminals, I have invested too much of my attention in their capture. Had I a spymaster, it would have been his duty to organize men and seek the thieves in the city's dens. Since I do not, I have led the initiative and because seeing this particular pair of thieves tried is of personal import to me. But it is now the burden of my would be spymaster to lure our presumed thieves into their next crime.

Across the ale saturated room, Regold makes a show of raising the bet on his hand of cards. The men at the table fold their cards. When he tosses his cards down to rake in his winnings, one card flips upright revealing his bluff. He merely chortles over his pile of silver and coppers at the three angry men. I can hear the healthy jangle of his coin purse as he tucks away most of the winnings, further inciting the men. It is bad form to pocket their money before the game is through. While Regold knows his two targets, if they are not whom we seek, he tempts all the opportunistic thieves in the alehouse with his behavior.

I fold my own hand of cards and draw lightly from the stale brew in my tankard. The paltry winnings before me keeps me in the game but as the poorest player. Several times I have folded my winning cards to keep me in that position.

A hand slides along my shoulders quickly followed by the scent of a sour body and the press of a woman bursting the seams of her bodice. "Looks like you could use some luck, my man, or something to soften the blow."

I glance up at her, masking both my pity and distaste. "'Fraid it's not my night. I've naught for me and less for you."

She moves along easily, not wishing to waste her time with a roomful of men available.

Keeping apace of Regold's game, I bet high on my next hand and lose half of what remains to me. The men at my table have enough of my coin that they will feel they have sufficiently fleeced me should I abandon the game.

Regold's gloating laugh turns heads. He sweeps the heap of silver into his purse and rises from the table.

"You don't mean to leave?" demands a man who is aptly described as wiry.

"Indeed, I do!" Regold pats the purse. "I'm off to find merriment with fairer faces than yours!"

The three come to their feet objecting, but he is deaf to them as he struts from the alehouse.

The grizzled one of the three fists his coins and stomps to refill his ale. The remaining two, one wiry and one brutish, confer.

I make my final wager at my table.

The big one drains his tankard while wiry clears both their winnings from the table then leads the way to the door.

Aye. That's our thieves.

"I'm done in," I say to my table, collecting my few coppers and following in the wake of the pair.

In the street, they stalk Regold while I stalk them. When Regold detours into a dead end alley ostensibly to relive himself upon a midden heap, the thieves "corner" him as planned. It is then that our soldiers posted in the shadows close the net around them.

I fall in with Regold as the complaining, bound thieves are marched toward the fort.

"That was enjoyable," he crows.

"I could tell. You played it heavy handed. I saw a score of other men move to help carry your purse for you. Fortunate those two were fastest to the door."

He laughs at the jibe. "Hard to believe you gave up such fun to be the esteemed commander."

Once, I felt as he. Those days are past. At present, my mind is sprinting ahead of my body toward the fort.

"You did well, Sergeant. Quite well."

TIRZAH

This is the fourth night my husband has gone into the city after taking dinner with me. Thrice he has returned tainted with the stench of sweat, ale, and once, perfumed oil. His beard has grown into a scruff of whiskers to further his disguise.

The increased patrols which Anders leads has deterred additional thefts—to the best of his knowledge—while Trent orchestrates the spies in the city. Each night he presses a kiss to my cheek then disappears till near dawn. During the day, he has assigned Regold to escort me to work with Matilda while he rests and attends to his responsibilities.

Matilda has much to say regarding my marriage, though I have expressed little of what transpired and nothing of the discontent I feel.

There has been no time to visit the harlots. Worry for the young harlot Aiyla gnaws at me. With Trent occupied by the thefts, he has not been able to plot her escape to Parse Kítaran, if he still means to. Perhaps it was the impulse of the moment or guilt speaking for him when he claimed he cared for her plight, that he would act.

"Not fair," I chide myself. "He meant it." It is my worry for her and worry for him fanning such ungracious thoughts.

I toss on the bed we have not shared. When I think of his kisses, of his touch that ignites my skin, an ache hollows my belly. Part of me regrets allowing him to end what I began on our wedding night. Then I remember his parable. His earnestness. How he reached deep into my past and embraced the woman who fell prey to her malleable heart. I am comforted and can trust he did not and never will use me. For that I can believe he wanted my best when he said it was too soon.

I count the chime of the bells echoing across Chishelm. Ten. Where is my husband now? Surely haunting a tavern. Perhaps an alehouse. How far will his disguise lead him? What must he do to maintain it? Surely nothing to dishonor our marriage. But the path right up to the door of dishonor has much to which I would object. I could not bring myself to ask him. He has worn the mantle of spymaster longer than I have worn that of healer. I know he will flush out the thieves. I simply pray it is soon. Will he then share more than a meal with me?

It is a strange thing. Before we wed, I felt his pursuit because he sent a letter nearly every day. Now that we are wed, I can keep company with him, and we share more conversation over a meal than could be contained in a letter—perhaps not of the same depth—yet I catch myself digging trenches of bitterness. I must then painstakingly fill them in with shovelfuls of gratitude lest I destroy the ground upon which I stand.

"I am protected. I am provided for. I am loved. He has not nor will he betray me."

The declaration does not unknot the cords of frustration and fear twisting my mind.

"I am my husband's treasure."

The scent of perfumed oil was confined to the shoulders and collar of his tunic. I am not proud to admit I know this. The temptation to press his discarded tunic to my nose proved too strong when I found it atop his trunk awaiting his next venture into the city. This comforted me for but a moment because I next tried to imagine how it came to be there and set about deducing it. Had he returned while the back of a chair was wearing his tunic and I was alternately touching and hugging it, I cannot imagine how I would have explained the irrational jealousy that possessed me to do such a thing. The ensuing question that my clever deduction afforded did not comfort me. Why was a woman draped on my husband's shoulders? I lost many hours of sleep tormented by the images that question provoked.

"He is no longer the spymaster. Why must he be in the alehouses acting as such?" My conversation with myself does not provide answers. It widens the trench of bitterness faster than I can fill it. I repeat my chant of gratitude to the empty room. The quietude mocks my assertions. "Protected. Provided for. Loved."

Surrendering to sleeplessness, I light a candle and open my anatomy book to the last place I read. I flop onto my stomach atop the covers to read about the mysterious workings of the body. It fully engages my thoughts that have become kinked around my husband's actions each day.

The candle is half spent when I hear the click of the lock. I look over my shoulder as Trent enters. He stops in the threshold, eyes fixed on me.

"Is something wrong?" I ask. It is nowhere near dawn.

"You are awake," he foolishly states.

"As are you," I drawl.

He shuts the door, slowly crossing to me. Unable to see his face, I roll to my back, looking up at him.

Wearing disheveled clothes and a layer of stubbled whiskers, he seems a man who has worked long, hard hours—which he has. Even as I look upon him, his gaze consumes me in my threadbare chemise. Heat rushes through me, making me tremble. Trent bends over me, bracing a hand on either side of my head. His eyes are bright with desire.

Will it be now? Has he returned to be with me through the night? Maybe even to love me? The intensity of his gaze says he has.

"My Tirzah. My delight. You are aptly named, Wife."

His words sing in my ears, nearly drowning the sound of my own tortured questions.

He lowers his head to mine, giving me a soft kiss. My fingers knot in the covers. He draws back to read the encouragement in my eyes then kisses me again. Firmly. Deeply.

The sourness of cheap ale ruins it. In a rush, I recall where he has been. Cloying perfumed oil stings my nose. I push him back, scooting to lean against the headboard. Offended, I drag the back of my hand across my mouth. "You smell of an alehouse."

He lets his head hang between his shoulders. "Forgive me. I forgot myself."

"Why must you always be sorry? Can you not do what you mean to do?"

My bitter accusation snaps his head up. He observes me with a furrowed brow, then straightens. "You are right. I will do better."

Why does it not feel as if I have won? He agreed with me, but I want to cry.

Trent moves to his trunk, pulling off his tunic by the collar. He sniffs it, grimaces, and chucks it in the corner. A few weapons land atop his usual complement. Finding the tooth powder I made of fine salt and herbs upon the dresser next to the wash basin, he pulls a small linen cloth from the drawer, dips it in the powder and cleans his teeth. He scrubs away the other offensive odors at the basin then pulls a folded knife from a drawer. He lathers soap on his face and begins to scrape away the bristles.

"You discard your disguise?"

He works the knife down his cheek, moving slowly along the curve of his jaw before saying, "The thieves are in our jail."

I stumble over the plain statement. "In the jail? You apprehended them?"

He stills. "I vowed that I would."

I rise to my knees. "Where? When? Are you certain it is them?"

"Tonight. In an alehouse. They fell into my trap."

The curved knife rasps as he moves it in quick short strokes on his chin, the sound matching how I feel at such abbreviated answers. "Cuyler! Please tell it in full. How did this come to be?"

When he remains silent, I slap my palms on my thighs with an impatient huff.

He rinses and dries his knife then collapses it upon the hinge before setting it beside the basin. I crawl on my knees to the edge of the bed, biting the inside of my cheek.

Finally turning toward me, he dries his face with a towel. "You wish to hear how it was done?"

"I do!"

Dispassionately, he explains where he has been these past nights and how he managed to locate the thieves and tempt them into committing a crime. "While I believe these are the same that stole from you and killed Crishoff, they have not admitted such, thus, it is imperative we positively identify them."

"How?"

He waits for me to comprehend what he is asking.

"You want *me* to identify them."

"I do."

I sit back on my heels. "I do not think I can. Twas deepest night. I know only the shape of them and their voices."

"You must hear them. This I know. In the morning, I shall escort you to the jail."

"What of tonight? Can we not have it done with?"

He looks long upon me then shakes his head.

We stare at each other till the awkward tension becomes unbearable. I return to my place upon the mattress, setting aside my book and slipping beneath the covers. "Have you more to do this night?"

"There is always more to do."

"Then I will say goodnight."

He sighs a disappointed sound. The rustle of cloth and jangle of his weapons follows as he dons both. "Goodnight, Tirzah."

In a moment, he is gone, leaving me to regret my biting words that I fear drove him away nearly as much as I regret not having congratulated him and telling him how proud I am of the work he has done.

CHAPTER FIFTY-ONE

TIRZAH

May 16th

If I thought once the thieves were captured I would see more of my husband, I was wrong. After escorting me to the jail where I was able to assure him he did indeed have the thieves that waylaid me, he spent the whole of yesterday preparing the charges against them even though their attempted theft of Regold before a passel of witnesses made things simpler. However, I am grateful that Trent has not forgotten to keep his promise. This is the day we will free Aiyla.

I move through Matilda's shop in a whirlwind, tidying, dusting, scrubbing. Anything I can help with, I do. I am bundling and hanging fresh herbs in her workroom to dry when the time comes.

"Well, that soldier is returned. Not your husband, the other one."

"Regold?" Did Trent change his mind? He is not a forgetful man.

She hums. "Suppose you'll be slipping off somewhere secretive."

I finish tying a knot around a fragrant bundle of thyme. It is wise of Matilda to purchase fresh herbs. Poor quality stems are easier to hide once the herbs are dried. "Regarding that…"

I face Matilda, rallying my courage to explain myself. I pray she hears it with the humble sincerity I feel. "I have the utmost respect for you as a midwife and healer, and I am deeply grateful that you sheltered me and allowed me to learn from you. However, I feel that you are wrong in choosing whom you are willing and not willing to help. My convictions would not allow me to abandon the harlots. Thus, I have been going to them and giving what aid I can."

Matilda is obviously affected by my speech, but it takes her time to reply. "You disregarded my decisive direction. Do you dare denounce that?"

"I do not."

She sighs, looking around at the workroom that I have thoroughly cleaned. "You are not naive, are you?"

I shake my head. "My mother was an unwilling harlot. Her skill with apothecary kept us alive through illnesses that would have otherwise claimed us because we were shunned by society. Had someone seen past the mistakes that landed her in that position and offered help without conditions, she may have been able to raise us out of poverty. But she could not."

Matilda listens earnestly, but I can see that her mind was decided long ago. "You have my sympathies for the sorry state of your childhood, and I respect your reasons for rendering aid, but I do disagree. Once a woman has wandered down the path of wanton living, she cannot come back."

"We shall see. I am on my way to try to bring a young woman out of that life into a new one."

"You're abandoning your apprenticeship." It is a statement which I acknowledge. Matilda opens her arms, embracing me without reserve. "I am sad to say farewell."

"As am I."

Regold follows me into the street. "Commander sends his apologies." He gives me a sealed letter. "Said I was to help you with your special task."

I crack the seal, anxious to see what possible reason Trent could give to excuse himself from this.

Tirzah,

I wanted to be with you to help free Aiyla as we planned. Instead, I have sent you Regold. He is at your command and has the purse you will need. If the proprietor is reluctant to let her go, I have given Regold a letter that I hope will ease your way. Do as you see fit. A dose of your beautiful candor may be needed.

All my love,
Cuyler

I fold the letter and shove it into my new basket that still needs to be stocked. *Gah!* He is not even sorry that he cannot be here because of circumstances! He has chosen this! I do not know which is worse, him apologizing constantly or him acting decisively. He had better be prepared to explain himself. "Infuriating."

"Not what you wanted to hear?" Regold guesses.

"No." I bite my tongue, refusing to speak against my husband or disrespect Regold's commander, though I very much feel disregarded. Trent wants my candor, he shall have it when next we speak.

Keeping pace with Regold, I pull myself out of my colliding thoughts when we reach the intersection that will lead to the market district of Old Main. "Why are we here?"

"I am following you. I do not know where we are going."

"You don't! How are you going to help me, then?"

He shrugs. "Commander said to do whatever you asked."

So help me, Trent, you'll never dare break your word to me after today…

Regold sniggers. "I wager he won't."

Woe's sakes! I must have said that aloud.

I set us on the correct path and in a low tone outline our mission to Regold. "There is a young woman that works at the Corked Raven. Her name is Aiyla."

Regold grins. "I've met her."

Ire builds under my skin. It was not fair of Trent to put me in this position, especially with Regold who could ruin it. "How recently have you 'met her'?"

"Whenever I am in Chishelm, I make a point to see her." He shrugs. "I like her. She's sweeter than most. Not so hardened."

People will confess anything to a healer. I huff. "Aiyla is sweet because she is obliged to be. And she is young."

Regold eyes me. "How young?"

"Seventeen."

He tries to bury his discomfort. "Not so young."

"She was younger when her family sold her to the proprietor."

He slows. "What do you mean?"

"They were desperate for money with a house full of children and their youngest ill. No one would offer for their daughters, thus, two years past, they sold Aiyla, the prettier of the two, to pay the physician and buy food."

Regold catches my arm to stop me. I wince at the pressure on my bruises, but he does not notice. "That cannot be true."

"Aiyla agreed to the arrangement, but she cannot stay there any longer. She is with child."

Regold stands rooted in place. "Women that are harlots wish to be so. They are wanton."

I snort and jerk my arm away, though it hurts worse for it. "If you will not aid me, give me the purse and wait for us outside."

He starts forward in silence and opens the door for me, following inside, when we reach the tavern.

"Ah, good day, Healer!" The proprietor greets me warmly. "I am glad you are here. One of my girls is not faring well. Stomach complaint of some sort. Hope you can sort her out."

"For free, of course," I say, in no mood to pander.

"Well," he props his hands on the counter. "You've never asked for compensation afore. I do pay for the girls' room and keep, but..." He scrunches his face, then brightens when he sees Regold. "You have a fancy for her, don't you, Sergeant? The golden haired girl? How about the Healer tends her then she tends you?"

His ribald suggestion has Regold turning shades of red.

"It is regarding Aiyla that I have come today. I know that you entered into an arrangement with her family. I would like to compensate you for the money you paid them. In exchange, you will tear up her sale agreement and not hold her family liable."

The proprietor gapes at me then laughs. He points at me, addressing Regold. "Is she mad?"

"I am quite sober. Aiyla is ill," *because of the babe*, "and I fear for her health if she remains here."

Gone is the proprietor's jovial facade. "Are you looking to open a stable by stealing my girls? The streets are not friendly to thieves."

Regold edges in front of me, finding his voice. "Are you threatening Healer Trent? The commander does not tolerate threats to his wife. Nor do I."

"She is sotted if she thinks I'll free my most valuable girl."

Regold pushes a letter against the man's chest. "Read it."

The proprietor knows better than to strike a soldier without provocation, but he wants to. Nevertheless, he reads the letter, a black storm brewing on his corpulent face. Regold motions me back. I obey, glimpsing a trio of eyes peeking from the brewing room.

"This is outrageous! I'll not abide this!" The proprietor slams the paper on the counter. Regold swipes it away from him.

"Are you defying the Hand of the King?" Regold asks.

The proprietor glares at him.

"Get the girl, Healer Trent," Regold instructs. "I'll square with him."

The older harlot that questioned my motives for helping them appears from the brewing room. "This way, Healer."

I follow her above stairs to an unlit room with the window flung wide, coaxing in a breeze to stir the fouled, stagnant air. Aiyla lies on a bed, a bucket near her.

Compassion hurries my feet. "Oh, dear girl! All will be well."

The older woman helps me get her upright, though we must pause for Aiyla to heave. Her stomach is worryingly empty.

"She cannot keep nothing down. I'm worried for her."

I pull the large cloak from my basket and cover Aiyla, drawing up the hood. It takes both of us to get Aiyla below stairs. Regold stands between us and the proprietor as we help her out the door.

"You'll take care of her?" the woman asks.

"I vow she'll be safe and cared for, all this a bad memory."

The woman nods. "You have made a friend in me, Healer."

Aiyla is too weak to go far. She makes it a block before collapsing into me. Regold scoops her up without a word, carrying her all the way to the fort and straight into the infirmary. He gently deposits her upon a cot then walks out.

Physician Therig appears in the doorway. "Whom do we have here, Healer Trent?"

TRENT

I lean my elbows in the window's embrasure as night closes out the day. Regold still stands guard against the wall of the infirmary. After returning my letter as requested and dropping my full purse in my hand as I hoped he would, he went to the kitchen and carried a platter laden with viands into the infirmary then took up his position against the wall. If he can wrestle his way to the other side of his mistakes, I have great hopes that he will become my aide and spymaster. I will need his help to enact my plans that extend far beyond Aiyla.

My only regret is that I did not personally help my wife. I hope the fact that I have not seen her this day owes to her preoccupation with her patient not her pique with me, though I am certain it did not improve her opinion of me. Again my conscience takes the scourge to my body for its unfettered desire that led me to break my vow to my wife and also offend her by trying to gain her bed smelling like a sotted knave. It undoubtedly put her in mind of the man I was, especially with the stench of that woman upon my tunic.

If I am being honest, passing off my duty to Regold was not only a means to prove his readiness, it was a means to keep Tirzah from seeing me in that place again, knowing I have bedded all those harlots, including poor Aiyla. I do not want to remind her of my past sins. She deserves a better man, but how can I prove myself worthy of her love when I continue to fail her?

By now, I hoped to be able to offer her good news regarding a new apprenticeship. All I have to show is a stack of rejection letters from the notable healers and physicians in Malsihra. I planned to see her settled in our house there with a new position to delve into while I am riding all across the kingdom for the next year. That no longer seems probable. I must expand my search on her behalf to other cities. Perhaps she would be happy living with my mother and sisters if the midwife in Gistin is willing to apprentice her. I must draft a request.

I return to the ledger on my desk that I have neglected. Between the sum for repairing the tavern in Malsihra and Tirzah's bride price, it will be at least a year before I am clear of those debts. I deduct them from my earnings as well as the cost of my house in Malsihra. If I continue supporting my mother and sisters—pray, let none of them soon require a dowry—I'll have less to live on than I did before becoming Lorennt's hand. Oh, my sins are costly in so many ways.

The note to subtract the sum for Aiyla's debt sits in the margin. I blot it out, since it was paid by another.

"He blotted out the charge of our legal indebtedness, nailing it to the cross." The Spirit of Truth recalls the verse of Holy Text to my mind.

I stare at Aiyla's debt. Blotted out. Paid for. I imagine it is mine.

If I truly believe that my debts were paid for by the Saving Son and removed from me, why then am I still bowing to those burdens? Why am I wearing guilt like an immovable cloak?

The longer you belong to the Almighty, the greater you realize your need of his grace. Tirzah's explanation holds true. I feel more aware of my past and present failings than ever before, nor can I excuse them as I once did.

More Text comes to mind. *"As far as the East is from the West, so far have I removed your iniquities from you."*

Being free of the debt and contending with the consequences, I should not bow to guilt. Grace frees me to walk forward, to forsake the cloak of shame incurred by my old self.

Tirzah's indictment prods me. *Why must you always be sorry? Can you not do what you mean to do?*

No more excuses. No more bowing.

It is time to begin living like a free man. A man who does not hide from consequences.

The night watch salutes me as I cross the bailey. Regold comes to attention from his arms-crossed stance.

"Any trouble?" I ask.

"None."

"Edric will take your post come morning."

"No. I have spent enough hours wronging that girl that I can dedicate a few hours to protecting her."

Aye, high hopes that I have found my man. "As you will."

The infirmary is dark and still. I go to the only convalescent room with a closed door. There is no noise within. I slip inside. Comforting herbal scents float atop the scent of bile. Aiyla is sleeping on a cot, a blanket drawn up to her shoulders. My wife is slumped in a chair, chin on her chest, drooling. I can only shake my head. She ought to have made use of a cot. If she is this attentive a caregiver to her patients, she will be unparalleled as a mother. The thought spreads warmth through my chest. An image of her cradling our babe floats in my mind.

Aye. She will be a wonderful mother. But someone must care for the caregiver.

I borrow a cot from an adjacent room and set it beneath the window. Tirzah is a deep sleeper. She does not rouse when I move her to the cot and drape a blanket over her. Perhaps that is why she insists on sleeping in a chair. I kiss her brow, then turn to leave. A pair of dark eyes watches me.

I kneel next to Aiyla. "I'm sorry to have woken you. Is there anything you need?"

Her eyes bounce to a mug on the nearby table, but she says, "No."

I reach for the mug. Mint wafts from the liquid. "Here."

She pushes herself up on an elbow and sips the drink before returning it to me.

"Anything else? Are you warm enough?"

She nods. "The healer has been kind."

"Good. I want you to know that I am sorry for what you have suffered and for adding to your misery. I hope one day you can forgive me. Even if you cannot, I want you to know you are safe—now and evermore. When you are strong enough to travel, my wife will see you settled in a place where you can heal."

"Thank you."

"Though it does not change what happened to you, I vow that I will see the laws changed so that no more women may be sold into prostitution, and I will fight to free those already bound to it."

"I agreed to the terms," she says, claiming responsibility for her state.

"You were a girl. You could not comprehend the depravity you would be subjected to, even had you been told. No, Aiyla. That burden rests on the shoulders of your parents and the proprietor."

She shudders through a breath and closes her eyes.

I pray the damage done her these past years will not take a lifetime to undo. Thankfully, Salome and Leelah will be with her through her trials. "Sleep well, Aiyla. You will not be disturbed again."

CHAPTER FIFTY-TWO

TRENT

May 17th

I enter the jail to collect the thieves for their execution. What Kragorn said buzzes in my ears. *The Almighty takes no pleasure in the death of the wicked.* I asked an elder this morning if it was true. He showed me where it was written and the rest of the text which says, *"'As surely as I live,' declares the Almighty, 'I take no pleasure at all in the death of the wicked. I would rather they turn from their wicked ways and live. Turn back!'"*

I confessed that I did not want them to live. I want them to perish. The elder showed me another passage that told of a prophet charged with delivering that message to a vile city. At first he refused to deliver the message. Then, when the king and whole city did sincerely repent, so angry was the prophet that he declared if the Almighty forgave them, he would rather die. I relate to that prophet. The thieves have wronged my wife and many others.

I feel the same now standing before these thieves as I did when Erianna granted mercy to some of the Ruphiri. Yet, much as I try to stifle what I have learned, I cannot be easy in knowingly disobeying. I wrestle to surrender my way of thinking to the Almighty in this.

A niggling voice tells me I will be less of a warrior if I say what I intend to say. I argue back that Kragorn is the greatest warrior and man I have ever known.

Iron clangs as the jailer brings the thieves from their cell at my order. With them standing before me, defiant in their wickedness, I feel very much like that prophet—like I will be made a fool if they do not repent but even if they do, I would rather they not.

"By Malesiir's law, you have been condemned to death by hanging. Naught you can say will change that verdict. However, if you—" The words lodge in my throat. Utter foolishness.

But the urging in my heart will not relent. *Tell them.*

"If you have a care for the soul within you, there is yet time to call upon the Almighty and ask forgiveness for the wrong you have done. His Son paid for the debt on your souls if you will believe in Him."

There is a prolonged silence. The thieves gape at me, then at each other. And erupt with laughter.

My pride stings. The confounded look the jailer wears worsens my humiliation. I clamp a hand on the arm of the brutish man who mistreated my wife and shove him ahead of me.

I march them through dim corridors into daylight where Anders awaits with a contingent to escort them to the gallows. Tirzah stands outside the infirmary alongside Regold whom I have officially assigned to guard duty. She nods to me then returns to her patient. When she told that she did not want to attend, I did not begrudge her for it. She is a healer. Witnessing a hanging would hurt her heart, just though it be.

The gallows are a short walk to the square of Old Main. Loading the prisoners in wagons seemed like more trouble than walking them at the end of a sword, thus, Sergeant Braun and I control the brute while another pair steers the wiry quick talker. Anders follows immediately behind ready to assist. The side street dumps us onto Old Main where a company pushes back the jeering crowd.

The thieves balk at the sight of death greeting them.

"Keep going," I demand.

As if planned, both men dart toward the crowd. I dig in my heels, but Braun is caught off balance. Feeling the give from that side, the thief throws his weight into me, slamming me into a stack of crates that collapse. I yowl as a shard of wood drives deep into my forearm, but I hang onto the thief, bringing him down with me. I wrestle him amid the pile of broken boards, refusing to release him though the shard digs in deeper. He flails, kicking at the soldiers who comes to subdue him. I flip him to his back, his arms pinned beneath him, and dig my knee into his throat.

"Cease! Or die writhing like a worm!"

He fights for breath but finds none. When his struggles weaken, I shove upright and allow Anders to haul him to the gallows. The other thief is already upon the platform, having been quickly subdued.

Perhaps Valor does not possess a fast temper. I have never fought as much in so short a time as I have since being named the king's Hand.

The frenzy of the crowd at witnessing a near escape drowns my howl of pain as I attempt to pull the shard from my flesh. It holds fast. Blood seeps from the puncture, soaking my sleeve.

"Commander?" Braun grips my shoulder and swears at the sliver a handspan long and the width of an arrow protruding from my forearm through my tunic.

"Went in sideways. Doesn't seem too deep," I say, though I cannot know.

"Would you have General—"

"No," I growl. "I will do this."

I attempt to detach my mind from the pain, focusing on the gallows. Anders has maneuvered the thieves into their spots over the trap doors, lowered and tightened the ropes over their necks. They have nowhere to run but into death.

My arm throbs with every beat of my heart. Blood trickles around my wrist, slicking my palm. I hold it higher, but pain spears through me like fire. Accursed depths! For all the men I have shot through with arrows, it feels I have finally taken one.

I stand upon the platform and proclaim the wrongs of the men wearing necklaces of rope. A vindictive shout echoes in the streets when I announce the penalty. There is no echoing cry within me. Only grim determination. I set my hand to the lever. I do not *want* to release it. I simply *must*. No satisfaction comes from the scrape of wood. The snap of rope. If anything, sorrow twangs in my chest. Sorrow for the victims of these men, perhaps sorrow that this is the path the men chose. I feel weak for it.

I want to blame it upon the injury but my head is not completely clouded with pain. Not yet.

"Get the commander back to the fort," Anders orders Braun. "I'll see to the bodies."

Fort Dead Wolf looms behind the buildings of Old Main, pulling my feet forward.

"Where you going?" Braun barks as I head toward the keep while he diverted to the infirmary.

"To tend this."

"You want I should send Old Therig? Or your wife?"

"Neither," I snap.

TIRZAH

"Healer Trent," Regold calls down the corridor ahead of his appearance. "You are wanted at the keep. Commander is injured."

I am flying out the door faster than I can remember to grab my basket. I return to grab it only to remember it is not stocked. "Injured how?" I ask on my way to the workroom.

There is a long pause.

"Sliver of wood in his arm."

I borrow supplies from the workroom then hasten past Regold who guards the door.

I push into our room to find my husband at his desk hunched over his arm like a dog licking its wound, glaring at the interruption. Except he is wielding a dagger.

"What do you think you are doing?" I scold and whip the dagger out of his hand. He has already worked his tunic off and prepared a needle with thread. "You could do much damage that way."

"I can manage," he growls.

"Oh, aye. See how well you manage." I trace a puckered scar on his upper arm. "If you can forbid me from ladders, then I forbid you from suturing—yourself or anyone, ever!"

I clear away his supplies and lay down towels.

"Very well, Healer," he complies like a sullen child and scoots the chair to make room for me to work.

"Do you want something for the pain?"

He points to a bottle on the desk. It smells of strong ale.

"So be it."

The sliver is embedded shallowly in his arm. It has jagged edges and cannot be drawn. It must be lifted. Which is what he must have been attempting when I entered.

I take a sharp, clean knife from my basket then prepare what items I will need. I offer him a thick bit of leather. He bites down on it then nods. I slice the knife into his skin, applying pressure till I feel the sliver. Trent groans into the leather. I feel him fist my skirt as well. Blood gushes from the wound into the towels beneath his arm. I work quickly to lift the wood free then pluck the remaining splinters. I position a basin beneath his arm.

"Catch your breath," I instruct and give him a few moments. "Steady now. This will be miserable but soon over."

He leans his head against the small of my back while his hand moves to my hip, holding onto me to brace himself. I rub his shoulder, waiting. He tenses. I pry open the lips of the wound and flush saltwater through the channel cut in his arm. He howls into the leather, clinging to my body as if attempting to leave his and enter mine to escape the pain.

I empty the pitcher. "There. The worst is over." I let the wound close and press clean towels to absorb and staunch the blood.

Trent spits the leather to the floor, shuddering back in the chair. "If it weren't my bow arm, I'd not have let you do that."

"I thought it was the sword arm you soldiers cared about."

"I care... both."

I look across my shoulder. "Are you with me, Cuyler?"

He is pale. Panting.

"Breathe slowly, Cuyler."

His hand tugs at my hip, pulling me down to his lap. He leans into me, his arm wrapped round my waist. "You... help."

Warmth spreads through me. I lift the edge of the towel to check the wound. Still bleeding too quickly. I adjust the pressure. "Do I help more than ale?"

"A fair comparison," he pants, his chest heaving against my shoulder. "You are also...intoxicating."

"You're shamming again," I banter, trying to take his mind off the pain. "It's unacceptable to sham your wife."

His breathing begins to slow. "Don't be gull. Why do you think I haven't shared your bed?"

A question I have not satisfactorily answered. "You have been busy?"

"Too busy to sleep?"

I shrug. I thought he worked through the night then slept while I was with Matilda. The past few nights I have slept in the infirmary.

"I cannot keep my word to you while lying next to you."

I let that settle. "Where have you been sleeping?"

"In the war room. No one knows."

To prevent ridicule of the man of him and the woman of me. Our hasty, near compulsory marriage is already too large a target.

But sleeping in the war room? Upon the floor? That does not befit a husband moreover the king's Hand. Were I to go to him, to ask him... No. Not until he explains why he sent Regold to fetch Aiyla.

I check the wound. Still too much blood. I increase the pressure.

Aiyla told me that he spoke with her last night after moving me to a cot, both things I regret sleeping through. The question buzzes in my mind, drowning all other thoughts till I must speak it. "Did you send Regold in your stead because you could not face Aiyla?"

He is slow to answer. When he does, his admission is quiet. "I told myself it was because I needed to test Regold. I want to make him my aide and spymaster. But the greater truth is... I could not face you."

"Me? But we planned—"

"Tirzah. You were repulsed by me when I came to you after catching the thieves, just as you were repulsed after I told you of my sins with those women. I did not want to give you more cause to remember the man I was when I so badly want you to know who I am—a man who has been redeemed."

Regret pools in my middle. His past is as unchangeable as my own, however, it was my present bitterness that hurt both of us. "There is truth in what you say, but I should not have spoken so harshly that night."

"I do not fault you."

"I drove you away."

He does not contradict me. It is my fault that I slept alone instead of in the arms of my husband.

I lift the towels. Blood seeps rather than flows. "I can suture it now."

He begins to release me then pauses to ask, "Can you do it from here?"

"If you'd like." He lets me adjust my position and his so that I may reach his arm from his lap. Settled, I take up the needle and thread. "How did this happen?"

He huffs. "I showed weakness."

The needle glides in and out of his flesh causing his hand to twitch with the pain, but his breathing remains steady.

"I cannot imagine that. Of all things you might be accused of, weak is not one of them."

He rests his forehead against my shoulder. "Did you know there is a verse that says the Almighty takes no pleasure in the death of the wicked? He wishes they would repent. So I gave them that chance."

I stop to look at him. "You did what?"

"I told them—" He grimaces, pulling away. "It does not matter."

"Cuyler." I set my hand on his jaw. "Tell me."

He stares across the room. "I told them though they must die, if they repented, their sins would be forgiven by the Almighty." He grunts, deriding himself. "They laughed. Realized I was weak. So they tried to escape."

I am stunned. He did something few would have the courage to do for their friends, knowing they would likely be scorned. He did it for his enemies. "That was not weak. It was brave."

He does not want to meet my eyes though he admits, "You told me it was wrong to withhold forgiveness."

I nod, amazed at this man. "Have you forgiven Silla?"

His face pinches. Then he looks at me. Runs my plait through his hand. "I forgive her."

I tend his arm, my pulse thrumming. Perhaps I can lay down my shovel. Walk away from my trenches.

I apply a salve atop his sutures to protect him from infection, follow it with a folded strip of linen to keep it clean. I encircle his arm with more linen to keep it all in place. Blood is dried on his wrist and hand. With a rag, I cleanse it, paying attention to the grooves of his fingers.

He seems content to hold me for as long as I will stay. Not kissing me. Not stroking my hair. Simply holding me.

"I do not want you to sleep in the war room." I turn to him, setting my hand on his bare chest, and feel his heart drumming like mine. "Cuyler, I want you with me."

He touches my face, admiring me. "Tonight—"

"No," I argue, feeling the audacity of my demand but not caring. "Not tonight."

His brow lowers till I borrow his words. "I mean this moment."

His hand sweeps up my spine to the back of my neck and pulls me flush with him. He kisses me with the unrestrained passion of a man kissing his wife.

I meet him kiss for kiss, touch for touch.

Suddenly, he jerks back. "Tirzah. I need you to be candid with me. Tell me what you want. I have twisted your words to make what I want of them before."

I touch my face to his, letting myself love him unreservedly. "I want to know and be known by my husband."

He groans and kisses me wildly. His hands drop to my waist to lift me.

"No!" I start. "You shall tear your sutures!"

He nuzzles my neck. "Then it is good I am wed to a healer."

"I'll not allow it!" I try to stand, but my husband won't let go.

He meets my eyes, stretches his injured arm out to the side, hooks the other around my waist, and lifts me without a single grunt. I wrap my arms around his neck, kissing him as he carries me to our bed.

CHAPTER FIFTY-THREE

TIRZAH

May 21st

"You cannot stop smiling," Leelah observes.

"Surely not," I argue even as a smile tugs at the corners of my mouth.

"She is right," Erianna says.

Leelah scoffs at her. "You are not much better. You look as pleased as if someone vowed to feed you cookies every day for the rest of your life."

Erianna hums at little Cuylah, far more enamored with Leelah's babe in her arms than our company.

"Is Valor jealous of your new love?" I tease her.

"*Hmm?*" Erianna asks, not having heard me.

Leelah leans near to confide, "She has come here every afternoon. Valor too. He is happy for the chance to eat from my kitchen after she nearly burned his house to the ground preparing a meal."

I grin. "The Warrior Queen has a missing talent? Seems fair."

The ping of steel glancing off steel echoes in the courtyard where Kragorn and Valor spar, the children entertained by watching, excepting Fialla who naps in a little bed in the corner.

"I am surprised you are not sparring," I say to Erianna.

"Babes are better than swords," she replies.

Not even when Cuyler's namesake begins to fuss does Erianna return her to her mother. The queen walks around the great room, soothing her with a gentle bouncing gait, her long unbound hair swaying at her back.

"Has Aiyla settled at Salome's?" Leelah asks.

"She has. Rest and good food has done wonders for her health. Salome's acceptance is doing more."

"When may we meet her?" Erianna asks.

I hesitate. The pair of them are intimidating.

Leelah says, "If being accepted by Salome was to her benefit, surely becoming acquainted with the Queen of Malesiir will waylay some of her shame."

"I promise to leave my weapons belt at home," Erianna vows.

I bob my head. "Of course. Will tomorrow suit?"

We make plans, then the women insist on hearing the full story of how Trent came to marry me. Erianna is greatly amused at the tale of how he caught the thieves. Then she tells me of Trent's brawl that destroyed a tavern.

Though Anders intimated there had been a fight, I had no notion of the scale, nor of Lorennt's fury. "All because someone spoke crassly of me?"

Erianna shrugs. "It was intolerable because he loved you, even if he did not know he did."

"But it nearly cost him his position!"

She shakes her head, rocking the babe with the motion. "Lorennt might have flogged him as public recompense, but he was hardly angry enough to dismiss him."

The thought does not cause her the least worry but my insides churn. "I consider flogging quite severe."

"Why did you not tell me!" Leelah objects. "I could have told her and resolved the matter of her marriage in time for her to attend me at Cuylah's birth!"

"Because it was not for us to interfere," Erianna explains, kissing the babe's downy head.

Kragorn and Valor enter from the kitchen, mopping perspiration from their faces and necks.

Leelah whips her gaze to her husband, stopping him in place. "And what of you? Why did you not tell me?"

Though he cannot know of what she accuses him, Kragorn cants his head then makes for the stairs. "I think Fialla has woken."

"She is in the corner," Leelah purrs.

Valor chuckles.

Rather than mounting a defense, Kragorn drags his friend into the mire with him. "For what are you laughing? Haven't you courted all the women in this room?"

That snaps Valor's mouth closed. He jerks his head at me. "Not her. Not truly."

Erianna arches a single brow at her husband. "Kragorn is right."

The men share a look then move toward the door.

Erianna's bright laugh cuts through the tension. "You would have done better to continue sparring with swords than match your wit with your wives."

Valor crosses to her and unapologetically kisses his bride.

Leelah groans. "Not again. These two have been unbearable when they are together."

Valor breaks away to say, "Not half as amorous as you were when you wed, Mistress Tareth."

Leelah considers her husband, amber fire in her eyes. "Perhaps."

"How fares Commander Trent?" Kragorn asks.

"Very well," Leelah interjects. "Tirzah has not stopped smiling since she arrived."

I tuck my hand in my pocket, still smiling as accused. "I am glad you asked. He has a message for you."

"What is it?"

I hand him the folded paper rather than repeating it. There were too many curses.

Kragorn summarizes, "Trent demands I take immediate control of the fort else he will give General Harkerse charge of it and return me to a mere weapons master."

Valor laughs louder than the rest of us. "Sounds like the commander misses his wife!"

Erianna winks at me across the room.

TIRZAH

May 26th

I bunch the fragrant mullein in my hand, snipping the stems near the ground. The early evening air hangs pleasant in the boughs of the forest. Some like to gather their herbs while the dew still clings to them, but given a choice I prefer the early evening when the stems are dry but recovered from the heat of the day.

With Aiyla on the mend physically, I have relocated to Leelah's home to give Aiyla space to contend with her new life. She and Salome have taken to each other with a fondness befitting grandmother and granddaughter. It surprised Aiyla, the unreserved way Salome accepted her. It outright astonished her when the Queen of Malesiir came to call on her. But as Leelah suggested, it made Aiyla feel important and seen in a way she has not in the past miserable years of her life.

A percussive thudding on the path to Leelah's house draws me from the edges of the forest. Has Kragorn returned already?

Reluctant as he was to leave his family, Kragorn set out for Chishelm this morn. I do not know how he will manage to pry Leelah from her domain, but I foresee a secondary home within Chishelm for the Tareth family.

I wait on the edge of the road beneath a rise for the coming rider. Before I catch sight of him, I spy black legs churning beneath a dusty, straw colored coat. A thrill races all the way to my toes.

The man draws his horse alongside me. "Your husband is either permissive or a fool to allow his wife to wander about at dusk without an escort."

I set my basket on the ground, the bunch of mullein atop it. "I would not describe him as permissive. He has forbidden me the use of ladders."

The rider loops his horse's reins around a branch. "Then he is a fool?"

I prop my hands on my hips. "Certainly not. He is the Hand of the King."

"Oh?" His arms curl around my waist. Armor forms hard planes between our bodies. "How would you describe him?"

I catch his face between my hands. "Missed."

"Tirzah," he murmurs my name like a benediction as he claims my lips. "It has been an age."

I laugh. "It has been a week." My body, however, agrees with him. Of its own volition, my spine arches bringing us closer together.

"A year if it's been a day," he argues, greedily kissing my neck.

I feel my skin warm as if touched by sunshine. His romance of me has been thorough. "You cannot count, Commander."

"Tis possible," he agrees, nuzzling my hair. His breath tickles the shell of my ear. "I am besotted by you."

Though I want badly to surrender to our passion, I say, "They will come looking for me if I do not soon return."

"Then best this waits, for I have no intention of soon releasing you."

Anticipation has me gripping his upper arms beneath his chainmail sleeves till a cloud casts shadows on this moment.

I must soon release him to his duties to the king. There will be weeks, perhaps months, between his returns to the capital. A selfish part of me wishes he was merely a farmer, then I might keep him to myself.

"Have we long before we leave?" While I will be permitted to accompany Cuyler, Valor, and Erianna on their two month tour of the kingdom prior to the campaign against Limba, the three of them will be engaged in meetings with city officials leaving me to find my own ways to fill my time. Then Cuyler will be at the king's disposal, going to the corners of the kingdom to fulfill his duties, and I must begin anew my search for an apprenticeship.

"Five days," he murmurs against my temple.

I hold tight to him, reminding myself that every day is a grace.

TRENT

June 2nd

The women are cohorts in mischief as we head southwest to Pillings where we will pass the night. Erianna procured a gaited palfrey for Tirzah and has been teaching her how to ride at a running walk. Clad in full armor, the fierce Warrior Queen and my droll, voluptuous wife make quite the contrast of feminine beauty.

While we are alert to our surroundings, the full company of soldiers surrounding us allows Valor and I to pass the easy hours discussing his contacts in Pillings and the nearby villages. Though I am acquainted with most of what he tells, I listen with an ear to retain. Ere long, he will be too distant for letters to reach him with speed or reliability. Regold flanks us, learning my responsibilities and deciding if he will accept the offered task of being my aide as I was Valor's.

The queen's standard bearers that enter Pillings ahead of us draw out those with whom we have come to meet. We dismount and walk the streets. The blacksmith, thatcher, and elders come for an introduction to the queen and her retinue. Tirzah stays at my side, amicable but quiet.

"Where are we to stay?" She whispers to me while the queen is speaking to the blacksmith. It occurs that I did not explain the size of

Pillings to her. There is not an inn or tavern within the town.

"We shall make camp outside the town and leave at dawn for Vinstead. That city is two days distant."

She attends thereafter and I am reminded of her deportment at court. Watchful. Ever learning. Often keeping her own counsel.

Part of the company makes camp and prepares the early evening meal while the thatcher waxes about the best method for drying rushes.

When finally we sit around a fire eating stew, we trade stories of good humor. Erianna shares one of her time in Grass Lake in the Commonwealth and another of Hellah and Jessup, the legendary healer and apothecary.

Tirzah addresses Valor. "You told me much of them, the woman and her father-in-law who raised you."

He props his elbows on his knees. "Aye. All that I learned of healing came from them, despite my being a poor student. They are the best on the Continent."

"They saved my life. A story I will share another time," Erianna says with a glance to the eavesdropping soldiers.

Valor asks Tirzah, "Have you thought anymore of where you will apprentice?"

She rubs her palms on her skirt, a morose furrow sitting between her brows."In the capital, I suppose. Cuyler will be returning there most frequently, and he owns a house there." Her tone does not convey her inherent optimism. It is determined, aye, but not happy. We have not spoken at length of her position, but something about our roughly sketched plan upsets her.

Tirzah nods to herself, the outward sign of her inward conversation. "It seems to make the most sense. In such a large city, I am certain to find someone in want of an apprentice."

I squirm. How am I to explain that I have already made inquiries on her behalf that was answered negatively? I pray I am able to find her a position in one of the central cities we pass through. I have not yet heard answer from my mother who was to speak with their local midwife. We shall learn firsthand in a little over a week when we pass through Gistin.

"It happens," Erianna says brightly, "that Hellah is looking for an assistant." A stone plummets through my stomach. "She is an expert midwife and healer, and she works extensively with the impoverished in Grass Lake—even the harlots. She shares your calling. And Jessup is a physician of great knowledge and gentle disposition. He is also an expert apothecary.

The stone continues to ricochet inside me when I dare look at my wife who is leaning forward, eager to catch every detail.

"Their home," Erianna continues, "is designed perfectly to accommodate their apothecary shop and rooms for patients. There is also the most beautiful herb garden in her courtyard. I think I still smell of mint from all the hours we passed there." Erianna steals a fond glance at Valor. "We will be passing through Grass Lake ahead of our campaign. It would be no trouble to ferry you to Hellah. You could remain with her while you complete your apprenticeship and return fresh with knowledge and experience to fulfill your vision for Malesiir."

Tirzah is grinning. "That would be a dream! To be able to learn from them in such a place? That would be..." My wife looks at me, such hope and energy in her expression. Then the stone within me crashes through her, demolishing that hope. She shakes her head slowly, mournful for harboring such a dream, short lived though it was. "No. I could not. I could not leave my husband, could I?" The question hovering behind her statement thrusts me away from the fire. I sling my quiver and bow over my shoulder and stalk into the forest, quickly losing myself on a game trail.

TRENT

Is it that simple to betray me? To see what she wants and risk our relationship to obtain it? That is what Silla did. She would not trust me to aid her. She made her own plans to protect herself and her mother. It nearly cost them both of their lives. It did execute what was between us. Not love, but the promise of a future.

Will Tirzah do the same?

I weave through the dark, not intentionally stalking game but merely *stalking*. The area seems picked clean of opportunity, however, to flush any.

Not once has Tirzah asked for my help finding an apprenticeship. Does she think me incapable? Or that I do not care? She is my wife! Her needs and desires are of the utmost importance to me! All along I have been searching for a position for her. Had she asked or discussed it with me in anyway, I would have told her of the inquiries I have made. Though they were fruitless, they must count for something.

What if neither of us can find a position for her? A selfish thought worms into my mind. What if I stopped taking care to prevent getting her with child? Would a babe occupy her sufficiently that she would stay at home, ready to welcome me between my missions for the king?

I feel a wretched knave for thinking such, especially when she expressed her desire to wait. No, that is not the solution. It would only increase the weight of the anchor that our marriage seems to her.

I couldn't leave my husband, could I? Her despondence while speaking that question bludgeons me.

Could you, Tirzah? I want to demand. *Would it be so easy to wave farewell to me and sail hundreds of miles away? Does our marriage mean so little?*

I could thrash Valor for allowing his wife to seed such an impossible dream in mine. *Go on a grand adventure to warmer climes where you will train with the most acclaimed midwife and physician known to us. All you must do is leave your husband behind. Tis a simple sacrifice. What is marriage compared to the fulfillment of your dream and life's purpose?*

But... *I couldn't leave my husband, could I?*

No, Tirzah! You cannot leave me! I will haul you off the boat if I must! You are my *wife*. I have indebted myself to provide for you. I would die to protect you. I love you.

I pinch the corners of my eyes against the bridge of my nose, combatting the burn of tears.

I will not let her go. She is mine. I will ensure she is happy. I *will* find her an apprenticeship in Malesiir.

CHAPTER FIFTY-FOUR

TIRZAH

June 12th

"Your mother is an easy woman to be with," I say to Trent as we settle into our tent for the night. From the moment Brea Trent burst from her front door, ran past her son and wrapped me in a crushing hug, I knew she was a woman of amiable kindness. Before Cuyler could utter a word to rein her enthusiasm, two fair haired young women flung their arms around him, squeezing the breath from him and chattering like jays.

Since that greeting, the restraint that has bound my husband since Erianna spoke of Hellah's want of an apprentice has begun to loosen. When he returned that night, I broached the topic, but he would not speak of it. Thus, I can only speculate why he was upended. Was it my enthusiasm for the impossible dream? If so, I do not understand why it bothered him. It is as unrealistic as saying, "I wish to own a castle!" Tis only a dream, no matter Erianna speaking as if it could be realized. She does not live in a world limited by the concerns of common folk.

Furthermore, Valor goes wherever Erianna goes, but Trent is bound to the king. The mere thought of leaving him rent my heart in two. I could not do it. And aye, though he must leave me in the capital while about his duties, he will return. We will have time together between his assignments. I would rather have those days to tuck away in my heart in the spans of time we are apart than to be without him altogether.

"She is," he agrees with my assessment of his mother.

"Your sisters are also great company. Between them and your younger brother, your mother must be constantly entertained."

He hums his assent and lowers to our plush bedroll while I brush my hair.

Knowing the fabric of our tent is merely a visual barrier to what goes within, I keep my voice low. "How unfortunate that your older brother is a boor, though his wife reminds me of a pixie for all her sweet smiles and how she flits about seeing to the needs of all her children. I can see why your were taken with her as a boy. She is charming. And got with her fourth child?"

"Fifth," he corrects.

"And still as tiny as the queen. Such a wonder."

He hums again, his simple answers revealing his distraction.

"What is amiss, Cuyler?"

He does not answer. The disquiet sitting upon his brow has me lowering next to him. I place my fingertips to his deep scowl. "Cuyler?"

He stares across the tent at his satchel. "Fetch me that."

I do as bid. From it he withdraws a stack of letters bound with string. He gives them to me.

"What is this?" I slide the string from the bundle.

"I have been making inquiries on your behalf."

"For what?" I move toward the candle to read the direction on the front of the topmost letter then unfold it.

"An apprenticeship."

My gaze startles toward his, but he is staring through the stack of letters.

Apprehension needles along my spine. I read quickly to the end of the letter. *No position available.* I move to the next. It says something similar. Then the third from a physician. *Will not apprentice a woman.* The fourth from a healer. *No time to train.* She recommends a particular midwife. The following letter is from that midwife. *Nothing available.* The final letter says it plainly. *I will not allow her to render services to harlots.*

I am stunned.

Cuyler intones, "Gistin was my last great hope. If you loved my family, perhaps you could stay with them and complete your training with the local midwife. I asked my mother to make the inquiry. She told me today that this midwife also refused you."

My eyes blur. How could I have been so thoroughly rejected? "Surely there must be someone willing... Perhaps if I make the inquiries in person?"

"The short of it is this—No one will apprentice you if you intend to help harlots."

He speaks true. It burns me with indignation and anger. "That is not fair."

"I agree."

I wave the stack of letters. "How can this be? I know this is what I am called to do. Why is it so difficult to find a teacher when I am called to do this?"

Cuyler's strange calm clashes with my nerves. My voice pitches higher. "Do you not find this upsetting?"

"I have been upset by this for weeks."

He still will not look at me. Shrilly, I whisper, "Cuyler! What am I to do?"

He does not have to search for an answer. He proposes, "Can you open your own shop as an apothecary and healer?"

Having thought long on such an idea myself, I can say with confidence, "No. I do not feel it would be ethical to do so when there is still a great deal I do not know. I am only an assistant."

His head bobs a slow nod, as if expecting that answer. He takes a deep breath. "Then there is only one solution left to us. You must go to Grass Lake to apprentice with Hellah."

I gape at him, certain I misheard or that he misspoke. He cannot have meant that.

"It is an answer to our prayers," he continues dispassionately. "You will learn all that you need and more. It aligns too perfectly with your needs to not be from the Almighty. With the queen able to escort you straight to Hellah's door, there can be no better solution."

I struggle to comprehend all that he is saying. "You think I should go to Grass Lake?"

"It is your dream."

I shriek, "It is across the Continent!"

The hum of conversation outside our tent falls silent. I press my hands to my mouth.

He sighs deeply, finally looking in my eyes. The misery in his puts instant tears in mine.

I lower to my knees, wrapping my hands around the crook of his arm. "I cannot leave you."

"You can."

I shake my head and fall into his embrace. "No! I do not want to. You are my husband!"

His hand cradles the back of my head as my tears break through my feeble grasp.

Into the veil of my hair, he murmurs, "Aye. Your husband. Thus it is my duty to help you steward the talents the Almighty has given you and help you fulfill your calling. I hoped to present you with a stack of letters requesting you as an apprentice so that you might choose the one that most suited, but I failed to secure you a single one." He continues overtop my protests. "Which tells me of the great need in Malesiir for you to fulfill your calling. The poor and the outcasts are woefully neglected if no healer will train you because you wish to serve them."

This is the source of the strain on him. All these weeks, he has carried this knowledge and protected me from the burden of worry until he could present me with a solution. Unfortunately, it is a solution I cannot accept. "What of Port Veritae? We could inquire there."

"I would rather you be in Grass Lake than that degenerate city." The vehemence of his answer forbids argument. He sets me back, softening at the uncommon tears streaming down my cheeks. "You have said training with Hellah would fulfill a dream."

"Aye, but—"

"It will also take the sting out of my absences."

I shudder and press his palm to my face as though applying pressure to a wound. His touch stems the flow of my tears.

"You are a better person than I, Tirzah. Though it hurts you for me to leave, you have encouraged me. When presented with the same, I grew angry and withdrew."

I understand, for I am not without my own boil of anger and desperation. The plea I have refrained from making finally escapes, though it sounds childish to my ears. "May I not come with you? I will become better at riding and not slow you down. I could be the cook for your contingent."

Though he knows I already know the answer, he does not belittle me for asking. "It would be too dangerous. I cannot allow the king's and my enemies to know your face. They would imperil you to bend me to their will. Tis why I have left you in Regold's care when I meet with the elders in these larger cities."

I nod my understanding.

"Verily, it may be safer to remove you to Grass Lake when I make enemies of Malesiir's base denizens by freeing those women and children who have been sold into slavery."

There is an ache in my breast for those people and an ache at what is being asked of us in order to help them. But there is no fear. Nor is there real conflict. Though it hurts, this is the path we must walk. Had there been another way, it would have been provided. "I know you are right," I take his face in my hands. "Still, I do not want to be parted from you."

"Nor I you. I have long fought this decision, but peace has stolen upon me without my consent. The timing of our marriage has enabled you to do what you must." He speaks slowly, ensuring I hear the veracity in his words. "I am proud of you, Tirzah. You have chosen to serve the poor souls other healers have condemned. If going to Grass Lake is what you must do to be equipped, then I shall support you."

The reflection of my own feelings in my husband moves me deeply. How grateful I am for this man!

"I am equally proud of you. Instead of fleeing from the darkness that mired you, you have declared war against it."

He slides my hands across his face, kissing my palms in turn. "With the help of a healer that showed me it was better to live in the light of grace."

My heart presses against my ribs, nearly paining me with the overflow of my feelings. "How is it that our callings have become inextricably paired? Especially when both of us sought to hide from those whose bondage negatively affected our lives. How is it that we have been set up as their champions?"

"Tis not the work of man. Our plans would have led us to a far different place. Even the desires of our hearts changed. Rather, they grew."

"It can only be explained by the grace of the Almighty."

Cuyler pinches the light of the candle, blanketing us in the soft night. The vow he then makes to me goes beyond words. We will cherish each of the days ahead and part knowing we will be reunited after a time, equipped for our future.

Salome was right all those months ago when she challenged me to see that I was not cherishing the love that already belonged to me. I wonder if she also recognized that my reckless pursuit threatened to deprive me of that which I have now found in my husband.

This love is holy.

EPILOGUE

SILLA

Two years later

The sun scorches my fair skin while the ocean breeze fights to cool it. Were the breeze not saturated with the briny scent of ripe fish, I would be more grateful.

"Not long now," Spymaster Regold assures me, despite my knowing the workings of this dock better than he. My narrow eyed smile says as much.

He ignores my sarcasm and notes my firmly middle-class dress and head scarf. I am utterly unremarkable among the other women waiting upon the dock for the approaching ship. My stiff but still slightly slumped posture also reflects the women around me who aspire to the carriage of noblewomen without knowing how to achieve it.

Regold remarks, "Can't get used to you changing skins as easily as I change tunics."

I bob one shoulder, conceding his point. Even the fine silks and life of a noblewoman, which I prefer, are but another skin. I abandoned the truest version of myself long ago. She would have gotten me killed.

The gangway lowers to the dock with an agonized groan. Regold draws my arm through his as people mill on the dock leaving little room for the disembarking passengers. I swallow the note of disgust that seeks release. Can they not hear themselves lowing like cattle? Mindless beings.

A crash of wood on a merchant vessel unloading near a warehouse inspires the dockhands to dip into their ocean of foul language. My mouth twitches in amusement as the cows around me moo their feminine protest. A broad shouldered man, agile despite his size, scrambles to correct the position of the hoist that led to the ropes slipping and dropping the cargo. Stepping into Regold's shadow lest I come to the man's notice, I admire his dark skin gleaming taut over pronounced muscles. Like many of his fellow laborers, he has removed his tunic. A flush bathes me as I watch him, wondering when next our paths will cross. If he persists in interfering with my mission, it will likely be soon.

Shoving aside my musings regarding the dockhand, I flick my eyes to Regold when he gusts an exhale.

"There she is," he intones. "Blazing depths! She's more beautiful than she was when she left two years past."

I follow his gaze to the woman descending the gangway on the arm of a helpful sailor.

Curse it. Regold is right.

"Trent'll be beside himself. Bet he holes up in that house with her and—"

At my quelling look, Regold leaves the thought unfinished. He weaves us through the crowd to the lone woman attracting the lusty stares of many a man. Something must be done.

"Cousin!" Regold exults, speaking over Tirzah Trent as he draws her into an embrace. While he whispers caution in her ear, I remove the extra length of fabric tied around my skirt and fold it in half crosswise.

"Hello, Cousin," I greet Tirzah. "Let us conceal you from the sun lest you burn." I drape the makeshift shawl over her head, tying the fabric so it casts her face in shadow and hangs down to her waist, making her look fat rather than curvaceous.

Questions leap from her wide eyes, but she holds her tongue. Regold takes her on his arm while I flank her to block inquisitive gazes. Together we herd her off the dock while a pair of soldiers disguised in common garb pass us to collect her trunks being offloaded from the ship. We make our way down military controlled streets, taking the long, safe way to the nondescript townhouse owned by the Rodiharians.

"The reprisal for freeing the harlots must be as bad as he said," Tirzah observes based on our careful movements.

"Likely worse," Regold says. "But Port Veritae has its own problems that make this city particularly dangerous."

"Thus, Trent's abundance of caution," she surmises.

"Aye."

Basking in the attention of the beautiful woman, Regold inquires,

"How did you find the Commonwealth?"

Her answering smile stuns him. Mimicking a mannerism of my favorite royal, I roll my eyes.

"It was incredible," she replies. "I loved everything there. Well, everything except the summer heat."

"Are you now a healer in full?"

"Truthfully, I completed my training and attained the level of Physician—not that the title will convey to Malesiir."

I feel another eye roll coming, so I lock my gaze to the street ahead.

"That is quite an achievement, Physician Trent."

She beams at his praise.

Oh, to be able to go back in time and convince Erianna murdering this woman would be justified...

We turn the corner mere blocks from the house and nearly collide with one of those dangers Regold forewarned.

"Governor Thorne!" I exclaim, drawing his notice as Regold diverts down an alley with Tirzah.

"Lad—" The Governor corrects himself, "*Silla*. Greetings. How fares your aunt?"

"Quite well, I thank you. Tis a fortunate thing I have stumbled into your path. My aunt wishes to extend an invitation to her dinner party in a fortnight. Would it be possible, do you think, to grant her request? It would be a grand favor to her if you would grace her table," I simper, buying time.

Puffed by my compliments, he juts his nose into the air. "Perhaps, perhaps. Send the formal invitation round, and I shall attempt to fit it into my schedule."

My poor aunt will be simply aghast to learn of a dinner party she must now host. Were I not so unsettled by Tirzah's return, I would have fabricated a simpler diversion.

Governor Thorne clears his throat, motioning to his path which I block.

"Oh!" I gasp, playing the flustered coquette and leaping to the side. "Forgive me, Governor." I press my fingers to my mouth, covering a smile.

The old lech smirks, eyes lingering where they oughtn't as he passes with his guard.

I continue on my way, casting affected glances over my shoulder at him on the chance that he does the same, which he does once, fluffing like a rooster at my attention.

I prolong the act until I turn down the alley leading to the townhouse. Regold guides Tirzah from the opposite street. I nod my assurance that I was not followed. He positions Tirzah between us. Through the kitchen door of the servant's floor, I enter the house first, ascertaining that none lie in wait while Regold guards our backs on the street. Only soldiers and the cook wait in the kitchen. I pull Tirzah through the door, Regold on our heels.

"I see my husband has trained his replacement spymaster well," Tirzah teasingly commends Regold.

"Come," I urge her to follow me up the stairs to the third floor. "He's waiting for you."

I knock on the second door off the landing and enter without waiting for a response. Trent raises his head, his hands still pressed to the table where he was pouring over maps. His expression is simultaneously fierce and soft as he moves toward us, making my heart flutter. His look, however, is not meant for me. I step aside, accepting the shawl Tirzah removes from her head. She nervously presses a hand to her hair, attempting to smooth the wind tossed strands, not that it matters. She could be disarrayed and covered in mud and Trent would still look at her the same. He catches her face in his hands and kisses her gently, again and again, before wrapping her in his arms. My heart spasms. I drop my gaze to the floor.

"Was there trouble?" Trent inquires.

"No, Commander," Regold replies from behind me. He sets a hand on my shoulder. "Silla diverted Governor Thorne. He did not see us."

"Well done."

Firming my countenance into neutrality, I meet his waiting gaze.

"Thank you, Silla," Trent murmurs. He holds his wife to himself, cradling her head against his chest with one strong hand. I lose track of my gaze, letting it linger on those blunt tipped fingers that once dove into my hair and held me just so.

I incline my head respectfully. "Of course, Commander." Even I marvel at the level indifference I masterfully purport.

Regold's gentle pressure on my shoulder tugs me backward. "I will report on schedule, as long as you don't forget we exist now that you aren't pining for your wife."

"I might forget," Trent says, restraining a grin.

Regold amuses himself with his ribald wit as we descend to the ground floor.

"Best leave those below stairs," he advises the soldiers hauling

Tirzah's trunks through the kitchen door. "Commander's not to be disturbed."

We fall in step in the back alley.

"You know, I am the spymaster for a reason." Regold lets the statement dangle. I do not comment so he continues, "You dealt with that admirably."

"You dearly love the sound of your own voice, do you not?"

Regold nods. "Aye, but I'm no fool." He hooks my arm through his. "What you need is a distraction. What about that dockhand that couldn't take his eyes off you?"

"What dockhand?" I scoff.

"The one that lost control of the cargo because he was watching you."

"That did not happen."

"Indeed, it did. You only took notice of him after the crash, thus, you missed his attention."

"You are daft. He was not watching me."

"I thought you did not know of which man I spoke," he taunts, revealing the snare he laid.

I must be more out of sorts than I realized. Regold never snares me. Tugging my arm loose when we reach the corner where we will part, I take a moment to disabuse him of his prurient notion. "While you may find time to chase skirts, I have been given a mission which occupies the full of my attention. Have you forgotten the short length of leash the king has provisionally given me? I will not test his patience by amusing myself with a dalliance."

"Test not his patience, but do have fun. He cannot have meant you to be miserable."

"Oh, but he can. You do not know him."

Regold raises his palms in surrender, backing away. "So be it. I will see you on the morrow?"

"In the gardens," I confirm.

He winks and disappears into the throng moving toward the city center. I swing around, leaving the lovely visages behind as I make my way back toward the docks then follow the sloping streets down into the underbelly of Port Veritae.

A Note from the Author

Dear Readers, thank you for spending time with me in the world of the Redemption Saga. I hope you enjoyed the tale of Tirzah and Trent. These two supporting characters from the previous books grew in my mind until I had to share their story. I hope reliving most of the plot of Redemption's Song from their perspectives and seeing their happily ever after develop was at least half as interesting for you to read as it was for me to write. You may have heard authors say this before, and I can attest to the truth of it—Sometimes, I am absolutely surprised by my characters and where the plot takes them. This story proved no exception. While writing, several times I audibly gasped and said, "Trent! I cannot believe you just said that! How could you?" My husband, who is used to my nonsense, rolled his eyes while I continued furiously typing. We authors are a silly bunch.

In the epilogue, we saw a peek into the complicated mind of Silla Hugler. She has been taunting me with her secrets while I wrote the last three books, and let me tell you, there is more to her than I ever knew when she stepped onto the pages for the first time in Redemption's Pursuit. I am champing at the bit to tell you more about Silla, the nefarious goings on in Port Veritae, and to get a good look at her hero. (He is being quite dodgy with me as I dream about their plot. If you figure out his name, would you let me know?)

But first! The story you have been anxiously awaiting! It is finally time for the conquest of Limba. Erianna's wicked father, King Arcto, must be held accountable for his actions. Leading the charge on that journey is our mysterious, somewhat antihero Torvarik cast alongside his first wife, Annekeh. Their story is fraught with turmoil, adventure, and a tenacious love. Look for its release in 2023.

If you'd like to be the first to know about teasers, bonus chapters, and books I recommend, subscribe to my website at www.elcrossbooks.com and follow me on Instagram @elcross_author.

About the Author

Erin L. Cross is a wife, homeschooling mother, author, and part-time landscaper. A native to Florida, she divides her time between reading, writing, and turning her suburban backyard into a homestead. Being a life-long learner, she is not satisfied until she has exhaustively researched a subject of interest.

This habit proved fruitful in fully developing the fictitious yet historically inspired medieval world and characters in her first novel *Redemption's Pursuit*, a story that was ten-years in the making. On that solid foundation, she dove into writing The Redemption Saga, a six book story arc that will conclude in 2023.

Erin's deepest desire is that in whatever she does, she will do it to the best of her ability, to the glory of God.